MORE THAN A KISS

His lips brushed hers gently, slowly. She held her breath, not daring to move. Part of her longed to cast caution to the wind, to kiss him back and damn the consequences. Part of her cried a protest, a warning that she was asking for heartache. But somehow that little voice seemed to have lost its heart.

He lifted his head and gazed down at her, his eyes dark and shadowed. She stared back, heart pounding. For a moment neither moved, then his fingers fell away from her chin. His arm around her waist eased.

"Don't," Hannah whispered before she could stop herself, and slid her arms around his neck, pulling him back to her. This time she kissed him, really kissed him. His grip tightened as he kissed her again, deeper and harder, as if his self-restraint had finally given way.

His mouth, which had been tentative a moment ago, took possession of hers ruthlessly. Hannah let him. He tasted of sweet tea and brandy, and he kissed her as if he'd been waiting forever to do it . . .

Books by Caroline Linden

WHAT A WOMAN NEEDS

WHAT A GENTLEMAN WANTS

Published by Kensington Publishing Corporation

WHAT A GENTLEMAN WANTS

CAROLINE LINDEN

ZEBRA BOOKS
Kensington Publishing Corp.

www.kensingtonbooks.com

*To my children,
who never leave me in any doubt
of what they want;
and to Eric,
who doesn't, either.*

ACKNOWLEDGMENTS

Writing a first book is pure fun; you can write one sentence at a time, whenever the muse wanders by, with endless time to rewrite and revise, and no one to please but yourself. Writing a second book is much harder. You can't wait for the muse to waltz in when she feels like it, you must track her down and beat the story out of her because you have a *deadline*. My eternal thanks to the following people for encouraging me, prompting me, and cutting me some slack during the writing of this book: Heidi Hermiller, who read it first and told me how to fix the first part; all my Romance Unleashed friends (Paula, Laura, Lori, Kristina, Flo, Sally, Sandy, Jackie, Sophia, Cynthia, Jessica, Eve, Teresa, Kate, Pamela, Kathy, Kathleen, Barbara, and Irene) for overflowing my inbox with friendship and support; Stephanie Kip Rostan, my wonderful agent, for keeping me sane and on-track; John Scognamiglio, for being a writer's fantasy editor to work with; and my husband and children, for thinking this writing habit of mine is pretty cool and exciting, even when it makes me crazy.

PROLOGUE

No one noticed the man who arrived last. The host and hostess had long since mingled with their guests. It was almost the supper dance.

The latecomer did not join them. He paused just inside the ballroom, his gaze sweeping the elegant, merry crowd. But after a moment he turned and went up the stairs, away from the ball. Moving quietly and quickly, he turned into the family wing, pausing at each door, every now and then opening one a fraction of an inch before easing it closed and going on.

Finally, almost at the end of the hall, he stopped longest, placing his ear right up next to the door. With a stealthy glance over his shoulder, he opened the door and stepped inside.

Anyone else would probably have backed out at discovering a couple occupied as this one was. Marcus Reece, however, was not embarrassed at all, and instead of backing out of the room, he closed the door behind him.

"There . . . oh yes . . . yes . . ." moaned the woman, rising and falling in sensual abandon, her head thrown back and eyes closed in ecstasy.

"There? Oh no, *almost* there," panted the man bucking beneath her thighs. His hands were wrapped about her hips, his trousers down around his still-shod feet.

The woman laughed, her breath catching in a gasp. "Almost? Wait for me, love."

"Can't," growled the man, shoving himself up on one elbow and taking her dark pink nipple into his mouth. "Come now."

"Oh . . . Oh . . . Oh oh *oh!*" Her exclamations rose into a shriek as she finally opened her eyes and realized they were not alone. "Oh my God!" She shoved her lover away from her breast and vaulted off his lap, grabbing up her loosened gown in a vain attempt to cover herself. "What are *you* doing here?"

Marcus regarded her stonily. "Saving your life, most likely."

The man on the chaise had recovered from his shock enough to sit up and turn. "Marcus, old man, how kind of you to join us," he said in a voice sharp with sarcasm. "To what do we owe the displeasure?"

"To Lord Barlow." The woman made a strange gulping sound and turned pale. "He has been drinking a great deal tonight, and it seems he is out of patience with the rumors of his wife's infidelities. Someone has finally broken the news to him that while he sits at his club, Lady Barlow graces other gentlemen with her private attentions. He is on his way here as we speak, to see for himself how true the rumors are."

The woman gasped, and began frantically adjusting her clothing. Marcus ignored her and turned back to his brother. "Barlow means to kill you, David," he said in a low voice. "He heard your name. Get up and get dressed."

"You said he didn't care," David accused the woman, yanking up his trousers. Her arms bent behind her as she tried to fasten her gown, Lady Barlow glared back at him.

"He doesn't care! Only . . ." She darted a quick glance at Marcus, who had retrieved David's discarded shirt and was turning it right side out. "Only when he drinks," she finished a bit sullenly.

"The man's a bloody sot!" Marcus flung the shirt at his brother, and David jerked it over his head. "You lied to me."

"As if you cared," she flung back.

"Quiet!" Marcus silenced them both. "That no longer matters. David, my carriage will be waiting in the mews. Get out of the house any way you can without being seen, and go directly there. Here." He handed David his waistcoat and jacket.

"Why?" David asked, pulling on the jacket.

Marcus smiled grimly. "Barlow may be close at my heels, and will raise an uproar if he finds you. Or believes he finds you."

"Oh." David stuffed his discarded cravat into a pocket and got to his feet. "Right, then. In the mews?"

Marcus jerked his head in a nod, already turning toward the mirror. The door opened and closed softly as David left, and Lady Barlow said, "Well!" Marcus ran his hands through his hair, ruffling it a bit. "What the devil am I supposed to do?" she exclaimed, when he ignored her. "I don't suppose you've some secret plan to allow me to sneak out."

"You, madam, are coming with me." Jocelyn Barlow pouted and crossed her arms under her bosom.

"I haven't agreed to any of this."

He barely glanced at her. "I don't recall soliciting your agreement, but considering your husband's temper, it would be in your best interest to persuade him you've been with me instead of with my brother."

"I hardly *was* with your brother," she muttered.

"I don't care whether you found it satisfying or not," he said in a dangerously quiet voice. "I don't care about *you*."

She snorted, and Marcus faced her. For a moment he was tempted to leave her here like this, still disheveled and unbuttoned. She was an unfaithful wife, apparently an untruthful lover, and Marcus truly didn't care about her.

But if he didn't, she would owe him nothing. Her husband was in a fury, had publicly declared his intentions, and Marcus didn't think she would raise a finger to calm him; she'd likely enjoy the notoriety of being the cause of a duel. Marcus hadn't raced across town and barged in on them just to have Barlow call David out before breakfast tomorrow. "Turn around," he ordered. She opened her mouth, looked at his expression, and turned around without a word.

"We will stroll downstairs and rejoin the guests," he said as he did up her gown properly. Thank God she was one of those daring women who didn't wear a corset. "We have been admiring the artwork in the salon, and David left hours ago. I don't think we need to mention anything that happened in this room." He turned her around and ran a critical eye over her. "Your hair is falling down." She flushed and turned to the mirror to fix it.

Marcus waited at the door, controlling his impatience. They needed to be seen together for a few minutes before Barlow arrived. Lady Barlow finally finished her toilette and took the arm he offered, and they left the room.

"May I ask why you're doing this?"

"No."

She was quiet for a moment as they walked down the hall. "Do you know, when you first appeared like that, it was quite startling, but also, I must say, rather

exciting to see you standing there, watching me. . . ."
She cast him a coy look from under her lashes. Marcus,
who was not easily shocked, could hardly believe his
ears. He stopped, waiting until she looked at him.

"You are sadly mistaken if you think the sight of you
riding my brother like a common strumpet was remotely exciting to me," he said. "I suggest you purge
the thought from your head."

She pouted again, and said nothing more as they
reached the stairs and went down to the ballroom.

Normally Marcus spoke only to people he knew and
respected, but tonight he purposely slowed his gait
and rolled his shoulders a little. When someone hailed
him, either by his name or by David's, he nodded in
greeting. A few people gave him odd looks, but he
ignored them. There was only one person he truly
needed to confuse, and Barlow had been drinking.

"You, sir!" A stocky gentleman and his companions
plowed to a halt behind them. "I demand satisfaction!"

With one last speaking glance at Lady Barlow,
Marcus turned. The rest of the room was already
facing his accuser, breathless with anticipation. Either
rumor moved even faster than Marcus's horses, or the
fool had been telling everyone here of his intentions.
"Satisfaction, Barlow? For what, may I ask?"

At the sound of his voice, Lord Barlow's eyes widened,
and he gulped. "Exeter. Oh. I say. I thought . . ." He
cleared his throat and shot a nervous glance at one of
his friends. "Exeter. How do you do, sir?" He gave a
wobbly bow.

Marcus looked down on him. "I am well, sir." He
waited a heartbeat. "And you?"

Barlow hiccupped at his frosty tone. "Very well,
sir." There was a moment of silence. "Jocelyn," muttered Barlow.

"Good evening, husband." She dipped into a slight curtsey, hiding her pallor behind her fan.

Marcus unwound her hand from his elbow. "Now that you have arrived, Barlow, I will return your wife, with my thanks for the pleasure of her company this evening."

"The pleasure of her company," parroted Barlow, taking his wife's hand. He looked completely flummoxed, thrown off his stride. "Yes. Mmph. Yes."

"She was kind enough to show me our hosts' gallery," said Marcus. "Quite illuminating." Lady Barlow was known as a patron of the arts. Marcus suspected she especially patronized handsome young artists, but that was beside the point.

"Quite." Barlow seemed incapable of conversation. He continued to glance between Marcus and his wife as though he didn't comprehend what they were saying. But there was nothing he could say without calling his wife a whore and Marcus a liar. And while he might be drunk enough to do the former, he wasn't about to do the latter. Marcus decided he had done enough.

"Good evening, Barlow. Lady Barlow." He turned and walked away, hearing Lord Barlow's complaint to one of his companions: "Greaves, you're daft! That was Exeter, not his wastrel brother."

To which Greaves whined, "I never could tell them apart!"

Marcus strode from the ballroom, ignoring the furious whispers that sprang up in his wake. With no apparent sign of hurry, he left the house without once looking back. His carriage was waiting at the bottom of the steps, the footman standing at attention next to the door. He pulled it open as Marcus approached, and closed it behind him. Marcus rapped once on the roof, and they were off almost instantaneously.

"I suppose I should thank you," came David's voice

from the shadows opposite. "I can't believe she lied to me."

"If you had any sense at all, you would have made certain of matters yourself."

David snorted. "Well, when have I had any sense?"

Marcus didn't disagree. David *had* no sense, carrying on with the wife of a jealous man and then making light of the affair to his friends. One of those friends had spread the tale, obviously having as little discretion as David did. "I suggest you take a holiday until the scandal dies down."

"Scandal?" David sat up. "How can there be a scandal? He didn't catch us together, or even see us together."

Marcus let out his breath slowly. "Barlow overheard that fool Brixton regaling some friends with the tale. He was too drunk to puzzle out why he saw his wife with me instead of with you, but he'll get there eventually. Enough people will know she was with you earlier."

David sat back with a huff. "Fine."

Marcus felt a moment of relief that David had agreed so easily, and pressed the point. "Tomorrow."

"Come now, that's extreme!" David protested. Marcus said nothing. "Surely that looks like running away," David tried again. Still Marcus said nothing. He didn't give a damn what it looked like. He cared what it would accomplish. Silence filled the carriage until they reached David's town house. The vehicle tipped slightly as the footman stepped down to get the door.

"Fine, then," snapped David. "I'll go. Enjoy the gossip in my stead." He jumped down from the carriage without a word of good-bye, let alone thanks, and stomped up his steps. Marcus leaned back and sighed. David would be gone before Barlow's headache passed tomorrow if Marcus personally had to set him bound and gagged on the public mail coach. Truth be told, Marcus had been looking for a way to get David out of London, and while this was not quite as good as any—how dare David carry on without a thought for his family's reputation, when their sister would be making her debut in less than a year—it would suffice. No doubt David would find something, or someone, just as disreputable in Brighton, but London society would be more engrossed in its own follies. Without a duel, any gossip about Lady Barlow and David would fade.

Suddenly tired, Marcus signaled the coachman to go home. He had no interest in returning to his club. Though it had taken barely an hour, riding to David's rescue had worn him out and utterly ruined the evening. He knew it was too much to expect gratitude, but he did wish David didn't resent him for it. Someday, Marcus thought, he wouldn't do it, and David would discover how cruel his interference had been. But first he must think of Celia and her future. Once his sister was well and safely married, Marcus promised himself, David would be cut loose, free to behave—and suffer—in any way he liked.

But until then, he was David's keeper. Marcus leaned his head back against the cushion and said a quick prayer that David wouldn't get into too much trouble in Brighton.

CHAPTER 1

The hamlet of Middleborough included less than two hundred souls all told, and although it boasted both a tailor and a dressmaker, a bootmaker, and two fine taverns, it could not by any stretch be counted a city. Its chief claim to fame, as well as its main source of revenue, was its location. Twenty-five miles of good road to the north lay London, twenty-five miles to the south lay Brighton, and nearly every traveler between the two cities came through Middleborough.

Thus the residents of Middleborough were accustomed to fine carriages and matched teams bowling through their town. Most stopped at either the White Swan or the King's Arms, but the straight, flat highway inspired more than a few drivers—gentlemen with flashy rigs, mostly—to race each other, at speeds which rendered Middleborough little more than a blur.

It was a fine early spring day when two such carriages appeared on the horizon. Walking along the road, her arms filled with packages, Hannah Preston heaved a sigh. Shifting her armload, she caught hold of her daughter's hand and pulled her to the side.

Moments later the carriages thundered past in a blur of glossy horses and brightly painted wheels.

"Fools," muttered Hannah, barely avoiding a muddy puddle. "One of these days, there's going to be a spectacular accident."

Her sister-in-law laughed. "You'll be sure to see it, situated right here at the bend in the road."

"Then it had better happen soon," she said. "The new vicar will be arriving in a month."

"Mama, do you want there to be a crash?" Hannah ignored Sarah's snicker, guiltily, and rushed to answer her daughter.

"No, Molly. Of course not."

"Oh." Molly stared after the departed carriages. "Uncle Jamie bet Uncle Tom a shilling there would be one this week."

Hannah frowned. "Your uncles should know better than to discuss that around you."

"Is wagering a sin, Mama?"

Hannah hesitated. Her late husband would have said yes, but as her own brothers were the guilty parties, she could hardly condemn it. "Now, Molly," said Sarah, "you must know Uncle Jamie and Uncle Tom love to tease. Did they know you were about when they said that?"

Molly pursed her lips and her chin sank almost to her chest. "I listened when they didn't think I was there. Don't be angry, Mama."

"How could I be angry? Is it your fault God gave you such good ears?" A tiny smile crossed Molly's face, and she shook her head. Hannah wrinkled her nose, making a silly face to encourage the smile. "I see our gate. Shall we race?"

As she hoped, Molly took off, squealing with laughter. Hannah hurried a few steps, then had to stop as a stone slipped through the hole in her boot. "Ouch," she said in exasperation.

"Time for new boots?" Sarah asked.

Hannah sighed. "Time for seeking employment, to buy new boots."

Sarah said nothing as they trudged the rest of the way down the lane. Hannah pushed open the gate Molly had left swinging. "You'll always be welcome with us," Sarah said quietly, but Hannah shook her head.

"You've four children of your own, Sarah. And living with Jamie might drive me around the bend." Sarah smiled sheepishly. Hannah forced herself to smile back. Sarah was trying to help. It wasn't her fault she had no room to offer. "It's enough that you helped me carry all this home today," she added.

"I wish things were different, Hannah."

She avoided her sister-in-law's gaze. "I do, too, but they aren't, and it can't be helped." She did wish everything was different. She wished the new vicar wasn't waiting to take possession of the vicarage. She wished she had funds of her own to purchase another cottage. She wished her husband hadn't died and left her alone.

Molly was sitting on the front step, clapping her hands in glee that she had won the race. Hannah wrinkled her nose at her little girl and laughed. Sarah took the packages back to the kitchen, Molly at her heels, while Hannah took her time scraping her boots.

Dark little footprints down the hall indicating that Molly had forgotten to scrape her shoes clean. Hannah heaved a bittersweet sigh. It was too much to expect a four-year-old to remember such rules, she supposed, and as long as it was Hannah's own house footprinted, there was no reason for dismay. In a few weeks, though, that would change. How she would miss this little house.

She sighed again, taking down the rag hanging

beside the door and wiping up the footprints. She didn't want to raise her child as a guest in someone else's house any more than she wanted to live as a guest in someone else's house, even if the someone else were her own father, but there was nothing to be done about it. She had nowhere else to go, and would just have to learn to accept it.

Behind her, the gate squeaked. "I beg your pardon, ma'am," called a slurred voice. "D' you know where I might find a doctor?"

Hannah turned, squinting to see the stranger with the upper-class accent. Tall, well-dressed, and decidedly drunk, she decided as he swatted at a pestering fly. "What's happened?"

"There's been"—he cleared his throat—"a bit of an accident, really."

"What sort of accident, and where?" The doctor lived on the other side of Middleborough, over a mile away. She hoped there weren't serious injuries.

The stranger flapped one arm toward town. "Over there, around the bend. Tremendous crater in the road, did you know? Very lucky to have missed it myself." The momentum of his arm had carried the man off balance, and he lurched into the gatepost.

"What happened?" Hannah asked. The crater had been a rock only a few days ago, when some men from town had dug it out after receiving numerous complaints. They must not have finished filling it in yet.

"Why, he hit it, of course. Flew right out of his rig."

Hannah nodded. She was accustomed to helping others, and although people flung from passing carriages were rather rare, they were still God's creatures, and entitled to Christian charity from the vicar's wife. Vicar's widow, she remembered with a pang. "I'll come see what I can do," she said.

Sarah appeared at the back of the hall, no doubt

drawn by the strange voice. "There's been a carriage accident," Hannah called. "I'm going to see if I can help. Could you stay a little longer and give Molly her tea?"

"Of course," said Sarah. Hannah hurried down the path to the gate, where the man was now tilting strongly to one side.

"Is he badly hurt?" she asked, starting off in the direction he had indicated.

"I've no idea," he said, not sounding very concerned. "Should I fetch a doctor?"

"Let's look at him first. I'm Mrs. Preston, the vicar's wife, and have seen all sorts of injuries." She could smell the spirits clinging to him, and suspected his friend would smell the same. In Hannah's experience, drunks seem to lead charmed lives. Hopefully this one would be so lucky.

Although he was several inches taller, Hannah's companion seemed to have trouble keeping up with her. She asked a few more questions, but he could offer nothing of interest except the fact that the carriages had been racing. They rounded the bend in the road, and came upon the scene.

The horses seemed unhurt. They still stood in the traces, quivering but otherwise calm. The carriage, a flashy yellow phaeton, was now a one-wheeled vehicle, the axle resting on the ground. Another carriage was parked nearby, the horses tied to a tree branch. There was no sign of anyone else.

"Where is he?" Her guide blinked owlishly.

"Over here." He led her down a gentle slope, away from the road and toward the field. A pair of legs in blue trousers and tall polished boots protruded from underneath a blueberry bush. "He rolled some way," explained the man.

"What's his name?" she asked, picking her way closer.

"Reece. Right. Lord David Reece." He didn't appear too lordly right now. Hannah went down on her knees next to the man and pushed aside the branches until she could see a dark head.

"Lord David?" she said loudly. "Can you hear me, Lord David?"

"Wake up, Reece," called her companion, kicking one of the prone man's boots. "I've brought someone to help."

"Please don't kick him, sir. His leg could be broken." Hannah turned back to the victim, reaching out to shake his shoulder gently. "Lord David, can you—?" As she touched him, he twitched, then erupted from under the bush with a furious bellow.

"God damn, that hurts! Leave me be!" He swung his arm in a wide arc, knocking Hannah breathless and backward. He howled again. "Bloody Christ! What the hell happened to my arm?"

"Sir!" Hannah scrambled to her knees. "I've come to help."

"You'll go to hell for sure now, Reece," said the first man, laughing. "You're swearing at the vicar's wife."

"My apologies," grumbled the injured man, cradling his arm to his body. "Christ, it hurts!"

Hannah ignored that. "Where are you hurt?"

"My arm," he moaned, hunching over. She put out her hand again, and he flinched. "Don't touch it, I think it's broken. This is all your fault, Percy!"

"Well, I like that!" exclaimed his friend. "You wanted to race. I never made you hit the hole in the ground."

"Sod off," snarled Lord David, turning a bit green.

"Gentlemen!" Hannah glared at both of them. "You may argue later, but for now shall we get out of the road? My cottage is just down the road, so we'll move you there, and I'll send for someone from the village." Lord David nodded weakly, and Hannah hoped he didn't throw up on her. "All right then. Mr. Percy, would you help him up?"

They got the injured man on his feet, only to have him go suddenly white as a sheet and topple back to the ground in a dead faint. Hannah sighed, directing Mr. Percy to lift him again, wedging herself under Lord David's side. His long arm dangled over her shoulder, his head hung forward, and Hannah staggered under his weight. There was no way they could lever him up into the surviving carriage, so they would have to walk. Thankfully Percy was as tall as his friend, and was able to take most of the load, but he was still drunk, and their progress was slow.

Finally they reached the cottage and Hannah kicked open the gate. They maneuvered Lord David's limp body through the garden, and Hannah called out to Sarah as they reached the door.

"In here," she said to Mr. Percy, indicating the parlor. She wasn't at all sure the sofa in there would be up to Lord David's height, but she couldn't go another step. Her shoulder felt like it had been sheared away. With a great thump, they deposited Lord David on the sofa, and Hannah flopped into a chair in relief.

"Goodness." Sarah surveyed the scene from the doorway, hands on her hips.

"Is there any tea left?" Hannah knew just was Sarah was thinking: we got to see the spectacular accident! Sarah had a sharp sense of humor. At Hannah's question, Sarah nodded, her eyes still fastened on the man lying across the sofa. "Will you bring it, please?" asked Hannah with exaggerated politeness. Sarah glanced at her, smirked, and went back to the kitchen.

Hannah turned to her visitor. "Mr. Percy, do sit down. Mrs. Braden, my sister-in-law, will bring some tea. I'll see if I can help Lord David." She got up and pulled the curtains all the way open so she could see better.

The light fell upon a strikingly handsome man. Lord David Reece was tall and well built, that much Hannah already knew, but he was also very attractive. Dark hair, almost black, worn long and tied back from his face with a slender leather thong. Sooty eyelashes, a high brow, sculpted cheekbones, wide, firm lips . . . Hannah couldn't help being impressed. He was one of the handsomest men she had ever seen, even if he did smell like a distillery.

She turned her attention to his arm. His coat was exquisitely tailored and fit him perfectly, which made removing it while he was unconscious a near impossibility. She settled for feeling his arm through the cloth, and came across the distorted lump of his shoulder. It was probably out of joint, a relatively mild injury, but not one Hannah knew how to fix herself.

She moved down to his leg. Something about the angle of his foot on the ground had made her think it was broken, and the way he fainted the instant any weight was put on it strengthened that suspicion. His boots, like his coat, were a perfect fit, but had to come off. If the leg swelled inside the boot, it would be difficult even to cut the boot off without further injury. She turned to Mr. Percy.

"I suspect his leg is injured, or perhaps his ankle. I think it would be best if we removed his boot."

"What? Oh. Right." Percy rubbed his hands together, going to his friend's feet.

"No!" Hannah protested, realizing what he intended. "His ankle may be broken. We should cut the boot—"

Mr. Percy looked horrified. "I should say not," he said indignantly. "These boots are from Hoby. Reece'd never slice them off. I'll get it off, never fear."

"No, please, Mr. Percy—" Hannah cringed as he seized the boot and yanked.

"Arggggg!" Lord David came awake with a roar. "God damn son of a bitch, Percy! What the bloody hell are you doing?"

"Keeping her from cutting off your boot, Reece." Mr. Percy dropped the boot on the floor, wobbling on his feet again as he staggered to a chair. Gripping his leg, Lord David turned to glare at her.

"Your leg may be broken," Hannah said weakly.

"I should bloody well think so! Jesus holy Christ, that hurt!" Hannah pressed her lips together at his language. "Who are you, anyway?" He scowled at her.

"I am Mrs. Preston. This is my cottage." Hannah looked up to see Sarah watching, a tea tray in her hands, her eyebrows halfway to her hairline. "Thank you, Sarah. Would you like some tea, Lord David?" He grunted and slung his arm over his eyes. Hannah turned to his friend. "Mr. Percy, perhaps you should see to the horses. Mr. MacKenzie at the White Swan or Mr. Edwards at the King's Arms will be able to stable them for you."

Percy jerked to his feet, relief washing over his face. He had been looking at the tea tray with a mixture of repugnance and resignation, and Hannah wondered if he had more liquor in his carriage.

"Right. Many thanks, ma'am. Reece . . ." He shuffled his feet. "I'll make sure your blacks are settled."

"Get out, Percy," muttered Lord David from under his arm. Hannah went over to Sarah.

"He needs the doctor," she whispered.

Sarah looked past her at the man sprawled on her sofa. "I could go, but will you be all right?"

"Well, I could always kick his broken leg," Hannah replied. "That would probably do him in if he tries to ravish me."

Sarah muffled a snort, reaching for her shawl. "I'll

hurry." Hannah rolled her eyes and went back into the parlor.

"Are you really the vicar's wife?" He sounded suspicious. Hannah poured a cup of tea, and carried it to the sofa.

"I was. My husband died six months ago."

He cleared his throat. "Terribly sorry." His eyes flickered toward the tea. "You wouldn't have any brandy to put in that tea, I suppose? For medicinal purposes?"

"Liquor got you into this position, Lord David; it would be very bad of me to offer you more."

"Call me Reece," he said, leaning back and ignoring the tea she set on the table beside him. "What's the village?"

"Middleborough. It's almost half a mile from here."

"Right. The middle borough." He turned pleading eyes on her. "Just a spot of brandy? My arm hurts like a . . . It's terribly sore."

Hannah hesitated. It would be a while before the doctor arrived. "I have some sherry."

"That's lovely," he said fervently. "Sherry would be capital." Hannah deliberated, but the man was clearly suffering; being drunk was the least of his troubles at the moment. She went to get the sherry.

When she returned, his eyes were closed, and she just set the bottle and glass down beside the tea. There wasn't much she could do for him, and if he could rest until the doctor arrived, so much the better. She went back to the kitchen, where Molly was just finishing her tea.

"Mama, why is that man here?"

Hannah brushed the bread crumbs from the table onto her hand and tossed them out the window. "His carriage was wrecked, and he was hurt. This was the closest house, so we brought him here."

"Will he stay long?"

"I doubt it, dear. Aunt Sarah's gone to fetch Dr. March."

"Oh." Molly was quiet. Hannah washed the cups and put them on the dishboard to dry. "He's drinking Papa's wine."

Hannah's hands froze over the teapot. For a moment she could hear Stephen answering Molly's questions, see him balancing his daughter on his knee, fair heads close together. And now someone else was drinking his sherry. "Yes. The gentleman's leg hurts very much, and the wine makes it feel a little better."

Molly thought about this. "It didn't help Papa."

Hannah's throat tightened and she couldn't reply at first. How to explain to a child that her healthy, sturdy father could catch a cold in the rain and die from it? Molly hadn't talked much about Stephen's death, and once Hannah had explained that her papa had gone to live with the angels in heaven, she had seemed content, her curiosity satisfied. Hannah didn't know whether this reassured her or not.

"Is he going to die, too, Mama?" Hannah shook herself. Molly was only four.

"No, Molly, I doubt he'll die. He's not terribly sick, and we'll take good care of him until he can go home."

"Better care than we took of Papa?" Molly gazed up at her with complete innocence, her arms on the table, her chin on her hands, her small legs kicking. The ache knotted in Hannah's chest again, that she had not been able to take care of her husband. It had been a cold, for mercy's sake. . . .

"Yes, Molly. We'll take the very best care of him, and not let him get sick."

Molly nodded, looking relieved. "May I go plant some flowers? Missy wants to dig." Hannah nodded, and Molly hopped down from her seat and ran into the garden, her rag doll in hand. Hannah put away the plates and wrapped up the last tea cakes.

She went back into the parlor to get the tray. Lord David still had his arm over his face, but the bottle of sherry was empty. Hannah added it to the tray and took everything back to the kitchen. She set the bottle aside and sighed. The last traces of Stephen were vanishing every day. She had given his clothes to the poor, as he had asked her to do, and his books would stay with the house. She had no use for sermons and theological texts. Soon there would be almost nothing left of him and her life with him. She put on another pot of tea, for herself this time.

By the time Molly ran into the house, shouting that Aunt Sarah had come with Dr. March and Uncle Jamie, Hannah felt better. Her moments of helplessness were getting rarer over time. The most important reminder of Stephen, her daughter, bounded into the kitchen, eyes glowing.

"Uncle Jamie is here! I told him he won his bet with Uncle Tom, and he said I could have the shilling!"

Hannah bent a sour gaze on her elder brother. "That was very noble, Jamie."

He grinned. "Make sure she gets something sweet from Mrs. Kimble in town," he said, winking at his niece. Molly shrieked with glee. Jamie rumpled her curls. "Run into the garden now, child. I need to speak to your mother." Molly darted out the door. "What happened?"

"Where's Dr. March?"

"In the parlor, with Sarah."

Hannah sighed. "A carriage race. One of them hit a hole and was thrown. I think his leg is broken, and his shoulder may be out of joint." A loud howl echoed from the parlor. "His friend came looking for help.

They're both deep in their cups." Jamie nodded, and she followed him down the hall to parlor.

Dr. March was bent over the injured man's arm. He looked up at their entrance. "Ah, Mr. Braden, I'll need your help. This arm is out of joint." Hannah hurried to Lord David's side. His eyes were closed, and a thin sheen of sweat covered his brow.

"How are you?" she whispered, feeling for a fever as Jamie took off his coat and Sarah fetched bandages.

"Bloody fine," he said through his teeth, squinting at her with bloodshot eyes. "But I do thank you for the sherry." Hannah smiled, and stepped back so the doctor could reset his shoulder. Lord David's face twitched once, but he didn't make a sound, even when Jamie accidentally bumped his injured leg.

"There you are, sir," said the doctor. "Keep it bandaged and rested for a week, and it will be fine. Now let me see this leg." Hannah sat down beside her patient and took his hand. He looked at her, startled.

"Are you from London, sir?" she asked, trying to distract him from the doctor's probing. He nodded once.

"Leaving it. Family orders."

"Your family lives near, then?" Hannah watched as a frown creased Dr. March's face. Lord David snorted.

"A sister and stepmother. And a brother in London."

"Mmm-hmm," said Hannah absently, trying to see what the doctor was doing. He had straightened Lord David's uninjured leg, and seemed to be measuring the two against each other.

"Is it very bad, do you think?" She tore her eyes away.

"I beg pardon?"

"My leg," he said, his color fading another shade as the doctor tugged on it. Hannah hesitated.

"I'm sure it will be fine. Dr. March is a fine physician."

"Well, sir, you've a seriously broken leg," said the

doctor then. "It will take time to heal. You're to put no weight at all on it for four weeks. I'll splint it and bandage it, and nature will do the rest." Lord David nodded, and his hand relaxed in Hannah's. She hadn't even realized his grip had tightened. The doctor gave her a significant look, and when he left, she followed him to the door.

"He shouldn't be moved, Mrs. Preston," said the doctor in a low voice. "Would it be a terrible imposition to leave him here?"

Hannah hesitated. "Of course not."

"See here, Dr. March," exclaimed Jamie, "he can't stay *here*. She's alone with a child. She can't care for a wounded man."

The doctor sighed. "Well, I suppose I could give him enough laudanum for a trip into town, but there wouldn't be anyone at the inn who could look after him. He won't be able to do anything for some time."

"Jamie," said Hannah, putting one hand on his arm. "I was about to ask if you might persuade Pa to send Willy for a while. He could help Lord David."

"I haven't agreed," said Jamie testily. "I'm not leaving you alone with a strange man, even if Willy's here. He could be anyone! He's hardly given a good account of himself so far—"

"Jamie, he's got a broken leg," interrupted Sarah gently. "And it's Hannah's house." He glowered at his wife.

"I can't throw him out," said Hannah. "He's in enough pain as it is."

"I agree, Mr. Braden," put in the doctor. "It may do the man further harm to move even into town."

Her brother said a few things under his breath about drunken idiots who threw themselves out of carriages, but stopped protesting. The doctor went to splint Lord

David's leg, and Hannah and Sarah were left in the hall when Jamie stomped out to tend his horses.

"Well, that's a rare bit of excitement in Middleborough," Sarah observed. "A drunken lord crashing on your doorstep."

Hannah sighed. "I could do without that kind of excitement. A trunk of gold sovereigns crashing on my doorstep would be more helpful." She glanced into the parlor. "But I can manage, so long as Pa lets Willy come."

Sarah pursed her lips. "We'll tell him the gentleman looks rich. That ought to do it."

Hannah choked back a laugh. Her father would agree to just about anything that might benefit him financially, including sending his youngest son to help a stranger. "Thank you."

Sarah grinned as Jamie called to her. "Good luck."

Hannah followed to the door and waved as they drove off. "I could use some luck," she said to herself. Her time was running out. When the new vicar arrived in a month, she would have to move back into her father's house unless she found another way. Into her father's house, with her father, his new wife, and her two younger brothers. A month sounded like a very short time. And now she would be tending an invalid during that month.

With a sigh and a silent prayer for help, Hannah went back into the parlor to help the doctor.

CHAPTER 2

Lord David proved to be a model houseguest. Thankfully, Willy was allowed to come, although he did admit to Hannah that if he were to get a reward from Lord David, their father would take half of it. Knowing the money would be lost at dice or drunk at the White Swan, Hannah almost hoped Lord David didn't give Willy anything. For his part, Willy was happy to be released from the farm, and attached himself to Lord David, whose horses Willy had seen in town. Every word Hannah heard from Willy was about those horses, and how desperately he longed to have some as fine. Hannah realized how attentive he had been one morning after Willy had gone into town to get some items for Lord David, taking Molly with him.

"Good morning. How are you feeling?" She smiled at her guest as she let herself into the parlor.

He lowered the newspaper. "This *Times* is two days old."

"I'm sorry. Middleborough gets them a bit late."

He tossed it aside and dropped his head back against the sofa. His hair was unbound, and spread around his shoulders, and his jaw bristled with dark beard. Hannah set down Stephen's shaving mirror and basin. "I brought you something."

He was unimpressed. "I was beginning to enjoy looking like a ruffian." Hannah laughed. He did look a bit dangerous in his white shirt, sans neckcloth and waistcoat. He was a very attractive man, and only if one looked closely did the signs of dissipation become apparent.

"You may use it or not, as you like. Is there anything else I can get you?"

"Some company?" he said, with a charming smile. "If I have to discuss one more horse, I swear I'll not be responsible for my actions."

"Willy's very persistent, isn't he?" said Hannah with a sigh. "This must be dreadfully dull for you. Perhaps you would care to sit in the garden?" He grimaced, but reached for his crutch.

That day David sat in the garden because he couldn't go any farther. The next day he sat there because he discovered Willy would leave him in peace if he sat in the sun and closed his eyes. The day after he sat there because it was too dark to read in the parlor, the day after that because it was too hot indoors, and the next because Mrs. Preston was cleaning the parlor.

His hostess was a very industrious woman. Just watching her made David faintly ill. While he sat among her roses and herbs, she baked bread, knitted socks, tended the garden, read stories to her daughter, mopped, scrubbed, washed, and mended until David thought she would drop. It was fascinating to him; women of his class never did half those things. Aside from the horse-mad Willy, though, there was no one else to do things, so he supposed she had no choice. The amazing thing was, she didn't seem to mind.

Of course, David hadn't seen any other damn thing to do in this village, since Percy had deserted him. The first few days he had thought he would literally die of boredom, but now he was beginning to see some attractions in the place. Except for the work, of course.

The air was fresh. The nights were quiet. The food was plain, but delicious and fresh. The garden was undeniably peaceful, just like Mrs. Preston herself. She was the first woman David had ever known who could sit beside another person and not speak. Today she sat on the bench opposite him, quietly, peacefully, sewing. Not nagging or chattering or complaining, just minding her own business. It made him want to talk to her.

"Do you do everything yourself?" She looked up, not surprised or pleased, but thoughtful. "About the house, I mean."

"My brothers help with any repairs, and my sisters-in-law come to help at times. Other than that, yes."

"That must be quite a burden for a woman alone."

Her fingers paused over her sewing. "My husband died only six months ago." She forced a smile. "The work isn't so bad."

David cast about for something to say. She still wore black sometimes, and gray when not. It was a pity, he thought, for she was an attractive woman, and couldn't be very old. "On the contrary, I think it must be very hard at times."

Her eyes sparkled with teasing. "Do you mean the work, or living in Middleborough?" He knew he looked guilty from her laugh. "You mustn't be too hard on Middleborough, sir. It may not have the entertainments of London, but life in the country can be very wholesome and refreshing. In just a week, you've gained some very healthy color in your face."

"Yes, the sun doesn't seem to shine as often in the city." David squinted at the sky, realizing that she was right. Middleborough was growing on him: the spare furnishings of the house, the fresh breeze that blew through the garden, the absolute silence that left a man no choice but to examine his own thoughts. David hadn't indulged in such introspection in years, perhaps never, and while it might have been the influence of living in the vicarage, he began to feel as though he should let the fresh air into his life as well.

He knew he was an irresponsible rogue—his brother had been telling him so for years, and Marcus was never wrong about anything—but David had never regretted a thing until now. Perhaps this was the turning point in his life, the crossroads he had been galloping toward. Perhaps being marooned in a vicarage was his chance at redemption.

Mrs. Preston went into the kitchen to tend to her bread. David watched her go, thinking that he wouldn't mind absorbing some of her calm self-possession. He could never picture her worked up into a fury over something like being outbid on a horse, nor racing down a dirt road and breaking her leg. Everything she did seemed to have a reason, a purpose. His moment-to-moment existence began to seem, at that moment, a trifle pointless.

For the first time, David began to consider the possibility that the broken carriage wheel was a blessing after all.

"Why are you moving house?"

Hannah looked up in surprise at the sound of his voice. David was watching her from the doorway, leaning on his crutch. In the two weeks he had been at the vicarage, they had become friends of a sort, and he had asked her to call him by name. Hannah had seen stranger friendships develop, when Stephen would help the town drunk or a servant cast out for being with child. While not quite as desperate as those souls, Hannah sensed a deep insecurity in David, one he took great pains to hide behind a brash, cocky front. Still, he was amusing and witty and very easy to talk to, and she found she genuinely liked him. "Why are you walking around? Dr. March said you should wait another fortnight at least before putting weight on your leg."

He hopped into the room and sat with a thump on the threadbare sofa. "Willy told me you're moving house soon. Why?"

Hannah resumed packing books. She couldn't take all of them with her, and was trying to choose which to keep. "This is the vicarage. The new vicar will be arriving the week after next."

He was silent. "And where will you go?"

"Back to my father's." Hannah weighed a well-loved novel against a volume of medicinal remedies, finally setting the novel aside with a twinge of sadness. She loved reading, and the novel was a gift from Stephen.

"Why are you leaving that book?" He had it in his hands before Hannah could stop him. He flipped it open and saw the title page and Stephen's note.

"I can't take everything." She took the book back. "Did you need something? Has Willy not returned yet from town?"

He shifted, propping his splinted leg on the sofa. "I was just seeking a little company. I found this in my room, and thought you might know how it came to be there." He held out a bundle of braided rags. Hannah smiled.

"I made it for Molly when she was getting her teeth. She chewed on it to help the pain. I expect she left it to comfort you because your leg is hurt."

"Ah." He turned the floppy toy over in his hands. "That was very kind of her."

"She's a very compassionate little girl," said Hannah. "Though rather shy." He laughed with her.

"I think she must have learned it from her mother," he said. "The compassion, that is, not the reserve. I haven't properly thanked you for taking me in, nor apologized for my behavior."

"I understand. The pain must have been terrible."

He shrugged. "What will you do at your father's house?"

Hannah put a dog-eared periodical into her box. It was two years old, but Molly had overturned a bottle of ink and printed her little hands all over it. Hannah expected she would keep it the rest of her life. "Admirable fortitude. Dr. March said the break was clean, but awkward. You don't want to be left with a limp."

"It wouldn't matter," he muttered, staring into the fire with hooded eyes. "A limp, a missing limb, it would all be the same." Hannah sensed that he wasn't speaking to her, and tactfully concentrated on her packing. After a moment, he shook his head. "Why didn't you answer my question?"

She quirked a brow. "Are you accustomed to getting an answer to every question?"

"I? No. But I would like to know the answer to that one."

Hannah sighed. "Well, the sad truth is, I've no idea. I have no other place to go. Jamie has four children of his own, Tom has three, and Luke and Willy still live with our father and his new wife. I don't mind so much for myself, but Molly . . ." Her voice tailed off. "I didn't want to raise my child under someone else's roof," she finished.

The firelight threw flickering shadows around him, illuminating the planes of his face, his hair black as night. He wore a blue silk dressing robe over his shirt and trousers, and the rich fabric glowed like a jewel. "You could marry again," he said in a quiet voice.

Hannah sighed again, but with a wry smile. "An excellent idea. I would cull my list of suitors, if I had any."

"I meant it seriously." Hannah threw him a reproving look.

"I didn't question the merit of the idea, only the practicality."

He was quiet for a long time, and Hannah went back to her sorting. A gardening almanac made the box, a book of poems did not. Her two favorite novels went into the box, handprint-free periodicals did not, nor did another book of poems. Her box was already over half-full, and she was only a third of the way through the shelves. She would probably have to go through the box again, she thought regretfully. If only she had her own cottage. . . .

"You could marry me."

Hannah dropped the book in her hands. "David—I didn't—"

"No. It's a serious offer, and you should seriously consider it." He leaned forward, bracing his elbows on his knees. Hannah met his dark eyes for a long moment.

"Thank you, but I couldn't. We're barely acquainted."

"It would solve your problem," he said as if she hadn't spoken. "I can support you. I like Molly very much, and would try to be a good father for her. You won't have to choose which books to keep, and you'll stay mistress of your own house."

"There's more to marriage than being able to support a wife," Hannah said, almost amused in her disbelief. He nodded.

"I understand. I wouldn't ask for any other comfort than you've already given me." Hannah cleared her throat and busied herself with the books in front of her, hardly able to believe that she was discussing marriage with a near-stranger.

"Why would you marry me? What do I have to offer you?"

"Salvation, perhaps," he said. "The goodness in life I've been so short of. The moral character I've never had."

"David, I can't offer you salvation, or goodness," said Hannah, dismissing the idea with a smile. "You must find those things within yourself. Why do you think you can't?"

He scratched his chin, thinking. "Because I never have. I've never tried, in case you were about to ask, but I can't even think how I would go about it."

"It's different for every person. Depending on someone else to do it for you will only delay the business."

His mouth crooked in a grin. "I've delayed it for thirty-two years."

"It's never too late to start." Hannah reached for another stack of books. "But I'm honored to be asked."

"I meant it. Perhaps what you say is true, but I'm not withdrawing the offer. I could take care of you. Did you love your husband?"

Startled, Hannah nodded. "Yes," she said in a husky voice.

"He was a lucky man. Do you think you could ever love another?"

Hannah didn't want to let herself think about it. After Stephen died, she had buried her feelings for him deep in her heart, resolving to be brave and happy for Molly's sake, and for the most part she had been. But the question caught her off guard. Could she ever feel that way about another man? Stephen was dead. He had once filled her heart, and while she would never forget him, the void was growing every day, and she didn't know if she should fight it or not. "Perhaps," she murmured.

"The possibility is all I would ask. I won't push you." She said nothing. "I promise the decision would be yours."

"I couldn't promise it would ever happen." Was she possibly considering this? "And I couldn't accept your offer if I thought it wouldn't." That didn't come out quite the way she had intended. It sounded as if she wanted time to think about it. "I think you should reconsider," she added gently. "I'm honored by your offer, but you should reserve it for someone you feel something for."

"I feel something for you," he said with a sideways look. "Friendship. Respect. Admiration. Do you know how rare it is to find that in another person?" He ran one hand through his hair, looking frustrated. "I could return to London and find the sort of wife my brother would take, someone young and stupid and wealthy. It's more like buying a horse than choosing a mate. Even if we only remained friends, it would be a better match than most. So consider it." He reached for his crutch and got to his feet. "Good night."

Hannah murmured a reply. She sat by the fire for a long time. His last words stuck in her mind. Perhaps it wasn't just an impulsive offer made out of pity or guilt. Even in the country, marriages were often based on more practical concerns than love, and friendship was often a hoped-for state.

He was a handsome man. Hannah couldn't deny that. With time and familiarity, she could develop an attraction to him. And if he could support them, how much easier things would be. She had divined that his family had money, even if it weren't in David's control, and that they would be comfortable.

And she wouldn't have to live in her father's house.

Before her marriage, she had filled her mother's shoes, cleaning and cooking and washing for her father and brothers. Now she was used to being much more, the head of her own small household. In her father's house, she would be little more than a poor relation, and an unwanted one at that. Now that her father had remarried, he didn't even need the labor she would provide, and saw only the burden she and Molly would be on him. Hannah didn't doubt that life in his house would be rather grim.

But she knew too little about David. It wasn't just her own future she was deciding, it was Molly's as well, and she couldn't put that responsibility into the hands of someone she had known only a fortnight. Hannah got to her feet and dusted off her skirt. She would finish the packing tomorrow, after she told David she couldn't consider his offer.

It was hard to forget it, though, especially when she tried once more to refuse and David refused to listen. He waved aside all her objections, promised it would be a marriage of convenience, and urged her to consider it a while.

So the next time Sarah stopped in, Hannah sent Molly into the garden and pulled her sister-in-law into the kitchen. She might be losing her mind, but David's suggestion was taking root, sounding better and better. Better than her alternatives, anyway. Hopefully Sarah would be able to bring her back to earth.

But Sarah didn't. "Now, that's a thought," was her first comment. Hannah stared at her in shock.

"But an impractical, foolish thought, right?"

Sarah pursed her lips. Outside the window, Molly was rooting stones out of the garden with a sharp stick, chattering away in her high, sweet voice to

David, who sat on a bench in the sun, his healing leg propped on a nearby rock. "What are your choices?"

Hannah looked down. "You know as well as I do."

"Isn't this choice more attractive?" When Hannah didn't reply, Sarah took her hand, leaning across the table. "You know it is. Remarrying would be the best solution to your problems. Mind, I hoped you'd marry someone nearer Middleborough. You must write me, when you're a grand lady in London." She grinned, letting go of Hannah's hand to reach for the teapot. "Yes, I think you ought to consider it."

Hannah chewed her lip and looked out the window. Molly was now ferrying the stones across the garden to David's side. Each time she brought him a new one, David took it and examined it gravely. He said something and held up one stone, and Molly dissolved in giggles. Hannah's heart swelled as she watched her daughter take the rock from David's large, elegant hand with her grubby little fingers. David listened attentively to whatever Molly was saying, nodded, then gently placed the rock back with the others. He was very patient with Molly. Could he be a good father? "Can I risk it?" she murmured.

"Can you not risk it?" Sarah asked meaningfully.

Hannah sighed, dropping her face in her hands. She knew what Sarah meant; if she refused David, she might never have another offer. She certainly wouldn't meet many eligible men out on her father's farm. Nor would Molly, when she was old enough. David's offer meant a world of difference to Molly as well as to Hannah herself. *Could* she pass it up?

"Perhaps Jamie ought to talk to him," Sarah suggested. "Just to see how sensible his offer is."

Hannah took a deep breath, and nodded. Jamie wouldn't hesitate to tell her if he thought it was a mistake, but he also knew how reluctant she was to return to their father's farm. Sarah promised to send him, and left.

That night Hannah watched David closely. He held Molly enraptured with a fanciful story after dinner, and Hannah didn't miss how happily Molly bade him good-night. Perhaps marrying David wasn't so farfetched. Perhaps it would be the answer to her prayers. Perhaps he would be a good father, and a good husband, and keep her in comfort the rest of her days. When Jamie rode over the next day and closed himself in the parlor with David, Hannah almost held her breath, waiting.

Footsteps made her look up. "Come with me," grunted Jamie, tramping through the kitchen. Heart in her throat, Hannah put down the basket of shelled peas and hurried after him.

Her brother was adjusting his saddle. "He's pledged to take care of you," he muttered. "Got enough of his own money to support a family. He promised to deed a small country house of his to me in trust for Molly, so you'll have a place to go if . . . well, just in case. Guess you'd be a lady, Han."

"What do you think, Jamie?" she asked. He shrugged.

"Could be worse, I guess." He glanced at her. "What do you think?"

Hannah bit her lip. "I don't know yet."

That night after everyone else had gone to bed, Hannah sat up with a pot of tea and thought through her options as coolly as she could. It was not an easy decision, but in the end there were too many arguments for it, and not enough against it. In the morning, hoping she was making the right decision, she told David yes.

The banns were read the following Sunday.

CHAPTER 3

Percy dropped into the chair with a groan. "Damn, Reece, you've put your foot in it this time." He held out a letter with a familiar seal.

David tossed it onto the bed and went back to scratching his foot. He had expected it would be completely better by now, and was annoyed by the bandages and the cane he still needed. "Not your damn business, nor anyone else's."

"Huh," snorted Percy. "I managed to avoid him for three weeks, and paid for it. An hour he had me in his study, Reece, an hour! Is he really your brother?"

"Sadly," said David under his breath. That must be why Percy had returned to Misbegotten Middleborough, as he had called it before bolting for London. "Many thanks, Percy."

His friend uncorked the bottle of brandy. David accepted a glass after a moment's hesitation. He had given up almost all drink while at the vicarage, but by the second glass the familiar warmth settled over him. Percy was full of news of town: Walker's new bays, which he expected to run at Ascot and earn back their extravagant purchase price, Hadley's fight with

Devere over an opera dancer, Brixton wagering and losing half his inheritance one night, and winning it back the next.

David listened moodily. He knew it had been a bad idea to invite Percy to stay for the wedding. As long as he was steeped in the pure air of this little village, he wasn't tempted to return to his old ways. Percy's stories, though, stirred those dark and wild urges within him that he had sworn to banish with Hannah's help. No more carriage racing, drinking, or whoring, if he was to be her husband. But the more Percy talked, the stronger the discomfort became, like spiders crawling under his skin. Could he never drink again? Never visit a brothel again? What was he thinking, getting married while he was still young?

As if reading his thoughts, Percy kicked his uninjured foot. "Why'd you do it? Marriage is one thing, but a vicar's wife! Christ, man, you might as well become a vicar yourself."

"Leave it, Percy." David tried to ignore the prickling feeling that his friend was right. "I gave my word."

Percy laughed. "Consigned to marital drudgery. It won't be the same without you." He upended the bottle over his glass.

"She's a very good woman," argued David. If Percy would just go away, he might still be at peace with his decision. Hannah could be the saving of him. Assuming he still wanted to be saved, which he thought he did. Probably.

"Been the end of more men than any other sort." Percy snickered "No more women, no more drinking, no more cards or horse races or fights. To your imminent demise!" He lifted his glass as David glared at him. Suddenly Percy stopped, a delighted look on his face. He leaned forward, sloshing brandy onto his trousers.

"You know who ought to marry her? His grace! No vice, no excess, no fun! They're a perfect match!"

"Stubble it," growled David. The wicked urges were waging war against the honorable ones, with Percy's help.

"Right." Percy subsided into his chair. "No doubt you'll learn the life soon enough, give up all your friends and habits to sit at home and read sermons." He produced a pair of cigars and offered one. "Last smoke, old boy?"

David snatched it from his hand. "Go away, Percy. I've a wedding tomorrow." Percy got to his feet with another snigger and staggered off to his room. David contemplated the cigar, and Percy's words.

All right, so he was beginning to regret his offer to Hannah. He still liked her very much, but he'd been seduced by the enforced solitude of the last few weeks. As long as he stayed here, her company might be enough, but he couldn't live the rest of his life in Middleborough. The mention of a horse race or a cockfight made his blood race; he wasn't cut out for the quiet country existence.

But she needed someone to take care of her, someone who would appreciate her, and love Molly, and protect them both. David had wanted to be that person, but finally acknowledged he wasn't ready to change that much. The prospect of reforming his life, which had so appealed to him two weeks ago, now looked fatally dull.

But how could he get out of it now? He had given his word, the banns had been read, she was probably laying out her dress right now. She would be humiliated if he backed out now. Not that a gentleman *could* back out, of course.

His eyes fell on the letter Percy had brought. His brother, damn it all, had found out where he was, although probably not what he was doing. Percy would have delighted in telling all about Marcus's reaction to that news. David reached for the letter and broke the seal.

It was a long indictment. There was barely a salutation before the recriminations began. David ignored them, skipping to the bottom of the page:

> *Your utter lack of consideration astounds me. To disappear for weeks without word is bad enough, leaving your household to apply to mine for their wages and funds, but to ignore Celia's birthday when you had most solemnly promised to attend is beyond contempt. She is a girl of seventeen, and strangely enough, dotes on you. I am disgusted by your disregard for her feelings. You have shown yourself irresponsible, reckless, and completely selfish. I will expect a full accounting of your activities and excuses when you return to London. My carriage will arrive tomorrow to convey you, since accomplishing the trip unaided seems beyond you.*
>
> *Exeter*

David put the letter aside with a grimace. Even to his own brother, he signed himself Exeter. Percy was half-right: his brother was Hannah's equal in matters of responsibility. Not that Marcus would ever look at a woman like Hannah, for all that she was attractive and intelligent and filled to overflowing with common sense. Marcus would have a woman of property and breeding who would obey orders. Wouldn't it be amusing to watch them cross swords, though? David thought with a grin. If only there were some way to throw them together without any danger to himself. . . .

An audacious idea came to him. Something that he hadn't done in years, something Marcus had threatened to kill him for if he ever tried again. But if he managed it, Hannah would be set, he would be free, and Marcus would swallow a dose of his own medicine. All in all, it sounded rather ideal. David seized his cane and hobbled after Percy.

"Oh, no," was Percy's assessment. "Really, Reece. That's too far. He'll horsewhip you for certain."

"I'll tell him you helped me, of course."

Percy swore. "No! Even I have more sense than that."

"Come on, Percy," cajoled David, warming to the idea with every moment. "It'll be better than when we convinced old Deveraux his mistress was sleeping with his son. How could you miss it?"

"I value my life, that's how. He's not my brother. He'll kill me."

"Let's go to Italy, then. If we're gone before Marcus finds out, everything will be fine." Percy grumbled some more, but David could see that he was weakening. It had been a long time since they pulled off such a prank, and perhaps if Marcus had given him any credit for that, David wouldn't have considered this. But he was the useless younger brother; Marcus was responsible and competent and did everything to perfection. David had been raised with the trappings of wealth and power, but no real hope of possessing them, and with a dry stick like Marcus hovering critically over him, there was absolutely nothing for him to do but enjoy life, in any way he could. In the end, Percy agreed, as he always agreed to David's suggestions, and they opened a bottle of wine to perfect the plan.

"David, is something bothering you?" Hannah asked. They were five miles out of Middleborough, finally free of the wedding guests, and heading for

London in a luxurious coach which had appeared mysteriously at the White Swan. David said only that it was his brother's, sent to bring them back to town. Hannah thought it very kind of his brother to send the coach even if he hadn't attended the wedding, but when she said so, David just gave her a curiously cunning smile. All day he seemed to hum with excited energy, as did Mr. Percy. If they weren't grown men and beyond such things, Hannah would suspect they were plotting mischief.

"No." He had propped his still-healing ankle on the opposite seat where Molly was curled into a sleepy ball, her doll clutched to her jam-smeared dress. "Why do you ask?"

"You seem very excited about something."

He grinned. "Why shouldn't I be?" Hannah colored.

"David, I hope that . . . perhaps I should—"

"Hannah," he said, taking her hand. "I promised I wouldn't ask. That's not what I meant." She breathed a faint sigh, ashamed of herself for being so relieved. The thought of the wedding night had given her some pause. On her first wedding night, Stephen had been almost as nervous as she, but there had been no thought of waiting. David was being generous.

"Thank you. I'm sorry I mentioned it." He nodded, releasing her hand. Hannah put it back in her lap. Curiously, she still felt no spark of attraction at his touch, just a strange sense of disbelief that she was someone's wife again. She hoped her lack of warmth hadn't disappointed him.

By the time they reached London shortly after nightfall, Hannah was exhausted. Once woken from her nap, Molly grew restive and cross. David had managed to calm her with a long story about a princess who tamed a dragon with strawberry tarts. He really was very good with her, but eventually Molly erupted

into a full-fledged temper fit. Hannah almost wept
with relief when they finally stopped outside a handsome town house, and Molly stopped crying. David
took Molly by the hand and asked if she would like to
see her new room. Hannah wearily brought up the
rear, not too tired to notice the quiet affluence of the
neighborhood. David knocked on the door, and the
man who answered it looked like he would faint with
shock. "L-L-Lord David?"

"Why yes, Walters, the very same. May we come in?"
His mouth still agape, the man stepped aside. David
swept Molly into his arms and carried her inside. Her
finger was lodged in her mouth as she stared at the
man holding the door. "This is Miss Molly Preston,
and her mother."

Hannah hesitated, watching David start up the
stairs. She had a nagging feeling something wasn't
right. "Mrs. Preston?" asked the man called Walters,
watching her worriedly.

"Reece," she corrected, wishing David had introduced
her. But they were all tired. "David is my husband." He
and Molly were out of sight now, leaving her alone. "You
are Mr. Walters?"

He gulped and bowed. "Yes, madam. If there is anything you require, notify me at once."

Hannah nodded, forcing a smile. "Thank you. I
should see to my daughter," she murmured, and hurried after David. She found him in a large, elegant
room, tucking Molly into bed. Her child looked small
and lonely in the middle of the wide bed decorated in
swathes of pink silk. White velvet drapes covered the
window, and the white and gold furniture was daintily
carved. It was a decidedly feminine room, and set the
alarm bells ringing in Hannah's head. She made sure
Missy was tucked in with Molly, and followed David
into the hall.

"Whose house is this?" she demanded. "That room is decorated for a woman. And who is Mr. Walters?"

He chuckled. "Walters is the butler. The house belongs to my brother; I have a sister, you know. But it's always ready, and much nicer than my rooms, so I thought we should stay here. It's just for a few days, until my other arrangements are ready."

Partially mollified, Hannah hesitated. "I'm sorry. But you might have told me."

"I know." Not looking very sorry, he kissed her hand. "I'll have your trunks brought up immediately."

"Didn't Mr. Walters expect us? He looked shocked to see us."

Again that secretive smile that had so disturbed her earlier. "No, I didn't have time to send word. But the house is always maintained, so nothing should be lacking. Don't worry, Hannah, everything will be fine." He squeezed her hand and released it. "I'll see you in the morning. Sleep well."

Hannah watched him stroll down the stairs, whistling softly, and had the feeling again that there was something he wasn't telling her. Mr. Walters brought her trunk a few minutes later, and she got out hers and Molly's nightclothes, then dressed her sleepy daughter for bed. By the time she was ready for bed herself, Molly was already fast asleep. Before climbing into bed, Hannah went to the window and pulled aside the drape.

The heavy fabric felt thick and lush in her hand, unlike the cotton curtains in her room at the vicarage. It would take her quite a while to get used to the vastly more comfortable circumstance of her new husband's family. A butler, velvet drapes, silk bedhangings. She peered out the window at the unfamiliar city lights and buildings. She had never been to London, or even expected to go. Perhaps she ought to start considering the adventure her new life might hold.

* * *

"May we see a circus today?" Molly asked over break-fast the next morning. David laughed, setting down his coffee cup.

"Not today, moppet. I've some business to attend to, and I'm sure your mother will want to explore a bit." He looked at Hannah. "Walters will be able to tell you how to get around."

"Is there a park or a green nearby?" Molly was already trying Hannah's patience. She had awakened to find her daughter standing on a lovely but precarious chair, going through the wardrobe, which contained some very immodest items. Hannah wasn't precisely sure what all of them were, but she thought they were really too decadent for a young girl like David's sister. Judge not, that you be not judged, she had reminded herself, shooing Molly out and closing the wardrobe door firmly.

"Yes, the park should be safe at this time of day. Go ask Walters how to get there, Molly." She slid off her chair and bolted from the room, ignoring Hannah's caution to walk. His merriment fading, David turned back to her. "Hannah. I have some business. Unfortunately, it will take me out of London."

"So soon?" Hannah was surprised. David had stayed in Middleborough for weeks with no sign of contact with anyone, and hadn't seemed to care about getting back in any rush. Although, perhaps that explained this urgency now. "When will you return?"

"I'll be gone several days at least. I'm sorry. I hate to leave you alone on your first day in town, but it can't wait any longer. I hope you can forgive me."

"Well, if you have to go, you have to go, and it can't be helped," she said practically. "I hope it won't take overlong." Sudden uneasiness clouded his face.

"I'm doing this for you and Molly. I want to provide you a comfortable life."

"Good heavens, David, I understand," she said. "We shall miss you, but I won't keep you from your responsibilities."

"I might have known you would say that." He grinned in relief, and she smiled. After breakfast he bade Molly good-bye and told her to be good for her mother. As he mounted his horse, a splendid gray gelding, Hannah fidgeted. It seemed unnatural to say farewell with just a wave; he was her husband, after all. He leaned down. "Good-bye," he whispered, kissing her cheek. "I shall hope you still smile at me when I come back."

"Of course I will," she said, glad that he had made it easy for her. She stood back with Molly and watched him ride away.

The rest of that day they explored the house. The cook was Mrs. Walters, and she took a liking to Molly immediately. Molly asked to help with the baking, which seemed to surprise and delight the cook, and by the end of the day they were fast friends.

While Molly made bread, Mr. Walters showed Hannah the rest of the house. He appeared recovered from his shock of the night before, and Hannah told herself she was being silly for imagining things. David had hardly left them in cruel circumstances, and even if they eventually settled in less elegant quarters, he had taken care of them thus far. The house verged on opulent, to Hannah's eyes, and the Walterses were very helpful.

Over the next few days, they explored the neighborhood. They went to the park every day, and walked along streets lined with shops boasting the most beautiful things in the windows, and crowded with carriages the likes of which Hannah had only seen passing through Middleborough. The ladies dressed in splendid clothes, as did the gentlemen, and Hannah couldn't help thinking that David's attire, which had seemed so fine in Middleborough, was actually unremarkable here. London was a far cry from home.

Mrs. Walters volunteered that there was a market several streets away, and Hannah decided to take Molly. They borrowed a basket from the kitchen, Hannah made certain she had some money in her pocket, and they set out. They watched a puppet show, three times at Molly's insistence, and then wandered through the stalls piled with vegetables and flowers and fruits. For the first time in years, Hannah didn't have to shop for dinner; Mrs. Walters had already done it. It was rather nice to walk slowly and aimlessly through the market, and to hold Molly's hand without having to scold her daughter to hurry. In the end they bought some strawberries from a fat woman near the opera house. The walk home was slow, because Molly was tired and dragged her feet, but finally Hannah cajoled her with the promise of tea and biscuits.

Molly dropped her shawl on the floor and began pulling at her bonnet the instant they were home. "I'm so hungry, Mama!" she declared, lifting the straw bonnet straight up with both hands. The bow caught under her chin, forcing it up.

"Be patient," said Hannah, setting down her basket and pulling the bow loose. "There, you may go ask Mrs. Walters for your tea."

"Thank you, Mama!" Molly flew toward the kitchen.

"Walking, Molly!" Without looking back, her daughter skidded to a halt and began taking tiny mincing steps. She rounded the corner and Hannah just shook her head with a smile as the tapping of Molly's shoes accelerated to a run again. She hung up her shawl and

Molly's, and was removing her own bonnet when Mr. Walters appeared, looking very uncertain. He cleared his throat.

"Pardon, ma'am, there's someone to see you."

"Oh?" Hannah didn't know anyone in London. Could it be someone from home? "Thank you, Mr. Walters. Would you please take these to Mrs. Walters?" She touched her hair, smoothing down any wind-blown curls.

He took the basket of berries. "Yes, ma'am." He cleared his throat again.

"Is your throat sore?" Hannah asked, concerned. His voice sounded very scratchy, too. "A cup of chamomile tea might help." His smile looked sick and weak.

"Thank you, ma'am," he murmured. Hannah twitched her skirt into place, and went to the drawing room.

At her entrance, a tall man turned from the window. "Oh!" she said in pleased surprise. "I didn't expect you back today." She started toward him. He didn't move. Hannah stopped, and took a closer look.

At first glance, he was the very image of David. A second glance revealed differences, though slight. His mouth was firmer, with none of the devilish grin that always curved David's. His posture was straighter, his figure leaner, his hair shorter. And when he moved a step toward her, it was with a pantherlike grace, and not with David's easy, ambling gait.

"Forgive me, sir," apologized Hannah as his eyes narrowed on her. "I mistook you for someone else." She hesitated, then moved forward. "I am Mrs. Pr—" Old habits died hard; she corrected herself, awkwardly, "Reece."

He stared at her for a long moment, one hand behind his back, the other tapping a leather-bound book against his thigh. "David, I suppose," he said at last. It was a frosty voice, smoother than David's but more forceful. Hannah put up her chin.

"Yes," she said. "You know him, then?"

A dry smile flickered, leaving his eyes unchanged. "Not as well as I once thought, but still better than you, I imagine."

Hannah stiffened. "He's not at home. I would be glad to tell him you called."

The man tilted his head, scrutinizing her. "Are you still a virgin?" he asked abruptly.

Hannah would have gasped, had she not been so shocked. Her mouth fell open and she could only look at him in dumbfounded outrage.

"Never mind," he sighed, casting his eyes upward. "It doesn't matter. What has David promised you?"

She felt fully absolved of any obligation to be polite. "I think I must ask you to leave my house."

He seemed amused by this. Another smile crooked his mouth. "Your house," he repeated. "Indeed."

"I'll have Mr. Walters show you out." Hannah turned her back on him and marched toward the door.

"I am Exeter," he announced, as if this would explain everything. Hannah stopped, slowly turning back to face him.

"Shall I have Mr. Walters summon your carriage, Mr. Exeter?"

He exhaled sharply through his nose, closing his eyes. "Not Mr. Exeter, girl, the duke of Exeter."

"What do you want?" she snapped. No one had called her a girl for years. She was a woman of twenty-six, after all, and a wife and mother. This man must have some reason for calling on her, and while she couldn't bring herself to be nice to him, she didn't want to anger David by throwing out a duke, especially one who looked enough like him to be his brother.

"I wanted to see you. We shall have some dealings

together, may God grant they be brief. What, precisely, did David tell you?"

"He told me nothing of you," she retorted. "And I'm not surprised, based on what I've seen of your conduct and character."

Something flared in his dark eyes. "My conduct and character?" he repeated. "You assault *my* conduct and character. That, madam, is the best joke I have heard all day." He flipped open the book he held, his piercing gaze making her suddenly wary.

"Who are you?" She retreated a step as he started toward her, paging through the book, his eyes never leaving her.

"I," he said with terrible precision, "am Marcus Edward Fitzwilliam Reece, duke of Exeter and elder brother, by ten minutes, to David Charles Fitzwilliam Reece." He turned the book around and thrust it forward so she could see it.

Her mouth went dry as Hannah recognized the register from the Middleborough parish church. She saw her own name, Hannah Jane Preston, halfway down the page, just as she had signed it five days previously. But the signature beside it . . .

"And according to the register of this parish of Middleborough, and therefore, according to the Church of England . . ."

Not the name David Charles Fitzwilliam Reece, but written in a precise, sharp hand . . . the name Marcus Edward Fitzwilliam Reece.

"I am your husband."

CHAPTER 4

She stared at it for a moment in shock. Then she pushed the book aside and met his hard gaze. "That's impossible. Just because your name is there—you are not!"

He closed the book with a loud snap. "But it complicates things enormously, and will cause me a great deal of trouble to correct. So I ask you again, what did David promise you? Tell me now so we can settle and you can go back to wherever you came from."

Hannah couldn't decide whom she was more furious with, David or his insufferable brother. "Please leave," she said through her teeth. "I will not stand here and be insulted in my own house." She remembered too late it wasn't actually her house.

He smiled sardonically. "Ah, yes, your house. Your house, as you like to call it, belongs to me. The last woman who lived here and called it her own was my mistress. Are you sleeping in her room, madam? How do you like Monique's taste? I never cared much for all that pink myself."

Hannah's mouth dropped open again, in shock and rage that David had put her child to sleep on sheets last used by this arrogant, pompous, fornicating beast. Never in her life had she wanted so much to hit someone. Another thin smile crossed his face. "David didn't tell you that, either? Pity."

"If you won't leave, I will." Hannah whirled and stormed toward the door. She didn't stop when he spoke, but she couldn't help but hear his sharp command.

"I expect your trunks packed and ready to leave at dawn." Hannah paused, hand on the knob.

"David's country home," she said to the door. "Is that also yours?"

"David's hunting box? No, that's all his. Is that where he seduced you?" Hannah opened the door and slammed it behind her with a satisfying crash. She went to the kitchen, shaking with anger. Molly, standing on a chair in front of the table, looked over and her eyes lit up.

"Mama! I've made a loaf!" She patted a mound of bread dough in front of her. "It's got cinnamon in it!" she whispered with a smile. "Mrs. Walters says it will taste so good with butter on!"

Hannah forced her mouth to turn up. The cook took one look at her face and turned away. "That's lovely, dear. Mrs. Walters, may I speak to you for a moment?" The woman nodded, wiping her hands with great care on her apron. Hannah beckoned her over to the corner, away from Molly's curious ears. "Who owns this house?"

Mrs. Walters cleared her throat. "Well, His Grace does. But once Lord David returns and explains, everything will be fine. Don't worry your head about it."

Hannah controlled herself with difficulty. She had a feeling none of them would see David anytime soon. "And your last—" She stopped, shying away from the word *mistress*. "Who lived here last?"

Mrs. Walters grimaced. "A Frenchwoman. Impossible to please and vain as Lucifer. Glad to see the back of her, I was."

Hannah nodded. Enough of it was true that the fine points didn't matter. David had lied to her and played her for a fool. She pressed her hands to her cheeks. How could she have been so stupid? How could she have walked into this?

"Ma'am, don't despair, truly. His Grace is a gruff one, sure he is, but he's a fair man. And he's right devoted to his family." Mrs. Walters's round face creased with concern.

Hannah let out her breath carefully. She wanted to throw something. She wanted to call David a very rude name to his face. She wanted to scream and cry in humiliation and anger. Instead she met Molly's wide brown eyes over the cook's shoulder, and swallowed her fury. "Thank you, Mrs. Walters."

"Pleased as plum pudding I was, to meet you," whispered the now-beaming woman. "A sensible woman is just what every rogue needs. Chin up, dear; Lord David was wrong to leave you here to face the duke, but he'll set things right when he returns."

Hannah forced another smile. Mrs. Walters patted her hand, and bustled back to her baking.

Hannah left Molly in the kitchen and went up the stairs to the bedroom. She closed the door behind her and covered her face with both hands. What was she to do now? How could David have tricked her so? How could she have allowed herself be tricked? What has seemed too good to be true was, of course, not true at all. A handsome, well-to-do gentleman crashing into her life to sweep her off her feet and carry her away to his elegant London town house? She should have known better.

But why, she wanted to scream. Why would David

do such a thing? What had it gained him? She hadn't tumbled into his bed, or brought him anything like a dowry. She pressed the heels of her trembling hands into her eyes. The only thing David had done was turn her life upside down. And anger his brother, she supposed, which must have been his intent all along.

She uncovered her face and swiped at her eyes. There was nothing to do but return home. She was a passable seamstress and cook; perhaps she could find employment and take a room somewhere. She would tell everyone David had died, she decided in a spurt of malice, died very violently. She would have no trouble thinking of some terrible fate for him.

She went to the wardrobe and began pulling out her things. The sooner she and Molly left London, the better.

Marcus tossed the register on the carriage seat beside him, wishing it were his wretched brother's head. David would pay dearly for this. The woman had looked shocked to see him, and she hadn't taken the bait when he offered to settle the accounts, but she would. He wouldn't give her a choice. The sooner she left London, the better.

He took David's note from his pocket and unfolded it. The arrogance of it had infuriated him, but until he saw the woman in the Holly Lane house, Marcus had really thought, deep down, that it was a joke. He held the letter to the window.

Dearest brother—Many thanks for your note reminding me of my numerous failings. You have awakened my sense of responsibility, and I shall try to be more aware of such things. In fact, since we brothers must look out for each other at all times, I have taken the lib erty of remedying one small oversight of yours. As you have not yet seen to the task of getting a duchess, I have found one for you. Apply to the vicar of Middleborough for details. I look forward to receiving your thanks when I return to town.

Yours ever, DR

Marcus threw the letter on top of the register. It had been a punishing ride to Middleborough and back, and his eyes burned from lack of sleep. Only fury was keeping him moving at this point: fury at a vicar who shook his hand and inquired after his bride, fury at a woman who told him to leave his own house, fury at a brother who could do this to him. It had been a long time since Marcus truly regretted having a twin. David's previous pranks had been limited to tricking creditors into transferring his debts to Marcus, and that time at Oxford when he had tried to pass as Marcus to avoid being sent down. Marcus had promised to cut his throat if he ever tried it again, and David hadn't, until now.

He wished David had at least had the courtesy to choose someone obviously impossible, who would realize her proper place and be glad to go back to it. Instead David found a woman who already had all the self-confidence and bearing of a duchess, just above medium height with glossy black curls, snapping blue eyes, and a full mouth that Marcus might have found appealing under different circumstances. As it was, he had to get rid of her and have the register altered before anyone else got wind of this.

The carriage stopped in front of Exeter House, and the footman swept open the door. Marcus unfolded himself from the seat, collecting the register and letter. The butler bowed as he strode through the door, the footman took his gloves as he removed them, and another servant was waiting for his hat. They operated in silent efficiency, the way Marcus preferred things, and he was turning toward the stairs when the butler broke protocol. He cleared his throat.

"Your Grace, Lady Willoughby is here." Marcus turned and looked at the butler. Harper bowed his head and waited.

"Was she told I was at home?"

"No, Your Grace. She insisted on waiting." Marcus waited. The butler bowed lower. "I shall tell her you are not at home for the rest of the day." Marcus inclined his head, and turned to go. Harper knew he didn't like people waiting for him when he returned home. He was halfway through the cavernous hall when the drawing room door opened with a resounding crash.

"How dare you!" cried Susannah, Lady Willoughby, in a dramatic tone. Marcus stopped, leveling a cool stare at her. God, he hated female theatrics. She crossed the hall with smooth, measured steps, her narrow skirts clinging to her legs. She came to a halt within arm's reach, drew back her hand, and slapped him full across the face.

"How dare you do this to me!" she hissed at close range. "You lying, arrogant, manipulating scoundrel!"

Marcus was glad he hadn't promised her anything. She had handed him the perfect excuse to get out of the assumptions she had drawn and he had not corrected. "Then I bid you good day, madam," he said coolly, turning on his heel.

"Exeter! Wait!" she screeched, flinging herself at him. "How could you? After all we've meant to each other—to find out like this—I'm humiliated in front of all society!" She pressed her face, and her breasts, into his arm and sobbed, her hands like an iron band around his wrist.

"And you decided to make a spectacle of yourself in front of my servants as well? I fail to see how that improves your situation." He had a sinking feeling he knew what she had found out, and wanted to know how.

She shoved away from him, her bosom heaving. "It was in the *Times,* of all places," she went on in the same tragic voice. "Everyone will know that I won't be your duchess. How can I hold my head up? How can you expect me to suffer this?"

"I myself never knew you were to be my duchess," said Marcus in clipped tones. "How, I wonder, did the rest of London know it?" She jerked backward, a flash of dismay in her eyes. "Perhaps you were indiscreet, and rash, in telling your friends of your hopes, for that is all they ever were. I make no apologies, for I made no promises to break."

"You're cold," she said under her breath. "You've ice in your veins, just as everyone says. I never would have taken you to my bed if you hadn't been Exeter."

"And I never would have gone had you not made it so freely available," he returned just as quietly. "Good day." He walked away, and Susannah shrieked at the butler to fetch her carriage. Marcus waved aside the footman who held open the study door and went to the desk where the newspaper lay. He spread it open and flipped though the pages until he found the announcement. David had made his little prank public. Marcus swore; a retraction would be almost as humiliating as this, and generate even more gossip, but a retraction he would get as soon as the woman was gone.

He dropped into his chair and rubbed one hand over his face. At least there was one side benefit: Susannah was out of his hands. Everyone in town knew of their affair, but she had crossed the line when she began spreading rumors of their impending engagement. Marcus never knew what on earth possessed women to try trickery to get a husband. First Susannah, then this Hannah Preston. Surely neither one had actually expected to end as the duchess of Exeter.

If only he hadn't gone into Kent for a few days to see those thoroughbreds. If only his secretary hadn't fallen ill and left all the work to that idiot Adams, who neglected to pass on Walters's message that David was at Holly Lane. Then he might have nipped this disaster in the bud, prevented the announcement in the *Times*, and caught up with David before he vanished from sight.

As he sat plotting a variety of bad ends for his brother, there came a quiet tap at the door. "Yes?" he growled.

Harper appeared in the doorway. "Mr. Timms, Your Grace."

Marcus closed his eyes and waved one hand in grudging assent. Harper left, and a moment later a bluff hearty gentleman who looked nothing like his timid name came in. "Well, Exeter, I would have thought you had your plate full. Congratulations are in order, I suppose."

Marcus opened his eyes to glare at the man. Timms, damn him, just chuckled. "I would prefer, Timms, that my private affairs remain private."

"Well! Ought not to publish them in the *Times*, then." Timms caught sight of the paper open on the desk and smirked. "I take it your investigations of Lady Willoughby are complete, then. I saw her leave, and she seemed rather displeased."

"She was never going to be pleased, at least not in the manner of her choosing." Marcus got to his feet, subtly taking charge. "But essentially, yes, my investigations were complete. She knows nothing, and cares for nothing beyond her own comfort. The money could be printed on tea leaves and she wouldn't notice."

"She's been used, then."

Marcus nodded. "I believe so. She hasn't the intelligence to conceive of a plan of this scope herself."

Timms sighed. "I don't know if I should be pleased or not. It would have been so nice to find the culprit."

Marcus shrugged. "Keep looking. Susannah Willoughby's not the only one who's been passing counterfeit notes." It occurred to him to find out if Hannah Preston had received any money from David, but he kept the thought to himself. Timms and the other bank directors had promised David would not face punishment if he were involved in the alarming amount of counterfeit money that had been circulating in London lately, but Marcus wouldn't go out of his way to incriminate his brother. David had done a fine job of avoiding him for the last few weeks, which was not unusual, but in these circumstances it was somewhat alarming.

"I suppose we've no other choice." Timms looked at the newspaper again. "I'll leave you to it, then. Good day, Exeter."

Marcus nodded curtly. When Timms had gone, he went around his desk and unlocked the cabinet behind it. He took out a slim file and opened it, arranging some pages on his desk. Drawing up the chair, he studied his notes.

First, he could mark off Susannah. Marcus made some notes next to her name, just as glad to eliminate her as a suspect as he was to lose her as a lover. He hadn't meant to have an affair with her, although once she proposed it, he had seen the advantages. Marcus didn't waste a moment on guilt over his ulterior motive; she had one as well, to judge from her visit this morning.

But if she weren't producing the banknotes—and Marcus was quite sure of that—where had she gotten them? His eyes moved over the paper, where more than two dozen names were arranged in clusters. Some of them had exculpatory comments, some incriminating, but only one name on the paper concerned Marcus: David Reece, written squarely in the middle of the page. Every other name on the paper could be linked to David, many entirely too closely. No one had any direct evidence David himself had been passing false notes, but a large number of his friends and associates had been doing so, and Marcus disliked a coincidence that glaring.

But the penalty for counterfeiting was death, or, for the upper classes, transportation. Regardless of David's personal failings, Marcus couldn't stand by while his brother faced that. Timms, acting on intuition and the complaints of his wife's brother, who had gambled with David only to find himself left with a handful of fraudulent banknotes, had come to Marcus and offered him a deal. If Marcus would use his influence and position to find the counterfeiter and put an end to his business, Timms would see David bore no public consequences for any role in the scheme. Marcus agreed, preferring to deal with David on his own. As he always had.

He went over the list of other suspects. Everyone on the list moved in the upper ranks of society; the forged notes had been passed at some of the finest establishments in London. Everyone had some connection to David: friends, school mates, former lovers. Otherwise there were no common factors, at least none Marcus had seen so far. All of them had been linked to the counterfeit money, although Marcus was sure many had had no idea. Whoever was printing the false notes was terribly good at it.

But if David were behind the scheme, how? Marcus had searched David's town house from top to bottom, taking advantage of his brother's absence and underpaid servants, and found nothing. Of course a man would be an idiot to print money in his own sitting room, but Marcus hadn't found so much as a smudge of ink. The servants had told him nothing useful, except that David continued to spend as much as ever, but not more. The wine cellar was still full, the deliveries from the butcher still came weekly. Marcus had watched David's every move for over three months, looking into everything from the contretemps over Lady Barlow to David's change of tailor. There was nothing even remotely noteworthy.

And yet, Marcus just sensed David had a part in this. His brother had grown more reckless of late, more careless than ever of his reputation. Lady Barlow had been only the most conspicuous indiscretion. Marcus replaced the pen and sighed. He had hoped David's absence from town would help matters. He had hoped the stream of forged money would continue unchecked. That would be a mark in David's favor. But as far as Marcus could tell, the supply had diminished to damning levels.

At least now he knew where David had been, and what he had been up to. Was the Preston woman an attempt to divert his quiet investigations, or simply revenge for Marcus's banishing him from London? The latter meant nothing to Marcus—she would be gone in the morning anyway—but the former possibility worried him. David wasn't stupid, and could have become suspicious. It was possible the woman was meant to distract him. It was hard enough to shadow David without his knowledge. It would probably be impossible if he were aware of it.

He never considered just asking David. His brother

reacted with violent affront to any suggestion of judgment, and since Marcus devoutly hoped David would be completely absolved in the end, he saw no point in bringing it up. Besides, he knew David, and knew that the worse the trouble was, the less likely his brother was to tell the truth about it. If he asked, David would deny it, and Marcus would still have to prove it to himself.

He rose and went to pour a drink. First he must deal with this Preston woman. She appeared to be a common country maid; a large enough settlement, and she would leave. The notice in the *Times* would attract some attention, but if no bride could be found and Marcus accused the paper of mistaking the matter, the gossip would blow over quickly.

He hoped.

CHAPTER 5

Hannah had intended to leave on her own, and Walters hadn't said that the plain carriage that came wasn't the one she had asked him to get. Only when the door was shut did she realize that it was far too luxurious to be a hired vehicle. She rapped on the driver's door, but got no response. Her worst fears were confirmed when the carriage halted in front of a monstrous mansion and a liveried footman let down the steps. With no other choice, Hannah took Molly's hand and let the servant march them inside, simmering with anger.

It was the largest building she had ever seen. The ceiling soared three floors above, its frescoed surface as distant and as beautiful as heaven. The floor was a milky veined stone Hannah decided must be marble, and it went on forever. The servant left them standing there alone, and Hannah hated the owner of this beautiful home more than ever. She would never have left a guest standing by the door, let alone kidnap someone and force them to call on her.

"Mama?" Molly's whisper echoed around the hall. "Where are we?" Her eyes were wide and round, and

Missy was clutched close to her chest. Hannah squeezed her hand.

"We have to say good-bye to someone," she said quietly, wondering if the abominable duke were listening somewhere. Even their whispers sounded like shouts in the tomb-like quiet. "We'll be leaving soon."

"Is David here?" Molly hadn't understood Hannah's explanation that David wouldn't be coming back, yet wasn't dead. Hannah hoped she never saw David Reece again.

"No, he isn't," Hannah began, but the sound of footsteps interrupted her. She straightened, expecting the servant again, and looked into the disdainful eyes of the duke.

"Good God, don't tell me that's David's bastard," he said in greeting, looking down his nose at Molly. Hannah's chest swelled with maternal outrage, and she placed her hands over her daughter's ears for fear of teaching Molly a very bad word in the next few minutes.

"I demand that my trunks be unloaded this instant," she said through gritted teeth. "I am not some object to be brought here and there at some whim of yours. You will apologize to my daughter, and you will call a carriage for us, or I will not apologize for the consequences." His dark stare didn't waver.

"Don't make threats you can't back up, girl," he said softly. "I might call your bluff."

"Oh, please do," said Hannah with absolute sincerity. Something flickered in his eyes, and he looked away first.

"Two hundred pounds," he said, holding out a paper. "Complete silence, and your permanent absence."

Hannah refused to look at the paper. "My trunks, please." She had enough money to pay for the trip home, and was angry enough to refuse every last pence he offered.

The paper didn't retreat. "Take it now," he said in a silky voice, "for you'll never see it again."

"I shall hope the same applies to you." Hannah turned, taking Molly by the hand. "Come, Molly, let's fetch our trunks and get our own carriage."

There was a loud banging on the door then, and another servant glided forward to open it in front of Hannah. A lovely young woman burst in, and headed straight for the duke.

"Oh, Marcus!" she cried, flinging herself at him in a froth of ruffles and ribbons. "You naughty man, to keep such a secret! How could you let David be the one to break it to us? I vow, I nearly fainted when I read his letter, and Mama thought it must be one of David's jokes, but we just had to come and see for ourselves!" The duke was untangling her arms from around his neck, looking grim, and Hannah slipped toward the door with Molly plastered to her skirt.

"Now, Celia, what are you talking about?" Hannah was surprised that the duke could sound capable of human kindness. His voice was almost pleasant with a little warmth.

"Your bride!" The young woman laughed, her eyes sparkling. She let go of him and whirled around, her eyes fastening on Hannah at once. "You must be Hannah," she said, a wide smile splitting her face. "I'm so glad to meet you." And she rushed over to enfold Hannah in a firm embrace.

Hannah froze. Over the girl's shoulder, her gaze collided with the duke's. His face was extraordinarily still, and she just knew he was furiously angry. Well, none of this was her fault, and she wouldn't stay to face any more of his wrath. She stepped backward. "I'm afraid there's been a mistake."

Still beaming, the girl clasped her hands in front of her, as if to restrain herself from further hugging.

"I'm sorry, I'm so happy I forgot my manners! I'm Celia Reece, Marcus's sister. Do call me Celia, for I'm so glad we're sisters. David told us all about you in his letter—Marcus, you are a reprehensible rogue to let our brother tell us all about your bride," she interrupted herself to scold the duke again. "But that's all past, and I'm so happy for you, and for Marcus! Mama and I nearly wept with joy!"

"No, I think—" Hannah tried to say, but Celia carried on without pause.

"And I do hope you'll forgive us for coming to town, but we just had to meet you, and of course since you're not from London, you might want some advice, just on where to shop, you know, and Mama knows absolutely everyone! Oh, Marcus! Shall you throw a ball for her?" She swung around again to her brother and Hannah tried to gather her scattered thoughts. Molly was whimpering into her skirts, and she leaned down to comfort her daughter, ignoring the duke's response to his sister's ludicrous suggestion.

"Don't be scared," she whispered. "We'll be leaving soon."

"I'm hungry, Mama," said Molly, her eyes glistening and her chin trembling. "When will we have tea?"

There was a rustle, and Celia was before them again, this time on her knees. "You must be Molly," she said tenderly. "I'm your new aunt Celia. I've brought you a gift. Would you like to see it?"

Molly turned large tearful eyes on Hannah, who hesitated. She didn't want to offend the young lady, or frighten Molly, but this 'aunt Celia' nonsense couldn't be allowed to continue. "All right," said Molly then, removing the finger from her mouth. She let go of Hannah's skirt.

Hannah realized another woman had followed Celia, an older woman who must be her mother. She stepped forward as Celia held out her hand to Molly. "Welcome, my dear," she said with genuine warmth, clasping Hannah's hands lightly. "I'm so pleased to meet you and your daughter. She's a lovely child."

Hannah tried again. "This isn't what you think. . . ." Molly squealed loudly as Celia produced a large box, brought in by another servant. Hannah stopped, transfixed. The wrappings alone were finer than anything she had ever seen.

"Mama, look!" Molly began shredding the paper and ribbons in excitement. Hannah rushed over, grabbing Molly's hands.

"Wait, Molly. I don't think you should open it. We— we're going to leave now."

"Oh, Mama." Molly's eyes filled with tears as she looked sadly at the lovely box. Celia knelt beside her. "There, don't cry. It's for you, really." She sent a worried look over Molly's head at Hannah. "I picked it out just for her," she pleaded quietly. Hannah's frantic gaze swept the room, searching for help from somewhere, anywhere. The duke was scowling over a letter, and Celia's mother was watching her with a concerned expression. As Hannah watched, the duke stiffened, and abruptly shoved the letter into his pocket. With two long steps he crossed the hall.

"Celia, take the child. I beg you excuse us for a moment." He seized Hannah's wrist and began towing her away. Hannah hung back, searching for Molly, disappearing behind the skirts of Celia and her mother.

"Mama?" she heard her daughter ask. "I want my mama!"

"It's all right," she called, even as the duke dragged her across the hall. "I'm here, Molly. It's all right."

"Mama? Mama!" Molly was struggling against Celia's embrace, who was trying to comfort her. "Mama!" she shrieked. Hannah tried to strip the duke's hand from her wrist and began resisting in earnest.

"Let me go! She's frightened!" He wouldn't let go, and when Molly bolted across the room and latched on to her legs, Hannah pitched helplessly forward, slamming into the duke's chest. With a startled exclamation, he caught her as she grabbed instinctively for his shoulders, and they collapsed into a heap on the floor, Molly wriggling her way up into Hannah's arms. Oblivious to all else, she held her daughter close and crooned soothingly in her ear. When Molly's sobs finally subsided, she slowly realized that she was sitting across the duke's lap, leaning against his chest, his hand at the small of her back. Molly's arms were tightly wrapped around her neck, and except for some lingering hiccups, the hall was totally silent. She lifted her head.

Celia had her hands pressed to her lips, her eyes horrified. Her mother looked shocked, and even the butler's mouth was hanging open. And the duke . . . She hardly dared look at him; his black glare was scorching enough to feel. Mortified, she scrambled to her feet, Molly still in her arms. Aside from one small push, the duke said and did nothing to help her. She wet her lips. "There's been a mistake."

Celia rushed forward. "Oh, no!" she protested, her eyes glistening. "The mistake was mine. I'm dreadfully sorry, I didn't mean to frighten Molly, I was just so excited! You're not hurt, are you?" Her anxious gaze flickered over Hannah and Molly both. "I'm so sorry, Marcus," she said, turning to her brother as he rose slowly to his feet.

"Quite all right, Celia," he said in the tight voice of someone who's been offended but can't admit it. "No one's hurt, I trust?" His wrathful glance flickered toward Hannah. "Then I hope you will pardon us, but your arrival was somewhat unexpected, and we were discussing some arrangements which must be settled today." Hannah opened her mouth for another protest, but the two ladies seemed accustomed to this behavior, and nodded. Molly slid to the ground, still sniffling, and allowed Celia to give her Missy, who had fallen to the floor. This time the duke took Hannah's arm, very firmly, and escorted her into a nearby room.

His temper seemed to get away from him for a moment. One hand plowed through his dark hair, and he swore under his breath, striding toward the large windows overlooking a garden. Hannah decided to try a brisker tone, to set things back on the proper foundation.

"I think it vital to explain to everyone that there's been a misunderstanding."

He swung around, his face set. "In the face of the evidence, madam, I hardly think it will be believed." He held up his fingers to enumerate. "First, there is my name in a marriage register, signed in a hand indistinguishable from my own, in a ceremony performed by a vicar willing to swear that I am the man you married. Second, there is an announcement of our wedding in the *London Times,* no doubt sent on my stationery in my hand. Third, there is a letter from David"—he whipped out the crumpled letter she had seen him reading earlier—"recounting in excruciating detail our supposed 'whirlwind romance,' the very sort Rosalind and Celia would adore, and when they show up to see for themselves, here you are, just as David described you." He turned abruptly to the window as Hannah recoiled in shock as his words sank in. "The only misunderstanding was mine," he muttered.

"Well, it simply must be corrected," she protested.

He slanted a dark look over his shoulder. "You prefer to spread the truth about? I have no such desire."

"What other choice do we have?" she exclaimed. "We've both been victims of a very cruel prank, and no one should think less of us for telling the truth."

He sighed impatiently. "It's hardly that simple."

Hannah raised her eyebrows. "Oh, no?" She turned and marched back into the hall. "I'm terribly sorry, madam, Miss Reece, but there's been a misunderstanding. The duke and I are not really married." From the corner of her eye, she saw him in the doorway behind her, his dark gaze fastened on her. She tilted her head toward him with a faintly smug look to say, see how easy it was?

After a moment of surprised silence, Celia gasped. "Of course! She's right, Mama, only a country church. We must have a real wedding here, before the ton. But goodness, do you think we can plan one for this Season? It's already a month gone!"

Hannah shook her head. "No, that's not at *all* what I meant."

Celia rushed to pat her arm. "There, it's no trouble! In truth, we would love it! You have no idea how Mama's despaired of Marcus ever marrying. Mama, do you think blue for her gown? It would look so well with her eyes."

"I don't want a blue gown," said Hannah in alarm. "Nor any gown at all!"

Celia's mother laughed. "Gracious, dear, don't let Marcus bully you! He shan't stint; Celia's right, you simply must have a proper wedding. Marcus, send word at once to the church."

"Hannah doesn't want one," he said, and Hannah started at the sound of her name on his lips. She whirled to face him, and he cocked one brow as if to say, not so simple after all. "You've caught us both off guard, Rosalind. Perhaps you would care to rest after your journey?"

Celia and her mother agreed at once. Hannah pressed her lips together. "I am not staying," she said loudly. "And I am not marrying that man!"

Rosalind sighed, putting her arm around Hannah. "Come, dear, Marcus isn't so bad. I know he snaps and frowns when he's in a temper, but you mustn't let it fool you. Think of all the reasons you married him in the first place." There was a moment of silence as everyone looked expectantly at Hannah and the duke, who were facing each other with the air of combatants about to duel. Rosalind turned to the duke hastily. "Marcus, don't stand there like an idiot. Say something to persuade her."

"I haven't anything to say," he said in a cool voice. "If she wants to go, let her."

"Marcus!"

"Oh, how could you!"

"*Thank* you!" Hannah glared at him. It was not her fault she was here in the first place, it was his, and he was making her look like a fickle ninny. Molly was starting to cry as Hannah's voice rose. She reached down automatically to comfort her child. "I most certainly will leave!" Taking Molly's hand, she started toward the door. The butler's wild eyes darted from her furious glare to a point over her shoulder, to the duke, no doubt. Hannah didn't care; she was leaving if she had to break down the door with her bare hands and walk to Middleborough with her trunk on her back.

"Oh, Hannah, wait! You can't go!" Celia wedged herself in front of the door. "Don't leave, please!"

"You heard what he said," she retorted. "I want to go, and he won't stop me."

"You're absolutely right," agreed Rosalind, coming up beside her daughter. "I don't know what's gotten into Marcus, but you must know he's had a streak of deviltry in him since he was a lad. Not quite like David, but impertinent in his own way. You mustn't take it to heart."

Two pairs of bright blue eyes smiled at her, one gleaming with excitement, the other with determination. With a jolt, Hannah realized she had fallen into the clutches of a romantic and a matchmaker. If she didn't get out now, she might be caught forever. She looked over her shoulder, appealing to the duke to step in and put his foot down. He met her eyes for a moment, his gaze dark and impenetrable, and then he lifted one shoulder a fraction of an inch.

"Harper, have rooms prepared. I'm sure the ladies will want refreshment as well." There was a triumphant look between mother and daughter, and they started toward the stairs as footmen began carting in enormous trunks. Standing back to let them by, Hannah thought she might just slip out the door behind them, and no one would be the wiser, until she saw her own trunk pass.

Increasingly frustrated by the willful obliviousness of everyone around her, she wheeled around, searching for the duke. He was standing at the bottom of the stairs, a very grand and lovely staircase that curled around the hall in a marble spiral. He met her eyes, and Hannah realized he was waiting there for her. The two other ladies were climbing the stairs, talking and laughing, and Hannah realized in astonishment that Molly was with them. Fists at her sides, she marched toward the stairs.

"I'll speak to you shortly," the duke murmured as she stomped past him. Hannah stopped on the second stair, pleased that now she was looking down on him.

"I have nothing more to say to you."

He sighed, closing his eyes in that expression of

pained affront she was already coming to hate. "Sadly, I have more to say to you." Hannah snorted and turned. "You should have taken the money," he said under his breath. She shot him a killing glance.

"Believe me, if I had known the alternative, I would have."

The room she found Celia and Rosalind in was almost unearthly in its beauty. She had thought the prostitute's pink-covered room richly decorated, yet in comparison to this room, it was tawdry and shabby. To start, it was huge, probably nearly as large as the entire vicarage. The furniture, which Celia and Rosalind were uncovering with great haste, was delicately carved in lovely, airy lines. The walls were covered in pale blue silk, and the high ceiling was painted even more wondrously than the one in the hall. Hannah's mouth dropped open as Celia swept open the drapes and the full light of day filled the room.

"Mama!" Molly crawled from under a shrouded table, her eyes shining. "I'm hiding!" Celia's light laugh rang out as Molly disappeared again.

"Oh, she's just the most darling child!" Celia dropped to her knees to peek at Molly from the other side. A muffled squeal pronounced Molly's delight with her new playmate.

"She's the very image of Celia at that age, except for the eyes," said Rosalind fondly. Hannah murmured something in polite acknowledgement, wondering if that explained the duke's assumption that Molly would be David's. Nothing would excuse the way he had inquired, though. "I can't think why Marcus hasn't had these rooms prepared," continued Rosalind. "I'll make sure he sees to it right away. Do you think you'll want to redecorate immediately?"

Hannah's eyes widened. Redecorate this stunning room, when the things weren't even worn out? Even if she didn't plan to leave at the earliest possible chance, she wouldn't consider it. "I think it's the most beautiful room I've ever seen," she said. Rosalind smiled with real pleasure.

"Thank you, my dear. I did so love this blue." Hannah frowned, wondering what about that statement made her uneasy, but the footmen came in then with her trunks. Her two small trunks were grubby and out of place in this lovely room. As was she. Molly tugged at her skirt.

"Mama, may I have that?" She pointed to the gift box, which Celia had brought upstairs. Hannah took a deep breath. She expected there was something terribly expensive inside, and she couldn't allow these kind women to give it to Molly under their mistaken belief that she was the duke's bride.

"Molly, it's very, very kind of Miss Celia to bring it for you, but . . ." Molly's face was so anxiously hopeful, as was Celia's, that Hannah hesitated. Rosalind touched her shoulder.

"Hannah, whatever disagreement you're having with Marcus, it doesn't affect Celia's gift to Molly. We want her to have it."

More protest would be rude; Hannah suspected she might have already been rude. Defeated, she nodded to Molly, who lit up like a candle and raced across the room to the box. Celia looked almost as excited as Molly ripped open the paper.

It was a doll, with a porcelain face and hands. Her hair fell in long golden curls, just a shade lighter than Molly's, and her painted eyes were brown. Hannah watched her daughter stare at the beautiful doll in rapt adoration. Celia moved the arms and legs, then took out some clothes, just as fine as the pink satin dress the doll wore.

"Celia always wanted a baby sister," murmured

Rosalind. "She's been so excited about meeting Molly. I do hope you'll forgive our intrusion."

Hannah shook her head. "No, not at all. I—I should apologize to you. It's a lovely gift, and very generous, but things—that is, I wouldn't want you to mistake things between the duke and me. They aren't what they seem."

Rosalind's smile was sympathetic. "They never are, dear. But David wrote us that you were a woman of uncommon sense, and perfectly suited to Marcus. He's used to having his own way, and everyone has bowed to his wishes his whole life. You'll just have to be strong and stand up to him, because that's what he really needs." Hannah smiled weakly at the reference to her sense. If she'd had any real sense, she would have seen through David's lies and not wound up in this mess. But Rosalind had one thing right: she most certainly would stand up to the duke.

Marcus watched the skirt of her drab gray gown swish past him, climbing his stairs, heading toward his suite. Harper was hovering nearby, waiting for his instructions, and Marcus didn't want to give them.

Damn David. It was one thing to dump a vicar's wife in his lap—with a child, no less, a truly charming touch—and it was another to set Marcus up for a fool not only in front of London society, but facing his stepmother and sister with a tale they would never believe. Where on earth had David even met a vicar's wife? Marcus would have sworn David would run screaming from that sort of woman. But here she was, and urging him to tell the truth. The truth, unfortunately, would break the hearts of the only people Marcus genuinely loved, and he couldn't bear to do that.

Against his will, he growled the orders to Harper.

Marcus did not like doing things against his will, and as soon as the butler hurried off, he began turning the situation around in his mind, looking for any possible way to use it to his advantage.

If the Preston woman stayed, he would have to acknowledge her as his wife, support her and clothe her and treat her as such. Rosalind would spend a fortune of his money on her. And she had a daughter who might as well be Celia's sister; Marcus knew just how much fun the gossips would have with that coincidence. Having three women and a child in his house would be annoying, to say the least, but he could simply spend more time away from the house, furthering his investigations and avoiding vexation all at once.

If the Preston woman left, he would have to explain why to Celia and Rosalind. Judging from what he had just seen, they wouldn't accept it easily. If Mrs. Preston played her cards right, she would soon have two devoted allies in his family. Marcus frowned slightly. As much as he didn't like it, perhaps it would be better to let her stay. She would divert Rosalind's attention, which was probably preferable to having his stepmother devote her considerable energy to mending a rift between husband and wife. At best Marcus would have to endure her well-meaning but unwanted matchmaking, and at worst, she would discover the truth.

Marcus sighed. Ironically, it seemed easier to lie to his stepmother and sister and hide the fact that David had brought Mrs. Preston to London to embarrass him, at least until the furor had died down and he could shuffle her out of sight and out of mind. Then he could deal with Rosalind, after this sorry mess with David was resolved. That, he reminded himself, was more important, even though saving David's neck was becoming more difficult and thankless with every passing day.

He went upstairs and into his suite, the unfamiliar murmur of female voices coming through the connecting door. Marcus tapped on the door to warn them, and pushed it open.

Three females turned. The fourth was bouncing on the bed, but was promptly hauled down by her harried-looking mother. Marcus took a moment to examine the woman he had decided to let stay on as his wife. Her gray dress didn't look as drab here in the pale glowing blue of the room, even though it was still unattractive, primly buttoned to her neck with long close sleeves. Curling wisps of dark hair had pulled loose from the knot, framing her face and brushing her neck, and her eyes had lost some of their snap. A shadow of hesitancy fell across her face as she faced him, holding her daughter by the shoulders.

"Do let us know if we can help you with anything," said Rosalind, moving toward the door. Celia went, too, and Marcus saw the little girl's eyes follow her. In the doorway, Celia turned.

"Hannah, would you let Molly come explore with me? Just for a bit." Without waiting for her mother's reply, the child flew toward Celia, who beamed. Mrs. Preston's composure slipped another notch as her daughter grabbed Celia's hand with a huge smile, but she only smiled when the little girl looked back and waved.

"Bye, Mama," she called, as Celia closed the door behind them. Alone at last with his supposed wife, Marcus watched the forced smile fade from her face. She drew in a deep breath, set her shoulders, and turned on him.

"How long do you plan to allow this to continue?" Hannah couldn't hold back her frustration any longer. "If you had told them at once, the unpleasantness would be already past, and I could be on my way home."

He said nothing, just remained in his rigid pose near the door. Hannah was tired, hungry, caught off guard by Molly's unexpected desertion, and at the end of her patience with the rude, autocratic duke. She had certainly done her best to be truthful, and he had done nothing to help her, even though she would have thought it in his best interest as well. "For someone who must wish me a hundred miles away, you're doing a shameful job of setting matters to rights."

"It occurs to me that there are advantages to your presence in London." He prowled away from the door, hands behind his back. "First and foremost, it will prevent a great deal of humiliation for both of us. Before you protest, think how it will look to your quaint little village when you return barely a fortnight later, alone and unwed. David might be rightly labeled a scoundrel, but I doubt you would escape completely unscathed by it.

"As for myself, I admit having a bride begins to look less objectionable than naming my brother a rogue and liar who deceived a woman into marriage for the purpose of embarrassing me. Sadly, David is quite able to copy my manner and handwriting, although he hasn't done so in years, and no doubt many would remain unconvinced that he was guilty. It would look like a selfish attempt to free myself of a rash attachment."

"You can't honestly mean to carry on with this lie," said Hannah in disbelief.

He gave a short bark of laughter. "Not indefinitely, I promise you. A month or so should do. Then I shall be well pleased to see you off to wherever you came from."

"I'm afraid I don't understand you, sir," said Hannah in just as frosty a voice. "Why wait a month? I would be well pleased to be off today." He turned from the window.

"I do not intend to deny the marriage."

"There is no marriage," she said furiously. "You can't keep me here!"

He gazed at her with something resembling a smirk. "I will not help you leave."

Hannah pressed her lips together. He didn't have to say the rest, that since everyone thought she was his wife, no one else would help her, either. She didn't want to live here for a day, let alone a month. "It will be obvious to everyone within a matter of hours that we're not married. Then what will you say?"

He lifted one shoulder. "I have said we are; why will anyone doubt it?"

"Because we don't know each other," she exclaimed. "Someone will notice that!"

"David has already taken care of that point." He started toward her again, and Hannah almost took a step backward. "He's already told Rosalind and Celia we fell in love at first sight. How acquainted can two people become in a week or two? They might notice, but they shan't find it odd."

"You're mad," she said incredulously. "Why is this easier than telling people the truth?"

He stared coolly down at her, hands clasped behind him. "I don't want to tell Celia and Rosalind the truth."

"I know it won't be pleasant, but—"

"They adore David," he interrupted. "He's rather good at gaining women's affections, and while that is a questionable talent, I can't bring myself to break their hearts."

Hannah paused. That was harder to argue with. She had a hard time believing the duke harbored such tender feelings for anyone, but he had been kind to his sister downstairs. And she was already disposed to like Rosalind and Celia, and it surely would be a difficult blow to them to learn how badly David had behaved. "I shall take the blame then," she said in a slightly kinder tone. "I'll tell them I'm homesick, or inconstant, or something. I can't fault you for wanting to protect them, but I can't lie to them for a month."

"Then I shall." He walked around her and headed toward the door he had come in through.

"How will that spare their feelings?" Hannah followed him, more outraged than ever. She recanted her moment of sympathy for him; he respected his family, perhaps, but obviously he didn't care for *her* feelings or opinions at all. "You would rather they think you so cold and unfeeling that your wife left you than that David tricked us both?"

His smile was cold. "They'll believe the first much sooner than the latter."

"Well—but . . ." Hannah floundered for a reply. What kind of sense did that make? "They looked very pleased to think you were married. Don't you think they'll be disappointed to find out you're not, and that you lied to them?"

"No doubt." He opened the door and glanced back. "This is my dressing room. Knock first, if you ever have reason to enter." Hannah stiffened in anger, and he closed the door in her face.

"Wretch!" she said under her breath, striding away from the door. What possible reason would she ever have to enter his— She froze. Dressing room? Then this room . . . must be the duchess's room. She looked at it again in alarm, then at the door more closely. Sure enough, there was no lock. Naturally Celia and Rosalind had assumed, if she were his wife . . . But she wasn't, and couldn't fathom why he wanted her to pretend she was. Surely any hurt Celia and Rosalind might feel now would be ten times worse later, even if they never discovered the truth and only thought the marriage had disintegrated. It seemed clear from what he said that they would lay the blame at his feet, and wouldn't that be just as likely to break their hearts?

And then Hannah realized he was sacrificing his own place in their affections to save David's.

CHAPTER 6

Her first inclination was just to leave. She ventured out into the hallway, intending to hail a carriage of her own, collect her daughter and her trunks, and go. The duke said he wouldn't help her leave, but she hardly needed his help. Before she had reached the stairs, though, a man who looked like a royal courtier but who must be a servant appeared out of nowhere, and inquired how he could help her.

Hannah hesitated. Perhaps, if she just said she needed a carriage summoned, he would do it. If he thought she was the duchess, after all, he would obey her, right? But in the end she didn't have the nerve, and didn't want to get the man in trouble with the duke—who was probably the sort to give the sack for the smallest thing—and so simply shook her head, and had to retreat. Trapped in the beautiful blue room, Hannah tried to calm her temper and think.

No matter what the duke said, it was better that she leave sooner rather than later. Since he didn't seem to care what she thought, she decided she didn't have to worry about what he thought. She would just leave, and he could make up any story he liked to explain things to his stepmother and sister. But how? She pressed her fingers to her forehead. Everything she owned was in the two small but heavy trunks near the door, and she didn't see how she could get them downstairs and into the street without anyone noticing and stopping her. She racked her brains; if she had a persuasive story, a reason, surely someone would help her. But what should she say? She wished she had some of Sarah's imagination at the moment.

She was no closer to a solution when the door opened a while later. Hannah spun around, relieved to see it was only Molly. Then Celia Reece stepped into the room behind Molly, and Hannah felt awkward all over again. The girl looked so happy to see her, her pretty face glowing. Uncomfortably Hannah smiled back.

"Mama!" Molly ran to her, and Hannah instinctively scooped her up. "Celia showed me a room full of mirrors, Mama! Huge, tall mirrors that go almost to the ceiling! She said we shall dance in there, and I may have a new dress. May I, Mama? Will it be prettier than the new dress I just got when you were mar—?"

"Oh, Molly!" Hannah burst out, a little too loudly. She wasn't quite ready to explain this to Molly, not until she had at least decided what she would do. "Be patient. We shall see if you need a new dress before getting all excited about it. And where are your manners?" she added in a whisper.

Molly looked over her shoulder. "Thank you, Aunt Celia."

Hannah closed her eyes at the title as Celia answered happily, "You are most welcome, Molly." She opened them as Celia went on. "Hannah, Mama would like to know if you would care to take tea with us. You must be hungry after your trip."

Molly bounced in her arms, smiling hopefully, and

Hannah's shoulders slumped. She lowered Molly to the floor, thinking frantically. Tea with a duchess! Whoever would have guessed such a thing would happen to her? And although the duchess seemed very nice, Hannah didn't see how she could enjoy it, unless . . .

Unless she could seize this opportunity, before matters got too far out of hand. The duke didn't want to hurt his stepmother and sister, and Hannah would respect that, for Rosalind and Celia's sake if not for his. But he clearly had nothing against lying to them. He'd even encouraged her to do it. A grim smile crossed her face. Well, then, she would lie to them— but not in the way he expected her to do.

"Tea would be lovely," she said, straightening and taking Molly's hand. "Thank you."

Celia beamed. "Mama has already arranged it on the terrace. Shall we go?" Hannah nodded, and they followed Celia out.

As they walked through the house, Hannah could barely keep her mouth from falling open in amazement again. It was magnificent beyond all her dreams. She had read stories in the newspapers about the grand entertainments and dinners given by the Prince Regent and the opulent furnishings in Carlton House, but surely this was every bit as fine. The floors were marble, the rugs were thick, the windows were tall and crystal clear. Everything was sparkling clean, even the servants who curtsied and bowed as they passed. Hannah felt very plain and poor again, but she kept her head up and tried to gather her thoughts for what she would say.

"There you are." With a brilliant smile, Rosalind came to greet them as they stepped out onto the terrace. She clasped Hannah's hands in her own. "I thought we could sit out here, as the day is so fine. Besides, we are family. We needn't stand on ceremony."

It was all Hannah could do to murmur a polite reply. It had suddenly occurred to her that if David hadn't tricked her, and they had been married in truth, she would still have had Rosalind for a mother-in-law and Celia for a sister. Then she could have accepted all their kindness and been delighted to call herself part of their family. But thanks to David and his wretched brother, she couldn't.

"And Molly!" Rosalind leaned down to look Molly in the eye. "Has Celia shown you the secret passage?" she asked in a loud whisper.

Molly's eyes grew wide. She had put her finger in her mouth when they reached the terrace, a sign she was as cowed as Hannah felt. Silently she shook her head.

"You must ask her after tea. The house is full of all sorts of hidden cupboards as well. Celia delighted in finding them when she was your age."

Celia laughed. "Yes, and David would always tease me that I'd find myself stuck in one some day."

Molly pulled her finger from her mouth. "Did you?" she asked in a little voice.

Celia made a face as Rosalind laughed. "Yes. I'd be stuck there still if Marcus hadn't found me and let me out."

"Marcus missed her before anyone else did," said Rosalind, smiling. "He searched the house from top to bottom until he found Celia in a hidden cupboard in the library."

"Well, enough about that, Mama." Celia rolled her eyes. "Shall we have tea? I'm starved."

"Yes, of course." Rosalind led the way to a delicate table already laid with tea for four. Again Hannah had to conceal her wonder. The lawn spread away from the terrace in a sweep of perfectly trimmed green velvet. She could see a large garden with a fountain in its center, and far across the lawn, the river ran past, glittering in the sunlight. It was every bit as gorgeous as the house. Dazed, she sank into a chair.

"Do you like it?" Rosalind handed her a cup of tea.

"It's stunning," said Hannah, still taking in the view. "As is the house. I'd never seen—" Abruptly she fell silent, remembering that it was not her view to admire. She subsided in her chair and stirred her tea.

"Now, Hannah, I must apologize," Rosalind said once everyone had a cup. Celia and Molly had their heads together already and were giggling about something. "We were so thrilled when we received David's letter, we simply couldn't wait to meet you. But of course you ought not to have to entertain the whole family when you're barely settled in. I'd no idea you were just arriving today. I do hope you can forgive us."

"Of course," murmured Hannah into her teacup. They had more right to be here than she did, after all.

"Now . . ." Rosalind lowered her voice with a glance across the table. "I must tell you the news of your marriage was like the answer to my prayers. Marcus used to tell me he would never marry, which of course he simply must do; he has the dukedom to consider. And while it caught us a bit by surprise, it shouldn't have." Hannah looked at her askance. Rosalind leaned closer, her blue eyes twinkling. "Marcus is the sort of man who doesn't hesitate when he wants something. Isn't it wonderful, when a man makes you feel so wanted?"

Hannah would have laughed out loud if she hadn't been absolutely mortified. The duke wanted her to go away, if he wanted anything from her at all. She had to get out of this mess. "I confess, I don't know the first thing about London."

"That is no trouble. You can learn." Rosalind offered a plate of tiny cakes decorated with sugar-encrusted violets. Hannah's mouth watered just looking at them. She took one, and nearly swooned in delight as it melted on her tongue. Clearly there were at least a few good things about being a duchess. "We shall look over your wardrobe tomorrow and remedy any deficiencies," Rosalind went on. "I don't mean to offend," she said at Hannah's startled look. "David wrote that you grew up in the country, with very little time in town, and I suspect fashions are somewhat different here."

"Oh, Mama, may I do some shopping, too?" asked Celia eagerly. She turned to Hannah. "May I get Molly a few gifts?" she whispered. "Just a few."

Only because she was not planning to be there to go on this mythical shopping expedition did Hannah not protest. She tried again to temper their enthusiasm. "I think perhaps I ought not to go out. I know nothing about being a duchess."

"It's a wonderful thing about being a duchess," confided Rosalind merrily. "No one wants to criticize you, so you can be anything you wish."

"The duchess of Devonshire gambles worse than any man and she's received everywhere," added Celia. "No one would dare cut Marcus's wife."

"Celia, that's gossip," chided her mother.

"I didn't even know he was a duke," said Hannah, a plan forming in her mind at last. If they thought the duke had misled her about himself, surely they would understand her desire to leave. "I had no idea of any of this." She waved one hand at the manicured landscape, the gleaming house, the fine china dishes. "He told me nothing of his life. It's very different from what I'm used to." Rosalind's eyebrows went up. Celia set down her teacup with a clank, her eyes wide. Hannah bit her lip and tried to look betrayed.

"Goodness," murmured Rosalind. "Marcus must have completely lost his head. You really had no idea he was a duke?" Hannah shook her head. This seemed to please Rosalind. Her smile grew. "What a lovely surprise it must have been. When did you discover it?"

"Ah, well, he told me . . . that is, not until I reached London," Hannah said uncomfortably. It didn't seem to be working the right way. Flustered, she leaned over to wipe Molly's chin, although her daughter was working her way through a jam-covered tea cake and seemed perfectly oblivious to her mother's unease.

Celia giggled, her hands clasped under her chin. "Oh, he must have been so in love," she cried, turning to her mother. "Imagine, he didn't tell her until they were married!"

At the thought of the duke being so in love with anyone, let alone with her, Hannah threw down her napkin. "He ought to have told me," she said firmly. "I'm very unhappy with him for deceiving me. We quarreled."

"Oh, but you must consider it a compliment. Marcus is usually very aware of his station. If he let you think him an ordinary gentleman, he humbled himself greatly. I do so love a man who does that for a woman." Celia nodded her agreement, her eyes misty.

"It was a terrible, terrible quarrel," went on Hannah in desperation. "I don't know that I can ever forgive him. You must have seen how cold he was this morning. He doesn't want me to stay! I don't see how we can go on, after this. It was all a terrible mistake." There, she had all but said she would leave.

Rosalind dismissed it with a wave of her hand. "Marcus doesn't show affection in front of others. You mustn't take it as a personal rebuke. As for the quarrel, it will blow over. Above all, Marcus likes peace. When he sees how much it upset you, he'll make amends. Now, if we're to plan a proper wedding for this Season, we must start at once."

Hannah shot to her feet, unnerved. "No, I—I really don't think I can discuss that."

"Of course not," said Celia. "Mama, we really must take care of the shopping first. How can she go about, if she has no clothes?" Rosalind agreed at once, and they decided between themselves that as soon as Hannah's wardrobe was complete, they would move on to the wedding, and perhaps even a ball to introduce her to the ton. Hannah ducked her head and let them talk around her, knowing she wouldn't be there for any of it, even though she still had no idea how she would leave—just that she would. Aside from the lies the duke wanted her to tell and the sting of David's betrayal, she suspected that becoming attached to Rosalind and Celia, and then having to leave them, would hurt worst of all.

When Molly put her hands on the table and rested her cheek on them, Hannah seized the reprieve. "Molly, it's time to rest."

"I'm not sleepy, Mama." Molly undermined her words with a wide yawn. Hannah got to her feet as Rosalind smiled and Celia giggled.

"Would you excuse us?" she murmured, lifting her daughter. "You may explore the secret cupboards after you have a little sleep," she said by way of enticement. Molly brightened then, and waved good-bye to Celia and Rosalind as Hannah made her way back into the house.

"Mama?" Molly snuggled against her chest, her small body a comforting familiar weight in Hannah's arms.

"Yes, darling?" She tried to remember how they had gotten to the terrace. She could see the stairs over there. . . .

"Are we going to live here?"

She didn't answer Molly's question as she climbed

the stairs. What should she say about this to Molly? She had to say something, after the way Molly had nearly blurted out that it was David and not the duke Hannah thought she had married, but didn't want to trouble Molly with more than she could understand. "No," she settled for saying. "We're only visiting."

"Oh." They reached the room where her trunks were, and Hannah pushed open the door. She pulled back the covers on the bed, surprised to find fresh linens, faintly scented with lavender. The room had been cleaned, in just the short time they'd been having tea. It would have taken her a week.

She took off Molly's shoes and deposited her on the bed. Missy was on a chair near the bed, and Molly wedged the doll under her arm before wiggling into the pillows. The new doll, christened Elizabeth, stood in a place of honor on the dressing table, visible but untouchable. Missy, the rag-tag doll with only one eye and no shoes at all, was in Molly's arm, and Hannah was somehow reassured by it. "Where is David?" Molly asked then.

Hannah sighed. "He's gone away. I don't know when he'll be back, or if we'll be here when he returns."

"But I thought we were going to live with him now, and he would be my new papa."

Hannah felt a fresh burst of anger. "I was wrong. He's changed his mind." She kissed Molly on the forehead. "Now, close your eyes and rest. You'll have plenty of time to explore when you wake."

"We aren't leaving tomorrow, are we, Mama?"

"I'm not sure yet." Hannah got up and headed for the door. That was another good reason to leave as soon as possible; the longer she stayed, the harder it would be on her daughter when they left. Molly's sleepy voice made her pause with her hand on the knob.

"I hope we stay. I like it here." With another yawn,

she closed her eyes and put her finger in her mouth. Hannah opened her mouth to reply, then thought better of it. Her gaze flitted over the painted ceiling, the carved furniture, the yards of silk on the walls. A very small part of her also liked it here, just a little. Who wouldn't like to live like a queen—or a duchess—even for just a little while?

She shook off the thought. She couldn't indulge in such nonsense. No matter how nice the house was, no matter how kind Rosalind and Celia were, she didn't belong here, and it would be better for them all if she didn't stay. The very luxury of this life drove home the point: it was best not to get too accustomed to things she couldn't have. She looked down at herself, not surprised to see cake crumbs and jam smeared on her plain wool traveling dress. That was her life, not this silk-covered, marble cool existence.

Someone had unpacked her things, the gray and black dresses discreetly moved to the back of a large wardrobe in the corner. She only had two other dresses, her best blue muslin and a warm winter one of red wool. She changed into the blue one, feeling a little bit better once she was clean and neat once again. She took a quick peek in the mirror, tucking a stray curl behind one ear, then slipped quietly from the room and went in search of the duke.

CHAPTER 7

The duke of Exeter spent every day the same way: working at his desk. He ate his breakfast there while he read the freshly ironed papers. After breakfast, his secretary brought the post, sorted according to urgency and nature, and Marcus dictated his replies. While his secretary withdrew to copy the correspondence, he met with his estate agents, solicitors, bankers, or any other employees as necessary. Then the secretary would return with his correspondence to sign, after which the butler served luncheon, also at his desk. Discipline and order were the hallmarks of a responsible man, after all, and Marcus made a point of being disciplined and orderly.

Or rather, he tried to make it a point.

The sudden illness of his secretary, the efficient Mr. Cole, had turned Marcus's well-ordered days on their head. Instead of Mr. Cole, he now had young Roger Adams, who was a cousin of Mr. Cole's. Mr. Adams wrote a fine hand and was eager to please, but these appeared to be his sole qualifications for the position. Adams sorted invitations to musicales and *soirées* with truly important letters. Adams lost track of which bills

Marcus supported in Parliament, and presented any and all petitions in favor of opposing bills. Adams always seemed to have more things in his hands than he could handle, tended to clear his throat too much, and, most damning, he had neglected to notify Marcus immediately when David's letter had arrived, despite explicit instructions to do just that.

Today, of course, order had been flung out the window, and he'd lost the entire morning with the to-do over the vicar's wife, but there was still work to be done and Marcus was doing his best to proceed as usual. Adams was as well; once again he was stumbling over an apology, this time for accepting an invitation to Lady Morley's hunt, which Marcus had no intention of attending. Marcus stared at him in stony silence until the secretary finally stammered himself out and just sat there, ears red.

"Mr. Adams."

"Yes, Your Grace?" The young man breathed like a cornered fox.

"You may send Lady Morley a regretful note informing her that an unexpected obligation will prevent me from attending the hunt."

Adams bobbed his head. "Yes, sir. I shall make clear it was my mistake—"

"No." Marcus wished intensely that Cole would come back to work. "It would be rude to imply that I only accepted her invitation in error. Make no mention of it. Just send my regrets." The last came out rather harshly, and Adams paled. Marcus wanted to throw up his hands in despair. No doubt Adams would botch the whole thing more than he already had, and Marcus would have to write the damn note himself. What was really the point of having a secretary if he had to do everything himself?

Adams nodded again, shuffling his pile of papers.

Some of them slid to the floor, and Adams ducked to get them, knocking more off in the process. "My apologies, Your Grace," he murmured. "Your pardon . . ."

There was a faint tap at the door. "Enter," Marcus snapped as the hapless Adams lost his hold on more papers. He rubbed his forehead wearily, debating whether to sack his secretary on the spot or wait until he had finished the day's correspondence. A soft throat clearing broke his thoughts.

His supposed wife stood just inside the door. Thank God she'd left off wearing that drab gray. Marcus disliked women in dull colors, particularly if they had any looks at all, and this one, surprisingly, did. Her deep blue dress was simple but flattering, and played up the warm tones of her skin. Her dark curls were pulled back, emphasizing the graceful lines of her neck and shoulders, even bare as they were of jewelry. Sadly, her eyes remained unchanged; if anything, she looked more ready than ever to defy him.

"Might I have a word, sir?" she asked. Adams leaped to his feet, trampling letters and invitations without care. He goggled at her for a moment before sweeping a bow that wouldn't be seen even in court. Marcus closed his eyes in disgust.

"Of course. Adams, stand up."

"Madam, pray forgive me," babbled his incompetent secretary, bowing and scraping, strewing papers all over the rug. He sent a desperate glance his employer's way. Marcus let him suffer. They were working, or trying to, and whatever she had to say could wait.

"Perhaps in a few minutes," he said to her. "I'll attend you soon in the library."

Her posture stiffened. "Of course," she said, dipping into a subservient curtsey. "Pray forgive my intrusion, my lord." She curtseyed again, and this time Adams looked at him curiously. Marcus cursed under his

breath. She had to go out of her way to show him up,
did she?

"Stay," he barked as she turned to leave. "Adams, a
moment." With a nervous smile at her, the secretary
fled, closing the door with a bang. The man could not
remember the simplest directions. Marcus turned a
frigid gaze on the intruder.

"What must you say that simply could not wait?" he
drawled, leaning back and lacing his fingers together
across his stomach.

Hannah glared right back. The duke's secretary
might be afraid of him, but she wasn't, not after the
day she'd had already. It had taken her a long time
to track him down, after being waylaid by Rosalind
about the dressmaker yet again, Molly waking up
bursting with energy, then luncheon served in a
cathedral-like dining room by a regiment of silent servants. Thankfully Celia had taken Molly off to explore
the house yet again, and Hannah had finally appealed
to Rosalind for help in locating the duke, help Rosalind was all too happy to give. Hannah could see the
woman was thoroughly over the moon about her stepson being married. Too bad it wouldn't be for long.

"If you cannot be appealed to with reason," she
began briskly, "perhaps money will work. Your stepmother intends to start shopping for a wardrobe
befitting a duchess. Immediately. Unless you tell her
differently, or allow me to, she is going to spend a great
deal of your money. *Hundreds* of pounds." The amount
was a wild guess, but Hannah had no idea how much a
silk ball gown would cost, let alone the fur-trimmed
cloaks and satin slippers Rosalind had mentioned with
such enthusiasm.

"And you object?" His expression didn't change in
the least.

"Surely *you* do," she exclaimed. "It will be a waste of money!"

He lifted one shoulder. "Not yours. Is it your concern at all?"

"It most certainly is! How can I deceive her like this? She already wants to discuss plans for a ball—here! If you let her buy the clothes, next she'll be ordering orchids! And that doesn't even approach what she's contemplating for a wedding. A legal one this time!" Hannah wanted to shake the man, she was so angry.

He sighed, watching her as if she sorely tried his patience. "Let Rosalind and Celia do what they will," he said in a voice one would use on a slow-witted child. "It is my money, my house, and my family. Pretend you enjoy it, or sulk about it, I don't care. I warn you, though, I don't want them to learn the truth, and if you think to force it from me, you should reconsider. Push me, and I will push back, harder than you expect."

"You are asking too much," she said, her voice shaking. His flat gaze didn't waver.

"All I ask is that you keep one fact to yourself. So long as you act moderately like a duchess, everyone will treat you as such. I would rather not have to make a display of husbandly discipline."

Hannah's lips parted, then clamped together in outrage. Husbandly discipline! Of all the nerve! "As you wish, my lord," she said through her teeth, whirling to go.

"Your Grace," he said distinctly. Hannah froze. What did that mean? She turned, eyes narrowed in suspicion. "One addresses a duke, or a duchess, as 'Your Grace,'" he said. "Never 'my lord' or 'my lady.'"

Hannah's temper started a slow burn at the reprimand. She had never known, nor expected to know, a duke. She did not even want to know this one. She turned all the way around again, raising her chin. "I was accustomed to calling my husband by his given name."

He made a small motion of impatience. "Very well. I give you leave to call me Exeter."

"That is your title, not your name," she said.

"That is who I am," he said, his voice even colder than before. "I will not permit anything more intimate."

Hannah cocked her head. "Very well. The next time Rosalind comments on our distant address, I shall tell her it's because we're not intimate."

He came to his feet in the blink of an eye. "You will not discuss our relations with her."

"Why not? That's all she wants to talk about. How did we meet, how did you win my heart, when did I first know I loved you?" Hannah began to enjoy taunting him. She widened her eyes innocently and smiled a little. "Besides, won't it make her more understanding when I leave, if she believes our marriage devoid of intimacy?" That should take some starch out of his arrogance, and wouldn't he be the better for it.

Marcus couldn't believe her nerve. Not only asking to call him by his given name—something no one save his family dared—but threatening him with this! She had no dowry, no property, no name, no breeding, no standing at all; the only possible reason for a man in his position to wed someone in her position was love, or desire. He had no problem with people thinking him incapable of the first, but no man in town would believe him innocent of the last, especially not with that sly, coquettish look on her face.

He circled her, studying her with new attention. Her figure, though not extravagant, was pleasing— quite pleasing, to tell the truth. When she wasn't glaring at him, her eyes were fine, and he remembered the smile that had lit her face the first moment he saw her. She was a reasonably attractive woman, and Marcus wasn't about to suffer the ton's amusement at the news that he would marry her and then not bed her.

He stopped behind her, so close her skirt brushed his boots. She had endured his perusal without a word, but when she started to turn, he laid his hand on the back of her neck to stop her, his thumb brushing the soft wisps of dark curls. Her skin was soft and warm, touched with golden color. "What else were you accustomed to doing with your husband?" he murmured in her ear. She felt surprisingly nice under his hands, and Marcus smoothed his other palm over her shoulder before he could think better of it. "Perhaps it would be more natural for you to call me by my given name if we were more . . . intimate."

Hannah jerked away, appalled at the way her skin tingled where he had touched her. He had lovely hands, large and strong, and capable of shocking gentleness. If only he had any similar gentleness in his character. . . . Then what? What would it matter, if he were kinder? Nothing, that's what, especially since it was a fancy anyway. He had just suggested—"How dare you!"

His eyes smoldered, with anger, she assumed. "You were the one who broached our intimate relations."

"We do not have intimate relations!" she hissed. "Nor will we! You are not my husband."

"What has that got to do with intimate relations?" He stepped forward, meaning to intimidate her, but she stayed where she was, chin high, eyes blazing with defiance.

"You're right," she retorted. "I wouldn't invite you to my bed even if you were my husband."

"But if I were your husband," he said in a soft growl, "it would be my duty to seduce you, wouldn't it?" And the look he gave her, as if he might be contemplating it right now, sparked an awful feeling in her stomach—not outrage, but worse: curiosity.

As Hannah stood there, just as appalled by her reaction as she was by his suggestion, salvation came. There was a soft scratch at the door.

"Come," said the duke. Flushed, Hannah stepped back, turning to hide her burning face from whomever was at the door. The door opened, then the butler's calm, quiet voice said, "Mr. Joseph Braden to see you, Your Grace."

The duke frowned. Hannah gasped. They both stared at the butler, then the duke said sharply, "Who?"

"Mr. Joseph Braden," repeated Harper. His eyes flickered toward Hannah for a split second. "He claims to be Her Grace's father."

That frosty gaze turned on her. She moistened her lips nervously. "Yes," she said. "He is." The duke's eyebrow went up slightly as he looked at her suspiciously. She took a step toward the door. "I—I'll see him."

"Stay." He raised one hand to stay her, his keen gaze never wavering. "Show him in, Harper." The butler bowed out of the room, and Hannah felt a rush of embarrassing color to her face. "Well?"

The disdain in his question made her want to flinch. And he hadn't even met Pa yet! What could Pa possibly want? Not that it mattered; his presence could only make things worse. "It really would be much better if I saw him, alone," she tried again. "No doubt he's come to bring me news of home, or . . . or . . ."

"News? Does your little hamlet produce such news in a se'nnight that your father must ride to London to tell you at once? It's a long journey." His voice had sharpened again.

"Well, I shall find out," she said, edging toward the door. Perhaps if she could head Pa off, in the hallway . . .

Too late. "Mr. Braden, sir," announced Harper, standing aside as her father clumped into the room. With another faint groan of hinges, the door closed behind him, and the room was silent.

Although not tall, her father was burly, with wide shoulders and thick limbs. Now he stood in the duke's elegant study, looking for all the world as though he'd come straight from his fields, in worn, rough clothing and dirty boots. Or from the pub, unless Hannah's nose deceived her. The contrast between the tall, aristocratic duke and her tavern-brawling father couldn't be harsher, even before her father spoke.

"I reckon you 'ave an apology fer me," he said, as if determined to offend. Hannah closed her eyes, mortified by association.

"On what grounds?" The duke's voice was ice-cold.

"On grounds yer a duke." She could feel the duke's eyes boring into her, so Hannah opened hers, caught between wanting to apologize for her father's rudeness and wanting to just bundle him out of the room before he could make things worse. No matter how much the duke's pride could use a little trimming, she didn't think a scolding from her father would do it.

Before she could say anything, though, her father went on. "I suppose it would ha' been too much to expect to hear that title when you was courtin' my daughter. Lettin' everyone think you were just a gentleman with empty pockets musta been a real joke to you. Well, I'm come to let you know I don't think it's funny, and you best be ready to fix things."

"Pa!" gasped Hannah. Clearly he didn't recognize that the duke was not David. They did look very much alike, but Hannah could easily see the distinct differences. Her father was insulting a man he had never met.

"What, pray, would setting things right entail?"

The calm set of his face belying the menace in the duke's words.

"You didn't ask proper permission to marry her."

The duke lifted one shoulder. "A bit late to raise that objection."

"She's still my daughter." Pa raised his chin. "You never made a settlement on her." Hannah felt sick to her stomach as she realized why her father had come to London. When she had decided to marry David, his main reaction had been relief that he wouldn't have to feed and house her and Molly. But now he had discovered that she was allegedly married to a wealthy man. Hannah lunged forward and caught her father's arm.

"That's none of your concern!" she whispered furiously. "Jamie worked it all out—"

"Jamie did a poor job," he snapped. "Men like him know it costs to take a wife, and I don't like being cheated."

"Cheated! How can—?"

"Girl, go on back to your women's things," he interrupted. "I've got business here with your husband."

"But, Pa—"

"Go on now. Can't you see you're not needed?" He shook off her hand and turned his back on her in dismissal.

For one second, her feelings registered on her face. Marcus felt an unexpected stab of pity for her; he had seen that look before, a child's realization that his father didn't want him. He couldn't stop the instinctive resentment of a man who treated his child that way. "Yes, my dear, you may leave us," he said, forcing a tight smile. "I wouldn't wish to bore you."

She started, looking at him with a searching intensity that surprised him. "No," she said in a similarly strained tone. "I wouldn't wish to interrupt." She turned and left, closing the door behind her. Marcus turned his attention back to the rawboned farmer facing him, no longer under any constraint.

"Precisely how much did you expect to wring from me?" He took his seat, without inviting his visitor to do the same, and sipped his coffee, without offering to ring for more. He didn't want to see this man, and certainly wasn't going to pay him. He didn't know what had happened between Braden and David, but Braden obviously thought he *was* David, and Marcus always had a very hard time forgiving people that mistake.

"I thought a thousand pounds would be a fair price for a wife." The older man's flinty gaze didn't waver. Marcus nearly laughed. A thousand pounds was a pittance. He'd come all the way to London just for that?

"Why should I pay anything?" Marcus asked, the corner of his mouth lifting. Really, this wasn't even a contest. "She wasn't living with you, providing any sort of assistance to your household. If anything, I believe her marriage spared you the expense of supporting her."

"That matters naught," growled Braden. "She's my daughter. I got nothing the first time, on account o' she wed the damn vicar. Daughters ain't worth much exceptin' when they marry, and she done fine this time. A thousand pounds I'll have from you."

"No." Marcus almost smiled as the man bristled visibly.

"I know my rights—"

"Your rights?" Marcus came to his feet again, leaning over his desk to emphasize his words. "Marriage settlements are concluded by mutual agreement before the wedding takes place. After that time, she belongs to me. Any right you might have had to request a settlement expired the day she wed, and any attempt you make to interfere with my wife will result in grievous consequences for you." He paused to let this sink in.

"I see no reason to give you a thousand pounds now when you didn't see the need to ask for it before."

"You never said you was a bloody duke before," Braden snarled, his beefy hands in fists.

Marcus's smile was as thin as the blade of a knife. "How careless of me." He pulled the bell.

Braden ground his teeth. "Arrogant nob," he said bitterly. "You take my girl from her home and won't even do your duty by her family." Harper glided into the room.

"Harper, see Mr. Braden out." Marcus turned his attention to the papers on his desk. Braden nearly howled with rage as Harper waited for him.

"I'm seeing my girl again! She'll do what's right."

"Harper, see Mr. Braden out," repeated Marcus, emphasizing the last word. "Good day, sir."

With another fierce look, Braden left, and Marcus sat staring at the papers in front of him. He poured more coffee from the silver pot and sipped it. Then he turned in his chair and regarded the window behind his desk. He frowned. The latch should have been closed, but it wasn't. He got up and closed it, then stood regarding the work still spread on his desk. He rang for Harper again.

"Where is the duchess?" He hadn't presented her to his staff as such, but after the scene this morning, there could hardly be a soul in his household who didn't think of her that way. Obviously he would have to encourage that, if he wanted the charade to last.

"Madam has gone to the garden, I believe," murmured Harper.

Marcus sighed and went to find her, arguing with himself every step of the way. It was none of his business if her own father hurt her feelings. She could have sent for the man to come, and staged the whole scene. She could be the one who wanted the thousand pounds. It was just that damned wounded look in her eyes that bothered him. It made him think of David, who had been cut to the quick every time their father had brushed him aside as useless and unneeded.

She was sitting on a stone bench, her back rigid, her eyes fixed straight ahead. He came to a stop beside her.

"You have a beautiful garden," she said after a moment. Marcus glanced around.

"Yes." She nodded without looking at him. He sat on the other end of the bench.

"Whatever you paid him, I will pay it back." Her words were so soft, he barely heard them.

"What makes you think I paid him?"

Her hands were clenched, white-knuckled, in her lap. "I know he came to ask for money."

"And just because he asked, I would give it?"

She still didn't look at him; he wasn't even sure she had blinked. "I know you want everyone to think we are married."

"I fail to see how paying a man I have never met will accomplish that." Her eyelids dropped, and she sighed.

"He will cause trouble if you don't."

"I doubt it." She just shook her head, eyes still closed. A bee buzzed around her hair, but she didn't seem to notice. He let his gaze drift over the garden around them, realizing he hadn't been out here once this spring. The gardener had planted roses where the lilacs used to be. Or had the roses always been there? "I expressed to him how upset I would be if anyone were to interfere with my wife. He shall sorely regret it if he causes trouble."

"He's my father." It was more apology than protest.

"And you, to all appearances, are my wife." Marcus didn't bother to hide the rather callous emphasis on the possessive. "There are benefits to that, and you might as well take this as one." She said nothing and didn't move, but she wasn't crying. He crossed his arms, watching her from the corner of his eye.

Marcus was accustomed to getting what he wanted from people just through the force of his position and name, resorting to intimidation only when necessary. It worked on people of rank, who wanted something from him, or at least feared what he could do to them. This woman, though, had the whip hand over him in that he needed her cooperation to keep David's lies secret. Any time she took it into her head to do it, she could ruin everything.

He would have to deal differently with her, he realized. He took another careful look at her, from her simple knot of hair to her plain dress. What would appeal to a country vicar's widow? "We haven't settled things between us," he said abruptly. "In light of this afternoon's visit, it is time we did."

Hannah turned warily. No matter how much she told herself she didn't care if the duke were offended or insulted, she did care that her father's words and actions reflected on her, and she hated it that he still could hurt her. Surely by now she would be used to the fact that she was only a poor excuse for a son to him. She tried to focus on what the duke had said. "Settled things?"

"Your . . . compensation." She sighed, her head beginning to ache. What a wretched mess this was becoming, first pretending to be married to a man she had never met, lying to a mother and sister-in-law she would have dearly loved to have, and now knowing her father thought she had somehow cheated him.

"I don't want your money." He put up one hand, his gaze trained on the opposite side of the garden.

"You deserve something in return for your assistance. Hear me before you refuse." Hannah nodded wearily, wishing she were still in her own cottage and subject only to her own conscience. "My desire to conceal David's actions remains unchanged. I cannot do it without your help, though, and I have been remiss in not making clear how grateful I will be for that help. Your father, I believe, was to have been your support, had David not made his offer." He turned those dark, penetrating eyes on her. She nodded again, somehow just knowing that he already knew that for a fact. He nodded curtly. "Then I offer you independence. A country manor, or cottage, whichever you prefer, plus housekeeping funds. I would not wish to insult you by forcing a large amount on you"— a mocking smile bent his mouth—"but it will be sufficient for your needs. Invested wisely, you should never need rely on anyone again."

"That's very generous," she murmured, her temples throbbing.

"In addition you may keep any clothing and other gifts Rosalind and Celia give to you or to your daughter. The cost shall be none of your concern; if there is anything to question, I shall discuss it with Rosalind directly." Hannah said nothing. She just wanted to go home, but where was home? She remembered then the small property David had deeded to Jamie.

"David deeded a country property to my brother, as a sort of marriage settlement," she said. "If that were in fact his to give, I shall live there."

"Ah, David's hunting lodge. It was his, and is yours, if you want it. I warn you that David never kept it in the best condition, and if I recall correctly it is a small, primitive shelter." Hannah thought her own dear vicarage would seem small and primitive to this man, but she hadn't made the time to go see David's property, so she ought to take heed of the warning. It was hardly in his interest to give her a house she didn't need, after all, unless . . . If he still owned the house, she would be subject to his whim and fancy.

"Had we actually contracted to marry, I would have provided a dower estate," he said, as if he could read her thoughts. "You shall have ownership of the house for my lifetime, and I shall name you the inheritor of it, for your daughter."

"And what must I do?" Her will to fight was gone. Everything and everyone was against her. For the first time, Hannah fervently wished she had left David Reece lying under the blueberry bush.

"Display a reasonable appearance of marital contentment. I don't care how you spend your time, so long as you are ready to attend such society affairs as Rosalind or I would normally attend. I have a great deal of work most of the time, and won't make great demands on you. Most marriages are distant, and ours need not seem any different." He paused, his gaze sharpening. "The only thing you cannot reveal is the true nature of our relationship. This includes letting Rosalind think you share my bed, or have in the past."

She had no other choice. No good one, anyway. "How long?" she heard herself ask.

He shrugged. "A month, two at most. The Season will end then, and Rosalind and Celia will return to Ainsley Park. You may keep in contact with them if you like, but only so long as you never reveal the truth."

"And what about you?" she asked, trying to think through the consequences of this decision better than when she had decided to marry David. If she could never reveal the truth, she would never be completely free of his control. Even estranged, everyone would think she was still the duchess, and therefore still the duke's to do with as he wished. "What contact will I have with you?"

"None but the most necessary," he said brusquely.

"Neither of us will be able to marry anyone else." She couldn't marry again without giving away the secret, and Hannah was not so old that she had no hope or desire to fall in love again. The duke had no heir, and she couldn't believe he wouldn't want one, given that he had not only property and wealth but a title as well. He would obviously need a real wife for that.

He stretched his legs in front of him, the sun gleaming off his boots, one crossed over the other. Hannah watched them, those boots probably worth more than she'd spent on clothing in her entire life, so polished they reflected most of the light that hit them. Stephen used to sit like that, in the garden at the end of the day, one foot wiggling gently. She used to tease him about it, that he couldn't sit still even when he tried. The duke's feet were totally motionless. He seemed a person of great will and control, every word and action deliberate and calculated.

Except he can't have calculated this, she thought suddenly. She realized that he was feeling his way along as much as she was—in different directions, but no more certain of the way. It somehow made her feel better, that this man who was used to getting what he wanted, when he wanted it, was as much at sea as she was. Perhaps the odds weren't so completely stacked in his favor. This made her smile.

"I shall take that as agreement," said the man next to her, and Hannah blinked. She hadn't been paying attention, and had missed what he said.

"I beg your pardon, my mind was wandering." He exhaled slowly through his nose, as if she tried his patience, and Hannah bristled. "It's been a trying day," she snapped. "Forgive me."

"I said," he repeated very slowly, "that I have no plans to marry. Should you wish to marry at some point, I would not object, although you would have to break any contact with Celia and Rosalind. It would most likely be prudent to alter our arrangements as well; a final settlement, perhaps."

"But you might want to marry someday."

"I won't." Then his mouth twisted mockingly. "Are you afraid I would use that as an excuse to cut off your funds?"

"No, I just think you might change your mind," she said, annoyed again by his absolute confidence that things would go the way he wanted. "You have no heir." He said nothing, but his eyes narrowed. "No," she amended slowly. "David is your heir."

"Yes," he said. "David is my heir. It seems fair, doesn't it? Another ten minutes and he would have been the duke. He's already demonstrated that he's able to get a wife, and I know for a fact he is capable of fathering a child."

Hannah jumped to her feet in outrage. "He hasn't demonstrated himself honorable enough to make a decent husband! He's a liar and a scoundrel, and I wonder that anyone would want something they valued passing into David's hands!"

The duke rose, a dark and forbidding figure in the bright, sunny garden. "A man in my position marries for one of three reasons: wealth, consequence, or connection. I am fully satisfied with my ability to create my own wealth, have as much consequence as I require, and would rather not burden myself with any more connections. I will not change my mind." Hannah could only gape in astonishment. He cocked his head as if listening for something. "Do my ears deceive me? Has a woman missed a chance to suggest love as the reason to marry?"

"Your ears do not deceive you, but your knowledge of women does," she managed to say. "I would have suggested companionship, but not love. Not to you."

"Oh?" He seemed interested, neither surprised nor offended.

"You don't want to be loved," she declared. "You've gone out of your way to lie to people who unquestionably do love you. You can't imagine how hurt they'll be when they find out—"

"When?" Wrath suddenly kindled in his eyes, replacing the condescending amusement. "Surely you meant to say 'if.'" Hannah would not let herself look away. She was determined to stand up to him. He was going to win this particular battle, but he was not going to think he had bullied her into it, or that she was cowering in awe of him. It was her own decision, even if only because she had no other choice.

"Yes," she said at last. "I should have said 'if.' Because I will stay in London, and let everyone, including your mother and sister, think we are married. I will try to act as a proper duchess might, and not embarrass either of us. In return, I accept your offer of a cottage and income, plus one other promise." His subtle gloating hardened into suspicion. Hannah glared back. "When my daughter is grown, if I haven't married again and am still considered your wife, you will provide a dowry for her and allow me to bring her to London for the Season if she wishes it."

"How large a dowry?" he snapped.

Hannah named a huge sum. "Five thousand pounds." Molly would never be homeless and penniless like her mother nearly was. If she had to do this, she would gain Molly's independence, too.

The duke's posture relaxed. "Done," he said. Hannah jerked her head in a nod. He held out one hand with a dry smile. Hannah took it, and his fingers closed around hers as if their hands had been made to fit together. A strange tingle raced up her arm again. Startled, she pulled her hand free. How awful she should have this strange and very unwelcome reaction to him.

"Yes. Very well, then. I must go—" Do what? Her mind blanked. "Unpack," she blurted out. He just looked at her with a dark, steady gaze. Did he know why she was so flustered? After what he'd said in the study, about intimate relations . . . "Excuse me," she gasped, then turned and fled before she could embarrass herself further.

CHAPTER 8

Marcus watched her go, hoping he hadn't just made a colossal mistake.

He hadn't thought so until that last moment, when she pulled away from him as if he scorched her. For just a second, he thought there had been a flash of something in her eyes—not anger, and not dislike. It was more like alarm, which matched his own feeling. For just that second, looking down at her upturned face lit with the glow of late afternoon, he'd been more than just satisfied she had agreed to his proposal. Which was wrong.

He cursed under his breath, striding back into the house, setting the lilies along the path bobbing in his wake. It had been a mistake to touch her in his study. He certainly hadn't meant to plant the insidious thought in his own mind of taking her to bed. That was the one thing he absolutely could not do; if she were to become pregnant with his child while posing as his wife, he would never be rid of her, and might even have to marry her in truth. Seducing her, no matter how tempting the thought, was the worst possible thing he could do. He would have to remember that.

Adams was standing outside the study door, his face worried. At Marcus's approach, he jumped to attention and bowed. "Yes, come," snapped Marcus, throwing open the door and resuming his seat behind the desk, still unsettled by unwanted desires. He took it out on the secretary, dictating letters at a furious pace and reeling off a long list of directions. Adams nodded nonstop, scribbling madly, although Marcus hadn't much hope that more than half of it would be completed correctly. Finally he dismissed the young man, watching in pained silence as Adams fumbled his notes and documents together and left, closing the door with a loud click this time.

Marcus stretched his legs out under the desk. One thing he had neglected to tell Adams to do was arrange for pin money for his "duchess." After her outburst this afternoon, he wasn't sure he should do it at all. The allowance a genuine duchess would expect would no doubt horrify her. A dry smile crossed his face at the thought of her outrage over the cost. Hundreds of pounds spent on clothes, indeed. Marcus had paid Rosalind's bills for years, and knew he was on the hook for several thousand pounds at least. Rosalind would spare no expense lavishing the finest wardrobe London could provide on his supposed wife.

But he had already made that choice. Rosalind would be overjoyed to do it, and if ordering clothes by the trunk kept both his stepmother and the vicar's wife out of his way, Marcus would pay the bill with relief. The two women would shop, Celia would play with the child, and he could go on with his life relatively unperturbed. There was no reason to let this . . . complicating attraction disrupt his plans.

He went into the hall, which echoed with laughter and squeals and doors slamming somewhere above. He stopped and frowned. "Harper."

"Lady Celia is playing hide-and-seek with young Molly," said the butler, long accustomed to answering unasked questions. Marcus sighed.

"Have my horse brought around." Another door slammed, and there was a loud shriek of laughter. Marcus winced. "On second thought, make it the carriage. I'll dine at White's."

"Yes, Your Grace," murmured Harper, bowing away. Marcus went up the stairs, grumbling to himself about being chased from his own home. Turning down the hall toward his suite, he was nearly run down by his sister. Her face was flushed, her golden curls were wild, and she caught his arm, her chest heaving. She looked twelve instead of seventeen.

"Oh, Marcus," she gasped "Have you seen her go by? Did she go down the stairs?"

"I've seen no one." He disengaged himself from her grip. "Not quite ladylike today, are you, Celia?" He pinched her chin as he said it. "What on earth is going on up here?"

"We're playing hide-and-seek," she informed him with a giggle. "Come join us!"

"No, thank you," he said. "I couldn't keep up with you." From the corner of his eye he saw a small figure race across the hall. "Your quarry is escaping," he murmured. Celia's eyes rounded, and she whirled about, chasing after the now-giggling child. Marcus watched her catch up the little girl in her arms and spin around. Shaking his head, but fondly, Marcus went into his dressing room and rang for Telman. It was good to see Celia again, he had to admit, and so happy, too.

He was shrugging out of his jacket when the door opened and closed behind him, not quietly but thankfully not slammed. "Telman," he said in a warning voice without turning around. Had everyone in his house decided to make as much noise as possible? There was no response. He looked over his shoulder.

It was the little girl, leaning against the door. He sighed in aggravation, and she put her finger in her mouth. "No hide-and-seek in here," he said firmly. "Go find Celia and tell her you must play somewhere else."

"Are you David?" she asked in a tiny voice. Marcus clenched his jaw to keep from swearing.

"No, I am not," he said coldly. "Where is your mother?"

"Then you're Marcus," she said, still staring at him. "Aunt Celia says you have a handsome horse."

He sighed again, and went down on his haunches to see her. She was wary, but not afraid. It really was uncanny how much she looked like Celia. "You may call me Exeter, or sir."

"Oh." Her big brown eyes didn't blink. "But your name is Marcus."

Obviously, though, she took after her mother. "What is your name?" he asked, resigned to reasoning with her as well.

"Mary Rebecca Preston."

"Well, since I don't know you well, it would be presumptuous of me to call you Mary, or Molly. I should call you Miss Preston. Celia is my sister, and knows me very well, so she calls me Marcus."

"And may I call you Marcus when I know you well?" He frowned, and she added, "You may call me Molly right now."

He stood up and went to the door, opening it and stepping into the hall. "Celia!" His sister popped up from behind a table down the hall. "Your playmate is lost," he bit out as she ran toward him.

"Oh, dear!" She clapped a hand to her mouth. "I'm terribly sorry, Marcus. I told her which doors she ought not to go into, but she must have forgotten."

"I was looking for my mama's room," said the child, skipping into the hall. "I thought it was that one."

"No, it's over there," said Celia gently, indicating the door to the duchess's suite. She glanced at Marcus's face. "Come, Molly, let's go see the horses now."

Molly took Celia's hand. "Oh, yes! Good-bye, Extera!" She waved at him. Celia choked on a giggle. "Extera?"

Marcus gave her a sour look. "Good-bye, Miss Preston." His sister laughed outright, grinning gleefully at him, but led the child away. Marcus went back into his dressing room and finished changing for the evening, now that Telman had arrived. Extera, indeed. Both Preston females seemed determined to make fools of him in any way they could. Perhaps it would be worth it to send them away. How long could gossip last, after all?

Years, he acknowledged. And next year would be Celia's debut. While no one would blame her, a scandal would taint her through association. An estranged wife was nothing interesting; many men kept their wives and families in the country. He would just have to put up with them for a few weeks.

The best way to do that, of course, was to spend as little time as possible around them. He went down the stairs to his waiting carriage, and left.

Leaving the house provided no respite, though. In fact, Marcus reflected grimly to himself that he had apparently leaped straight from the pan into the fire by going out.

Men he scarcely knew and never spoke to stopped to greet him. His dinner was interrupted several times by people pretending to congratulate him, and in reality fishing for gossip about his sudden marriage. By the time he finished dining, Marcus was seething.

Was this a gentleman's club, or a women's sewing circle? He called for his carriage and set out for one of the most notorious gaming hells, seeking refuge in the company of men too dissolute to notice anything printed in the *Times*.

"Exeter!" said Robert Milleman, a slight acquaintance. "Join us? We require a fourth."

Marcus cast an assessing eye over the table near the door. Milleman, a portly gentleman with thinning hair, and Sir Henry Trevenham. Trevenham was on his list of possible suspects. He didn't gamble with anyone not on the list. Marcus nodded once, taking the chair opposite Milleman. Here, he devoutly hoped, he would have peace, and could accomplish something useful. In his current temper, he would be delighted to catch Trevenham with false bank notes, just so he could have an excuse to hit someone.

Milleman cut, and the portly man beside him dealt. For a few moments the table was quiet, as players examined their cards and a servant refilled everyone's glass with port. Marcus stole a quick glance at Trevenham, to his left. The man could be a counterfeiter; he had the hard eye of a gambler, and his fingers caressed the cards with familiarity. Perhaps this long day of frustration would yield something after all.

"Heard you were interested in Camden's thoroughbreds," remarked Trevenham idly.

Marcus led the first hand. "Perhaps."

"Good blood." Trevenham played. "His Dashing Dancer placed in the Ascot two years ago."

"Dashing Dancer, out of Starry Night?" asked the other man eagerly. Trevenham nodded.

"A lovely filly that was, Starry Night." Trevenham took a long drag on his cigar. "Planning to add to your stables, Exeter?"

"Perhaps," said Marcus again. Trevenham took the

trick. Marcus kept one eye on the man as the play continued. This time Trevenham passed, as did Milleman. Marcus took the trick.

The portly man pulled a handkerchief from his pocket and blotted his forehead. Milleman laughed. "Feeling the heat already, Redley?"

Redley grinned, but gruesomely. Marcus had the sense he'd been at the tables a while. He had the look of a man down, and trying to get back up. Somewhat scornfully, he diverted his attention back to Trevenham.

Redley was looed; he grumbled as he paid the pool. Milleman, who also had to pay, just smirked. Redley cut, and Marcus dealt a new round.

Blessedly, Trevenham and Redley were true gamblers. Any topic not indirectly related to gambling was promptly squashed. Thanks to the weeks of his investigations, they assumed Marcus was the same. Aside from a few bawdy comments on his new wife—which Marcus tolerated in bored silence—the talk was mostly of horses, cards, and various other wagers of interest at the moment.

At some point the play changed to vingt-et-un. Milleman left after the clock chimed one, and two other gentlemen, Bowden and Lane, joined them. They were not on Marcus's list, but played seriously, and pushed the stakes higher and higher. Marcus silently thanked them; a lot of money could change hands in a short time, and he would rather not spend the whole night at the tables.

Trevenham, though, continued on a steady course, winning a little and never losing too much. He stayed cool and unruffled, despite the enormous quantity of port he poured down his throat. Marcus played like a devil, past caring if he came out ahead or not. He wanted Trevenham's money. He wanted to see what color the man's notes were, and if Timms would pronounce them unfit. Redley was all but sweating blood, his collar dark with perspiration and his cards limp from his pudgy hands.

Another hand. Trevenham bowed out at once. Marcus stayed in only to keep from making the man suspicious. Bowden flipped the next card. Marcus barely noticed he won. Frustrated and running out of patience, he scooped up the winnings and thought how to draw out Trevenham. Perhaps he could take the man in piquet. . . .

Trevenham pushed back his chair. " 'Night," he said with a wide yawn and an indelicate scratch. "Done in, m'afraid." He shoveled his money back into his purse.

Marcus also got to his feet. His back was stiff from the strain of lolling about so indolently. "I'm done here as well." He cast a glance Trevenham's way. "Fancy a few hands of piquet, Trevenham?" *Say yes,* he willed the sot.

Trevenham laughed. "Not tonight, eh? Like playing a bloody sphinx." He patted his pockets, looking puzzled, then smiled triumphantly. "Taking my leave while I can," he said. His attempt at a bow wobbled gracelessly off balance. "P'rhaps another night."

Marcus inclined his head as Trevenham wove an unsteady path toward the door. Damn; another opportunity lost. Or was Trevenham onto his plan? If so, Marcus would be lucky to see so much as a ha'penny from Trevenham's pocket, let alone a nice pile of crisp, newly printed banknotes. With more violence than necessary, he reached for his own winnings. He was so sick of this.

"Exeter." A pale plump hand covered his own. Marcus glanced up coldly. Redley looked almost green as he stared at the pile of money under Marcus's outstretched hand. His upper lip was damp. "If I might . . ." He cleared his throat. "If I might have another hand . . ." There was desperation in his tone, lurking under the obsequiousness.

"Not tonight." He disengaged his hand from Redley's grip.

Redley persisted. "I deserve a chance to change my luck, don't I?"

Marcus glared at him. Redley should have changed his luck hours ago by leaving the table. Marcus hadn't especially wanted to win his money, but Redley seemed determined to lose it to someone. "Another night," he said with steel in his voice.

Redley lurched to his feet. His round face was mottled red and purple. "See here," he said, his voice rising. "I deserve a chance to win back my stake, surely!"

"You've had hours of chances."

"Damned cardsharp." Redley's voice slurred as it rose in volume. "Knave! Villain!"

Marcus straightened and directed an icy stare at the man. "It almost sounds as though you're calling me a cheat," he said.

Redley swallowed. He wanted to, everyone could see it, but didn't dare. His eyes fixed on the money still on the table. "My deed," he choked. "My deed."

Marcus glanced down and realized the man had thrown a deed into the pot at some point. Christ. If everyone hadn't been staring, he would have tossed it back in the little weasel's face.

But the duke of Exeter did not brawl, and he did not respond to threats. Deliberately, Marcus picked up all his winnings, including the deed. God knew he certainly hadn't tried to win it; what did he have to feel guilty for? Redley should have known better than to wager it in the first place. Redley's eyes bulged, and he swelled again. "Bastard," he whimpered.

The word hung in the air for a few seconds before Redley crumpled to his knees. As Marcus strode away,

Redley screamed a few more oaths at him, some in languages not English. His face set in stone, Marcus walked on.

The sound of the man's wails followed him all the way to the street. Marcus climbed into his waiting carriage without looking back. He was furious with both of them, Trevenham for not being a more gullible mark and Redley for being too gullible. God, this was why he hated gambling. Such a filthy, degrading business; he didn't know how David could stand it.

Once home, he dismissed the servants and went to his suite. He cast a quick glance at the door to the duchess's room, but like the rest of the house, all was silent within. Thank God. He didn't particularly like the idea of a woman, let alone a strange woman, having free run of his rooms. Another burst of resentment toward David filled his chest. It was bad enough that he had to worry about his only brother being transported or hanged, but he couldn't even call his home his own anymore. He stared at the duchess's door with loathing—not so much for the woman on the other side as for the terrible feeling of creeping helplessness her presence embodied. He was being outmaneuvered, boxed in and manipulated by events and people beyond his control, and Marcus did not like it at all.

He lit another lamp and poured out his winnings on the table. Normally he would examine every note, checking each one against the sample forged notes from Timms. Then he would catalog what he had learned in his file, adding to the body of evidence against some member of society, weaving a noose that would hopefully tighten around the throat of someone, anyone, other than David.

But tonight he was finding it difficult to focus. He glared at the door again. Tonight he couldn't quite care as much if David turned out to be the culprit. He didn't quite care if his brother were revealed as a liar, a troublemaker, and a thief. Just so long as he could have a little peace again.

He braced his hands on the edge of the table and let his head fall forward in exhaustion. His shoulders were stiff from tension, his eyes stung from the closed, smoky air of the gaming club. He was tired and sore and sick unto death of groping in the dark like a blind man, never knowing when he would be blindsided by yet another problem he must solve for someone else. It was past four in the morning, and he wished he could just go to bed and not worry about anything, just for tonight. . . .

But he couldn't. If he didn't worry about those things, no one would. His brother would go to prison. The Exeter name would be tarnished for years to come, weighing down his sister's and stepmother's reputations. The responsibility for his family sat thick and heavy on Marcus's shoulders. He was only making himself more tired by putting off what he had to do. With a weary sigh, he pulled out the chair, took up his magnifying lens, and bent over the pile of money.

CHAPTER 9

The next two weeks were some of the longest and most tiring of Hannah's life. Pretending to be a duchess was quite a lot of work, it turned out.

The duke gathered the entire staff and introduced her as the new duchess. His smile to her was dark with irony, but she ignored him, stepping forward and trying to learn as many names as she could. After the first twenty, though, she realized she ought to learn instead what all their positions were, for she had no idea what made one girl a downstairs maid and another an upstairs maid, not to mention the 'tween stairs maid. They were all neatly dressed in blue and gray, which Rosalind had told her were the Exeter colors, and Hannah realized self-consciously that their clothing was finer than her own. When she finally reached the end, she stood by the duke's side, not certain what to do next. He looked at his butler, and everyone left, quickly and quietly.

"Goodness," she murmured, watching the dozens of servants return to their posts without the talking and whispering she would have expected in any other group of people that large.

"Well done," said the duke with a tinge of surprise.

"I'll never remember all their names," she whispered. He frowned.

"There's no need. The butler, the housekeeper, and your lady's maid are all you'll deal with for the most part."

"How can you not know their names? They live in your house."

"That hardly means I speak to them all. I prefer my household to run smoothly, and that is easier if Harper is in charge of the servants." At another glance from the duke, the butler stepped forward. "Who will act as Her Grace's lady's maid?"

"Mrs. Potts recommended Lily," murmured Harper. The duke nodded, and the butler turned, looking at a slim girl waiting at the back of the hall. She came forward and curtseyed, and Hannah nearly curtseyed back. "Lily, you will be lady's maid to Her Grace," the butler told her. She bobbed her head.

"Thank you, Harper," said Hannah, unnerved by the silent communication. Didn't these people have voices? "I am pleased to meet you, Lily." The girl looked startled, but nodded, and murmured something in reply. At another look from Harper, she backed away, curtseyed again, and left, all in near total silence.

"Mama!" Molly's cry echoed in the quiet. "Celia showed me the nursery! Mama, there are toys in there! Come see!" She put her arms through the balusters at the top of the stairs and waved. Beside Hannah, the duke let out a pained sigh.

"I'm coming, dear," she called to her daughter. "Don't do that," she whispered angrily at the duke. He just looked at her, and it made her furious. "Don't sigh and close your eyes as if you can't stand everything Molly or I do. This was all your idea. If anyone is at fault, you are, so please stop acting put-upon!"

"I am acting like any man would act if he had four unwelcome females in his house!" he snapped back. "Fear not, I hold David entirely responsible, but I am not pleased by this situation!"

Hannah took a step, thrusting her chin forward until their faces were mere inches apart. "He may be responsible for creating it, but you have perpetuated it! I wanted to go home, but you made me stay."

"Impertinence in a woman is a very unwelcome quality," he said. Then, as she was opening her mouth to tell him what she thought of *his* manners, he reached out and put his finger under her chin, with a piercing look. "Pity, for it becomes you." She closed her mouth in confusion, and he turned on his heel and walked away, Harper trailing in his wake. Hannah stared at his back. Had he complimented or insulted her? Both, she thought. Molly called to her again, and Hannah hurried up the stairs to see the toys, all the while wondering what he could have meant.

The next morning Hannah was just unbuttoning her nightgown to get dressed when a flutter of movement caught her eye. Whirling around, she gasped in relief to see it was Lily, standing inside the door with a heavily laden tray in her hands.

"Goodness, you startled me," she said, clutching her gown closed. Had the girl knocked, and Hannah simply hadn't heard?

"My apologies, Your Grace," murmured Lily, lowering her eyes as she crossed the room to put the tray on the dressing table. "Harper instructed me to bring breakfast, even though you've not yet rung for it. He noted you to be an early riser." Frantically redoing buttons, Hannah only paid half attention.

"Ah, thank you, that's very nice." She scrambled

into her dressing gown, wrapping it protectively around herself. She was not accustomed to having visitors in her nightdress. Lily was moving about the room with quiet efficiency, pulling back the drapes and opening the wardrobe to survey Hannah's small collection of dresses. Hannah remained on the far side of the bed, uncertain what to do.

"Shall you dress before you take breakfast, Your Grace?" Lily laid out the nicest of her dresses, the blue muslin again. She proceeded to fetch stockings and undergarments, sorting through the drawers as if she knew exactly where everything was stored.

"Well, I hadn't thought . . ." Hannah glanced again at the tray, where several dishes steamed gently in the morning sun. It had been ingrained in her from childhood that lying in bed awake was sloth, and only for the infirm and lazy. Still, it was a tempting thought, given that the tray was already here, and emitting smells that made her stomach growl. "After," she said, making her way toward the table where the tray sat. She couldn't lie in bed and eat, but surely sitting at the dressing table to eat couldn't be that sinful.

"Yes, Your Grace." Lily was somehow across the room ahead of her, uncovering dishes and arranging things. Hannah marveled at how neatly it was done. She picked up her fork to taste a plump little sausage, but stopped as she noticed Lily tidying the room.

"Really, there's no need for that," she said. "Please sit for a moment."

Lily paused and stared, her arms filled with bedclothes. "Your Grace?" Hannah motioned to the other chair near the table.

"Please, sit down."

After a moment, Lily obeyed, her surprise disappearing behind her usual calm. She sat on the edge of her chair, tucking her feet under it, and folded her hands in her lap, as if she were sitting only on the expectation that she would soon be on her feet again. Hannah finished the sausage, and took a sip of tea. "Is the duke a good employer?" she blurted before she could think better of it. While none seemed mistreated, there was something unnatural about the Exeter servants.

Lily didn't blink. "He is a fair master, Your Grace. I am honored to serve his household."

"But do you like it here?"

"I have been quite content, madam. I hope to please you."

Heavens, no wonder the duke had an inflated opinion of himself. He was surrounded by people who practically kissed his boots, even in his absence. Hannah pushed aside the poached egg and took a slice of toast. The cook really did make divine bread; she would have to ask for the recipe before she left. Lily's eyes moved quickly to the tray, as if cataloging what she ate and what she skipped. Somehow Hannah just knew the tray Lily brought tomorrow—and she had a feeling Lily would, unless told not to—would only hold those things she had eaten.

"Well, Lily, if you wish to please me . . ." Hannah paused. She had never, in the entire course of her life, been able to command another person to do her will and know that it would be done. "You must always speak your mind, when I ask your opinion," she said firmly. "I am not the duke, and you do not have to whisper in my presence. I shan't need your aid for everything, and will ring when I do require it. Other than that, you may attend to your own business."

That seemed eminently reasonable to Hannah. She didn't need or really want Lily coming into her room every morning to put out her clothes or to bring her breakfast. Those were just many of the luxuries she would be wise to avoid, if she were to return to her former life with any ease. This was only for a few weeks, she reminded herself.

Lily blinked. "Your Grace, it is my purpose to help you in every way. . . ."

"And when I need it, I shall ask for it."

The maid's eyes widened. "Yes, madam."

"In fact," Hannah confessed, "I don't even know what a lady's maid does. I wouldn't know what to tell you to do, anyway."

"Anything you wish, Your Grace. I have some talent arranging hair, and my cousin is the dowager duchess's maid. She has been training me to assist you." Lily still spoke in a soft, even voice that would be almost unheard by anyone not attending.

"Why does everyone whisper?" The question came out before Hannah had fully considered it.

Lily's impassive face didn't change. "His Grace prefers the servants not call attention to themselves, madam."

"What a pity for him you can't turn yourselves invisible," said Hannah under her breath. Lily said nothing, but the slightest catch in her breath indicated the maid had heard. Hannah winced; she wasn't giving a very good account of herself, mocking the duke behind his back. She suddenly realized Lily would be out of a job when the fraud marriage ended. "What did you do before?"

"I was responsible for the more delicate items of the laundry, madam, and assisting the dowager duchess's maid and Lady Celia's maid when they were in London."

Heavens above, even the servants had servants. But then that meant Lily had been promoted to her new post, and Hannah began to feel rather bad that she would lose her new status fairly soon. She straightened the dishes on the tray, more and more dismayed by this arrangement. She didn't want to feel responsible for Lily, but it was an undeniable fact that the maid would suffer from her departure. "And what does this new position mean to you?"

Finally, Lily seemed at a loss. "In what way, Your Grace?"

"Well, are your wages higher?" Hannah wished she hadn't said anything. What could she do about it, even if Lily were reduced to blacking boots? "Better quarters, or . . . or something?"

The maid looked thoroughly perplexed now. "I have no complaint with my room or my salary, Your Grace."

"Well, very good!" Flustered, Hannah drained her teacup and pushed back the tray. "I think I shall get dressed now." Without thinking, she began ordering the tray, replacing covers and stacking the dishes so they would be less likely to fall off going downstairs. The duke would probably prosecute her for damages if she broke anything.

Lily sprang to her feet and reached for the tray. "I'll see to it, Your Grace."

"Oh, yes, of course." Hannah paced across the room, all her discomfort returning. Could she tell the duke she didn't want a maid? He would probably insist upon it, for appearances' sake. She opened the wardrobe and got out her sturdy gray wool, as well as her walking boots. Perhaps doing something ordinary like taking Molly for a walk would restore some order to her life.

She had barely unbuttoned her nightdress again when there was a tap at the door. It opened and Rosalind sailed in before Hannah could say a word. "Wonderful, you're awake!" she said gaily. "Madame Lescaut, my dressmaker, will be here shortly. We must begin your wardrobe."

"Oh, but . . . but . . ." Hannah clutched her dress in front of her protectively. "I was planning to take Molly to the park."

"Good heavens, we haven't time! Perhaps later we'll have time for a stroll." She eyed the gray dress in Hannah's hands. "Much later." Another tap on the door came, and Rosalind called, "Come!" Two servants carried in a large copper tub, and several more followed with buckets of steaming water. "I thought you might like a bath," Rosalind confided quietly. Hannah mustered a smile. A bath did sound lovely, but she didn't like being overruled on going to the park.

After she had bathed—while Rosalind sat and talked her way through several fashion periodicals, much to Hannah's discomfort—Molly bounded in, down the private staircase that connected the duchess's suite to the nursery. Molly had been enchanted by the thought of her own room and her own stairs. Hannah caught her up gratefully; this was normal, she thought, breathing deeply of Molly's little girl smell as her daughter hugged her.

"Mama, may we go to the park today?" Molly's brown eyes shone. "Celia says there is a pond with ducks."

Hannah smiled. "Of course we may." Rosalind made a soft noise behind her, and Hannah flinched. For a split second she almost said she didn't want a new wardrobe. But then Rosalind would probably go to the duke, and he would be sure to come scold her again. "Later," she told Molly, trying to hide her feelings.

Molly pouted. "Now, Mama. You don't have to cook, and Celia told me we must not dig in the garden, for Mr. Criggs—he's the gardener, Mama—will be angry with us, but the garden belongs to Extera and we might ask him if we may dig—"

"Later, Molly," Hannah cut in. Extera? She didn't even want to know what the duke would say if she asked permission to let Molly dig in his beautiful, formal garden.

"We must hire a nursemaid as well," said Rosalind in an undertone.

"No," said Hannah at once.

The duchess's eyebrows went up. "But, Hannah, you'll be very busy. Molly will need someone to mind her."

"I will," said Hannah firmly. "I am her mother."

Rosalind stared at her with a mixture of curiosity and surprise. "Molly will be fine. Celia had a nursemaid, and I never felt less than a mother."

"No, no—I didn't mean to imply that." Hannah closed her mouth in frustration. She didn't want Molly used to someone else taking care of her, and she didn't want to lose her one last link to her real life. Some things were inviolate, after all.

Molly looked at her with big eyes. "What is a nursemaid?"

"Someone to play with you, and fetch your tea, and give you baths and help you dress," said Rosalind.

Molly frowned. "That's Mama."

Rosalind sighed as Hannah beamed, pleased beyond words by Molly's response. "Well, we'll decide that later. For now—" She turned to Lily. "Take Miss Molly up to the nursery this morning. We've a great deal to do."

Lily curtsied. "Yes, Your Grace."

Hannah felt a bit better. It would give Lily something to do when Hannah didn't need her, and it would spare another employee in the duke's household whose position was only temporary. Lily held out her hand to Molly, who slid out of Hannah's arms and regarded her hopefully.

"May we go outside?" she asked.

A faint smile crossed Lily's face. "Perhaps," she said in her quiet voice. "We mustn't get you dirty."

Molly's face lit up. "Oh, Mama won't mind! So long as we scrape our shoes before we come in. May we, Mama?"

Hannah laughed and bent to kiss Molly's forehead. "You may, but mind Lily. Best manners, Miss Preston."

Molly nodded, her blond curls bouncing. She took Lily's hand and all but dragged the maid from the room.

"It's not a perfect solution, but it will do for now," said Rosalind. "Lily will be needed here. Come! We've so much to do." Satisfied with her victory about the nurse-maid, Hannah docilely went, unaware that it was the last inch Rosalind would yield for the next fortnight.

Being a duchess, it turned out, was a great deal more complicated than being the wife of a duke, or even just the pretend wife of a duke. One must look the part. Hannah's long never-been-cut hair was snipped and trimmed into a more fashionable tumble of curls. A wide variety of cosmetics and perfumes soon covered the top of the dressing table, including creams to turn the work-roughened skin of her hands and the tanned skin of her face and neck into a duchess's soft white skin. Hannah didn't think they were necessary, but Rosalind insisted.

One must act the part. Good manners were not enough, Rosalind advised. One must know not only a person's rank, but also their social standing and whether they were scandalous or not. Some of the gossip she related made Hannah's ears burn. Of course there had been gossip in Middleborough, but Stephen had believed it quite wicked, and most of the chattering hens had taken care to gossip away from the vicar and his wife. Hannah wished Rosalind would do the same. But she had given her word, and she didn't want to embarrass herself, so she listened, hoping she would be able to forget the most scandalous parts when she left London.

But most importantly, it seemed, one must dress the part. The dressmaker came every day, measuring and fitting Hannah for more clothing than she could wear in a lifetime. Only by keeping in mind the duke's statement that he would discuss any overspending with Rosalind did Hannah keep quiet. Once he got the first bill, she was sure, he would step in and put a stop to things.

She was standing on the dressmaker's stool, being pinned into yet another gown, when the duke did come. It was the first time she had seen him in a week, and that time had been only across the vast dining table, with Rosalind and Celia as buffer, to say nothing of a dozen hovering servants. He'd barely said a word, and his glowering silence had oppressed the whole table; even Celia's irrepressible chatter had gone quiet. It was also the first interruption in a day that was following the same monotonous pattern Rosalind had established, and as such, Hannah didn't react to it at first. She just stood there, stupidly staring back at him, thinking one thing: at last.

The room fell abruptly quiet as Rosalind, the dressmaker, and her assistants noticed his presence. Hannah wondered what sort of self-possession it took to walk into a room—without knocking—and simply know that everyone would pause to acknowledge his entrance.

"Might I have a word?" he said, in that same cool, deep tone she remembered too well, his impenetrable dark eyes on her. Hannah flushed as Madame Lescaut and her seamstresses rushed for the door like a flock of sheep being herded by a half dozen collies.

"Naturally!" chirped Rosalind, sending Hannah a

sly smile. "I quite understand." And she slipped out with them, closing the door behind her.

For a moment Hannah didn't move, frozen in awkward silence. The duke was just staring at her, his expression unreadable, his hands clasped behind his back. Gingerly she climbed down from the stool, trying to avoid being speared by all the pins holding the half-sewn gown together. "Yes?"

"I see your wardrobe is progressing."

Hannah started to lift one shoulder, but had to stop. "I did warn you. Rosalind seems to think a duchess cannot have too many clothes."

He raised one eyebrow. "Indeed. And you've not yet expired under the strain. Remarkable."

The sharp retort was on Hannah's lips almost before she caught herself. But she did, just in the nick of time. She caught the odd light in his eyes, and realized he was needling her, and so she managed not to snap back at him. "Not yet, no," she agreed calmly. "Though it's been a near miss, I can tell you."

His eyes gleamed. "Then it is time we made a public appearance." He crossed the room and handed her a thick ivory card.

It was an invitation to a ball, to be held in two days' time by Lord and Lady Throckmorton. Hannah rolled her lower lip between her teeth, studying the exquisite calligraphy. A London ball! And she would be going dressed as beautifully as a duchess. It was enough to bring a rueful twist to her lips.

"I trust that meets with—with your approval."

Hannah looked up at the catch in his voice. It did, she supposed, because she didn't have a reason to argue against it. What were all these clothes for, if not to go out and be seen in them? But the duke did not meet her eyes. His gaze was directed lower.

The pins holding the gown together in back must

have slipped. The bodice, daring as it was to begin with, had slid down. The new corset gave Hannah a figure she hadn't thought possible, and now it was on full display. And the duke's eyes were fixed on her newly prominent bosom.

She didn't dare try to cover herself. She could barely move her arms as it was, with all the pins holding the bodice together. No doubt if she tried to, the whole dress would just fall apart. Hannah could only stand in mute awareness, her breath strangely shallow as his eyes slowly rose to meet hers again. He wasn't at all embarrassed that she'd caught him looking. Her skin tingled. What was he thinking, staring at her with heat in his gaze? What would he do now? And why did that question make her heart race and her stomach knot?

She shifted her weight, horrified again at her reaction to him. Good heavens, what on earth was wrong with her? She barely knew this man, and didn't even like him, but he had only to look at her in that smoldering, knowing way and her every nerve tensed in anticipation. *Of nothing,* she told herself sternly, gripping the invitation.

"Does it?" he murmured. She blinked up at him. "Meet with your approval." Although his voice was as detached as ever, she was sure he sensed every awful thing she was feeling. When he looked at her that way, she was sure he could see right into her mind. Which was possibly even worse than his seeing her half-undressed like this.

"Yes!" She thrust the invitation back at him. "Yes, that will be perfectly fine."

He didn't take it. "You may keep it. Adams has already entered it in my diary."

Hannah lowered her hand. "Oh. Yes, of course. I—I'll tell Rosalind as well."

"She already knows. She chose that engagement."

Color flooded Hannah's face. And Rosalind hadn't said a word to her. She must have insisted he tell Hannah himself. Hannah pressed her lips together. She could survive this well enough, if only Rosalind would leave off her persistent matchmaking. It was embarrassing, and none of Rosalind's concern, and Hannah was having enough trouble keeping her thoughts off dangerous ground without Rosalind un-helpfully pushing her there.

"Well, what else is there?" she snapped, catching him staring at her again. "I shall do my best, if you're agonizing over being seen in public with me."

The harsh set of his mouth softened a tiny bit. "On the contrary, my dear wife," he said softly. "I wasn't thinking of that at all." And he turned on his heel and left her there, stunned speechless. He was quite good at that, Hannah reflected, holding up the skirt of her gown to stomp to the door and call Rosalind and Madame Lescaut back. Just once she would like to end a conversation with him not feeling tongue-tied and stupid. Or perhaps she should wish to feel only that, and not any attraction to the wretched man.

She showed Rosalind the invitation when the seam-stresses had finally peeled the gown off her. "Why, how wonderful," gushed Rosalind, as if she'd never seen the invitation before. "How eager he must be to show you off!"

"He told me you chose it," Hannah said.

Rosalind's face fell. For a moment she looked wildly annoyed, but she mustered another cheery smile. "Yes, I had forgotten. Which gown shall you wear? Madame Lescaut has finished the blue silk with the Brussels lace—"

"Please don't pester him on my behalf," said Hannah in a very low voice, barely moving her lips. Madame Lescaut and her entourage were on the other side of the room, but sound carried very well in these high-ceilinged rooms with their polished floors and acres of windows.

"Nonsense." Rosalind waved one hand. "Every man needs a little push."

Hannah let out her breath slowly, ducking her head as if to read the invitation again as she struggled with her temper and her conscience. There was genuine warmth in Rosalind's voice when she spoke of the duke, and Hannah didn't doubt Rosalind was only trying to aid his happiness—and Hannah's. She didn't know everything was a fraud. She didn't know they were lying to her.

Guilt crashed in on Hannah. Rosalind was exerting enormous effort to make Hannah into a well-mannered, well-dressed duchess, and even trying to push the duke into love with her. And in return, she was destined for bitter disappointment on all counts.

"Rosalind, I must tell you . . ." The words flew out before she could stop herself.

"Yes?" Rosalind smiled brightly.

"The duke and I . . ." Hannah couldn't do it, she just couldn't. She had given her word. It was not her fault the duke had a generous and loving stepmother. "That is, he's already told me certain affairs of his are none of my concern," she mumbled. "I'm afraid—I'm afraid you mistake the nature of our marriage—"

"In what way, dear?" Rosalind asked, her eyes probing. Hannah closed her mouth, trapped. "There, I suspected as much," went on the other woman in a soothing tone. "I'm not blind, you know, and I could see that things were . . . well, let's say I thought a little push might be beneficial. I don't wish to interfere in your marriage, but if Marcus has fed you some nonsense about society marriages, you must not listen to him."

"No?" echoed Hannah stupidly.

"No," said Rosalind firmly. "It's not a very admirable thing, that society expects a man like Marcus to have a wife and a mistress, but you must not accept it."

Hannah felt like a rabbit with one leg in the snare, knowing she was doomed and helpless to save herself. "I don't think I have the power to change his mind," she said, thinking frantically for a way to change the subject. Perhaps what she should wear to the ball . . .

Rosalind laughed. "No power! A woman always has a great deal of power over a man who wants her, and as for a man who loves her, well! Marcus is the sort to care deeply for someone, or not at all. Nurture the feelings that led you both into marriage, and he'll never stray from your side."

"If he doesn't care to be loyal, I shan't go about nagging him not to stray," said Hannah, speaking absolute truth. The duke would laugh in her face if she suggested such a thing, and if he wanted to have mistresses and flaunt his affairs, there was little she could do, especially since she wasn't even enjoying his attentions now. No. She frowned a little. That sounded wrong; more rightly, she wouldn't suffer from the continued lack of his attentions. Not a bit.

"It's not that I believe he wants to betray you," Rosalind was explaining. "Men are simply expected to do it, even men who claim to respect their wives. But what a man wants and what will make a man happy are often two different things. Mark my words, he'll be happier if he's not spending his nights in the arms of another woman."

Without warning, the thought of the duke spending the night in her arms filled her mind. Hannah shrugged, trying to banish the image before it could wreak any more havoc on her composure. "I don't see how I can prevent him, if that's what he wants."

"Make sure he's in your bed every night," said Rosalind promptly. Hannah choked.

"Well—I—it's not that . . ."

Rosalind laughed lightly. "Nonsense, my dear. He may be my stepson, but he's still a man."

Yes, a man who had stood looking down her half-stitched gown with a great deal of interest. Who had suggested they might share intimate relations. Who made her heart jump and her skin tingle just by looking at her. He was the very last man in the world Hannah should even think of having in her bed for one night, let alone every night. "Thank you for your advice," she managed to squeak, before forcibly turning the conversation to ball gowns and other, less dangerous, topics.

CHAPTER 10

At precisely two minutes before nine, Marcus left his suite and went downstairs. He was not looking forward to this evening, and hadn't been since the moment Rosalind stormed into his study and demanded that he take his duchess somewhere.

"You've married a wonderfully intelligent and sensible woman, Marcus, but you are treating her like a child," she'd accused him. "People are beginning to say you are ashamed of her."

He'd bitten his tongue to keep from suggesting he might be. The vicar's wife might be passably attractive, but it was clear she was not a society lady. She wasn't a lady at all, he had fumed to himself, cursing David yet again. She greeted servants like equals and allowed her child to run wild all about the house and garden, instead of being tucked away in the nursery. When he had dined with the ladies, Marcus had been appalled to discover she apparently wasn't very educated, for she made no effort to lead the conversation, displaying none of the witty banter society would expect in a duchess. As little as Marcus valued public opinion, he didn't particularly care to look like a fool, either, and he had a bad feeling that keeping Hannah Preston might have been a very foolish decision indeed.

Still, when he had gone to inform her that they would attend the Throckmorton ball—again at Rosalind's prodding—she'd looked vastly improved. Shockingly improved, he grudgingly admitted. And he was mildly relieved to see that she didn't appear to be intimidated by the prospect of going out. He hoped this evening went off without a disaster. He hoped Rosalind had taught her enough to survive. He hoped it would all be over quickly.

The hall was empty, though. He waited a moment, then beckoned Harper. "Where are the duchess and dowager duchess?" Rosalind knew he expected prompt departures.

As Harper opened his mouth, Rosalind appeared at the top of the stairs. "Marcus! There you are." She hurried down, and Marcus frowned. She wasn't dressed for the ball. "Celia has a dreadful stomachache. I can't leave her."

His frown turned ferocious. "Rosalind," he warned. She patted his arm.

"There, I know you're worried about Hannah. You can endure one night without going off and playing cards, surely? It's her first ball, dear. You must know how important it will be for you to introduce her to society." He exhaled sharply.

"Rosalind, you cannot expect me to stand at her side all night. Celia will be fine. I'll wait for you to dress." If the completely uncharacteristic acceptance of tardiness surprised his stepmother, she didn't show it.

"Marcus, she feels wretched. Men don't understand these things." He slapped his gloves into his palm, realizing she had tricked him. He had counted on Rosalind being so delighted to present a daughter-in-law to the ton that he had underestimated her matchmaking instincts. He couldn't let the same mistake happen twice. Rosalind smiled brightly over his shoulder.

"Oh, Hannah, how lovely you look!" Marcus turned, slowly, reluctantly. Hannah was picking her way down the stairs, holding her silk skirts very carefully, unintentionally exposing her legs almost to the knees. At Rosalind's greeting, she smiled.

"How kind of you to say so. I feel like I've been made a princess for the evening." She stepped off the bottom stair and let her skirts fall. Marcus raised his eyes to her face, having looked his fill at her very lovely legs. Unfortunately, this view was just as unsettling. Her midnight blue gown with white lace trim was low-cut and close fitting, setting off her figure to unexpected advantage. Her hair was no longer pulled into a plain knot, but was arranged more loosely, with curls artfully teasing her rather graceful neck. She was far more than passably attractive tonight. She glanced at him. "Good evening, sir."

"Madam." Aware of Rosalind's scrutiny, he lifted her hand nearly to his lips. Her fingers flinched, but she didn't resist. "Shall we go?" Harper stepped forward with his hat and coat, and a footman swirled a satin cloak around her shoulders.

"Good-bye! Have a lovely evening," said Rosalind, beaming at them. Hannah stopped cold.

"Are you not coming?" she asked. Marcus almost smiled at the dismay in her voice. Rosalind sighed, steering her toward the door.

"No, sadly, Celia is unwell, and she's not so old that she doesn't want her mother about. I shall be so sorry to miss your debut, but Marcus will stand in my stead, and really, who better to introduce you than your husband?"

"But . . ." She swung around, her alarmed gaze seeking his. Marcus quirked one brow, knowing better than she possibly could what Rosalind was up to, and merely offered his arm. What did she expect him to do, decide they should all stay home with Celia?

"Do give my regrets to Lady Throckmorton," Rosalind added. Slowly Hannah put her hand on his arm. Harper opened the door, and Marcus led the way out to the carriage.

Hannah let herself be handed into the carriage. She wasn't sure, but she suspected she'd just been tricked. Rosalind hadn't looked terribly worried about Celia, and the duke had that grim expression he so often wore when displeased. "Is Celia really ill?" she asked when the door was shut and they were alone.

"No doubt she would say so, if asked."

That sounded like confirmation. She couldn't suppress a frustrated huff. "I am quite tired of being maneuvered like this."

"Aren't we all," he muttered.

Hannah pursed her lips. "We could turn the tables on her, you know. Return early, or not even go at all."

He sat motionless. "I beg your pardon."

"After all," she went on recklessly, "Rosalind tricked us; why shouldn't we repay her in kind? If we return home and sneak up the servants' stair, no one need know."

"Except the servants," he replied dryly. She waved one hand.

"Then we could climb the large tree outside my windows. I certainly needn't summon a servant in order to go to bed."

"Climb a tree?" he said incredulously. "To get into my own house?"

"Of course," she said with a laugh. "Surely you did it as a boy."

"Indeed not." He paused. "Surely you didn't, as a girl."

"I most certainly did. My brothers taught me." She was growing attached to the idea now, even though she knew she could never bring herself to shred the glorious silk gown she wore by climbing a tree. It was strangely fun to twit His stuffy Grace about it, though. "I would go first, to show you how it's done," she offered innocently.

Marcus clamped his lips together to keep from replying. He could picture her all too well, hiking up her skirts and climbing a tree with those long, slender legs in white silk stockings. He was disgusted with himself for even letting himself imagine sneaking through the dark garden with her, then watching her—from below—as she climbed into her bedroom window. Which he would also have to climb into, since there was no tree outside the duke's suite. And then . . . Did she really not need a maid to undress?

"We shall attend the Throckmortons'," he said, more harshly than intended. Her lips parted, then tightened into a thin line, and she turned to look out the window. Marcus silently cursed his stepmother again, watching the moonlight shine on the dark curls and slender white throat of the woman opposite him. Her skin was nothing less than luminous in the moonlight, but he remembered that warm sunny tint he had seen last week in his study. Just how much of her skin was golden, he wondered, and what did she do out in the sun anyway? He looked away. Climb trees and behave like a hoyden, no doubt. "What a mistake," he muttered under his breath.

Her head whipped around. "What? Why?"

Marcus sighed. He hadn't meant for her to hear that. "Nothing," he said repressively.

"Are you afraid I'll embarrass you?" Her voice lifted in angry astonishment. "If so, I assure you I shall have to do far less acting than you to fool everyone into thinking we're happily married."

"Indeed," he said. "I shall be myself."

She snorted. "As shall I."

"You gave your word," he warned her.

"And I intend to keep it." Her eyes widened, although Marcus didn't for a moment believe her words completely innocent. It sounded almost like a threat to him.

"You shall take your cue from me. Do as I do, and we'll survive."

This time she laughed. "Now *that* would be acting! People will think it a wonder we can bear to be in the same room with each other, let alone be married."

Marcus frowned in affront. "I have been very busy."

She tilted her head, a funny little smile playing about her lips. Marcus felt a stab of worry; she didn't look like a duchess, she looked like a temptress. "That's the reason? What a relief. I was sure you were avoiding me." He closed his mouth into a thin line. He hadn't avoided her so much as he hadn't sought her out. "Well, you've nothing to fear," she went on. "I shall do my best to be a poised, gracious, happily married duchess."

And again, he worried that he had made a mistake.

They arrived at the Throckmortons' before either spoke again. Marcus disliked arriving on foot, and the driver maneuvered right up to the wide stone steps before halting the carriage. She avoided his eyes as he helped her out, again lifting her skirt carefully as she climbed the steps, and this time he refused to let himself look down.

The footman carried away her cloak in the front hall, and as she smoothed her gown one more time, Marcus realized something he had missed at home, when she had distracted him by lifting her skirts.

"Where are the pearls?" he asked under his breath, offering his arm and heading for the receiving line.

She looked puzzled. "What pearls?"

"The Exeter pearls, of course," he hissed. The pearls were over three hundred years old, and unusual for their perfect uniformity of size and luster. Everyone would expect his duchess to be wearing them, and she didn't have so much as a single strand on. He would look like a tightfisted miser, not even giving his bride a betrothal ring.

"What are they? No one told me about them."

He sighed, wishing Rosalind had remembered to ask for them. "Never mind. It can't be helped now." He handed over the invitation and joined the line. "The next time we go out, you must wear the pearls. They belong to the duchess of Exeter."

"I'm not really that person," she whispered. "I'd rather not wear your necklace and risk losing it."

"Nevertheless, you are supposed to appear to be that person."

"Well, how much simpler this all would have been if I had just known a pearl necklace was all that was required to fool people," she said under her breath. Marcus forced a half smile for the benefit of anyone watching, ducking his head nearer hers.

"Stop it."

She smiled tightly. "Stop what?"

"Defying me under your breath and behind my back."

Hannah kept her expression fixed although she yearned to turn her back on him right now and walk out the door. How on earth had she defied him? The wretched man had gotten everything the way he wanted it, and she had had to make all the accommodations! "You would prefer I do it to your face?" she whispered, smiling sweetly up at him.

His answering look was deadly. "Do not. Remember, darling," he added, with a dangerous smile, "our whirlwind romance."

She could hardly believe him. Their relationship was a whirlwind, all right, just not a romantic one. Not even looking at her like that was going to convince people otherwise. But then they were before the Throckmortons, so she merely smiled.

"Good evening, Exeter," boomed the host. "Delighted you honor us with your presence."

The duke, Hannah noticed, merely inclined his head as if such a welcome were his due. "May I present my duchess, sir," he said, placing his hand on top of hers where it rested on his arm and giving it a light squeeze. "My dear, Lord and Lady Throckmorton."

"A great pleasure." Lord Throckmorton bowed over her hand.

"A divine pleasure," interrupted lady Throckmorton, examining Hannah avidly. "We are so honored you chose our ball to make your debut before the ton, Duchess."

"My mother had hoped to attend with us," said the duke as Hannah opened her mouth to reply. "She sends her sincere regrets, and begged me to remember her to you."

"As if I could forget dear Rosalind!" Lady Throckmorton laughed lightly. She was about Rosalind's age, Hannah guessed, and quite likely her friend; Rosalind must have had a reason for choosing this engagement, after all. This impression was confirmed when Lady Throckmorton leaned slightly forward and said, her eyes twinkling, "And how is my goddaughter Celia?"

"Very well, ma'am," the duke said, again cutting off Hannah's reply. She closed her mouth quickly, hoping she didn't look like a fish, opening her mouth then closing it without a single word. "And anxiously awaiting her first opportunity to attend one of your balls."

Lady Throckmorton laughed. "Then next year I shall have one just for her!"

It appeared Lady Throckmorton would have talked longer, but other guests were waiting, and the duke was urging her forward, so Hannah simply smiled again and nodded, letting herself be towed into the grandest, most beautiful room she could ever recall seeing.

Ladies in glorious gowns every color of the rainbow swirled in the dance and curtsied to gentlemen in elegant evening wear. Enormous crystal chandeliers glittered overhead with dozens of candles. Billowing panels of pale green silk draped the walls, and a virtual forest of greenery made the ballroom look like a garden. Servants in scarlet coats carried gleaming silver trays of wine about the room. Her footsteps slowed unconsciously. Never in her life had she seen such an amazing sight.

"What is the matter?" asked the duke from one side of his mouth.

"It's so beautiful," she whispered, tilting back her head to see everything.

"Stop gaping," he said in an undertone. "You look provincial."

She pursed her lips in annoyance, but did stop trying to look at the ceiling, and gazed around the room instead. "Goodness, are all balls like this?"

"Yes." He stopped and took two glasses from a footman's tray. "For God's sake, try not to stare."

"I'm not staring," she said, watching an enormously fat woman lumber past, a dozen orange plumes waving in her headdress. One certainly didn't see that in Middleborough.

"You are." He handed her a glass.

Hannah took the glass, mentally reviewing his commands. Don't stare. Stop gaping. Don't even speak, apparently. She wondered if he wanted her to stroll about on his arm, smiling and not speaking, all night. She suppressed a snort. He didn't want a happy bride, he wanted a mechanical doll, one with strings he could control. "Is there anything you *would* like me to do?"

she asked, taking a sip of her wine. Bubbles tickled her throat, and she almost gasped aloud in surprise. She'd never had champagne.

Scanning the room over her head, the duke barely glanced at her. "You know. I hope I need not repeat myself." This time she couldn't stop a quiet huff, and he looked down at her, his eyes narrowed. "Don't drink too quickly. It will go to your head."

Instead of obeying, to Marcus's irritation, she took another sip, and raised her brows at him. "That's certainly not the way to convince anyone we're happily married."

He frowned, then quickly forced his brow to relax. "Whatever do you mean?"

She drank some more, looking at her half-empty glass with pleasure. "You look ready to give me a frightful scold. You wouldn't even let me speak to our host and hostess. Anyone with eyes can see you'd rather be anywhere other than here."

He'd rather be in the card room. He'd already spotted Grentham and Evans, two notorious rakes he'd had little luck tracking down thus far. If he hadn't been saddled with the vicar's wife, he could be in there with them, winning their money and delicately digging into their affairs. His temper, already strained by Rosalind's trick, was not in a state to tolerate a scolding. "Are you lecturing me, madam?"

To his surprise, she leaned closer, a mischievous smile on her face. "Now what good would that do? Would you even listen? I was merely trying to help you."

He stared at her. She was pushing him again. And again he found himself taking up the challenge. "In what way?" he asked, taking her elbow and turning her away from the crowd and closer to him, so that her hair almost brushed his chin. She smelled as enticing as she looked.

Her smile widened, and she lifted her chin as her eyes half closed. "If you treat me like a halfwit, people will think you're ashamed of me," she murmured. "If you scowl every time you look at me, people will think you regret our hasty marriage."

"Hmm." Marcus put his head to one side, watching as she finished off her champagne with obvious enjoyment. His throat seemed to close up as she flicked out her tongue to lick a stray drop from the corner of her lip. She glanced up at him, eyes glowing, and he found his voice. "You think I'm not persuasive?"

She tilted back her head and gave a throaty laugh. Even though he had already figured out she was acting a part to tweak his nose, Marcus found himself unable to stop her. She looked him straight in the eye. "No."

A gauntlet had been thrown down. Marcus snatched it up, disregarding any possible consequences or repercussions. Some things could not be ignored. He couldn't do a thing about Grentham or Evans, but he could do something about this. "Let me . . ." He paused, taking up her hand and bringing it to his lips. "Prove you wrong," he finished in a low voice. No one insulted him and got away with it.

She stared back at him. "I should like to see you try."

The thought of what he would like to try sprang unbidden to mind, in unfortunate detail. Marcus squashed the thought and pasted a slight smile on his face. "Shall we?" He beckoned toward the crowd, slipping his arm around her waist to urge her forward. Proving himself a devoted husband would also allow him to keep an eye on her, which was just as well. Who knew what havoc the woman might cause if she cast that sultry look on other gentlemen?

Hannah felt her face warm as a sea of curious faces seem to stare back at her. For a moment there, with the duke looming over her in his focused, intent way, she had completely forgotten where they were, and what she was supposed to do. She had let her irritation get the better of her, and gone and goaded the duke into . . . something. What had she done, she thought nervously, as his hand lingered at the small of her back. He paused, taking a fresh glass of champagne for her, giving her a measuring look with one eyebrow arched. She took the glass, hitched her courage back into place, and stepped brazenly toward the assembled guests. How difficult could this be?

The answer to that question depended on how one looked at it, she thought some time later. A great many people stopped them, but ordinary good manners seemed sufficient to satisfy them. No one seemed to want to ask too many direct questions about her background or their apparent marriage, although Hannah was sure many were dying to know. But they didn't ask, and she didn't volunteer. The duke never left her side, his hand at her waist or on her elbow at all times.

He was the other side of the question. Although his manner remained formal, there was much more easiness to him than she had ever seen. He smiled at her. He introduced her as his darling. He listened when she spoke, as if he cared to hear what she had to say. He was actually being nice to her, and Hannah almost wished she hadn't provoked him to do it. She was finding it far too enjoyable.

Something must have addled her brain, she told herself in disgust. The man was simply being nice because he wanted to fool everyone. He wasn't being solicitous because he cared if she had enough wine, or if she wished to sit down. He was acting, just like she was, Hannah told herself, even as she wondered how much she *was* acting. She certainly didn't feel aware of changing her behavior, although perhaps that was due to the champagne. She wasn't used to drinking more than one glass of wine.

Still, she felt a wave of relief when she excused herself to the powder room. An elegant salon had been set aside for the ladies, and she relaxed into a quiet corner. It seemed they had been here for hours; her hair was falling down and her feet were rather sore even though they had yet to dance. Hannah loved to dance, and the dance master Rosalind had hired had only had to teach her a few dances. Hannah had to admit, she was looking forward to dancing. The thought of the duke taking her in his arms, looking down at her with his curious little smile, sent a shiver through her that she refused to analyze. She opened her eyes and began to fix her hair.

"Did you see how plain she is?" hissed a voice from the other side of the screen as Hannah tried to poke her unruly curls back into the pins Lily had so expertly secured them with.

"Not a single pearl," said another voice, delightedly scandalized. "Not a one!"

"But Exeter hasn't left her side all night," said a third voice. Hannah's fingers slowed as she began paying attention in spite of herself. "He must see something in her."

"A drab little mouse," sniffed the first voice. "She looks terribly old."

"Drab, perhaps," said the third voice, unconcerned. "She looks no older than I, though."

"Precisely my point! He could have had anyone in London; why would he choose her?"

"She must be carrying," suggested the second voice. "I'll wager she seduced him."

The first woman snorted. "How? What on earth would make Exeter take *her* to bed?"

"The same thing that drives men to make love to governesses and parlor maids," said the third woman carelessly. "They do it because they can. You should wonder rather what made him marry her." The first woman cursed and the second woman giggled. "Never mind Exeter; he has a heart of stone anyway, Susannah. Fix on someone you can control. Now, I, on the other hand, have my sights on a certain rogue just returned to town . . ." Hannah sat motionless as the conversation behind her turned to other people, her drooping hair forgotten. So that was what people thought of her: drab and plain and old, a schemer who trapped a duke into marriage. Suddenly she wasn't sure she was enjoying the ball so much after all.

"Do you require assistance, madam?" A maid appeared at her elbow, startling Hannah out of her thoughts. "A cup of tea, perhaps?"

"Er . . ." There was a burst of laughter from the unseen women. Hannah leaped to her feet. "Thank you, no." She edged past the curtseying maid, not wanting to run into those women, and hurried back to where the duke was waiting for her, at the bottom of the grand staircase.

He was standing, tall and elegant, his eyes moving over the crowd. As she reached his side, he turned, his intense gaze fixing on her. Hannah took his proffered arm, flushing to the roots of her hair, very glad he had stayed by her side all evening, realizing just what he had protected her from. She held her head high and tried to smile graciously at the other guests, whose curious stares now made her feel gauche and awkward and very, very exposed.

"Everyone is talking about us." The duke shot her a glance.

"Yes," he said. "The whole reason we attended tonight was to give them something to talk about."

"They have certainly found something," she whispered back. "When shall we leave?"

Marcus barely kept from frowning. What was the matter now? Things had gone rather well so far, he thought, much to his surprise. The vicar's wife had excellent manners, and seemed to lack the propensity to rattle on and on as most women did. He could sense the mood of the room, once seething with curiosity about them, had begun to shift. People were falling for the illusion they were presenting, losing interest in them. This might yet prove to be a wise decision. The evening had been such a success he couldn't even regret too much missing Grentham and Evans in the card room. "It's early yet," he replied. "Supper's not been served."

She inched closer to his side. "I wish to leave."

He couldn't stop the frown this time, and cut short their circuit of the room to turn her into a sheltered corner. "Why?"

"I'm tired." He quirked a brow, and she flushed. "I'm tired of being stared at and whispered about. We've attended, and made a proper spectacle of ourselves. How much longer must we stay?"

Marcus cut a quick glance around the room. Even tucked back here, people were watching them. He hated it, too, and wasn't terribly disposed to argue with her about leaving. But it would be pointless to leave early, when public opinion was still undecided. "A little longer," he said. "We haven't danced yet."

She blinked up at him with snapping blue eyes. "If you wished to dance, you ought to have said something earlier. What will our dancing do, that hasn't already been done? I think people have gotten quite an eyeful of your plain, provincial duchess!"

Marcus looked at her. If it had been any other woman, he would have thought she was fishing for compliments. Plain? Whatever else she might be, no one here could think that. He was mildly surprised to realize she was one of the more attractive women in the room, especially animated as she was with anger. Her face was flushed, her full mouth rosy from being pressed into a thin line, and her bosom heaved with every breath. Even her hair was tempting, some of the coal-black curls trailing down her ivory neck, almost as if an impatient lover had mussed her in a frantic kiss . . . after pulling her into a secluded corner such as this one. . . . An alarm sounded faintly in his head. Perhaps it was time for them to leave after all.

"Ah, cousin! I thought that was you."

Marcus started out of his thoughts. In front of him, Hannah gasped, her cheeks growing pinker. Marcus instinctively reached for her, pulling her back to his side before turning.

"Good evening, Bentley."

His cousin laughed. "And a good evening to you, Exeter! I see you've brought your duchess out of hiding at last."

"Indeed." Marcus had never much liked Bentley, but one couldn't be rude to family, especially not publicly. "My dear, may I present my cousin, Bentley Reece. Bentley, my wife."

"How do you do," she murmured, letting Bentley bow over her hand. Marcus saw how his cousin's eyes moved over her face and then down, and the interest that sprang into his face. Something visceral and primitive made Marcus want to wipe that interest away. She might not be his real wife, but Bentley didn't know that. Marcus absolutely refused to sit back and watch his cousin make love to the woman everyone in London thought was his adoring wife.

"What a very great pleasure it is to make your acquaintance," Bentley was saying to her. "My cousin has long been suspected of being a monk; he's frustrated many a hopeful young lady. But I see now he was merely biding his time until the loveliest woman of all crossed his path."

Marcus shot him a black look, but Bentley's admiring attention never wavered. At his side, Hannah's hand crept around his arm. "Thank you, sir," she said, sounding more breathless and flustered than he had heard her sound tonight.

"Felicitations, Exeter," said Bentley with a roguish smile. "There's no end to your luck, it seems." That was Bentley, always ready with a compliment and a subtle jibe. Bentley turned back to Hannah, his avid interest undimmed, particularly in the neckline of her gown. "Might I beg the honor of a dance?"

"So sorry, Bentley, I've not even had the honor yet myself," said Marcus before she could reply. "Do forgive me."

Bentley laughed incredulously. "Come, man, you've not released her the entire evening! Allow the rest of us a chance to appreciate your good fortune, even if only for a waltz."

On no account did Marcus intend to allow Bentley to get her alone and quiz her. She could say something completely innocent that Bentley would twist around into a shocking little tidbit to scandalize the ton. Bentley was a notorious gossip and dandy, and his reputation with married women was even worse than David's. Marcus was quite sure that Bentley, contrary to implicit rules, would take even greater pleasure in seducing his wife than any other woman, if he were allowed the chance. Marcus absolutely refused to allow it.

"Not tonight," he said coolly. Thankfully the next dance was beginning, and Marcus gave Bentley a curt nod as he led her toward the dance floor. "One dance, and we can leave," he murmured in explanation. She nodded, letting him draw her into his arms without protest. She felt soft and supple beneath his hands, and that alarm sounded in his head again, louder and more strident. He forced his eyes away from the stray curl that looped around her ear, tickling her neck.

Hannah kept her eyes fixed on the duke's top waist-coat button and concentrated on her steps. She liked to dance, and found she liked the waltz, although dancing it with Celia and her dancing master was one thing, and dancing it with the duke another. She tried to take the opportunity to bring her temper back under control, while ignoring how easily his hand spanned her back.

She considered what people in Middleborough would have said if the most eligible man in town had married suddenly. There would have been a great deal of curiosity, to be sure, and some gossip, although not this rabid prying and sniping. She thought so, anyway. She must try to ignore it, Hannah told herself with a philosophical sigh.

"Now," murmured the duke, interrupting her thoughts, "what happened?"

She lifted one shoulder. "I overheard some gossip." He arched a brow. "In the retiring room," she explained.

"Ah." He swept her around the floor very easily. Hannah stole a peek over his shoulder; people were still staring at them. She raised her head and met the duke's eyes. "Women," he said with a wealth of understanding

Hannah waited, but he said no more. When she couldn't bear it any longer, she asked, "What about women?"

A dry little smile bent his mouth. "You overheard women talking," he clarified. "No wonder you heard what you did." She frowned. "More than one woman here wanted to be a duchess. There aren't nearly enough dukes for them all, let alone unmarried dukes of relative good fortune. It was jealousy you heard."

Of course. Hannah felt a little bit better. "They did say you could have had any woman in London." A flicker of irritation crossed his face. That made her feel even better. He didn't like being gossiped about any more than she did. "They think you chose badly."

He shot her an unreadable look. "Do they."

She nodded. Of course he must be right. She was silly to take it to heart. "One even suggested we must have married only to ensure a legitimate heir."

The duke paused midstride. "More champagne?" he said abruptly, pulling her off the floor and lifting his hand at a passing servant. Hannah took the glass he handed her and sipped, even though she'd already had a great deal more than she should have.

"May we leave now?" she asked. "We've danced."

"Yes." The duke drained his own glass. "Absolutely."

Relieved, Hannah took another sip—that champagne was lovely, just lovely—and handed her glass back to the footman. The duke offered his arm without looking at her, and they started for the door.

"Good evening, Exeter." Hannah felt the duke's arm flex under her hand before she located the speaker. She swung around, too fast, and had to hold on a bit tighter to keep her balance. It was a woman, and she was smiling at him familiarly. An involuntary frown knit Hannah's brow for a second. She didn't like the woman for some reason. It wasn't just the way she was looking at the duke—heavens, no—but there was something else. . . . What was it? She was a very beautiful woman, so fair she seemed like an ice maiden. Her light blond hair was fashionably styled—Hannah could recognize that now—her skin was a creamy white, and even her gown was a pale violet.

Her only fault was her eyes, which seemed to protrude from her head just a bit too much.

Then those eyes moved to Hannah, managing to assess her from head to toe in a single glance, and her smile turned vaguely condescending.

"Good evening," said the duke in his usual cool, remote voice. "May I present to you my wife. My dear, Lady Willoughby."

Lady Willoughby's eyes snapped, but her smile didn't waver. "Good evening," she purred, bobbing ever so slightly. "How delightful to meet you."

The voice did it; Lady Willoughby was the woman in the powder room who thought her plain and old. Something, probably the champagne, cut through Hannah's restraint with an almost audible snick. She straightened, gripping the duke's arm, and beamed back at the hateful woman. "Lady Willoughby. How do you do?"

"Very well, thank you." Lady Willoughby turned back to the duke. "I wanted to offer my congratulations on your marriage."

"Thank you so much," said Hannah. "How very kind of you to be so happy for us."

Lady Willoughby shot her a sharp glance. "Indeed. It was quite a surprise to a great many people."

Hannah raised her brows and turned to the duke. "Whyever so?"

He appeared caught off guard. "Er—I am not usually hasty."

Lady Willoughby trilled with laughter. "No, never! Everyone knows Exeter is the very soul of caution and calculation."

"Oh, dear, are you, darling?" Hannah tipped back her head to give the duke a fond smile. "I must confess, I haven't seen that side of you." He seemed frozen, staring down at her as if she'd gone mad. She turned back to Lady Willoughby, enjoying herself a great deal. "I'm so sorry," she said gaily, "it's been such a whirlwind"—she tapped her fan on the duke's arm—"we're constantly discovering new things about each other."

Lady Willoughby blinked. Twice. "Yes, of course," she said in a stilted voice. With a visible effort, she smiled again. "It was a pleasure to make your acquaintance."

"And yours, Lady Willoughby," she replied with a smile. The duke's arm was like iron under her fingers. He was going to blister her ears for this, but she didn't care, just for the pleasure of putting that sour look on Lady Willoughby's face.

"If you'll excuse us, madam," said the duke, through his teeth from the sound of things.

"Of course," she replied, in the same manner. "I do hope we shall meet again." Hannah wanted to giggle at how furious they both sounded. She hadn't meant to anger the duke, but he had said he wanted people to think theirs a love match. How else did he expect her to persuade people? Especially gossiping people like Lady Willoughby.

Marcus hustled her out of the ballroom as fast as he possibly could. What on earth was she trying to do? In his arm, she hurried along, picking up her skirt and giving him a sparkling glance brimming with laughter. She looked like a woman sneaking away for a passionate rendezvous, and Marcus cast an apprehensive glance behind him. The duke of Exeter did not sneak away, with anyone, for any reason.

But when they reached the front steps and he'd sent a footman running for his carriage, she turned her face up to his, and he suddenly didn't know if he meant to reprimand her or kiss her. "What are you about?" he settled for asking, annoyed at himself for even considering it, no matter what she looked like in moonlight.

His supposed wife lowered her eyes, although her pleased little smile belied any contrition. "I'm sorry, it was too much to resist. She was so spiteful." She raised those flawless blue eyes to him. "But it's what you wanted, isn't it? I'm just trying to do what you want me to do."

Marcus took a deep controlled breath. That was not what he wanted her to do, not if he wanted to keep his head. "I asked you to play a proper duchess, not a clinging vine."

Her merriment was unaffected. "I was not a clinging vine. And you asked me to play your wife, not a duchess. I told you I don't know how to be a duchess." To his shock, she smiled and stepped even closer, until they were practically in each other's arms. "Don't worry," she whispered, resting her hands on his shoulders. "It's just a part. I shan't expect you to act on any of it." And with another secretive smile, she turned and let the footman help her into the carriage, leaving Marcus staring after her in mingled amazement, horror, and . . . worst of all . . . desire.

CHAPTER 11

The Exeter pearls did not consist of a mere necklace. The box that Adams brought to her room the next day looked very like a pirate's treasure chest, and Hannah eyed it with some alarm. Rosalind, though, seemed delighted to see it.

"Ah, Marcus has finally remembered," she said. "Over here, please." The secretary set the chest on the dressing table chair, then bowed several times before he made it back out the door. Hannah caught the edge of Rosalind's smile. "Poor lad. Marcus terrifies him."

"I had noticed," said Hannah dryly. Rosalind quirked a brow at her, and Hannah changed the subject. "So! These are the famous pearls, I take it."

"Oh, yes." Rosalind opened the lid of the trunk. "I thought Marcus would give these to you himself."

Hannah lifted one shoulder, thinking that he was probably trying to find a way out of this fake marriage, after the way she'd acted last night. Not only flirting with him in front of Lady Willoughby, but then getting carried away with herself and stepping into his arms and practically daring him to— "No doubt he was too busy," she began, but her reply faded as she glanced into the box. Ropes of pearls were coiled in velvet-lined compartments, no less than four pairs of earrings gleamed up at her, and when Rosalind lifted out the top tray, hair combs, shoe clips, and a small tiara added their luminescence to the room. Hannah knew her eyes must be leaping from her face, but she couldn't help herself; the jewels in the trunk must be worth the entire income of everyone in Middleborough. Over a century's time. "Good heavens," she said faintly.

"Yes, I always thought the tiara was a bit much myself." Rosalind lifted it from the box and held it up. "Although it would look striking in your dark hair. It just blended into mine." Hannah doubted anything just blended into Rosalind's magnificent curls, still blond with only a trace of silver. And she was certain the tiara would look miles out of place in her own curly mop. "Try it," said Rosalind, holding it out.

"Oh, no," began Hannah, but Rosalind waved aside her protest.

"You must try it on, if only to see that everything is in order. I haven't worn these in several years, and they've doubtless been sitting in the vault ever since."

"I really don't think . . ." Hannah's weak protest died as Rosalind settled the tiara atop her head, adjusting it with a critical eye before reaching for the ropes of necklaces. Hannah stood stock-still, afraid to harm the priceless treasure being draped on her, and just the tiniest bit thrilled to have a chance to wear it. How often did an ordinary woman like her get a chance to wear a king's ransom in jewels?

Five necklaces, three bracelets, one pair of earrings and three rings later, Hannah felt like a queen. She faced herself in the mirror, disbelieving, as Rosalind fussed over the stubborn clasp of another bracelet.

"Goodness, this may need to be sent to the jeweler

for fixing," she said. "Everything else seems to be in order, though."

"Rosalind," asked Hannah in a dazed voice, "where might one wear all this?"

"Anywhere, my dear, although perhaps the tiara only for special occasions. Your first ball, for instance, although Marcus may give you something else for that. William, Marcus's father, gave me a sapphire necklace for our betrothal ball, and I only wore some of the smaller pearl pieces."

"Oh," Hannah murmured, turning to see herself better. The pearls seemed to glow with a light of their own, and if Hannah did say so herself, they flattered her coloring a great deal. Perhaps, with the money the duke had promised her, she could get herself a small necklace. Nothing like this splendid collection of course, just a simple strand as a reminder . . .

But when she left, she wouldn't need jewels at all. She would go back to her quiet life again, and without the balls and other events, jewels would be not only vain but wasteful. The money would be thrown away on something as frivolous as a pearl necklace she wouldn't have any reason to wear.

Aware that her expression in the mirror had become quite tragic, Hannah shook herself and forced a jaunty tone. "This whole set could come in handy, though; no one can even see my gown." It was true. The longest ropes of pearls hung to her waist, and wearing five at once presented a solid luminous mass that completely obscured the bodice of her dress. "I need never stand for another fitting again, if I only wear these to cover myself."

Rosalind erupted in peals of laughter. "Oh, Hannah, how droll! You must tease Marcus with that idea tonight, the economy of covering yourself with jewels instead of silk!"

"Perhaps not quite frugal, but he's already got the jewels," she played along, grinning.

"I think he would find the idea enormously intriguing, on one level," said Rosalind, her blue eyes bright with mischievous delight.

"Really?" Hannah turned to admire herself, unabashedly preening. If the pearls weren't so perfectly elegant, she would consider it vulgar, but as it was . . . she had to admit she liked it very much.

"Oh, yes. Wouldn't you, Marcus?"

"Indeed," said the duke's dry voice, nearly sending Hannah leaping out of her skin. She whirled around, only to see him standing there watching her admiring herself in his family heirlooms. Scarlet with self-consciousness, she fumbled with a bracelet.

"It was a jest, of course," she said, avoiding his eyes. "I only meant that because there are so many of them, and they're so magnificent, no one would even notice the clothes underneath. . . ." She could have bitten her tongue, and jerked the bracelet from her wrist. "I should put them back, before something gets damaged or lost. Rosalind, would you?" She sent Rosalind a glance of mute appeal before turning her back to the duchess and going to work on the rest of the bracelets.

"Of course it was a jest," said Rosalind lightly. "Don't think for one moment you'll not have to buy any more gowns, Marcus. Which reminds me, I must remind Celia of her appointment today with the dressmaker." And without another word she whisked out of the room, leaving Hannah gaping after her in disbelief.

"I'm sorry," she said too loudly, as the silence wore on and the clasp she was fiddling with still refused to open. "Rosalind insisted I try everything on at once."

"I see." His voice was closer than before. Fingers shaking, heart thumping, Hannah kept her eyes fixed on the blasted bracelet. If her face got any hotter, her hair might catch fire. She could sense rather than hear him approaching. "Is it broken?"

He was directly behind her. Hannah took a deep, steadying breath, then turned and faced him, wrist outstretched. "It may be," she said, relieved that her voice was almost normal. "I can't open it."

He took her hand in his and studied the clasp. Hannah stole a quick peek at his face, then had to look away. "You like the pearls, then?" he asked idly. She blushed.

"They're beautiful. Stunning."

"You must wear them the next time we go out."

"All right," she mumbled, not wanting to meet his gaze but feeling it on her.

"Hmm." He released her hand and stepped back. Hannah hesitantly looked up. He was studying her, his expression clinically cool as his eyes moved over her. "They suit you," he said, surprising her. "You look very well in them."

"Thank you," she said, her voice gone scratchy and husky. She cleared her throat. "Thank you."

He continued to stare at her. "Yes, I do see what you mean," he murmured.

Hannah straightened her shoulders nervously. "Oh?"

The glance he sent her was full of subtle amusement. "One can hardly see the bodice of that gown."

He was laughing at her. Hannah bristled. He had sent her the pearls and insisted she wear them; it was only a bit of fun on her part. "Don't be ridiculous," she said with a wave of her hand. "Anyone who looks closely can clearly see it." His brow arched. He pointedly looked at her chest again. Hannah could have kicked herself. "Well, I shan't ever wear all these at once anyway, so it doesn't matter." Trying to ignore him entirely, she went back to working at the bracelet.

"Wear some of them tomorrow night." Another invitation appeared in front of her. Abandoning the clasp again, she took it and read.

"Another ball?"

"Yes. This one should be more reasonable. Lady Carlisle has a bit more care for her guests' comfort."

"Will it be like the Throckmortons'?" She looked up, right into his piercing gaze. For a second she was caught. He had a way of staring at her that seemed to make her freeze.

"Very much so." Finally his eyes shifted, moving over her in a way that was almost worse. His gaze slid slowly over her from head to toe, not skipping a single inch. "This time we'll be prepared, hmm?"

"Yes." She put the invitation on the dressing table behind her. Pearls rolled down her wrist, the stubbornly closed bracelet. "Have you decided which pieces I should wear?"

He took his time replying, and Hannah flushed. She must learn to control her tongue; a man like the duke couldn't seriously be expected to help her choose which necklace to wear. What did it matter anyway, when they were all so elegant? "But I'm sure Rosalind will be able to help me decide," she exclaimed, and reached to the back of her neck to take off the necklaces.

"Quite so," he said, brushing her hands aside. "Allow me."

Hannah wanted to argue. She wanted to step away and not feel his hands on her. But she was not a coward, and refused to let herself squirm away. She forced herself to hold still as he moved behind her and his fingers brushed the sensitive skin at the back of her neck, unfastening clasps. One necklace slid forward, the pearls rolling over her bosom. Hannah gasped, and the necklace stopped. The duke lifted it over her head, as coolly as ever, and replaced it in the chest. Hannah closed her eyes as he turned back to release another clasp. Stupid girl, she scolded herself furiously, why must you put on all five necklaces?

Another clasp gave way, another strand of pearls fell away from her neck. Another. Another. Last one, she thought in relief, opening her eyes. Her knuckles were white where she gripped the back of the dressing chair. She had grown so attuned to his touch, she swore she could feel his breath on her. Even her hair felt alive with nerves.

Not that he noticed. Without thinking, Hannah raised her eyes to the mirror. She looked reasonably normal, at least, standing stiffly with her shoulders back and her head bowed slightly forward. And he looked—

He stood very close behind her, his head cocked to one side as he worked at the last clasp. Although she knew he was looking at the necklace, the image in the mirror appeared for all the world as if he were concentrating on her, on the bare curve of her neck and shoulder, as a man might contemplate his lover.

Her breath came shallow, part alarm and part desire. What was she thinking? She was not his lover, and he was not about to lean forward and press his lips to her neck, to that spot right below her ear that drove her wild, probably wild enough to forget all the very significant reasons why she shouldn't even want him to kiss that spot, at least for a little while . . . or maybe even a moderately long time, if she were honest about it. . . .

As if he could hear her struggle, his eyes slowly lifted, to meet hers in the mirror. Something changed in those dark eyes, so subtly she couldn't have said what it was. He knows, she thought in sudden panic. He knows what I'm thinking.

Marcus would have paid a great deal of money to know what she was thinking at that moment. Part of it he knew; it was desire, hot and bright, in the depths of her gaze. But something else shielded it, dimmed it. Fear? Dismay? Regret that nothing could ever come of that desire? Because it most certainly couldn't . . .

Could it?

"Thank you," she said breathlessly. Marcus blinked, realizing he was just holding the ends of an unfastened necklace. He pulled the necklace over her shoulder, deliberately letting the pearls slide across her skin. She flinched, then stepped away, her cheeks flushed. In the mirror he could clearly see the outline of her nipples against the thin silk of her gown, standing firm and tempting. He shouldn't do things like that. Her revealing response was almost worse than his own wonderings.

She tugged at the bracelet, until with a small ping it flew apart. The color left her face, and she stared at the broken strand with horror. "I—I broke it," she said, holding it out to him with trembling fingers.

He took it without looking at it. "It was already broken." She met his gaze, her face almost frightened, then turned away. Marcus watched as she pulled off the rings and earrings and remaining bracelets and put them back in the chest. When she raised her arms to take the tiara from her hair, he finally tore his attention away. He had only come to give her the invitation and make sure she knew to wear some of the pearls. It was just his luck she would have covered herself with them, and been laughing with Rosalind about the possibility of going naked beneath them. The pearls would indeed suit her perfectly that way, and he couldn't erase the image from his mind.

He contemplated the bracelet in his hand. Instead of having Adams see to getting it fixed, perhaps he could take it himself. Perhaps he could choose something for her; she liked pearls. Or sapphires, to match

Take A Trip Into A Timeless World of Passion and Adventure with Kensington Choice Historical Romances!
—Absolutely FREE!

Enjoy the passion and adventure of another time with Kensington Choice Historical Romances. They are the finest novels of their kind, written by today's best-selling romance authors. Each Kensington Choice Historical Romance transports you to distant lands in a bygone age. Experience the adventure and share the delight as proud men and spirited women discover the wonder and passion of true love.

4 BOOKS WORTH UP TO $24.96— *Absolutely* FREE!

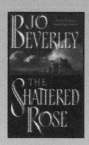

We have 4 FREE BOOKS for you as your introduction to
KENSINGTON CHOICE!
To get your FREE BOOKS, worth up to $24.96, mail
the card below or call TOLL-FREE 1-800-770-1963.
Visit our website at www.kensingtonbooks.com.

Get 4 FREE Kensington Choice Historical Romances!

♥*YES!* Please send me my 4 FREE KENSINGTON CHOICE HISTORICAL ROMANCES (without obligation to purchase other books). I only pay $1.99 for shipping and handling. Unless you hear from me after I receive my 4 FREE BOOKS, you may send me 4 new novels—as soon as they are published—to preview each month FREE for 10 days. If I am not satisfied, I may return them and owe nothing. Otherwise, I will pay the money-saving preferred subscriber's price (over $8.00 off the cover price), plus shipping and handling. I may return any shipment within 10 days and owe nothing, and I may cancel any time I wish. In any case, the 4 FREE books will be mine to keep.

NAME_____

ADDRESS_____APT._____

CITY_____STATE_____ZIP_____

TELEPHONE (_____)_____

E-MAIL (OPTIONAL)_____

SIGNATURE_____

(If under 18, parent or guardian must sign)

° Offer limited to one per household and not to current subscribers. Terms, offer and prices subject to change. Orders subject to acceptance by Kensington Choice Book Club. Offer Valid in the U.S. only.

KN096A

IIı.ı.ıIIı.ıIIı.ı.ıIı.ı.ı.ıIı.ı.ıIIı.ı.ıIIı.ı.ıII.ı.ıI

KENSINGTON CHOICE
Zebra Home Subscription Service, Inc.
P.O. Box 5214
Clifton NJ 07015-5214

her eyes. He could picture her wearing sapphires around her neck, and nothing else. . . .

Marcus stopped. What was he thinking? She was not his mistress, nor would she be. Lust was a transient emotion, and it would pass. He simply had to keep himself in check until it did. He laid the bracelet on the dressing table. "Rosalind will want to give the jeweler directions." And parade a fortune in jewels under Hannah's eyes. Marcus knew his stepmother. But he'd gladly buy a diamond bracelet or ruby earrings to keep from losing his head over her. He just wouldn't have any part in choosing them. "Or Adams can see to it." He gave a half bow, barely glancing at her. "Good day, madam." And he turned and left.

Hannah raised agonized eyes to the ceiling as the door clicked shut behind him. She shouldn't have teased him into being nice to her the other evening. It made impossible things seem possible. She put away the rest of the pearls, closing the lid gently but firmly. Out of sight, out of mind—just like the duke.

She hoped.

"Of course we shall take it!" said Rosalind when Hannah asked her later about the bracelet. "You may see something you like for your ball."

Hannah shifted uncomfortably. "No, I think the pearls are more than sufficient."

"For now," said Rosalind lightly. "Come, let's to Bridges at once! It really is one of the loveliest shops in London."

Since it would preclude receiving callers, or even worse, paying calls, Hannah agreed, and endured Rosalind's chatter all the way to the jeweler's without complaint. She had no intention of buying anything, or even touching anything, but it couldn't be so awful to look at the jewels. And since the dressmaker had come to Exeter House, and the wardrobe had taken so much of her time, it would also give her a chance to see a bit more of London.

When they reached the small shop with a simple sign saying "Bridges," Hannah stepped down first. The footman turned to help Rosalind down, and Hannah looked around in interest. The street was lined with shops, as far as her eye could see, it seemed. Liveried servants, their arms full of packages, hurried after elegant ladies. Gentlemen in gleaming boots and starched collars strolled along, pausing now and then to examine something—or someone—through a quizzing glass. It was quite unlike anything ever seen in Middleborough, and Hannah turned her head from side to side, trying to see everything at once.

Coming down the street toward them were Lady Willoughby and Mr. Bentley Reece. Lady Willoughby was smiling in a rather feline way, her heart-shaped face glowing with satisfaction. She was obviously enjoying whatever he was murmuring in her ear. Hannah felt again a prickle of dislike; seeing Mr. Reece with that woman only reinforced her instinctive feeling from the other night.

"Rosalind," she said on impulse as her companion stepped down. "Who is that couple?"

Rosalind turned. "Which—? Ah." Annoyance flickered over her face before she composed it. "That is my husband's nephew, Mr. Bentley Reece," she said in a carefully neutral voice.

"And the woman?" Hannah pressed. "We met Lady Willoughby at the Throckmorton ball the other night," she added. Rosalind's head snapped around, and she looked shocked.

"You did?"

Hannah nodded. "Yes, she came and spoke to us."

Rosalind's mouth settled into a thin line. "Did she," she murmured, her eyes flashing fire. "That scheming, grasping—" She broke off, drew a deep breath, and lowered her voice. "I do not care for Susannah Willoughby," she said, very fast and low. "She's Gerald Willoughby's widow. He was twenty years older than she, and terribly wealthy. He was barely dead a month before she was carrying on with the earl of Manning, trying to move up from baroness to countess." Hannah felt an uncomfortable stab at that; she had agreed to remarry only six months after Stephen died. It wasn't pleasant to think that she was the same as Lady Willoughby.

"She pursued Marcus like a hound after a fox," Rosalind went on, unaware of it. "She was . . . involved with him," she added delicately. "Fairly recently." Hannah felt a flush burn up her neck. Of course. Lady Willoughby had been the duke's lover. And he had treated her like any society acquaintance the other night, while Hannah had gone on like a lovesick girl. What an idiot she was.

"It's very unseemly of me to tell you this," Rosalind said, whispering now. "But I have never met a more sensible person, Hannah—I mean that as a compliment—and I think you should know. She's a very petty person, and I have heard from friends that she was telling everyone she would be the next duchess of Exeter. She may try to make trouble for you."

"I see." Hannah fought down an irrational flare of anger. Whom the duke carried on with was none of her business, after all. Hannah refused to act like a jealous wife, since she wasn't one. In fact, it might make her life easier if the duke carried on with Lady Willougby and anyone else who caught his fancy, for then everyone would understand why Hannah left in a few weeks, not to mention put to rest her overheated imagination. And yet . . . "What sort of trouble?"

"The sort I can combat," Rosalind said, shooting a glacial glare at the woman in question. "Never fear I won't stand with you. She's done herself in, you know; by telling everyone she was to be Marcus's wife, she's left herself to appear bitter in rejection." Rosalind paused, seeming to weigh her words. "There are many women in London who threw themselves at Marcus solely because of his wealth and position, and it made him very hard toward women in general. That's why I was so delighted to hear that he hadn't even told you he was a duke until after you were married, for it meant he wanted to be sure of your affections for him alone. I'm happier than I can say that he's found someone like you, who will appreciate him for the man he is. Quite unlike that Willoughby woman, who only wanted his money and his title, I promise you."

Hannah smiled weakly. "And the gentleman?" Mr. Reece and Lady Willoughby had seen them. She appeared to return Rosalind's low regard in spades, from the way she stopped cold and glared rather poisonously at them, although Bentley's face lit up and he tipped his hat. Rosalind's brow cleared at Hannah's question.

"He is much more acceptable," she said warmly. "Bentley is my husband's nephew. Such a charmer! Half the women in London have been in love with him at one time or another. His father had no head for business, poor, dear man, so Bentley was often at Ainsley Park as a boy. He practically grew up with Marcus and David as a brother."

"Then . . . they are friendly?" Hannah watched as Lady Willoughby said something to Mr. Reece, then turned on her heel and went back the other way, swinging her parasol violently.

Rosalind laughed lightly. "Perhaps not always! Bentley, I fear, came to feel the difference in their positions as the boys grew. He stopped coming to Ainsley Park shortly after Marcus became the new master." She looked up, a pleased smile blooming on her face. "And here he is now, my neglectful nephew."

Bentley lifted Rosalind's hand to his lips. "I confess it, to my shame, and implore you to forgive me. Had I known you had arrived in town, nothing on earth could have kept me from Exeter House."

She laughed. "Nonsense. I know you better than that, Bentley. You've been out seducing some poor woman into falling in love with you, I wager, and never once thought of your family." She turned to Hannah. "But this time, you have only punished yourself, for I have had dear Hannah's company. Have you met my daughter-in-law?"

"I had the pleasure the other night, at the Throckmorton ball," he said, turning his dazzling smile on Hannah. "Although not, unfortunately, the pleasure of a dance."

"Perhaps another time," she murmured, wishing again that he wouldn't look at her that way, as if he were picturing her without any clothes. He had all but leaned over to look down her gown the other night, and it made Hannah uncomfortable. No one had ever looked at her with such casual lust.

"It shall be my fondest hope," he replied, his voice dropping a tone. "We are family now, and I shall be heartbroken if you forget."

"No," she said. No, she wouldn't forget, but she would try everything to avoid it. She shouldn't have asked Rosalind about him until he was well away.

"And is the rest of the family well?" Bentley asked Rosalind. "How are all my cousins?"

"Celia, as you well know, will be making her debut next Season," Rosalind replied. "She longs to thank you for the lovely birthday gift you sent, Bentley. Do call on us soon. David is away from town at the moment, I'm not entirely sure where, but you know David, always here and there on a whim. And Marcus"—she cast a knowing little smile at Hannah—"is quite well."

"Excellent," said Bentley, although his smile looked a trifle tight now to Hannah. She doubted he truly cared how his family fared, but perhaps that was uncharitable of her. "I see you are for Bridges," he went on. "Not unescorted, I hope? Surely my cousin hasn't lost the famous Exeter pearls?"

"Of course not," Rosalind said sternly. "We're on a simple errand, having a bracelet repaired. Marcus never loses what he cares to keep."

He laughed. "No, no he wouldn't. It would give me the greatest pleasure to escort you on your errand and then for ices, but alas"—Bentley laid one hand over his heart, his expression growing mournful—"I have an appointment I cannot miss."

"I suppose we must let you go, then. Do try to make time to call." Rosalind offered her cheek, which Bentley dutifully kissed. He cast a quick glance at her, and Hannah forced a polite smile in reply, clutching her reticule with both hands. He understood, and merely bowed. His eyes gleaming, Bentley bade them farewell and walked on.

Hannah watched him stride away, wondering just what it was about him that bothered her. Rosalind, who knew him much better, thought him just a flirt, and no doubt she was right. Hannah told herself to stop worrying about him. Bentley wasn't even, as he had said, truly her family at all. At the end of the season, she wouldn't have to worry about crossing his path again, whether he unsettled her or not.

She heaved a sigh. This wouldn't be the first worry she had kept to herself. If overly attentive cousins were the worst thing she had to endure, she should be very glad indeed. She turned away and followed Rosalind into the jeweler's.

CHAPTER 12

"We simply must have answers! The bank cannot wait forever on this question."

Marcus stared coolly at Mr. Timms. The man had come to call on him yet again, to badger him, it seemed. Marcus was growing tired of that. "If I had answers, I would have already informed you," he said, watching Timms drink his brandy. Perhaps that was the reason the man was always cornering him at home: the brandy.

"Yes, yes, I know." Timms set down his empty glass. "But the other directors—"

"The other directors knew my terms," interrupted Marcus. "They agreed. Are they sending you here for weekly progress reports, or do you come on your own?"

Timms's round face flushed. "We must know," he said stubbornly. "The bank is losing money."

"The bank should make its notes harder to duplicate."

Timms eyed his glass, as if hopeful there might be something left in it. "Yes, well. Hmmph. Understand, Exeter, we're trying to be patient—you're a newly married man, after all, and we do appreciate—"

"I shall call on you in a week or so." Marcus got to his

feet. His personal affairs were no concern of Timms's, nor any other bank director's. "Good day, sir."

Timms flushed again, lurching to his feet and bowing. "Yes. Thank you, Your Grace. Good day."

Marcus stood until the door closed behind him. If consideration for his bride got Timms to stay away, perhaps he should be glad. The man was like a terrier with his teeth in something. Marcus supposed that was good, from the bank's point of view, but he preferred not to be prodded and queried at every turn as to why he hadn't solved the mystery yet. It wasn't his fault the bank made their notes laughably easy to duplicate.

And speaking of his bride . . . He wondered what she was doing this morning. Her child had been sliding down the banisters this morning with Celia. His sister was making the most of her last summer of childhood, to be sure. Marcus had watched them for a while, remembering when Celia had been so small he could carry her atop his shoulders. It had been a long time since Exeter House had echoed with childish laughter. It was loud, occasionally very loud, but less annoying than he'd expected. And the little girl had flashed him a smile so joyful, he had even smiled back without realizing.

But he hadn't seen her mother. Rosalind had gone out to pay calls, and Marcus knew she'd left alone. Celia and the child were out in the garden—he could hear them shrieking and laughing through the open window—which meant his supposed duchess was wandering about the house on her own.

Without bothering to examine the impulse, he left his study and went to the drawing room. It was empty. He frowned a little. Perhaps in the music room, although he had no idea if she played an instrument. She was not. Perhaps the library? Rosalind said she liked to read, and his library was an extensive one.

Halfway up the stairs, he met Albert Redley. He had a plump, plain woman on his arm, and their heads were together in excited conversation. Marcus stepped aside to let them pass, wondering why on earth Redley was in his house, and the couple noticed him. The gentleman's mouth dropped open in dismay, but the lady fairly leaped at him.

"Oh, Your Grace, how kind your wife is! The most generous, compassionate lady I've ever known! Thank you!" And she seized his hand as if she would kiss it. Marcus pulled free just in time.

"Thank you," he said coldly. "Lady Redley, I presume?"

She bobbed in acknowledgment, hands clasped before her, face beaming with joy. "She's just wonderful, wonderful! How fortunate you are, and we, too, are, and I simply must say—"

"Constance!" Red-faced, Redley lunged forward and hauled in his wife. "I'm sure his grace has other things to attend to—good day, Your Grace. Let's be on our way, Constance." And he rushed her down the stairs. Marcus stared after them with a growing feeling of dread, and anger. He went upstairs and found Hannah in the library.

She was sitting in front of a tea tray covered with the remains of tea for three. She looked up at his entrance and smiled at him, so brightly he knew she had done something he wasn't going to like. "Good afternoon. Would you care for some tea?"

"Thank you, no." He closed the door and leaned against it, watching her. She sipped her tea and smiled some more. She was far too pleased with herself. He pushed his hands into his pockets and started pacing across the room. "I met Redley and his wife on their way out. Did you have a nice visit with them?"

"Lovely." She picked up a scone and bit off a corner. From the corner of his eye he watched her lick a crumb from the corner of her lip. Marcus stopped near the window, glancing out in time to see the Redleys get into a carriage at the end of the street.

"They thanked me," he murmured absently. "Quite profusely. I wonder why." No reply from behind him. "Doesn't it seem odd to you? Redley was cursing me in three languages when last I saw him, and today his wife practically threw herself at me." China clinked, but otherwise silence prevailed. "You wouldn't have any idea why, would you?"

"Wagering is immoral," she said primly. "Taking a man's home and livelihood because a card came up a three instead of a ten is the cruelest, most despicable thing I've ever heard of."

"Albert Redley is fifty years old," he said. "I never thought to hear a woman barely half his age defend his vices."

"I think it very Christian to give him another chance to redeem himself, change his ways, and learn from his misadventure instead of being left penniless."

"Oh?" Marcus turned from the window. The Redleys were gone, and he wanted to watch her performance. "Then you know of his gambling debts."

She made a soft tsk. "I know about his mistake."

He leaned his shoulder against the window. "A mistake. Is that how one refers to drinking heavily and wagering every possession, including one's hearth and home, on the flip of a card?"

"I should call that a mistake, yes. Have you never made mistakes?"

"I have never in my life risked what I couldn't stand to lose, particularly not on something as random as cards. I call that stupidity, not a mistake."

She shot to her feet. "Then perhaps you shouldn't have been playing cards with him, if he's so stupid.

Perhaps you took advantage of a man not used to drink. Perhaps you ought to—"

"I took advantage of him?" Marcus was thunderstruck. He advanced on her, noticing with great pleasure that her holier-than-thou attitude slipped a bit. "If anything, Redley took advantage of others, playing at a table with stakes beyond his means. Why do you think he did that? Was it perhaps in the hope of winning a fortune from those who had one?"

"You took the deed to his home," she retorted, her chin rising.

"Do you know how much he lost?"

"No." Her blue eyes sparkled with defiance, and Marcus continued his steady prowl toward her. Christ, but who would have guessed the vicar's wife would look so stunning in silk and lace? As he got closer, she turned away, strolling across the room. "It doesn't matter anyway. I counseled him on the error of his ways, and forgave the debt."

"You did what?" He stopped, thunderstruck again. "It was not your place to do so."

That wicked gleam was back in her eyes as she swung around by the table. "Oh, but as your wife, we are one, are we not? The twain shall become one flesh. As the half of the whole who happened to receive Lord Redley and his wife, I decided to forgive the debt."

The twain becoming one was a terrible metaphor to use at that moment; similar thoughts had been plaguing Marcus for several days now, and the way she was standing, arms braced behind her on the table, the sun hitting her from the side and bathing her figure in light, unleashed the devil in him. She stood her ground, looking unconcerned, until he was within a foot of her. "Twenty thousand pounds," he said. "Redley lost twenty thousand pounds. He didn't stop when he had lost five thousand, or ten, or even seventeen. I didn't want his deed, but he wagered it and lost."

"You were going to sell it!" She inched backward, but the table was right behind her. He tilted his head to enjoy her discomfort.

"What would I do with his property?" Marcus hardly even remembered telling Adams to send it to the solicitors to sell.

"His widowed mother lives there!" She moved back another inch. The table must be digging into her back, but she didn't falter. "His children! Where would they go if you sold their home?"

He shrugged. "To relatives who might be more careful with their money than Redley? They aren't my concern, but since you've already forgiven him, I suppose there's nothing I can do now."

She blinked. "No. Isn't there . . . ?" Now she didn't look quite so superior.

"Of course there isn't," he said softly, resting his hands on the table on either side of her hips. "The only question that remains is, how are you going to make it up to me?"

She flushed. "You don't need that money."

He arched a brow. "Don't I? Do you know that?" She opened her mouth, then closed it, her defiance mixed with uncertainty now. "After all," he said, laying a finger on the shoulder of her gown, "as you have made me well aware, I've spent a great deal of money lately on things like this." He trailed his finger along the neckline, just barely touching the silk. The pulse in her neck throbbed rapidly. "Surely you have a plan to make good on Redley's loss for him. All twenty thousand pounds."

Hannah felt faint, no longer sure she was teaching the duke a good lesson. It was more money than she could imagine having in two lifetimes. "You know I haven't that much money," she retorted. He must be joking, she told herself nervously, shifting her hands behind her and trying to inch farther away from him without falling flat on her back.

"Oh, no, I'm not joking," he said, as if he could read her mind. "You thought to teach me a lesson on the depravity of wagering; very well, I shall consider the point made. But now, perhaps you need a lesson in keeping your promises."

"I've promised nothing," she protested in a strangely weak voice.

"You promised him he would not have to repay the money. Perhaps I was counting on that money to pay my servants. Perhaps now I shall have to let some go. Perhaps we'll be dining on soup for the next year because you graciously forgave an inveterate gambler's debt." Hannah bit her lip. She hadn't thought he might need the money, certainly not more than poor Lady Redley and their children.

Then she shook herself mentally. The duke of Exeter, scraping for funds? Nonsense. Rosalind shopped like a woman made of gold, and there were legions of economies that could be made in the housekeeping alone. He was harassing her about her actions, which in hindsight she allowed were a gross violation of their agreement, but which were still the right thing to do.

"What do you want me to do?" He really ought to notice the uncomfortable position he had forced her into, and spare her the trouble of pushing him away. How on earth was it possible that she had absolutely no reaction to David, who was charming and friendly even if he were a lying rogue, and yet suffered from this horrible awareness of his brother? "Shall I scrub the floors for you? I can cook, you know, and wash and mend."

His eyebrow went up. "Admirable talents. However,

I already have people tending to those tasks. We shall have to devise something else you might do which isn't already done."

Hannah's mind drew a complete blank. She couldn't think of what she could do to repay him, couldn't think of anything at all when he was angling over her this way, his eyes dark with the promise of something she couldn't even allow herself to consider. "I can't think of anything you haven't already got three servants doing," she said, trying to brazen her way out.

He grinned, a suddenly dashing expression that threw her off guard. Had she never seen him smile before? "Now, really. I can think of a few things neglected. . . ." His gaze dipped to her mouth. "Things which might be adequate recompense."

Hannah groped for her wits, which all seemed to be swooning in delight at the transformation of his face with that grin. It made her want to smile back at him, even though she suspected she knew what he was thinking. And even though it was wrong and she shouldn't allow this to continue, when she opened her mouth to speak, it wasn't a protest that came out. "Such as what?"

He moved a little closer, his arms beside her waist now. Hannah felt her equilibrium shift, tilting dangerously off balance. He was practically holding her in his arms; her feet were barely touching the floor, and she was only just holding herself up. He had held her at the dance, but that was different, in public, where they were presenting a happily married front. But now they were alone, and anything that happened would be just between the two of them.

His eyes were dark and deep, and the pulse in his throat was almost as fast as hers. Hannah felt her stomach take a plunge, and her heart a leap. If he kissed her, it would mean nothing but change everything. She shouldn't let him. She couldn't. She wet her lips and searched for words.

A trace of that grin bent his mouth again. "This, for example." He smoothed a loose curl from her forehead. "This." He stroked her cheek, and Hannah waited for him to kiss her. She didn't know exactly why she was waiting for him to do that, as it could only cause trouble, but she stood there and waited for it the way a child waits for his Christmas pudding, afraid to move for fear of being sent into the corner without any, but trembling with anticipation inside.

His fingers brushed along her jaw, and Hannah let her eyes slide shut. She was idiotic to feel any sort of attraction to this man who wasn't and wouldn't be her husband. He kept a house fully furnished and ready for new mistresses to move right in. He lied to his mother and sister and all his friends and acquaintances. He would have sold the home from under Lady Redley and her family. He was cold and remote and not above using her to avoid embarrassment. He had already gotten her to lie to her family, his family, and dozens of perfect strangers.

"Twenty thousand pounds for a kiss?" she blurted out as she felt the first faint brush of his lips on hers. He went utterly still, and Hannah opened her eyes to meet his gaze, once again opaque and distant.

"One thousand pounds." All Hannah's good sense had deserted her. She already regretted her crude question, both for the way she had treated another person and for the way it had driven him back into the icy persona that she so abhorred. The glimpse of a warmer man inside had shaken her, and drawn her, more than she wanted to admit.

"I'm sorry," she murmured, turning her eyes downward. He straightened, removing his hands from the table and stepping away from her.

"Quite all right." She hadn't realize how much his tone had thawed until now, when his words all but dripped ice. She jerked her head up, suddenly realizing he had misinterpreted her apology. He straightened his cuffs and glanced at her. "No doubt we can devise a less painful method of repayment."

"I'm sorry I asked how much," said Hannah as he strolled to the cabinet and got out a glass and a bottle of whiskey. "It was very rude. I apologize."

He filled the glass over half-full. "No, no, I prefer to keep these things honest. Nothing is free, is it?" His mouth curled in a tight, humorless smile, not at all like the engaging one she had seen just moments ago. Hannah felt worse than she'd thought possible, but what could she say now? *Won't you please be nice, the way you were just before I spoiled it?* He lifted his glass to her, the sunlight flashing on his signet ring, and then he turned away, facing the window.

"I'm sorry," she said helplessly. He said nothing, and she hurried toward the door, glancing back again as she left. The sunlight was blindingly bright around him, obscuring everything but the general shape of a man, standing straight and tall and uncompromisingly alone.

He was meant to be alone. Marcus stared out the window at the street below, swirling the cool comfort of his whiskey. What was he thinking, to flirt with the vicar's wife? Trying to kiss her when it was clear she would never regard him with anything but suspicion and mistrust? He must have gone mad. She could have sympathy for Redley, and enough spirit to set down Susannah, but he, clearly, was still a cold-blooded monster to her. Strange, how that thought could be so dispiriting.

He shook his head, trying to erase the image of her

arched under him, her eyes closed, her lips parted, looking for all the world like a woman ready to be kissed. Just not by him.

He wondered if she had felt anything for David. His brother obviously hadn't felt anything for her, to have abused her as he had, but women were capricious creatures and didn't always react rationally. Hannah was better than most, though, or so he had thought. Forgiving a twenty-thousand-pound debt was highly irrational, in Marcus's opinion. And she had agreed to marry David on barely three weeks' acquaintance. At one point, Marcus had discarded the theory that she had done so out of greed; a greedy woman would have taken him up on his offer of money. Right now he almost wished she were one, for he could have offered her the twenty thousand pounds, for just one night in his bed. . . .

His glass was empty. Marcus put it back on the tray with a sigh. Three fingers of whiskey and it was barely tea time. He was turning into David in more ways than one. He turned and went to find his secretary.

CHAPTER 13

Hannah couldn't stop thinking about the near kiss for the rest of the day. It wasn't even so much that the duke had obviously wanted to kiss her, but that she had wanted him to kiss her. She had been trying to rationalize her attraction to him for some time; it was a purely physical reaction, brought on by having to live so near him and pretend an intimacy they didn't have. Even as she repeated to herself that she really wasn't his wife, it was too much to expect that she could act like his wife and not have a few wayward thoughts. After all, she had been married before, and had enjoyed lovemaking.

But now she had also been deprived of it for several months, and perhaps the lack of it had made her long for it. That, she told herself, must be why she wanted the duke to kiss her, even though she didn't like to think of herself as a lusty widow. It pleased her femininity to know he admired her, and since that admiration was closely linked in her mind with a husband's attentions, her body was simply reacting out of habit. Yes. Habit, that's all.

So even though it was a good thing she'd stopped

herself from letting things happen that shouldn't happen, she was still on edge and out of sorts about it. Perversely, it only made things worse when the man in question disappeared for the remainder of the day.

At first she was relieved. What would she have said to him anyway? Best she had some time to calm herself and think about how to handle their next meeting. Then she was uncomfortable, as the day wore on and she couldn't concentrate on anything else but where he might be and what he might be thinking. Perhaps he was more put out by her actions that he'd let on. Perhaps he was angry at her. Perhaps he didn't really care. Hannah didn't even know why this made her upset. If anyone had a right to be angry, she did, after the way he had tried to . . . to . . . She shifted in her chair uneasily, remembering. He had only tried to do what she had been wondering about for days, and she obviously wouldn't be able to forget it any time soon.

She thought about his reaction, worrying over every little detail. Was he angry that she'd stopped him? Surely a man like him must have women falling into his arms. Perhaps it was just his pride that was injured. Well, then she had nothing to be ashamed of! But perhaps . . . perhaps it wasn't his pride. Perhaps it was something else, a possibility that made Hannah's stomach knot.

That settled the matter. She simply must speak to him, and apologize. She needed this masquerade to continue successfully as much as he did—more so, if she were honest—and thus it behooved her to set things right. She tossed aside the book that she'd done nothing more than hold for the last half hour, and got to her feet. Molly and Celia were flying kites in the garden below the terrace where she stood, and she waved at them before turning back to the house. A footman appeared out of nowhere to open the door for her, and she murmured her thanks as she went in, only belatedly thinking how accustomed she was becoming to things like that.

Her palms were damp as she walked through the corridors toward the study. She hoped he wouldn't be annoyed, as he had been the last time she interrupted his work. That would start things off on the wrong note entirely. And if she had guessed wrong, and he'd only been annoyed she hadn't thrown up her skirts for him right there on the library table, she was about to make a complete fool of herself. She came to a halt outside the door, her hand in a fist, and hesitated again. She reminded herself that this would clear her conscience, that she would much rather know than not know, and forced herself to knock.

The door opened almost at once. Mr. Adams blinked at her from over his clutch of papers, then bowed. Deeply. Hannah gave a shaky smile. She knew just how he felt, intimidated and nervous about making a mistake.

"Good day, Mr. Adams. How are you today?"

"Very well, madam," he replied, fidgeting. "How may I help you?" He stopped, looking alarmed. "That is, I hope you are well as well. And how may I help you?" he repeated anxiously.

Her lips trembled. "Very well, thank you." He bowed again, jerkily, as if he didn't know what else to do. A few letters slid from his grip to the floor, but he didn't notice. "I was seeking—" She hesitated; it felt so odd to call him her husband, even if that's what he was pretending to be, and yet she didn't dare use his Christian name. "The duke," she said. "Has he a moment to spare?"

Adams wet his lips, shifting his weight from side to side. More papers fell. "No, madam. That is, he is not at home at present, I believe."

"Oh," she said, nonplussed. Somehow she didn't feel reprieved.

"I believe he will be out for the rest of the evening as well," offered Adams. "He instructed me to finish my work and return tomorrow."

"Oh," she said again. Dining out. Could he be avoiding her? Or perhaps . . . She blinked. Perhaps he had gone to a woman who didn't stop him from kissing her. Not that it should bother her. Not that she had any right to know, let alone care. She forced those thoughts aside. "Thank you. I shall speak to him later, then."

Adams smiled nervously, bowing and scraping again. Two more letters fell to the floor, and this time he noticed, his face going white. Hannah took pity on him and knelt to help him collect everything.

"Your Grace!" With a horrified gasp the young man fell on his knees beside her, raking at the papers he had dropped. Hannah started to hand over the papers she picked up, then paused, her attention caught by one of them.

"This is the deed to Redley Hall." She looked at Mr. Adams in question. The secretary blinked repeatedly and nodded.

"Yes, madam. His Grace instructed me to return it to Lord Redley. I had just retrieved it from His Grace's study in order to send it off at once, as His Grace instructed." She let him take the deed from her hand without protest. "He asked that I return it with your compliments, madam," added Adams shyly. Hannah looked at him for a moment, speechless.

"Thank you, Mr. Adams." He bowed again, twice, and hurried down the hall. Hannah watched him go, then turned and walked slowly back out to the terrace. He was returning the Redleys' deed—with her compliments! After what he had said, she hadn't expected that. Her steps faltered a bit as she remembered what he'd said, and what he'd almost done. Surely he didn't think—that is, he wouldn't expect her, in recompense, to . . . ?

"Mama! My kite!" Hannah started out of her reverie. Molly was tugging on her hand, pointing toward the garden. "Look, Mama, my kite is stuck in a tree!" Molly's worried little face was flushed pink as she peered up at Hannah. "Get it down, please, Mama?"

She smiled, taking Molly's hand. "I shall do my best. Celia couldn't get it?"

"No, she couldn't! Celia doesn't know how to climb trees like you do, Mama. We need you to help." Hannah laughed and let herself be pulled into the garden, to where Celia stood looking sheepishly up at the stuck kite. Later, she told herself, she would simply ask him about the deed. And apologize. And promise to be more circumspect in the future, at least in front of other people.

And she didn't let herself think about what she would do in the future, in private.

It was rather late that night before her opportunity arose.

He'd been gone all evening, as Mr. Adams had said, but he must come home eventually. It was now very late, but she couldn't sleep. Hannah paced back and forth in her dressing gown, eyeing the door to the duke's suite. He had warned her to knock, if she ever had reason to enter. She bit her lip uncertainly. Did she have reason? Was it a good idea to tell him now? Was it a good idea at all to approach him?

At long last, though, she heard the unmistakable sounds of someone stirring in that room, the low rumble of his voice, no doubt talking to Telman. With her ear pressed against the door, she heard another door open and softly close, and it was quiet. Her stomach fluttered. *Do it and be done with it,* she told herself. She took a deep breath and knocked.

There was no answer. He might have gone into his bedroom already. Her heart skipped a beat. She tapped on the door once more, then gingerly opened it. She would take just one quick peek, just to assure herself he was not there before she went to bed with a clean conscience.

He looked up from his seat at the table. In front of him was a large pile of money, separated into banknotes and coins. A thin book lay open next to a small glass of amber liquid. At the sight of her, he put down his pen, his eyebrows arched in surprise.

She licked her lips. "Good evening." She had never seen him like this before, clad in only his shirt and trousers with a silk dressing gown over them. "May I have a word with you?"

For a moment he said nothing, then nodded once. He got to his feet and waited, his face expressionless.

Gripping her hands together, Hannah stepped into the room and recited the speech she had planned while pacing her own room. "I want to apologize for my actions earlier today. What I did was utterly inexcusable, and I want you to know I am very sorry. It won't happen again. I give you my word."

He tilted his head to one side and looked at her with unmistakable cynicism. Oh, dear. She rushed on. "I can only say that I was very much in sympathy with Lady Redley's plight, having almost lost my own home, and when she told me about her children, I . . ." She lifted her hand helplessly. "I couldn't help myself. But it wasn't my right to forgive the debt. I promise I won't trespass on your authority like that again."

"Ah," he said quietly. "The Redleys."

"But I must also add my sincere thanks for your kindness in returning the deed to them," she added hurriedly, before his words sank in. When she realized what he'd said, and what he'd meant, her cheeks turned pink. Did he think she was apologizing for the kiss? Or rather, for stopping him from kissing her? Oh—and she had said she was sorry, and sworn it wouldn't happen again! She didn't know whether to laugh or run back into her room in embarrassment.

Marcus looked at the floor and sighed, trying to distract himself from looking at her in her luminous dressing gown of violet silk and lace, with those wild black curls spilling over her shoulders. He didn't want to see her in her nightclothes, not after he'd spent the whole day trying not to think about her in no clothes at all. It was deeply alarming, how unsuccessful he had been at that. He was the duke of Exeter; women chased him, not the other way around. But today he had been unable to control his thoughts, unable to stop thinking about what might have happened in the library, what could happen if he ever came that close to kissing her again, what *would* happen if he ever took her to bed. And the truly alarming part wasn't that he wanted to do all that, but that he was having trouble remembering what would be bad about it. It was so unsettling, he fled his own house for the entire day, resolving to keep his distance and his sanity.

But here she was, speaking of the Redleys. "I accept your apology," he said, "and consider the matter at an end." With luck she would take the hint and go back into her room, slip off her dressing gown, lie down on the wide, soft duchess's bed, alone— He stopped his thoughts with an edge of aggravation. "You should consider, though, that Redley pledged the deed freely, and he should have kept his word instead of hiding behind his family."

"Of course," she agreed at once. "I completely understand." Then she stood there, oblivious to his silent urging for her to leave.

"Was there anything else?" he asked, turning away from her fathomless blue gaze.

"Yes," came her hesitant reply. "I was wondering why you instructed Mr. Adams to return the deed with my compliments."

Damn Adams, he thought. The man must learn to be discreet. "I had no more use for it."

"Of course," she murmured. "But . . ."

Marcus waited until he could face her dispassionately. "I returned the deed to Redley because you told him the debt was forgiven. As my duchess"—he lingered over the word in spite of himself—"your promises are backed by my word as well. It would be both insulting and embarrassing to you if I did not honor your well-meant words. I would never humiliate my wife in that way."

Hannah felt her heart give a little sigh. She had prepared herself for a proper scolding, or at least a pointed reminder that she had violated their agreement and should mind her tongue. He had forgiven a debt of twenty thousand pounds because he didn't want to embarrass her, even though she wasn't his wife at all. It was charming and wonderful and dangerous all at once. "Thank you," she said softly.

His gaze never left her. "It was my pleasure."

Of course it couldn't have been—he'd been angry with her when she first told him. But then, just as now, a different look had come over his face. There was a focused intensity in that look that should have made her nervous. Why, she already knew he thought she had come to apologize for stopping him from kissing her, which meant he had been thinking about that from the moment he saw her step into his room. His dressing room, which led straight into his bedroom.

Hannah had disliked the duke of Exeter virtually from the second she'd met him. He had been rude to her, insulted her, and coerced her into doing something she hated. But he had also held up his end of the bargain. She and Molly were housed, fed, and clothed in grand style. He had presented her to London society as a duchess, sent her a chest of jewels suitable for a queen, and forgiven an enormous gambling debt to avoid embarrassing her.

She had thought about what Rosalind had told her, about Lady Willoughby. At first his relationship with that woman had seemed a very black mark against him. The duke could have any woman he wanted, surely, so why would he choose the scheming Lady Willoughby? But something about this morning had pestered her, and it finally came to her. If he had meant to seduce her in the library—and she was fairly sure he had—why did he retreat so quickly at her thoughtless comment? A true rogue would have recognized it for what it was, a panicky attempt to avoid giving in to her desires. If he had brushed it aside and pressed his advantage, even a little bit, Hannah was uncomfortably aware that she probably wouldn't have stopped him a second time. Instead he had literally backed away, right into the cold forbidding manner that made it easy for her to walk away from him. She rather thought, after some reflection, that had been on purpose. She knew it was a tremendous assumption on her part, one which could come back to haunt her, but Hannah was beginning to think the duke was actually rather lonely, and that she had hurt him.

"I didn't mean to interrupt," she said hesitantly, catching sight of the table behind him again. He lifted one shoulder. She wondered what he was doing with a pile of money. Counting it, in the middle of the night? Was this what the wealthy did?

"I was going to have a cup of tea," she blurted on impulse. He arched a brow, then glanced toward the bell. "Oh, no, don't ring for one. I go to the kitchen myself and get it," she babbled on. "The servants have mostly gone to bed by now."

His other eyebrow went up, but without looking disapproving. He looked merely surprised. "I see."

She smiled uncomfortably, steeling herself. If she were wrong . . . if she had merely annoyed him by coming to apologize . . . But he was looking at her in that intense way again, as if he wanted to see inside her mind. She nibbled the inside of her lip for a second. The worst that could happen was that he would say no, and think her a provincial simpleton. "Would you care to join me?"

He didn't move. "I wouldn't wish to intrude." But he was still looking at her.

Hannah shook her head, the largest movement she could manage under that piercing gaze. "You wouldn't be."

For a moment he remained where he was, unmoving, and she thought he wouldn't accept. "It would be my pleasure."

CHAPTER 14

They walked down the stairs together, side by side but silently. Marcus knew he ought not to have accepted her invitation. He was flirting with danger as it was, his prized self-control perilously close to snapping. What in God's name had come over him?

So she was an attractive woman; London was full of them. So he wanted her; she wasn't the first. But she also confounded him and tipped him off balance nearly every time they met. He didn't understand why this drew him to her again and again, why he hadn't already dismissed her and put her firmly in her place. The irony of it was almost enough to make him smile, that the one woman in London who couldn't wait to be away from him was the one he couldn't stop thinking about. David would shout himself hoarse with laughter to know his joke had taken this twist.

Without thinking he glanced down at her. It was unsettling, that she hadn't filled in the silence with mindless chatter, like every other woman he knew would have done. He hated chattering women, but somehow this was even more disturbing. He felt as though his thoughts must be audible to her, that she was quiet because she was listening in on the torment in his mind.

She glanced up as he stole another look at her. For a moment their eyes met, before her lashes fell. Marcus jerked his own eyes to the front, his heart thumping erratically as he realized he couldn't take his eyes off her. She was always the one who turned aside; she walked away from him on the Throckmortons' steps when all he could think about was kissing her, and she stopped him in the library when all he could think of was making love to her. What in God's name was happening to him?

He had to stop this. He was a duke, a man of reason and responsibility and control. He would not act like a besotted fool over any woman. He could not. He must not.

In the kitchen he deliberately stayed back, watching as she stirred up the fire and hung a kettle over it. She moved around the room as if she knew it well. Marcus was quite sure Rosalind would never come down to the kitchen at midnight to make her own tea, and he was positive ladies like Susannah wouldn't even know where to find their kitchens. But Hannah appeared very much at ease here, just as she had appeared at ease in the Throckmortons' ballroom.

"Would you like some biscuits?" she asked, cutting into his thoughts.

"Er, no. Thank you." He stepped back out of her way as she set out a teapot and measured out the tea. It wasn't the polished silver teapot normally used for tea. It must be the servants' crockery, he realized in surprise. What an odd turn his life had taken lately. Who would have guessed the duke of Exeter would be sitting in his kitchen in the middle of the night, drinking tea out of stoneware cups?

"Do you come to the kitchen often?" he asked, still

adjusting to the thoroughly novel concept of being there himself. She smiled ruefully, pouring the water into the teapot.

"Oh, no. I think the cook's heart couldn't bear the strain. But I was accustomed to doing it at home, and—" She stopped abruptly. "Do you take sugar with your tea?"

"Yes," he murmured. He followed her lead and took a seat at the long wooden table, its top worn smooth from years of use. She sat opposite him, preparing his tea before handing it across the table. Home. What was her home like? What had her life been like? He sipped his tea without tasting. What had her marriage been like? For the first time, Marcus admitted he was curious. "What was your home like?" he asked before he could stop himself.

She smiled and shook her head. "Nothing like yours. Very small and plain, but cozy."

No one would ever call Exeter House small or plain. Marcus suddenly wondered if she liked it, or preferred small and cozy. "Do you miss it?"

"Home?" The question seemed to fluster her; she picked up her tea with a jerk, then set it down. "Well, yes, at times. But I won't be returning to the vicarage in any event, so there's no point in missing it."

Ah. The vicarage. Home of the late vicar. Her husband. Marcus took another great swallow of tea, damning his own curiosity. "What was he like? Your husband."

"Stephen?" Her face softened, and an unfamiliar feeling squeezed his stomach. "He was kind, and generous, and gentle. Understanding, almost to a fault, and so very patient." Unlike him in every way. Marcus stared at his tea and sighed. "He came to Middleborough when I was sixteen," she went on. "He was only twenty, and the previous vicar had been there for over forty years. Stephen worked hard to win the people over, working in the fields, helping with the sick, always willing to lend a hand. Everyone realized soon what great fortune it was to have him in our town."

"Including you."

"Of course. My mother died when I was ten, and I had two younger brothers to care for. Stephen would often walk me home from town. I got very lazy, counting on him to help carry my baskets." She smiled as if remembering, and that strange squeezing inside him grew tighter, almost painful. "When I was eighteen, he asked me to marry him, but my father wouldn't allow it until I turned twenty."

"Why not?"

"If I left, there would be no one to cook, and clean," she said with a rueful smile. "But finally he relented, when my brothers convinced him I might never get another offer, and he might be stuck with me forever."

He couldn't imagine her not getting another offer of marriage. And of course she had, from David—which she had accepted. Why was he even asking these questions, Marcus wondered morosely. He ought not to have come. Nothing good could come of his curiosity about her home and family and husband. The less he knew of her and her life, the better, he told himself. "I see," he said.

Hannah fussed with her teacup, hideously torn. The conversation seemed to have ground to a halt. Perhaps she should respect that and drink her tea in reserved silence. But she didn't want to be reserved at her nightly tea, she wanted to be herself after a day spent pretending to be a duchess. She wanted to be . . . friendly with the duke, she told herself, shying away from anything else. If they had to continue this pose for several more weeks, they might as well try to get along. Crossing her fingers that this wouldn't earn her another scolding for unduchesslike behavior, and that the glimmer of interest he'd betrayed wasn't just a few polite questions, she took a deep breath.

"But the more I see of London, the more I like it. There's ever so much more happening here than in Middleborough. Molly is just delighted with everything in Exeter House."

"Indeed." His grim expression lightened. "Although hardly designed for children, I recall Celia loved it as well."

Hannah smiled. "The secret passages and hidden cupboards! I imagine every child would like them." She paused, considering. "Why are there so many in the house?"

"One can only suppose my ancestors had something to hide," he said dryly. Hannah glanced up, caught the telltale twitch of his mouth, and burst out laughing. "I believe one proud Exeter hid an entire battalion in the bowels of Ainsley Park," he went on. "In case Cromwell had decided to cross him again."

Then as now, the duke of Exeter brooked no opposition. Hannah repressed her smile. "I didn't know Ainsley Park had hidden passages as well. That may be the only thing Rosalind hasn't told me about."

"Oh?"

"Goodness, yes. She's very fond of the place." She chuckled. "Of course, Rosalind is under the impression I shall live there—that is, that we shall . . ." She stopped, wishing she'd not said that.

"Ah." The duke looked into his tea. "I see."

Rosalind had told Hannah she was already making plans to remove to the Dower House, that she hoped to remain near enough to see Hannah and Marcus a great deal, not to mention their future children. Rosalind was quite sure the duke would resume his residence there, now that he was married and would soon have a growing family to house. He cannot raise children in London, she'd exclaimed. "She's certain you'll take up residence there, now that you're married," Hannah said carefully.

His mouth twisted. "Rosalind wants this supposed marriage to succeed."

That was true. No one knew it more than Hannah, who had to endure all Rosalind's matchmaking. She wondered if he knew about it. "You're very fortunate to have a stepmother who loves you so," she said instead.

One corner of his mouth hitched upward. "Yes. So I keep telling myself. It's impossible to be angry at her whilst I remember she only wants me to be happy."

"She's harangued you as well?" Hannah asked without thinking. He glanced up, eyebrows raised, and she flushed deep red. "That is, I—I knew she had spoken to you about the Throckmorton ball, but . . . but I didn't know . . . or rather, didn't expect that she would have . . . said . . . more." She stopped, wishing she had done so sooner.

"She has most definitely said more. I misspoke earlier; she wants *us* to be happy, and is determined to do anything and everything to achieve that end." He paused, watching her with an odd expression. "She's spoken to you, then?"

"You have no idea," said Hannah honestly. The duke would be livid if he knew half of what Rosalind had confided about him and his affairs. "The only one worse is Celia, but at least Celia confines herself to singing your praises, and not to advising me on the best way to—" Again she stopped, horrified at the way her mouth was running on ahead of her brain. She had almost told him Rosalind was urging her to seduce him!

"The best way to what?" he asked.

Hannah ducked her head and concentrated on stirring her tea. "Have a happy marriage," she mumbled.

After a second he seemed to understand. He coughed once, then again, and finally murmured, "Indeed," in a rather strange voice.

"It's part of the reason she's ordered so many new clothes," Hannah blundered on. "The only way to distract her is by shopping."

"She seems to have combined her efforts, then."

For a moment Hannah blinked at him in confusion, still distracted by remembered conversations with Rosalind about fulfilling her marital duties. Then realization hit her, with a bloom of heat low in her belly. It was the same feeling she'd had when he brought her the first ball invitation and had seen her in her half-stitched gown. Her skin seemed to tingle and tighten with awareness of the two thin layers of silk that were all that covered her. They covered her rather well—she hadn't been daft enough to wear one of the more daring negligees—but it was one more thing she didn't need to think about.

Refusing to let herself avoid the issue, trying to keep the conversation on a friendly but not too friendly track, she gave a slight shrug. "You did tell me not to argue with her."

"And on this you decided not to defy me," he said wryly.

She widened her eyes. "How dare you imply that I've been obstinate and uncooperative."

"Have I implied that?" He frowned. "If I have, I apologize. I should have said reluctant and unwillingly cooperative."

"That's much better," she replied at once. "If I'm to be accused of something, let it be the right thing." She sipped her tea, meeting his startled eyes over the rim of the cup. She winked, and grinned.

"I see." He leaned forward, resting his arms on the table. "Then let me add to that judgment the far greater point that you have been remarkably persuasive in your role." Hannah only just kept her mouth from falling open in surprise, which seemed to amuse him. He lifted his cup to her in salute and inclined his head.

"Why—why, thank you," she said, flustered. "I've done my best to follow directions . . ."

"Or not, as the mood may take you," he murmured. She blushed.

"I have *tried* to keep my word."

He hesitated. "Has it been every bit as dreadful as you feared?"

She wasn't sure if he were laughing at her or not. "I never feared it would be dreadful." Well, she had, but she had thought he would be the dreadful part. "I've come to like Rosalind and Celia a great deal," she rushed on. "Molly and I shall miss them both very much."

"Ah." Marcus tried to fight a rush of disappointment. He'd almost forgotten that part of the bargain. He was becoming rather accustomed to her presence, he realized; he even liked it. His life would return to the well-ordered, monotonous existence he'd always had when she left, and he would no longer be distracted from everything else by the way she put her head to one side and smiled that wry little smile, as if she were amused by some secret joke only the two of them knew. He would no longer sit and stare out his window when he should be working, wondering what was so entertaining in the garden that he could hear her laughing all the way in his study. He would no longer find himself coming home at odd times just to see what she was up to at the moment.

But he couldn't forget that she was leaving, not when she obviously hadn't forgotten. She was already thinking of how she would miss Celia and Rosalind. Not him. "They'll return to Ainsley Park in Kent for the winter," he said. "London is quite deserted once the weather turns cold."

She fiddled with her teacup. "But you shall not go with them?"

He shook his head, watching the way the candle-light gleamed on her loose hair. "No. I visit for the Christmas season only."

She looked up. Her skin was radiant and golden in the dim kitchen. "Why only then?"

He shrugged. "Ainsley Park is Rosalind's home. I don't wish to intrude on her."

Hannah glanced at him in surprise as she refilled their cups. Ainsley Park, of course, belonged to him, not to Rosalind. "I—I thought it was your home as well. Rosalind told me you were raised there."

"I was. But it was my father's favorite residence; when he married Rosalind, he brought her there. David and I were soon sent off to school, and . . ." He stopped. "Then after my father's death, responsibility kept me in London more often than not."

That wasn't quite what she had expected to hear. The responsibility, yes, and no doubt it was true. Hannah knew how much work it took to run a modest farm and a small cottage. She could only imagine the effort it must take to keep an estate the size of Exeter running—and not just running, but running smoothly and serenely.

It struck her then that she and the duke weren't so different after all. She had married a man she didn't know to avoid living where she would be out of place, while he merely ceded possession of his main estate. She knew from Rosalind that the previous duchess had died when the duke and David were five, and that Rosalind had married their father when the boys were only ten, and Rosalind a mere eight years older. Perhaps it had been hard for two boys to feel included in their father's new family, especially once Celia was born.

She ducked her head and stirred her tea. "I can understand that." She smiled wistfully, adding a small lump of sugar to her cup. "I didn't want to live with my father and his new wife, either."

His brows went up. "Indeed."

She flushed. "Yes. I was to move back to his house when . . . when I met David." That caught his interest; she could practically hear the air crackle with it, could almost feel it in his intense, direct gaze. He didn't ask, but Hannah took a fortifying breath and told him. "That was why I accepted David's offer, you know. Molly and I would have been an unwanted burden on my father, who was recently remarried. David offered me a marriage of convenience that was, well, too convenient to refuse. I did so want to remain in control of my own household." She raised her eyes and looked around the massive kitchen, finer than the one she had left in the vicarage, and thought of all the elegance and finery beyond it. Her lips quivered. "Obviously I miscalculated a trifle." He sat frozen, stiff and still. She leaned forward, letting her amusement show more plainly. "I'm not very much in control of anything, am I?" she confided with a laugh.

Slowly the corners of his mouth turned up. "More than you think, probably."

Hannah shook her head. "Not a bit!"

"No one would ever guess," he told her.

Hannah blinked. "Thank you." Then she laughed ruefully. "I should say thank heaven! I've been certain I would make a monumental fool of myself from the very first day."

"Nonsense. If anyone would have looked a fool, it

would have been I. How many men will insist they're married to a woman who appears ready to walk halfway across England to escape him?"

Her cheeks flamed at his wry tone. "Not quite halfway," she hedged. "Just back to Middleborough."

He flipped one hand. "Far enough to persuade everyone he wasn't a good husband."

Hannah gave a very unladylike snort. "I don't think that's what they would believe. More likely, that the lady had lost her mind."

"Perhaps then it was a bit of both," he replied, a small smile hovering on his lips as he picked up his teacup again. "I gave a very bad imitation of a husband, and you suffered a lapse in judgment in agreeing to it."

That was a very kind way of putting things. Hannah bit her lip, but not enough to hide her smile. "May I ask you something?" she said on impulse. "Why did you want me to stay?" The light in his eyes disappeared at once. His teacup stopped halfway to his mouth. "I know you didn't want a scandal," she hurried on. "But there must be more than that. I'm . . . well, I'm simply curious."

He replaced the cup very precisely on the saucer. "I did not want there to be a scandal. That is absolutely true. But mostly, I did not want to explain to Rosalind. Not only would it have been humiliating for her, after the welcome she gave you, but it would have destroyed her affection for David." He paused. "Rosalind was always David's champion. My father . . . suffice to say he did not expect much from David. David was only the second son, and for years my father still expected to have a third and a fourth. David was for the church—a profession he was spectacularly ill-suited to," he added as Hannah couldn't restrain a gasp of laughter at the idea. "Or perhaps the army—again, not something David embraced."

"No, I can see not," she murmured.

"Then, when my father began to accept that David might be his last son, he tried to impose some sense of duty. David grasped the finer points—an excellent tailor, a ready wit, a certain reputation among the ton—and discarded the less interesting ones. He got himself into more tight spots—" He stopped again, then shook his head. "I needn't hesitate at telling you, I suppose. I daresay this won't be any surprise to you, that David has a knack for mischief. When my father charged me on his deathbed with keeping David out of trouble, I'd no idea how monumental that task would be."

"Do you always save him?" she asked.

"Of course," he said evenly. "What else should I do? Watch my brother be taken off to debtor's prison? Sued for fraud? Called out for defaming a woman of very questionable morals?" He lowered his voice, throwing her a significant glance. "Cause a scandal by ruining an innocent woman and making a fool of his entire family?"

"Instead you would take a woman you'd never laid eyes on into your household and try to pass her off as a duchess." Hannah grinned as he opened his mouth, then closed it, with a piercing look at her.

"Yes."

"David would be impressed," she went on, thrown off balance by the way he was looking at her. "That seems like a jest he would appreciate." For a moment he stared at her in affront, his gaze sharp, then the expression faded. His mouth curved up.

"You are absolutely right." His grin grew wider, almost sheepish, and Hannah sat entranced by the transformation again. "I never thought of it that way." He shook his head. "So I'm no better than David, am I?"

No, she thought with a pang. *You're much better* David

caused a mess and the duke put his own position and status on the line to repair the damage—not for his own sake but for Celia's, and Rosalind's, and David's, and even Hannah's and Molly's. All this masquerade had brought him was inconvenience and expense. People thought he had been duped into marrying a poor, unattractive country widow, Rosalind pestered him about being a dutiful husband, and Hannah had meddled in his affairs worse than if she *had* been his wife.

"You're certainly no worse," she said, forcing herself to keep those thoughts to herself and maintain the cordial, lighter atmosphere.

"It is an enormous relief to hear that." He smiled again, and Hannah's heart turned over. "Now that you've set my conscience at ease, may I ask you something?" he asked. "Why . . . if I may be so presumptuous . . . did you accept my proposition?"

Hannah filled her teacup again very carefully. She added a lump of sugar and stirred very carefully. She could answer quickly and lightly, or truthfully. She decided on truthfully. "You promised Molly a dowry. She won't ever have to make the choice I did, to marry for security. You promised her a Season in London, so her choice of husband needn't be made from a small country village. There is so much in the world I could never offer her in Middleborough, and now, thanks to you, I can."

"Ah." He regarded her thoughtfully. "We are the noble martyrs for our families, then."

"I should hardly equate living as a duchess with being burnt at the stake," she retorted. "I'm certainly no martyr. You at least have suffered some inconvenience for others."

For a long moment he just looked at her. Hannah would have given anything to know what he was thinking. Impertinence becomes you, he had told her once.

"Well," she exclaimed, jumping to her feet. "Let me just tidy up. It's late." She cleared away the dishes, half wishing he would leave, half hoping he would stay. He stayed.

When she had put the last washed cup back on the shelf, he was still standing by the table, still watching her. She smiled nervously, pinching out the candle out of habit. As soon as she did, she cringed; of course the duke of Exeter wasn't trying to conserve candles, and would probably have lit a whole candelabra to light his way back to bed. But the dark was also comforting, so she said nothing and hurried past him through the door he held open for her.

He walked beside her, not touching and yet very close. His dressing gown billowed behind him and against her legs. The informality of the situation—she was only wearing a nightdress beneath her robe, for heaven's sake—unraveled another thread from her composure. Instead of leaving her warm and sleepy, the tea seemed to have left her hot and flustered. What had come over her?

He glanced at her with a faint smile then. Hannah smiled back, nervously, and quickly looked away. Thank goodness it was so dark. Hopefully he couldn't see her blush. He was handsome when he was stern and aloof; when he smiled at her, it made her knees go weak. This was not supposed to happen. She had only meant to make things a bit more cordial between them, not fan the sparks of awareness that glowed within her. It didn't matter that she was attracted to him, or that he was attracted to her. They were too different in station and background for this to be anything other than a charade.

Marcus was glad she was silent as they walked through the dark house. He was too discomposed by their conversation. He had been surprised when she

invited him, and then shocked by how much he hadn't
wanted it to end. Although he would have sworn they
didn't have a thing in common, for the first time in his
life that he could recall, it seemed as though someone
had understood him completely. It was shocking, and
unnerving, and utterly irresistible.

That, he decided, was a problem. He was finding
too many things about her that were irresistible. She
was not his wife. Being kind and understanding did
not give him leave to seduce her.

There was the crux of the matter: he wanted her, but
couldn't have her. With every other woman he had
known what they wanted from him, and what he
wanted from them. He rather feared, though, that
making love to Hannah would only be the beginning
of what he wanted. He feared that once he made love
to her, he would never be able to let her go. But the
longer he resisted his desires, the stronger they grew,
until his very soul seemed to roar and rage with frustration and despair. How much worse would it be to have
her for a little while and then lose her? Or even worse,
to suspect that seducing her had hastened her leaving?
It was better, for both of them, to do nothing. Sometimes it was best not to know what one was missing.

They had just reached the stairs when Marcus
heard a noise. That was unusual; the servants did not
wander the hallways so late at night. Perhaps Rosalind
or Celia had awoken and gone in search of a book
from the library. Still, Marcus glanced down the corridors to see who was about.

A shadow slipped through the back of the hall,
going toward the east wing of the house. Whoever it
was carried no lamp. Marcus came to an abrupt halt,
instantly alert. Something about that figure was not
right. It moved too stealthily. Beside him, Hannah
continued a step or two before realizing he had

stopped. When she noticed, she, too, stopped and turned. In the faint light he saw her brows rise, and heard her draw breath to ask what was wrong.

In a flash he caught her around the waist with one arm, clapping his free hand over her mouth. She jerked, then started twisting against his grasp with a muffled gasp. "Quiet," he breathed in her ear, still straining to see and hear, and she went still. A door opened with a faint yawn of hinges. Marcus's eyes narrowed; he knew that sound. It was the door of his study, a heavy oak door that wouldn't operate silently no matter how much oil the servants dripped into the hinges. Pulling Hannah with him, he moved a few steps to the right, placing them in the deep shadow of the spiraling stairs and opening a clear line of sight toward the study.

For several minutes they waited, not moving, barely breathing. *Come out,* Marcus silently dared the intruder. *Come out and reveal yourself.* No one had any reason to go into that room, especially not at this time of night, and a thief would surely not have walked through the house. There was a spy in his house. This could be the one piece he needed to fit the rest of the puzzle together, the last bit of information that would make everything else make sense.

The door groaned softly again, as the figure slipped back into the hall and closed it. Then he started back down the hall, just as quietly as before, but this time, Marcus was in position to see the intruder's face.

It was Lily.

He felt Hannah gasp against his hand; she had seen her maid, too, and was just as surprised as he was. Lily was quite possibly the last person on earth he would have expected to see. But he had no doubt of her identity, and even now she was hurrying toward the servants' stairs. Could Lily be some sort of spy, planted in his household for some purpose? He was sure she had worked for him for several years, though. Only a trusted, proven person would have been selected as the new duchess's maid, and Mrs. Potts herself had suggested Lily.

He looked down at Hannah, who still stood quietly in his arm. She gazed up at him, her blue eyes wide and questioning. Abruptly he realized how tightly he was holding her, how closely her body pressed against his. How well he could feel soft, womanly curves through the thin silk of her nightdress and dressing gown. And why he had sworn not to touch her again.

Hannah saw the change in his face as he looked down at her. She had been astonished when he grabbed her and pulled her into his arms, but then she saw Lily, and realized he was not acting on any sort of attraction. And the sight of her maid, sneaking around the house well after midnight, was unsettling in and of itself. Lily had to know it was enough to get her dismissed, even had she not gone into her employer's private study. The girl was up to something, and it couldn't be good.

But when Marcus lifted his hand from her mouth, she knew he wasn't thinking about Lily. It wasn't anger in his eyes, but hunger. His fingers drifted under her chin, lifting her face, and this time, Hannah didn't say a word.

His lips brushed hers gently, slowly. She held her breath, not daring to move. Part of her longed to cast caution to the wind, to kiss him back and damn the consequences. Part of her cried a protest, a warning that she was asking for heartache. But somehow that little voice seemed to have lost its heart.

He lifted his head and gazed down at her, his eyes dark and shadowed. She stared back, heart pounding.

For a moment neither moved, then his fingers fell away from her chin. His arm around her waist eased.

"Don't," Hannah whispered before she could stop herself, and slid her arms around his neck, pulling him back to her. This time she kissed him, really kissed him. His grip tightened as he kissed her again, deeper and harder, as if his self-restraint had finally given way.

His mouth, which had been tentative a moment ago, took possession of hers ruthlessly. Hannah let him. He tasted of sweet tea and brandy, and he kissed her as if he'd been waiting forever to do it.

He peeled the silk away from her shoulder, shoving aside the dressing gown to slide his palm over her bare arm and up her neck, back into her hair to hold her head and angle it just so for another ravenous kiss. Hannah's body ignited under his touch. Being in his arms felt exactly right, even if it really were exactly wrong.

But she didn't care. After so many weeks of lying about everything, this, even beyond the sheer exhilaration of his kiss, this was honest; this was true to herself. And when his hands slid down her back, pressing her against the physical proof that this was no charade on his part, either, Hannah let her head fall back in surrender, practically begging him to kiss her more.

Marcus lifted his head, searching for a sofa, a chair, a table, anything. She was warm and willing and he couldn't fight his desire any longer. His body was in agony, his soul was exulting. She was his. . . .

And then he realized what he was thinking. He was not her husband, only playing at it, and he had no right to ask this of her, or even to take it if she offered. Would she offer? He stood very still, holding her tightly, and tried to pull his mind away from that thought. Even if she led him to her bed and whispered *"Don't"* in that husky, inviting voice again, he would be honor-bound to say no.

For the first time Marcus allowed himself to consider what would happen if she stayed past the end of the Season. All England thought they were married, after all. He had been acting the part of a husband—with one notable exception—and not found it as onerous as expected. Indeed, he rather liked it. She was nice to talk to, when he felt like talking. She was not a chatterbox when he didn't feel like talking. She didn't know anything about running a household like his, but she was practical and intelligent and besides, Harper really ran the household. His stepmother loved her, his sister adored her, and he—

Marcus couldn't complete the thought. He wanted her, yes, and he liked her. Was that enough reason to allow their fraud of a marriage to slide into reality? If he gave in to this desire, he could father a child on her, his child, his son and heir. The next duke of Exeter would be the grandson of a farmer. Of course, the first duke had been a soldier, and as landowners all the dukes of Exeter had been farmers in some sense, and at least his son would have a good mother.

But it was the rest of his life he was considering, the future of the dukedom. He couldn't let a night's pleasure, no matter how desperately wanted, overcome a lifetime of duty and responsibility. He couldn't decide such a thing while he was half-insane with lust. Things might look vastly different in the morning, when he was his normal, rational, self. And Hannah— It wasn't fair for him to trap her into a life she might not want. He had done it once, but then he hadn't cared a whit whether she hated him for it or not. Now, though . . .

He forced himself to take a deep breath, and then

another. He made himself let go of her. "Hannah," he said softly. "I—"

"Shh." She touched his lips. Her fingertips trembled very slightly. "Don't."

His arms fell away. He was glad she had stopped him. He didn't even know what he was going to say. Apologize? That would be a first, particularly since he wasn't even remotely sorry. Point out the utter impossibility of any future for them? Hard to do, when he had been doing his damnedest to rationalize it.

"What was Lily doing here?" Hannah whispered, trying to change the subject and get her mind off whatever he had been about to say. If he had been about to point out the foolishness of their actions, she didn't need to hear it; she already knew that. If it had been a proposal to carry things further . . . Her heart thudded wildly. She might have said yes to that, with who only knew what consequences.

He took a step back and cleared his throat. "I've no idea." He paused, then narrowed his eyes at the study door. "But I intend to find out." Silently he moved down the corridor, staying in the shadows. Hannah fell in step behind him, half relieved and half disappointed. Of course she mustn't let him kiss her—or kiss him herself—right in the middle of the hallway, even if it was past midnight and no one was about. Of course she should be glad he hadn't pressed her—figuratively, not literally, she told herself with a renewed tingle—because she was clearly not in her right mind now. But she had a feeling they had crossed an important line tonight, not just here but in the kitchen, and she didn't quite know if things could go on the way they had been.

At the study door she obeyed his gesture to wait back a few feet, and watched as he listened intently for several seconds, then turned the knob and eased the door open. He seemed to lift it up as he opened, and the hinges were silent. Marcus stuck his head inside, looked from side to side, then stepped in and motioned her to follow.

Once in the study Hannah strained her eyes to look around, but she couldn't tell if anything were missing. Lily hadn't been carrying anything large, but money or something small could have fit into her apron pocket. Hannah turned to Marcus.

"Is anything out of place?" she whispered. He was also scanning the room, a thin line between his brows. He didn't answer at once, but walked around the desk to the window and peered out without stepping in front of the glass. Weak moonlight filtered in, barely giving enough light to see the furniture. Hannah stayed where she was, afraid of knocking into something.

"No," said Marcus at last, thoughtfully. "Nothing except the window latch."

"The window latch?"

"It is unlatched." He prowled away from the French window over to a set of casements. "These are still latched, as I require all windows to be at nights."

"Why . . ." Hannah was surprised. "Was she letting someone in?"

He went back to the windows in question. "Perhaps. Perhaps she was sneaking out herself, and used this room to avoid being caught. Perhaps someone met her here, and she passed something out to them."

"Money?" Hannah guessed.

"No," he murmured. He was still in the deep shadows, and she could barely see him. "I don't keep money in this room. It is no secret among my staff, so I doubt she didn't know."

"What, then?" Hannah asked when he said nothing more. Whispering in the dark, afraid to move, wondering if someone were hidden behind the settee ready to spring out at them . . . Her nerves, already tightly wound in the hall, felt ready to snap.

"It could be . . ." He paused. "It could be something far more important than money. Information." This answer meant nothing to Hannah. Information about what?

"Do you think anyone is in here?" she whispered.

"Here?" He sounded surprised. "No, I am quite sure not. But do stay away from the windows, in case someone is outside trying to see in."

Hannah felt her way toward his voice, around the massive desk. Her outstretched hand brushed his sleeve, and his own hand closed around hers as he drew her close to his side. Feeling immensely better now that she didn't feel alone and could even see a little, Hannah studied the window latch curiously and found nothing noteworthy except that it was, as he said, unlatched. What sort of information would a maid be sneaking around looking for, and to whom might she mean to pass it?

"As to whom, I don't know," Marcus replied when she asked. "As to what, I have an idea. Although I never would have guessed a maid's involvement."

"What is it?" Hannah asked again. It might not properly be her concern, but Lily was her maid, and had free run of her room and her belongings, not to mention the care of her daughter at times. Hannah wanted to know just what the girl was capable of before she started sleeping with a chair wedged against the door. Still Marcus hesitated, and Hannah couldn't bear it any longer. She went for the bell. "Summon her down at once. She should explain herself."

He grabbed her hand. "No. Say nothing to her."

She stared at him. "Why? So that she may continue to spy and do who knows what else?"

His mouth tightened. "So that she might lead me to

the others involved. There's more to this than a maid wandering the halls at night."

Hannah's eyes rounded. "What do you mean?" He didn't answer, and appeared to be deep in thought. "Whatever is going on?" she whispered, searching his face. "What are you worried about?"

His gaze focused on her again, and he let go of her hand. "David."

Hannah started. "Why? Where is he?"

"I don't know." He let out his breath in a hiss of frustration. "Would to God that I did."

"What has he done?" she asked, her voice low.

For a moment he said nothing. "Nothing I can prove," he growled. "I suspect, but I don't *know*. Until I know, I cannot do anything."

"What do you suspect?"

Again he hesitated. "Counterfeiting," came his quiet answer at last. "He could be transported if convicted."

Hannah was speechless. "David?" she squeaked.

One corner of his mouth slanted up bitterly. "Yes, David. I don't know why, or how, or even if it's true, damn it." He sighed.

"But—but what can you do, if he is?"

"I have assurances," he said obscurely. "But they mean nothing if I cannot learn the truth."

"Why must you do it?" she protested. "Surely the government or the Runners would be better able—"

He held up a hand to stop her. "The notes are being passed in the highest society. The Runners would not be able to investigate discreetly enough. I asked for the job; David is my brother, and I would prefer to act rather than sit and wait for others to hold his fate in their hands."

"Oh." Hannah subsided. She had no argument with that, really. "Is there anything I can do to help?"

He closed the window latch securely. "Watch. I have no idea what Lily was doing in here, or why. The best thing you could do is keep your eyes on her, and inform me of anything that seems out of the ordinary. It may mean nothing to this problem, but I would still like to know what she's been doing."

Hannah nodded. "Of course."

He looked around the study once more. "There's something missing," he murmured to himself. "Some piece I'm missing. Everything I've learned is disconnected; the central link is still a mystery." Then he heaved a sigh and turned to her. "Shall we?"

She nodded and he ushered her out of the room. All the way up the stairs and back to her room, Hannah racked her brains for anything that might be useful. Had Lily done or said anything revealing? She thought not, mostly because Lily hardly said anything and Hannah only summoned her when she absolutely couldn't avoid it. Perhaps she should start allowing Lily to help her more often. Perhaps she could get the maid to warm up to her, reveal some helpful scrap of information. It would be the least she could do, to help.

She was so absorbed in her thoughts, she simply followed him blindly, only coming to a halt when he did. Then she looked around and realized she had followed him into his dressing room. "Oh," she said stupidly, feeling her face grow warm.

"Yes." He didn't move, but his face assumed that dark, intent look she had seen before, down in the hall, just before he dipped his head to hers and kissed her. Remembered feelings raced along her nerves, and she was acutely aware of how near they were to not one but two beds. She felt again the hunger in his kiss, the way he had handled her, the urgency of his hands sliding over her body. More than her face felt warm now.

He saved her, turning away first. "Good night," he said. "Thank you for agreeing to watch Lily."

"Yes," she said, flustered. "Good night." She scrambled for the door to her room, glancing back just once. He was watching her again. She flashed an awkward smile, and closed her door before she completely lost her mind.

Marcus closed his eyes as the latch clicked closed behind her, saving him. Good night, indeed. It had been both spectacular and excruciating. And he didn't know if he would ever be able to forget it.

CHAPTER 15

Plink.

Plink plunk.

Hannah grimaced, aiming another stone at the rippled surface of the pond. The grounds of Exeter House were enormous, quite hiding the fact that they were in as large a city as London. She had found this little pond with Molly, who liked to watch the frogs. Far from the manicured terrace and formal gardens near the house, this little glen had been left mostly as nature formed it. Molly loved it, and was currently catching tadpoles in an old bottle supplied by the cook, up to her knees in green water. Hannah was throwing stones into the pond, trying to think.

It had been a week since Marcus kissed her. For the most part, things had gone on as before. He had dined with the family every night, and even sat with them in the drawing room after dinner. He seemed much easier, smiling and even laughing more. Rosalind and Celia didn't seem as surprised at this as Hannah sometimes was, so she believed it was his true nature—when he was at ease, with his family. She had been the outsider who spoiled that, most likely. . . .

Only now she wasn't. Or at least, she didn't feel like an outsider anymore. She no longer jumped when servants appeared out of nowhere to do the slightest thing for her. She no longer worried every minute that she would do something wrong and humiliate herself. She no longer even blinked when someone called her "Your Grace." And she could no longer deny that she was coming to like Marcus very much.

Hannah drew back her arm and flung the next rock. It skipped twice before plunking into the water. She'd completely lost her touch at this. In Middleborough she'd been able to skip it five or even six times. Duchesses, she supposed, shouldn't even make it skip once. But she wasn't a duchess.

Plink plunk.

Not even if a duke draped her with pearls and escorted her to balls.

Plink plink plunk.

Not even if a duke drank tea with her in the kitchen at midnight and then kissed her until her toes curled.

Plink plink plunk.

Not even if a duke did look as if he'd like to kiss her again every time he said her name.

Plunk.

She flung the rest of her handful of stones into the pond in disgust, then plopped down in the tall grass. She didn't know what she was anymore, she thought morosely. Was she still here just for the financial reward Marcus had offered her? Was she still here because she liked Rosalind and Celia? Or was she still here because she liked it?

She was fairly certain she could become accustomed to doing her own cooking and cleaning again. Wearing sturdy cotton and wool would feel different after weeks in silk and lace, but she would be taking the silks with her, and could indulge herself from time to time if she wanted. And she and Molly would be well provided for and independent, which would be an enormous burden lifted from her shoulders. She would miss Rosalind and Celia, but that would fade with time. And as for Marcus, well . . . Hannah sighed, drawing up her knees and resting her chin on them. Sunlight glared off the pond's surface, and she closed her eyes against it.

The only option was to ignore her feelings. Kissing him again wouldn't make her his wife. Letting him seduce her wouldn't make him feel anything for her in return. She must remember this was all a lie, and she mustn't let herself start believing in it.

"Mama, hold my tadpoles!" A dripping bottle filled with greenish water and a few nascent frogs appeared in front of her face.

Hannah opened her eyes and took the bottle with a grimace. It probably was a good thing she wasn't a duchess, because she clearly wasn't raising her daughter as a lady. Molly loved all the creeping crawling swimming things her male cousins liked. "Mama, will you make me a daisy chain?" Molly dropped a handful of squished flowers in her lap. Hannah laughed wryly.

"I shall try. But these stems are crushed, Molly."

Her daughter's lower lip went out. It was near her nap time. "Try," she said mutinously. Hannah raised her eyebrows. "Please, Mama," added Molly with a suddenly sunny smile. "And I'll put flowers in your hair!"

Hannah couldn't help smiling as her little girl ran around picking more flowers. Almost without thought her fingers split the wilted flower stems and wove the daisies into a chain, then joined it into a circle for the crown. At least she hadn't forgotten how to do that.

When Molly had sprinkled her head with buttercups, and was proudly wearing her own floral crown, Hannah got to her feet, swatting grass from her skirt.

The sun has faded behind the clouds. "Time to go back, Molly."

"Oh, yes! May I show Celia my crown?" Molly jumped up and down, clapping her hands.

"Yes, but then it will be time to rest." Molly was either too excited about showing Celia or too tired to protest, and she ran on ahead, leaving Hannah to collect Molly's shoes and stockings and release the tadpoles back into the pond. She turned toward the house, her thoughts turning toward Marcus again.

Perhaps she ought to consider leaving London early; surely by now they had presented a good enough front to avert scandal. Since the Throckmorton ball, she had attended half a dozen balls, several soirées, some dinners, and even a masquerade with Marcus. Although both of them had maintained the air of polite fondness, an unwanted tension seemed to sizzle just below the surface. Often she would catch him looking at her almost curiously, as if he couldn't decide what to make of her. Off her imagination would go, wondering about that look. Was he puzzled by something she'd done? Was he wondering what on earth she would do next to shock him? Or was he considering something else, something related to that kiss, and the way she had thrown her arms around his neck and pulled him close when he would have retreated? She wanted to know, and more than once nearly blurted the question out, but luckily had not. She wasn't at all sure she wanted to know his answer, no matter which way it went.

It was a long walk back to the house. She took her time, lifting her face to the breeze that smelled of rain. She trudged up the gentle rise toward the terrace, clutching the tadpole bottle in one hand and her skirt in the other, only to stop cold, just short of running into the man who stood with his back to her. Before she could move, he turned.

"Ah," he said, sounding pleased. "There you are. Harper said you'd gone walking."

"Yes." Flustered, she dropped her skirt, hoping it wasn't covered with grass stains. "I took Molly out."

His eyes fell to the bottle in her hand. "To the pond?"

Hannah's face felt warm. "Yes. Tadpoles," she said, lifting the bottle. He smiled a little.

"David used to catch frogs there to put in the tutor's boots."

She laughed in spite of herself. "Why am I not surprised to hear that?"

He continued smiling. "The tutor was very surprised."

"Unpleasantly, I expect."

"I believe the frogs were preferable to some of the other things the poor fellow found in his belongings."

Hannah laughed again, trying to tuck a loose lock of hair behind her ear discreetly. Her wayward heart had jumped again. Simply standing here laughing with him shouldn't make her so unaccountably happy.

"Would you care to take a turn about the garden?" he asked. "I wanted to have a word, if I might."

She wet her lips. What could he want? "Of course." She put her things on a nearby bench. He cocked his head, and she fell in step beside him, their steps crunching on the gravel.

For a few moments Marcus said nothing, just walked beside her. She looked absolutely lovely today, with her cheeks pink and her hair charmingly windblown. He would like to have Lawrence paint her, just like this, so he could forever remember it.

"You have flowers in your hair."

Her hand flew to her head and she stopped. "Oh!

Yes, Molly put them in." She ran her fingers over the black curls, plucking out the little yellow flowers.

Marcus watched her, enchanted. Without thinking he reached out and pulled a blossom loose. The stem snagged in her hair, and he reached out to work it free. Her fingers tangled with his. She glanced up at him, her cheeks flushing a deeper pink and her eyes sparkled with rueful laughter. Marcus just stared down at her, helplessly caught by some force he couldn't name and wasn't sure he wanted to know about.

"It's a frightful mess," she said with a hint of apology, breaking the spell that held him. "I'm afraid I—I haven't spent as much time fixing it. . . ." She lowered her voice and looked around. "Have you discovered anything else about Lily?" she asked in a bare whisper.

Marcus blinked. He had come after her specifically to ask what she might have observed Lily doing, but the thought had gone straight out of his head when he had noticed the flowers in her hair. "Nothing much, more's the pity," he said. "I was hoping you might have."

She sighed. "No. I can't look at her without thinking of it, though. I have the most awful feeling my thoughts show on my face and she'll know we saw her."

"That would almost be fortunate if she suspected." Marcus resumed their stroll. "If she began to fear she was about to be found out, she might do something that would help us." He hadn't meant to say "us"; he had meant to say "me." Hannah wasn't involved in his investigation.

"Yes, I suppose." She heaved another sigh. "But now I cannot bear for her to come and go as before. I would much rather do my hair myself"—she tugged at her tumbled hair with a grimace—"than summon Lily to brush it out."

It looked as though it would come out of its pins and cascade down her back at any moment. He cleared his throat. "It's charming."

She pulled another tiny yellow flower from it. "You flatter me." But she smiled.

Marcus twirled the buttercup he still held. Not many people accused him of flattery. He let the flower fall. "Perhaps you should have another maid," he said, trying to get the conversation back on the topic he had intended. "I don't want to put Lily on her guard yet."

"No." Her profile was somber. "Molly does love her. I haven't been able to forbid her to go with Lily, although I've finally given in and allowed Rosalind to send around for a nursery maid."

He raised a brow. "Finally?"

She didn't look at him. "I didn't want her to hire another servant who would only be temporary."

Marcus looked down. Ah, yes. There was that. That was not the topic he wanted. They had come to the edge of the formal gardens, overlooking the carpet of lawn leading down to the river. A hedge of rambling roses bordering the garden had been allowed to run a bit wild, and the scent of June roses drifted around them on the damp air. On impulse he picked one of the roses and held it out.

She gave him a surprised glance. "Thank you."

The petals were the same deep pink of her lips. He wondered if they were as soft. Instead of handing her the rose, he ignored her outstretched hand and tucked the flower into her hair, behind her ear. The smile she flashed him was almost shy, but pleased. Marcus felt a great rush of pleasure himself, just for having made her smile.

"Lily rarely leaves the grounds, and when she does it's unexceptional. She walks out with a young man who's a tailor's assistant, but has no other family. She's been with my family for years, as was her mother before her. Nothing she's done has been obviously suspicious."

She blinked up at him, her blue eyes puzzled. "But if she were a spy, wouldn't that also be the case?"

"Yes," Marcus conceded, still not sure why he had told her everything he knew about the maid. He must have felt sorry for her, worrying about whether to trust the girl or not. It was only natural that she didn't—Marcus himself didn't—but after being watched every moment of the last week, the maid had done absolutely nothing faultworthy. She hadn't even snuck around the house after dark anymore. Marcus had honestly expected her to do at least that again, at which point he would have been ready to pounce, and question her within an inch of her life. It was yet one more frustration among the many that were mounting by the day.

"However," he went on, as Hannah still looked uncertain, "she's done nothing else to cause alarm. Her history is exemplary—as it must have been, to be chosen for your lady's maid—and as she's done nothing else, that night may be supposed to have been a momentary lapse."

"Perhaps." She pushed her hair behind her ear again, jostling the rose. "That's all reassuring, but still . . . it was a serious lapse, if it were a lapse at all. Perhaps she's just a really clever actress who's been plotting and planning for years, so slowly no one's ever figured her for a thief—" Hannah broke off at the surprise on Marcus's face, and blushed furiously. Her wretched imagination again. What was wrong with her? She was normally so practical and level-headed. "Have you any idea where David's gone?" she blurted.

His gaze slid away from hers. "No."

She gave a frustrated huff. "If only he would show himself and explain things! I can't help but feel

Lily's behavior is somehow connected to David's disappearance."

"Perhaps." He still wasn't looking at her, but gazing out across the lawns with a remote expression. "It could also be pure coincidence. David has a knack for making a hash of things for everyone except himself. No doubt he's hidden away in some country house with a few of his friends and a great deal of whiskey, having a good laugh at my expense."

Hannah felt her mouth fall open. "Would he really do that?"

He shot her a dry look. "He would. Trust me."

"Oh, I do," she assured him, then didn't know where to look as his gaze turned probing and thoughtful. Hannah didn't want to venture down that conversational path. She did trust him; she just wasn't sure she trusted herself around him. If he made it clear he wanted to kiss her again, she didn't doubt he would stop if she told him to. The frightening part was that she wasn't at all sure she would stop him. Last time she hadn't. Last time she had thrown herself at him and kissed him first.

"But if David hadn't gone missing, would you have treated Lily's actions any differently?" she asked, tearing her mind away from such thoughts. She would not think about kissing him in this secluded, rose-scented corner of the garden, the air electric with a threatening rainstorm.

"Yes," he said, still staring at her. "I would have dismissed her at once."

"So don't you think it's all connected, too?"

"I cannot eliminate the possibility," he replied after a moment. "So, you are correct, it would make things a great deal easier if David would return and simply explain what he's been up to. If I knew without a doubt—" He hesitated, then started walking again.

Hannah followed. "But I don't. I've had men looking for David since the moment I realized he had disappeared, and they've not found him. He seems to have vanished from the face of the earth."

"Are you worried?" she asked quietly. Perhaps she shouldn't ask. But, she decided, he would certainly have no trouble telling her if she were out of line.

He sighed. "More than I can justify."

Hannah ducked her head and nodded. She was, too, especially about Lily. She couldn't shake the thought that Lily was up to no good.

"But David's done this all before," Marcus went on. "He's tweaked my nose, broken his word, caused some scandal, and then taken a holiday in a more hospitable port. If there weren't this question of forgery, this time would be no different than most others."

"Perhaps you ought to consider telling Rosalind," she suggested. "He might have written something to her that would help."

He shook his head. "No. I read the last letters he wrote her, and there was nothing helpful in them." He turned to her as if on a sudden thought. "Did he by any chance say anything before coming to London?"

Hannah thought hard. The trouble was, she hadn't known to suspect anything then, when she had been caught up in her own worries. "Not that I can think of," she answered at last.

"Ah," he said. "I thought not."

They walked in silence for a while. Hannah had no idea where they were going, nor did she care. The sun was completely gone by now, and distant thunder rumbled in warning, but she would have walked with him even if it had already been raining. Away from any watching eyes, she felt she saw the real Marcus, not the duke, and that man grew more and more intriguing by the day. And as they strolled farther from the house, her silly heart sped up in excitement.

"And things are well . . . otherwise?" he said, his voice lifting in question.

"Yes," Hannah said cautiously.

"Ah. Excellent." They walked some more. "No troubles at all?"

Hannah darted a sideways glance at him just as he did the same at her. They both looked away at once, almost guiltily. "Not that I can think of," she replied, keeping her voice even. "Should there be?"

"No, no," he said hastily. "I merely wanted to make certain you were content."

Content with what? With the fact that he had kissed her? That nothing else had happened? Or something else entirely? "What do you mean?"

He stopped, and she did as well a step later. "I wondered if you had any . . . reservations about the other night."

Her heart skipped a beat. "The other night."

"Yes."

"When we saw Lily?"

"No!" He winced. "Yes. That night. But not seeing Lily."

Hannah rolled her lower lip between her teeth. "You mean when I kissed you?"

He blinked. His eyes fell to her mouth. "Yes," he said, his voice gone low and raspy.

Her throat was dry. He wanted to kiss her again, she could see it in his eyes. Hannah felt rooted to the spot, tongue-tied with anticipation. "No," she said breathlessly.

He could kiss her. There was no reason why he shouldn't. Marcus gripped his hands behind his back. She would let him, he knew it; he could see it in her eyes, that she would let him and even wanted him to kiss her. What would be the harm, if he did? Besides, that is, losing himself completely.

Thunder rumbled, closer than before. The breeze kicked up, blowing loose curls and rose petals around her upturned face. For the first time in his life Marcus couldn't make a decision. One kiss could be dismissed as a mistake, an indiscretion. Two could not. Did he care? Did she?

"It's starting to rain," she whispered as a few fat drops spattered down around them. One hit her cheek, right beside her mouth, and he wondered what her skin would taste like, warm and wet. He could find out, just by leaning forward and pulling her close before the rain had a chance to soak them both. . . .

He closed his eyes for a split second. "Yes," he said. "We'd best go back."

"I think we'd better run!" she exclaimed with a shaky laugh as the sprinkles turned into a steady rain. Pulling her shawl over her head, she picked up her skirt and started running. Regretfully, Marcus followed.

Some things, perhaps, were never meant to be.

CHAPTER 16

"Then we are agreed, are we not? Exeter?" A pause. "Your Grace?"

Marcus turned from the window he'd been staring blindly out of and faced Nathaniel Timms and Mr. John Stafford, chief clerk of Bow Street. "I beg your pardon," he said. "What were you saying?"

"That since your brother seems to have gone missing, and your investigation has reached a blind end, we shall pursue other avenues," repeated Timms.

Marcus took his time replying. It was the sensible course. David had been missing for well over a month, and Marcus had learned next to nothing useful in a fortnight. He was tired of it all—the gambling, the worrying, the watching. Let Stafford do his best. "Yes," he said at last. "By all means. I only ask that if new evidence turns up indicating my brother, I be kept informed."

Stafford knew which side his bread was buttered on. "Yes, Your Grace," he said, bowing his head. "Of course."

"Of course, of course," said Timms a little too heartily. "Much obliged to you for all your efforts thus far, sir."

Marcus just looked at him. He hated to think he

had failed in what he set out to do—always had done—but this had been a quixotic pursuit from the beginning. This time, it seemed, David had out-smarted him. Either that, or David was innocent and it had all been a waste of time.

He got to his feet. "Then I bid you good day, gentle-men." Stafford and Timms returned his brief bow, and Marcus left, collecting his hat and walking stick from the servant who hovered outside Timms's well-appointed office. He emerged from the bank into the last sunlight of afternoon.

He paused to take a deep breath. It was a lovely day, and he no longer had to plan an evening crawling through gaming hells and crowded card rooms in search of suspects. It was quite a relief, actually. David had won; Marcus surrendered. Let David be his own man, unencumbered by Marcus's spying and over-sight. *You've finally got your wish,* he told his absent brother silently. *Enjoy it in good health.*

The footman swept open the carriage door as he descended the steps. As precise as ever, his servants. "Home," he said as he stepped into the carriage.

"Yes, Your Grace," said the footman. A moment later the driver snapped his whip, and they were off. Marcus leaned back, a faint smile spreading across his face. He felt rather free. He wondered what the ladies had planned tonight. With any luck, a quiet evening at home. He was tired of going out every night. Rosalind would be pleased, although she didn't know why he had ignored her every scolding about staying in more. He hoped Hannah would be pleased as well. Perhaps she would invite him to sneak into the kitchen for tea again. Perhaps he would invite himself.

The carriage stopped. Marcus jumped down lightly and strode up the steps, feeling a strange urge to whis-tle. The moment he stepped past the butler into the hall, a slim figure in blue stopped pacing and whirled to face him.

"Marcus," Hannah said, as he crossed the hall to her. He drew her hand to his lips, his heart lifting at the sight of her. As it always did. Yes, the feeling was most definitely in his heart. Distracted by that realization, he almost missed the worry in her voice.

"What is it, my dear?" He turned his back to Harper, wanting to take her in his arms and banish the anxiety from her expression. He wanted to hold her and shelter her and protect her from whatever had dimmed the light in her eyes. Instead he held her hand firmly between his two, and when she put her free hand on top of them, something warm and comforting filled his soul. Now he was home. With her.

Her somber blue gaze didn't waver. "David is here."

For a moment he didn't move; of all the times for his worthless brother to return and upend his life, he had to come home now, as Marcus realized he was losing his heart to the woman David had dumped on his doorstep. "Where?"

She wet her lips, glancing over her shoulder. "He's ill, and drunk."

He released her hand, the warmth inside him fading as the contact was broken. "Where is he?"

She reached for his arm as he started toward the stairs. "Wait, please! I want to warn you—" The drawing room door swung open, David leaning on the handle. His eyes glittered feverishly, and were bloodshot from the liquor Marcus could smell even from ten feet away. There was a crust of dried blood on his forehead, and his hair hung past his shoulders in a tangle. He was filthy from head to toe.

"The prodigal returns." Hannah flinched in dismay at Marcus's tone, the hated frosty hardness. He never used that on her anymore. In fact, she hadn't heard it at all in a long time.

"Marcus," she pleaded in a whisper. He seemed unaware of her presence, his attention wholly on his brother.

"Yes, dear brother. So sorry, but I have returned. A bit worse for wear, but still in one piece." David punctuated this with a mocking bow, then stopped short, one hand pressed to his ribs.

"What do you want?" Hannah bowed her head and squeezed her hands together miserably.

"What do I want?" David repeated, blinking owlishly. Hannah noticed his knuckles were white where he gripped the door, and that he seemed to sway the tiniest bit on his feet. He squinted at his brother, then at her, and focused on her hand, reaching out to touch Marcus's arm. Hannah self-consciously pulled back. All she meant to do was warn Marcus that David might collapse.

"David! Oh, Mama, David's here!" Celia's excited cry rang through the hall, and Hannah nearly ran around Marcus to intercept her. Whatever the brothers needed to discuss, they needed to do it without Celia or Rosalind about, and neither looked inclined to wait. David glanced up at his sister just as Hannah caught her.

"Celia, they need a bit of privacy," she said in whispered rush, trying to stop the younger girl as Rosalind hurried down the stairs toward them.

"Oh, David, how could you stay away so long?" Celia shook off Hannah's hands and flung herself at her brother, who had limped forward into the hall. David staggered, and only kept his feet thanks to Marcus's hand on his elbow. "I've missed you so! Mama and I came all the way to London as soon as we got your letter, and you are so terrible not to be here to see us!"

"Sorry, Celia," David mumbled. "Rosalind." His stepmother was crossing the hall to greet him, Hannah's weak protest lost in the noise of Celia's greeting. She watched helplessly. Marcus's face had set in the same grim lines she remembered from the last time Celia and Rosalind's untimely arrival had upset his plans. She stared at him, but he didn't meet her eyes.

"We'll discuss it later," Marcus said. He snapped his fingers. "Harper, prepare a room at once." He turned on his heel and started toward the stairs.

"I came to ask your pardon," David went on, his words slurring slightly. Marcus kept walking. "And Hannah's, for what I did." Marcus stopped. Hannah's stomach took a horrible plunge as she realized what was about to happen, but she couldn't seem to move or speak. Marcus wheeled to face his brother again, his face absolutely fearsome.

"Not now," he said in a terrible voice.

"I shouldn't have tricked either of you that way," rasped David, now leaning on Celia. He ducked away from Rosalind's hand as she reached out to feel his forehead. "I didn't expect you to be such a sport about it and keep her, though, really I didn't."

"David!" said Celia in bewilderment. "What are you talking about?"

"Nothing," bit out Marcus as he strode back across the hall, waving aside Celia and hauling David none-too-gently toward the stairs. "Harper!" Everyone jumped at his roar.

"I wanted to help her so much, but I knew I wasn't the right man," David babbled. His glittering eyes found Hannah, still petrified at the foot of the stairs. "God help me, I'm so sorry, Hannah."

She shook her head, actually praying for a man to lose consciousness. "No, really, let's talk about it later."

His face crinkled in a smile, as if he were almost proud. "That's what I like about you," he said. "So bloody practical! Everything in its proper place, at its proper time. Just like Marcus, eh?" He swung his fist, landing a feeble blow on his brother's chest. Marcus grunted, nearly dragging his passive twin up the stairs. "I knew she was the one for you, the moment I saw her, old man."

"Marcus!" demanded Rosalind from below. "What on earth is he talking about? David, what's happened to you?"

Marcus hesitated, which was his undoing. David tried to turn around, throwing them both off balance. Marcus grabbed for his brother's coat, barely managing to keep them upright. Celia screamed, and David sank to his knees.

"It's simple, Rosalind," he said, his voice suddenly clear again. "I signed Marcus's name in the marriage register. Hannah never met him until I brought her to London."

Complete silence filled the hall. Hannah felt her face burn with shame and awareness of every lie and deception she had committed these past weeks. When she finally managed to lift her head, Marcus's gaze was the one she sought.

"Marcus, is this true?" gasped Rosalind.

His eyes caught Hannah's, flat and dark and utterly expressionless. He didn't say a word, but the damning silence seemed to ring in the hall. David coughed weakly, sliding out of Marcus's grip. His damage done, the prodigal collapsed to the stairs, flat on his back, out cold.

"That's nasty stuff," said David with a grimace. Hannah put the lid back on the bottle of tonic and set it on the table.

"If I had anything nastier, I would pour a whole bottle of it straight down your throat."

"No doubt you would," he said with a faint grin. Hannah pressed her lips together, then reached for the bowl of broth. He had refused it earlier, but the doctor said he needed to eat it. David took one look at her face, and pushed himself up against the pillows and took the bowl.

"I'm terribly sorry, Hannah," he said when it was gone. She said nothing, stacking the dishes back on the tray. When David had fainted on the stairs, the household had seemed to come apart at the seems. Between Celia shrieking, Rosalind calling out dozens of hysterical orders, and the servants suddenly running everywhere, Hannah hadn't known what to do. She stood frozen at the bottom of the stairs, while Marcus just watched the pandemonium with his face still and closed. He had disappeared into his study soon after, and when Rosalind broke down after the doctor's examination of David and had to be helped to her room by a maid, Hannah silently slipped into the room and took over the nursing duties.

David wasn't in as bad shape as she had thought at first. Once he was cleaned and dressed in a nightshirt, he looked remarkably like the man she had first met. There were pouches under his bloodshot eyes, and he had a hacking cough, which the doctor said didn't seem to have settled into his lungs, and a fever. A broken rib was the worst of his troubles. And now that he was somewhat sober and rested, he was anxious to make amends, or at least apologize. Hannah wasn't ready to hear any of it.

"I think sorry is a poor recompense," she said. "What you did is unforgivable."

He winced. "Unforgivable? By you, or by Marcus?"

"Both, I think," she said evenly. His hands moved restlessly, plucking up the coverlet.

"It doesn't seem to have ended so badly." His tone was wheedling, imploring. Hannah stood up.

"You are not in any position to judge."

He cleared his throat, frowning, as though he were trying to think how to talk his way out of this spot. "You're still here," he pointed out at last. She shook her head, and picked up the tray.

"I'm not listening. You see nothing wrong with what you did. Good night." She went to the door.

"Will Marcus be up soon, do you think?" he asked almost plaintively. She paused.

"Are you sure you want to face him already?"

"Hmm, that bad, eh?"

Hannah met his eyes for a long moment, until his hesitant grin vanished. "Worse, I expect." She closed the door and left.

Marcus sat and drank, staring blindly at the window. It was all over. All his efforts to keep David's betrayal secret, undone by his ungrateful brother in person. Rosalind had been stunned, he saw, appalled by David's actions but also by his. Celia was just shocked, but betrayal would come. That disillusionment had hit him hard, but not as hard as the look of utter mortification on Hannah's face.

He smiled dourly. The three women whose happiness he cared for above all else had just been humiliated and horrified by what he'd done.

A sharp tap sounded on the door, and it opened before he said anything. Marcus didn't turn; he knew who it was. He had been waiting for her.

"Marcus, I have never been in the habit of taking you to task for your decisions," said his stepmother in a low voice. "You are a grown man, and if I haven't always been pleased by your actions, I have told myself you were competent to judge for yourself, and I have held my tongue." She paused, and Marcus heard her breath catch. "But I couldn't live with myself if I didn't ask *why.*"

"I did it for you," he said calmly. "And for Celia."

"Oh, Marcus," she whispered in dismay. He continued to stare out the window, his voice still devoid of emotion, as he related every detail.

"I thought to spare you the realization that David had used her so abominably," he concluded. "Hannah was nothing to me, and I was nothing to her; a few months of uneasy pretense, and she could return to her life, comfortably settled, and I could return to mine, with no one the wiser."

"You thought this would spare me?" Her voice rose incredulously, and Marcus closed his eyes as she repeated every argument Hannah had made. "To think you were indifferent and unhappy in your marriage? To think your bride had left you, and you cared nothing for keeping her?"

A telling silence filled the room. Marcus made no reply, refusing to cover for his brother any longer. Rosalind drew a long breath. "But I would never have blamed David," she said in wonder. "I would have scolded you, and been disappointed in you, but never once thought David at fault. Oh, Marcus, how could you?"

"Habit," he muttered, tossing back the last of his drink. No one knew how many times he had saved David, not even David. From the examinations he took in his brother's stead at Eton to the fortune in gambling debts paid and the angry husbands paid off and intimidated, Marcus had always acted to preserve the family name, and David's along with it. He had thought this would be no different, but it was. David had tried to wreck Hannah's life this time, and Marcus couldn't pretend that was a trifle to be brushed aside with a bank draft and some placating words. David deserved to suffer, and Marcus wouldn't mind administering the suffering himself this time.

"And David— Oh, I cannot even imagine what he was thinking!" Rosalind's voice rose as she paced back and forth. "I've a mind to go take a switch to him myself. What a trick to play on someone! And to lie to all of us! I hardly know him anymore— Oh!" She seized a glass from the sideboard and flung in into the fireplace with a small crash of broken glass. The fire licked hungrily at the shards of fine crystal.

Marcus refilled his glass and said nothing.

"This cannot be allowed," said Rosalind firmly when she had mastered herself again. "You've got to make amends, and David as well, though what he deserves will little repay what Hannah's lost."

Marcus had a guess what Rosalind was going to say. And to tell the truth, the thought of marrying Hannah sounded rather appealing. In fact, it had a great deal more than a little appeal. If Rosalind encouraged her, even told her she must, Hannah might overlook all the things she disliked about him and his life, and accept him. Or at least give him a chance; that was probably as much as he had a right to hope for, after what he'd put her through. That was all he deserved, and, Marcus vowed, all he would need. For the first time in his life, he waited with bated breath for his stepmother to suggest he marry.

"You've got to let her go."

He started, nearly dropping his whiskey. "What?"

"Tomorrow," said Rosalind. "She was persuaded to come to London under false pretenses, and should be allowed to return at once. Now that I look back, there were several signs she wanted to leave—oh, goodness, I was so blind, insisting everything would be all right if she only stayed!"

"She wants to go home?" he echoed numbly. He had really thought she was warming to life in London, and to him. Naturally she had wanted to leave at first, but he hadn't heard a word from her about it in some time. And at the same time, he had stopped thinking about when she would be gone. He couldn't imagine life without her now.

"What is there to keep her here now?"

Marcus said nothing. There was nothing *to* say. What was there to keep her now? No need to deceive Rosalind or Celia, no façade to present to the ton. David would be sure to venture out and dine on the tale sooner or later, if it hadn't already leaked from the servants' quarters, and then life in London would become a torment for Hannah. He desperately wanted a reason to argue, but didn't have one. "She's lived as my wife," he murmured.

Rosalind sucked in her breath. "Has she? Have you and she—?"

"No!" He lowered his voice. "I meant she's been presented to society as my duchess."

"Ah." Rosalind sighed. "Then you have to let her go. She's not your wife, and having lied about it for two months won't change the fact that you have no claim on her."

Marcus stared out the window, cold and desolate inside. *I do have a claim on her,* he wanted to shout. *I lied until I believed it for truth. I'm used to her, and I like her, and I want her to stay.* But that was what he wanted. What did Hannah want? He had bent her to his will once before, when she wanted to leave. He hadn't cared what she wanted then. But now . . . "Of course. I'll tell her tonight."

CHAPTER 17

Hannah asked Lily to bring her dinner to the nursery on a tray. She didn't know if the family would dine together as if nothing had happened, but she didn't want to risk it. She played with Molly for a while, trying not to think of what must happen next. The servants must be gossiping like mad about this afternoon's spectacle. They would all know she was an imposter, and soon all of London would as well.

Lily came to retrieve the tray. She kept her eyes averted, as if she didn't want to look at Hannah, and Hannah was both relieved and mortified. It was a sign she should leave as soon as possible, if even the servants couldn't bear the sight of her. So when Molly went to bed, Hannah went back to her own room.

There was too much to do. In less than two months Rosalind had filled the wardrobe with more clothes than Hannah would ever need, even though Marcus had said she could keep them. But her heart twisted as she studied the beautiful gowns and lacy shawls, the delicate shoes and all the gloves, stockings, bonnets, and other things a duchess must have. Her own plain clothing that she had brought from Middleborough had long since been buried behind all the finery.

She pulled out a nightdress at random, caressing the soft silk. It was the basest kind of vanity, but she liked wearing gorgeous clothes. She loved the feel of silk next to her skin. She loved being beautiful. She loved . . . she loved . . . She turned the silky gown over, sighing as she recognized the gown she had worn the night Marcus kissed her.

Oh, dear.

Who would have guessed that they would turn out to be so much alike under it all? Who would have guessed that her feelings could take such a complete turnabout regarding him?

It all made her head ache. She dressed for bed, hoping sleep would calm her thoughts and emotions. There would be time for packing tomorrow.

There was a rapid tapping at her door just as she was about to put out the lamps. Hannah went to open it, surprised to see Celia.

"What is it?" she started to ask, but the younger girl slipped into the room and closed the door, her eyes huge.

"Marcus has told Mama everything, and she's told him he has to let you leave," Celia said rapidly. "She's trying to push him into admitting that he loves you, regardless of David's tricks, but it won't work, not on Marcus. Oh, Hannah, you've got to tell him!"

"Calm down," said Hannah with authority. "What are you talking about?"

Celia sucked in a huge breath and held it for a moment. "Marcus told Mama what David did. All of it, how he pretended to marry you, and brought you to London and left you in his mistress's house, and then wrote Marcus that his new duchess had been delivered.

Mama was so angry, I thought she might go upstairs **and thrash** David herself. And then—"

"How do you know all that?" Hannah asked sharply. Oh, heavens—this would be even worse than she'd expected.

Celia shook her head. "I listened at the door. Honestly, I couldn't not listen! Oh, Hannah, what you must think of us, after the way we badgered you! And when I think—"

"Celia." Hannah squeezed her hands to get the girl's attention. "That's none of your concern, or your mother's. It is between Marc—your brothers, and if you have any affection for them, you won't repeat anything you heard."

"Of course I won't!" she cried. "But Mama is going to push Marcus into a corner, and he'll never admit it if you don't say something first! I know you shouldn't have to, but if you love him, you have to, or he's going to send you away!"

Hannah released Celia's hands, staring at her. "Oh."

"Back to your home, Hannah. Mama is telling him he has to send you home, since you're not really his wife. She thinks he won't be able to do it, and will admit he loves you to keep you. Because you do love him, don't you? You don't want to leave, do you?" Celia was crying now, silvery tears streaking down her face.

"No," said Hannah very quietly. "I don't."

"And you do love him?" Hannah said nothing. Celia grabbed her by the arms. "You do, don't you?" she demanded, on the brink of hysteria. Still Hannah said nothing. Celia sniffed, then burst into loud, noisy sobs as she flung herself into Hannah's arms. "Oh, Hannah! I'm going to miss you so."

And I will miss you, thought Hannah, so heartsick she almost burst into tears herself. She would miss Celia, and Rosalind, and most of all Marcus. She would miss everything about this life she had expected to hate. It was a bitter irony that she was allowed to leave, now that she didn't want to. She wrapped her arms around Celia and let the girl cry.

She managed to get Celia calmed, and sent her to her room to wash her face. Then she sat down and thought. Celia's account rang true; Hannah had known all along Rosalind was determined to see Marcus happy with her, and it scored her heart to realize how much she had begun unconsciously cheering Rosalind's efforts. She knew she had fallen in love with him—not when, not how, and sometimes not even why—but she had.

But he was going to let her go, Celia said. Rosalind's manipulations wouldn't work on him, he would send her home just to prove he could. If he didn't love her enough to humble his pride and ask her to stay, didn't it leave her no choice but to go?

Well, I could always tell him I want to stay, she reasoned. *There's no reason why he must humble his pride first. It might make a difference. It might not. If it doesn't, then I'll know. If it does . . .*

Then I'll know.

He knocked on her door an hour later. Her heart leaped into her throat, but Hannah squeezed her trembling hands together and responded at once. "Come in."

He stepped into the room, his jacket and waistcoat gone. He looked tired. "You weren't at dinner."

She managed a half smile. "I thought it would be awkward."

"Right." He sighed, rubbing his jaw. "I've told Rosalind everything."

"Celia came and told me," she said in a low voice. He nodded.

"I thought that was her shadow outside the room." He hesitated. "No one holds anything against you. Rosalind knows I forced you to play the part, and to lie to her. She knows David brought you to London under false pretenses, and that you have been an honest woman every moment." He stopped again. "No one will hold you here any longer. You have but to say when, and I'll have the carriage prepared to take you home."

She cleared her throat. "Is that what Rosalind said you should do?"

"Yes."

"Is that what you want to do?" she whispered. His chest filled, and something kindled in his eyes, but then the light died, and he let out his breath.

"I promised you could leave when our charade was over. I will not break my word and keep you here against your will. You are free to go at any time you wish." Hannah's knees gave out, and she collapsed onto the dressing table chair. This was it. If she said nothing, he would let her walk away. If she said something, he still might send her away.

"What if I didn't want to go?" She could barely bring herself to look at him. What if he said she should leave? What if he reminded her that she had promised to leave?

He was quiet for a long time. "I won't make you go, if you don't wish to." Was that hope in his voice? It could be. It might be.

She raised her eyes to him. "I want to stay." He didn't move. "Marcus . . ."

"Yes?" His voice sounded hoarse, but it might just be the blood roaring in her ears.

"What do you want?"

"I want you to stay," Marcus said, without knowing when he had decided it was true. She turned, half rising from her seat. He never knew how he had thought her ordinary. "Forever."

With a choked gasp, she put out her hand, and he crossed the room in two strides, yanking her into his arms and burying his face in her hair. Her arms slid around him, and he shuddered as he kissed her neck.

"Will you?" he demanded, pressing kisses up her jaw and around her ear. "Will you stay?"

"I will," she said, placing her hands on his cheeks and drawing his lips to hers.

"Forever?" he demanded against her mouth, holding her against him so that she realized his intent. He couldn't take it any longer, living this close to her and not touching her, kissing her, loving her. She pulled back, her glorious blue gaze as hot as lightening.

"Yes." And she moved against him, letting him know he was welcome—even required—to make love to her.

With one arm he lashed out, sweeping perfume bottles and brushes from the dressing table before lifting her onto it. Her knees parted, and he pressed between them, wanting to drive himself into her until neither existed alone anymore. He kissed her desperately, his hands shaking as they raced over her, too wild with urgency to linger anywhere. God in heaven, how long has he wanted this, to have her straining against him, her legs around his hips, her own hands gripping him with the same desire?

Hannah felt his hands sweep her nightgown up her thighs and she trembled. The fact that she had never stood beside him in a church and spoken her vows didn't matter, something that ought to have surprised her but didn't. He wanted her to stay, forever. From Marcus, it was a statement as meaningful as a wedding vow might be to another. He had no reason now to keep pretending she was his wife unless he wanted it to be so.

"My God, I've wanted you for so long," he groaned in a rough voice, cupping the curve of her breast, his thumb rough and insistent over her silk-covered nipple. Hannah moaned, wriggling closer, reaching for the fastenings of his trousers. She hadn't undressed a man in a long time, and her hands shook. Finally the material gave way, and she slid her palms flat over his hips, around to his back, pulling him closer. The trousers loosened, slipped, and his bare flesh met hers, thigh to thigh. He sucked in his breath, then pressed against her, and Hannah tilted her hips in silent, desperate urging.

Marcus swept one hand down her belly, over the silk folds of her nightdress. Her skin was softer than the silk, and he moaned. Or perhaps that was her voice, ragged and breathless in his ear. He kissed her, his fingers exploring, hungry and impatient. She sagged in his arms, her hands tightening convulsively on his shoulders, and he bent her backward. It barely even penetrated his fastidious mind that he was making love to her on a table, both of them still clothed. She was under him, her eyes glazed with desire, and Marcus had reached his limit. Then she reached between them and curled her hand around his erection, and he tumbled over the precipice. He closed his hand over hers, helping her guide him.

"I never meant to let you go," he breathed. Hannah's lips parted in surprise, and he thrust into her so hard she gasped, astonished at the raw strength of his desire. He cupped her hips in his hands, holding her in place. "Did I hurt you?"

"No," she gasped, still adjusting to the feel of him inside her. "Do it again." He did, and she moaned, throwing back her head as the first ripples of impending climax tightened her belly. His arm slid under her thigh, spreading her open, and Hannah bit back a scream as he drove into her again, so far she could swear he touched her heart. There was nothing gentle about it, but Hannah felt it in her soul like she never had before. She came with a shattering sense of splitting open, biting down on Marcus's shoulder to keep from shrieking. He growled, moving once more before grasping her by the back of the neck and bringing his mouth down on hers in a kiss so hard she didn't even realize he was shaking until he tore his lips from hers with a gasp.

"Holy God," he rasped, his shoulders heaving, his face pressed into her neck.

Hannah smiled without opening her eyes. She could feel the hard, heavy beat of her heart against her eyelids. "Yes, indeed."

The rumble of his laugh vibrated through her, making her laugh, too, even louder when he scooped her into his arms and carried her to the bed. He set her down, then just stood there, gazing at her, his hands on his hips and his eyes burning with desire. Hannah wet her lips. "We're a little overdressed for this."

He was already tugging his cravat loose, peeling off his shirt. "We shall have to remedy that." For a man accustomed to being dressed and undressed by a valet, he made short work of his clothing, Hannah thought, her eyes roaming over his chest, his arms, down his waist and hips. He was lean and hard everywhere, his skin sleek and golden in the candlelight. Dark hair covered his chest, narrowing down his stomach. His eyes never left her, those dark, dark eyes she couldn't look away from. He put her in mind of a powerful animal, muscles taut and coiled, ready to spring—at her. Her breath caught in her throat as he sat down beside her and pulled off his boots and trousers. The duke of Exeter was naked, in her bed. Her stomach contracted with desire, and fluttered with excitement at the same time.

"Laggard," he said softly, getting to his feet and pulling her to hers. Hannah blinked, realizing she had done nothing but watch him undress. And now he was undressing her. She shivered as he untied the satin ribbon laced up her side, loosening the nightdress. He kissed her as he dragged up the long skirt, the hem trailing along her thighs with a sensuous whisper, then broke the kiss to turn her around and whip the gown over her head. Dazed, Hannah felt his fingers running through her hair, combing out whatever remained of the neat braid she'd put it in for bed.

"I wondered . . ." he murmured, sliding a hand down her spine.

"What?" she managed to gasp. He wound her hair around his fist and tugged, turning her head to expose the side of her neck.

"I wondered how far," he breathed in her ear, releasing her hair to fall over her shoulder. "Your skin . . ." He kissed that place right below her ear and Hannah sucked in a ragged breath, trying not to melt on the spot. "Was golden." His hands swept up her sides to close over her breasts. "And what you did outside to make it so."

"I . . ." Hannah's head fell back against his shoulder as he kissed her neck again, his hands on her breasts, kneading her flesh, rolling the nipples between his thumbs and forefingers. "I always . . ." He nipped her earlobe between his teeth. "I . . . Oh!" He pulled her back full-length against him, and she felt him, thick and hard, against her bottom. Her knees felt weak.

"Yes?" He released her breasts, his palms skimming

down her ribs, until his hands wrapped around her waist. "What did you do, darling?"

"I forgot my hat," she blurted. His arms were around hers, and she couldn't move them. She wiggled her hands ineffectually—or so she thought until he exhaled sharply and pushed her forward. The carved wood of the bedpost pressed into her belly as he held her in place.

His mouth lingered on her neck; he seemed to know how it affected her. His fingertips raked lightly down her back, and she gasped. Her back had always been virtuously in contact with the mattress every other time she'd made love. But Marcus was making love to her back, with just his mouth and the tips of his fingers, and it was driving her wild.

He kissed her shoulder, tracing her collarbone with his tongue. Hannah looped an arm around the bedpost to keep her balance. He kissed his way down her back, his palms sliding over the curves of her hips, his teeth nipping at her spine. Hannah rested her head against the post, her breath coming in short, shallow sighs. Then he dipped his head—she felt the brush of his hair on her waist—and licked the crease at the top of her thigh.

Hannah moaned. He gripped her hip with one hand, still kissing every inch of her back, as his other hand slid between her legs, easing them apart. Her legs trembled, and she made a halfhearted effort to move, but he merely took advantage of her off-balance weight to push one knee forward, so that her foot now rested on the bottom rail of the bed.

She had never felt anything like this. She had to put her other arm around the post, or fall over in a paralysis of ecstasy. Now he was pushing his fingers inside her, touching her even more insistently, his mouth still moving over places that had never been kissed before. A shudder ripped through her, and she gulped back a sob.

Just when it seemed he would drive her over the edge, he stopped. Swaying on her feet, her head swimming, she let him turn her, until she looked down at him kneeling at her feet.

There was something almost fierce in his expression, concentrated on her. "Why are you frowning?" she whispered.

His brow cleared at once. "Frown? That was no frown." A wicked smile curled his mouth. "I was merely deciding which part of you to devour first."

She couldn't stop a smile, even as her breath caught in anticipation. Just the sound of his voice did wicked things inside her.

"That settles it, then." He surged to his feet and caught her around the waist, tossing her onto the bed. "It will have to be all of you."

"All at once?" she managed to say as he lifted her leg up and hooked it over his shoulder, driving into her in one smooth motion and causing her to arch like a bowstring underneath him.

"As near as I can manage." He brushed the hair from her forehead, those piercing eyes searching her face. "I can't seem to help myself." He leaned down to kiss her, letting her knee slip down his arm until Hannah curled both her legs around his waist. And then neither spoke again for some time, too caught up in exploring each other.

This was not the gentle joining she had known before; this was possession. Only, she wasn't quite sure who was conqueror. One moment he would stretch her beneath him and drive into her with long hard thrusts that left no doubt who was mastering whom, and minutes later their positions would be reversed, and she would be straddling him, fully in command.

It was thrilling, she found, to be in control, to hold him in her thrall and know that he knew it, too.

When they finally lay, sated and spent, Hannah truly did feel devoured. Her legs felt like jelly. Her insides felt like warm butter. Her mind was incapable of forming or holding a thought, it seemed, and when Marcus pulled her into his arms, nestling her against him, her only response was to snuggle closer and yawn.

"That's that, then," he said with a sigh.

"Hmm? What's what?" she murmured, fighting off sleep. After all the excitement of David's return, then this . . . discussion with Marcus . . . She giggled softly to herself, calling it a discussion when they'd barely said two words all evening. . . . What had she been thinking? Oh, yes . . . she was utterly exhausted.

"Nothing, darling," he said with a rumbling laugh. He curled his other arm around her waist. "I've just decided which country manor I should give you. I did promise you one, after all. I believe Ainsley Park would suit you very well." He yawned. "Very well indeed." Hannah just smiled without opening her eyes, and fell asleep with his breath warm on her shoulder.

CHAPTER 18

The first thing that crossed Hannah's mind when she woke the next morning was what a wonderful dream it had all been, Marcus telling her he never wanted her to leave, taking her into his arms, making love to her on the dressing table with a raw passion that made her body tingle in remembrance. She could swear she still felt the glide of his hands along her skin. . . .

His fingers moved along her arm up to her shoulder. When he turned her over onto her back, she shivered. Not a dream, but a fantasy come to life. He kissed her lightly, his lips lingering on hers.

"Good morning," she whispered. He smiled down at her.

"A very good morning indeed." She twined her arms around his neck, pulling him back to her. He came into her arms very naturally, very easily.

He lowered himself onto his elbows above her, his body settling atop hers. His hands slid over her arms, until his fingers insinuated themselves between her own. As his kiss grew hotter, deeper, as he moved over her in potent foreshadowing, he pried her hands apart, stretching her arms above her head until she was stretched flat beneath him.

"Hold on," he murmured, his voice barely audible over the blood pounding in her ears. She dimly felt him winding her fingers around the carvings of the headboard. "Don't let go," he added, his eyes crinkling in a faint grin. Hannah could only nod once, jerkily, as his hands swept down her arms, his fingertips scoring the sensitive undersides. Her body arched all on its own, and she thought he chuckled softly as he palmed the swells of her breasts. Then he bent his head, and Hannah lost whatever awareness of such things she had left.

This was . . . Oh, heavens. This wasn't making love, this was worship. He knelt between her knees, head bowed over her as his wicked, wonderful mouth moved down the contours of her throat, over her shoulder, and onto her breast. He didn't just kiss her, there was an insistent pull in his lips, as if he were dragging her with him deeper into a whirlpool of sensation, drowning her. . . .

Even though she went willingly, Hannah knew a moment of fear. She was out of her depth here, with him. Her first marriage hadn't prepared her for the intensely physical reaction she had to this—to him. Just from his kiss, and the look in his eyes, her body had reacted with astonishing speed; he could make love to her this instant, easily, even though he had yet to touch her intimately. It was dangerous, and frightening, how fierce and visceral her response to him was. It was more than the natural reaction of a female to a male. It was more than the emotional bond she'd had with Stephen. It was . . . rapture.

His teeth grazed over her nipple, and every nerve in her body jumped at the shock. Unconsciously, her grip on the headboard loosened. He sucked once, gently, and she gasped for air. He shifted his weight, pushing her knees higher and wider, and she shuddered at the image of herself open before him, waiting for him, ready for him.

She must have said his name, or made some similar sound, because he stopped then, looking up at her. His dark hair was tousled every which way, his face taut. He looked dangerous and reckless, not at all like his usual controlled self. "You have no idea," he said, "how much I want you."

"I think . . . I think I may have some idea," she said breathlessly. His hand had moved down to rest lightly between her legs. She could feel the warmth of his skin against hers, and it wasn't enough. Her hips rocked involuntarily.

Without taking his eyes from hers, Marcus touched her. Her eyelids dropped as her neck arched, her body undulating to push his fingers deeper. For a long moment he stroked her, but she was already slippery wet. It was wildly exciting to realize her desire for him matched his for her—or nearly so, Marcus thought, bracing himself on one arm and pressing into her. He didn't think anything could compare with how much he wanted her.

He meant to be gentle—gentle and patient and kind, a gentleman. More like the man she had once loved. Last night had been so frenzied and desperate because he had been . . . frenzied and desperate. After yesterday, when he had thought he would lose her forever, he'd utterly lost his mind and made love to her with a ruthlessness that shocked him; he wasn't like that. A *gentleman* wasn't like that. He had never lost control of himself that way, with a woman or with anyone else. But her uninhibited response had also shocked him, not only for being unanticipated but for being more arousing than he had thought possible.

That had been the moment he realized he had fallen for her, unexpectedly and inexplicably—but also, he suspected, irrevocably.

He had woken in the middle of the night, Hannah sound asleep in his arms, and lay awake a long time trying to figure out what had happened to him. She wasn't the woman he had ever pictured at his side— two months ago he would have laughed at the idea of even knowing such a woman—but she was the one he found he couldn't do without, the one he wanted more than anything or anyone he had ever wanted in his life. He didn't give a damn what society said about him for it. She was good for him, he had realized; she was perfect for him. And he meant to do anything to keep her with him.

But as he moved slowly, gently, inside her, Hannah wasn't having it. She didn't want him restrained and proper, she wanted the hungry, devouring lover he'd been last night. Like champagne, she liked the taste of it at once, and wanted more. She raked her nails lightly down his back to clasp his backside. He stiffened, looking down at her in surprise. Hannah flexed her spine and pulled him tighter against her. "I'm not made of glass, you know," she whispered.

"I see that." He cupped her cheek in his big hand, rubbing his thumb over her lips until she took it between her teeth and bit him. He blinked, then pressed her face to the side, baring her neck. Hannah heard a faint squeak—goodness, had she made that sound?—as he nipped her back, right on that spot below her ear, just as he thrust powerfully into her. The next thrust rocked her hips off the bed, and then his fingers were between their bodies, and Hannah almost screamed as he pressed with exquisite delicacy. "Better?" he breathed in her ear. Hannah tried to move her head yes, as he came into her again. She dug her toes into the sheets, straining even closer to him. He groaned, but didn't speed up. Hannah felt desperate; almost, almost, almost . . . until release splashed through her. And then his restraint seemed to snap, and he drove into her again and again with long hard thrusts that probably should have hurt but instead only pushed her farther into the waves of pleasure that kept coming until she thought she wouldn't survive it. She could hardly breathe—she saw stars dancing before her dazed eyes. . . .

Just when it seemed too much, Marcus stopped, shuddering with his own release. His forehead touched hers, his breathing ragged against her lips. "Not glass," he said on a sigh. "Fire."

The intense pleasure burst, like a bubble popping inside her, the last ripples swirling against her bones. She couldn't have moved if she wanted to, her strength completely washed away by the sense of complete contentment coursing through her. Marcus shifted, adjusting his weight, then relaxed with a sigh on top of her, as if he, too, couldn't—or didn't want to—move.

Slowly her heart returned to a normal rhythm. He still lay motionless across her, his arms around her and his head on her shoulder. It was, quite simply, perfect. Here, alone with him, Hannah forgot about the outside world, the explanations that would be required, the difficult choices that must be made. Here in his arms, it only mattered that she loved him.

Hannah didn't hear the door open on the other side of the room. She didn't hear what, if anything, Lily said. She did hear the crash of the breakfast tray hitting the floor, as every cup and dish slid off and shattered. She gasped. Marcus lifted his head.

"Go," he ordered. Hannah peeked around his arm to see Lily, her face white, her wide eyes fixed on them. Hannah flushed, realizing how obvious it was what they were doing.

Abruptly Lily blinked, then fell to her knees and began stacking the broken dishes back on the tray. Lily must be even more embarrassed than she was, and probably feared getting sacked as well. And yet, as embarrassing as it was to be caught in this position, Hannah felt a horrid urge to laugh. She squeezed Marcus's shoulder in mute appeal.

He glanced down at her, banked desire still warming his eyes. "Leave it," he said, almost lazily. The clink of china continued unabated. "Leave," he said again, with an edge. The clinks stopped immediately, and a moment later the door opened and closed softly.

"Oh, dear," Hannah whispered.

His eyebrow arched, and he draped one arm across her, sending a thrill through Hannah that had nothing to do with Lily. "What?"

"I should have told her to knock," she said, her voice shaking with suppressed laughter.

He shrugged. "No doubt she will, from now on." Hannah lost her battle against the giggles, and she laughed until her side hurt. Marcus just watched her, smiling. When she finally calmed down a bit, he leaned down, his palm caressing her hip suggestively, and murmured, "We must use my bed next time. No one would ever disturb us there."

She laughed again. Marcus was teasing her, still a rare and unexpected thing. He grinned, wiggling his eyebrows and looking like a naughty boy plotting more mischief. How she loved him like this. And what he'd said: from now on. *I want you to stay forever,* echoed his voice from last night. Hannah pushed away the question, almost before it could form, what precisely that meant. She wasn't going to let that worry ruin this moment; there would be plenty of time to ask him later. Instead she looped her arms around his neck and gave herself over to that happiness.

"I suppose we shall have to go down to breakfast," he said sometime later. "Now that every maid in the house will have been warned to stay out of this room."

Hannah laughed, rubbing her cheek against his chest. His fingers were playing in her hair, which felt like one great tangle. "I suppose. Although it sounds like too much work, getting up, getting dressed . . ."

"Hmm. There was that suggestion of wearing only the pearls." He stroked all the way down her back. "I should like to see that sometime," he added, making Hannah blush. His hand slowed to a stop just above the curve of her bottom. "Alas, I have other pressing matters this morning."

Of course. David. His name lingered unspoken between them. She could sense Marcus's withdrawal as the silence lengthened, and she touched his arm, clinging to the closeness of a few moments ago. "What will you do?" she asked quietly.

His eyes focused on her again, and he sighed. "I don't know. I vowed David would be his own man after what he did. I told myself I would let him go his own way, any wicked way he chose, and suffer the consequences. I fear I have contributed to his actions by saving him too many times."

"But someone beat him very badly." David ought to bear the consequences of his actions; Hannah was all in favor of that. But he didn't deserve to be killed. Marcus should at least know what his brother was involved in, given what he had suspected.

"Yes. I know." He kissed her. "So I am suspending judgment until David has told me his story."

Hannah could only kiss him back. For all his exacting, strict ways, he had the heart to suspend judgment for his brother, who really had behaved abominably.

"As happily as I could stay here with you all day," he broke off the kiss to say, "I cannot." Hannah heaved a sigh, but didn't protest. She started to sit up, but he caught her arm. "David also wronged you. Is there anything you wish to say to him?"

She turned to him, unable to keep the silly smile from her face. "Despite his trickery, things have come out rather well, don't you think? I'm feeling rather lenient toward David at the moment."

His face softened again, and he grinned back. "An excellent point." The grin faded. "I shall only hope his other actions turn out so fortunately."

Marcus went to David's room, bracing himself for what he might hear. Or not hear. Would David tell him anything? Would he take offense at any questions? Marcus just didn't know.

He tapped at the door, then opened it at the muffled summons. David reclined in bed against a mass of pillows, the *Times* in one hand and a coffee cup in the other. A breakfast tray at his side was covered with empty dishes. He put down the newspaper at the sight of Marcus.

"Good morning."

David took another sip of coffee. "Is it?"

Marcus checked the quick spike in his temper. "Thus far."

His brother put the cup back on the tray, a grim set to his mouth. "I expect you've spent the night planning how to tell me off, so have a go." He sat back and folded his arms with a look of sullen martyrdom.

A smile came to Marcus's face in spite of himself. "To tell the truth," he replied, "I've hardly thought of you at all since last evening." David's eyes narrowed warily. "I came to see that you are well, and, should you have anything to tell me, to listen."

A variety of expressions crossed David's face. Surprise, followed closely by suspicion, then dawning interest. "Hannah," he said at last. "That sounds like something she would say."

Marcus said nothing, and could only hope his thoughts didn't show on his face. Hannah, indeed.

"Well, well," said David, sounding rather pleased, "don't say she got to you, old chap."

He refused to take the bait. "She sends her sincere wishes for your recovery."

David waited expectantly, but when Marcus said nothing more, he gave a cynical laugh. "She'd best save them until you finish with me. What sort of penance shall you exact?"

"None. I meant what I said. I'm through nagging and scolding you. It appears you've already taken a thrashing from someone for something"—David scowled—"and I have no interest in finishing you off. You're welcome to stay until you are well, and then go. But this is the extent of my forbearance," he added. "For what you've done to Rosalind and Celia, not to mention to Hannah, my patience is at an end. The slight to myself I can disregard; we've always treated each other as squabbling boys. But no more. I won't respond to it in the future. Should you ever decide to deal with me reasonably, I shall be more than glad to reciprocate in kind, but until then . . ." He shrugged. "You are your own man, David."

His brother's mouth was hanging open. "I say," he began in an awed voice.

"So, now that I have seen you are well, I leave you to your rest." He inclined his head, and turned toward the door with a much lighter heart than expected. All the times he had scolded David, he'd always left with a dread of what David would do next to spite him. This time, he didn't care. Hannah was right; he couldn't save David from himself. If his brother really didn't want his help, why should he keep trying to force it on him?

"Wait." Marcus stopped in the doorway at David's voice. "You're not even going to ring a peal over me?"

"Would it do any good?" Marcus shrugged. "I see no point."

"You're not going to do anything at all?"

He met his brother's incredulous gaze. "Aren't you relieved?"

David cleared his throat, looking severely disconcerted. "Yes, I suppose, but . . . ahem. But the thing is . . ." He paused. "The thing is, I'm in a bit of a difficult spot, and to tell the truth, I was . . . Well, I intended to accept whatever you decreed, because I may need a bit of advice." Marcus waited. "Or rather, help," David muttered.

"What sort of difficult spot?"

David shifted uncomfortably. "With some bad fellows. Over money."

Marcus moved into the room and took a seat. "Oh?"

David fiddled with the dishes on the tray. "I suppose I should start at the beginning," he said. Marcus nodded once in assent. His brother fidgeted some more, then took a deep breath. "The trouble is, it isn't just about money, not in the usual sense. I seem to have fallen in with"—David sighed—"counterfeiters."

"Hmm," said Marcus quietly. David shot him a piercing glance.

"You don't seem at all surprised." Marcus just shook his head. "But then—then you knew, all along? And you didn't say anything?"

"I suspected," Marcus corrected. "And I attempted to discover the truth for myself, until I unexpectedly found myself married." David actually winced. "My efforts to investigate further were somewhat hampered by escorting a wife about town."

His brother groaned. "Shouldn't surprise me," he muttered. "You always were smarter than I was." Marcus was inwardly shocked by that admission, but didn't react to it. For a minute David stared morosely at his hands, then roused himself again.

"It was the tailor's assistant," David said. "Weston refused my custom, out of some snit over bills, and I had just begun patronizing Horrocks. Slocum, the assistant, was fitting a new jacket for me one day and began telling me about a mill he had heard of from another gentleman. I was interested—this was before the Season had begun, and life was dull—and Slocum said he would try to discover more."

"A tailor's assistant?" asked Marcus. David flipped one hand, annoyed.

"Dash it all, I know! I wasn't thinking clearly. It had been a while since I'd seen a good fight, and . . ." He sighed. "But Slocum put me in contact with a chap named Rourke, and we went out to see the fight. It was a smashing one, too, two bruising fellows. Of course everyone was wagering, and Rourke and I were no different. Every now and then he would joke with me about raising the stakes, depending on how his fellow was doing, and I laughed along with him. It seemed a very close contest, but at one point, one chap—his— fell to the ground bleeding heavily. Rourke said at once he was out, but I pressed him." David shuddered. "I challenged him to double the stakes. No sooner had he agreed than the bloody fellow got to his feet and laid into my man. Not ten minutes later he was declared the winner. When I tried to settle my debt with Rourke, I was shocked to discover all his trifling remarks about the stake had not been in jest, and he considered that I had lost . . ." David closed his mouth and looked away.

"How much?"

David dragged one hand over his face. "Twelve thousand pounds."

Marcus could only stare in amazement. "And did you challenge his claim that the stake had been raised so often?"

David wiggled his shoulders, his brow lowered moodily. "There wasn't much I could say, was there? Gentleman's honor."

Marcus clamped his mouth shut to keep from yelling. David's honor wasn't the issue at the moment. "And how did you get in with the counterfeiters?"

There was a flash of regret and disgust in his brother's eyes. "Soon afterward. While I was scrambling for a way to make good my vowels, Rourke called and told me he had a way out of my predicament. Some associates of his were looking for someone to render some small service; a trifle, he called it, not difficult or disruptive to one's way of life. Naturally I was interested." He paused. "I should have known, when Rourke said he would consider the debt paid," he said bitterly. "What they asked was too simple. They wanted me to gamble. To flush out a cheat, they said, someone who had robbed them of something priceless. It wasn't all that clearly explained, but I gathered he was a person of some importance, someone they couldn't name publicly without fearing retribution from him. They said they didn't want to tell me his name, to prevent me from giving it away.

"In any event, they wanted me to gamble with the highest society possible. They would bankroll it entirely, they said, so I wouldn't feel constrained; winning was not important to them. And Rourke vouched for the fellows, and assured me he would consider our wager settled. So I agreed."

Marcus had been trying not to say anything for some time. "All you had to do was gamble," he repeated carefully. "They would give you the money, and didn't even mind if you lost everything. What on earth made you trust them?"

David swore. "I'm getting there," he muttered. He shoved another pillow behind him. "Slocum was the conduit. He sent rolls of notes with the clothing I had ordered. Huge, fat rolls of notes." He sighed. "It was too easy, I know, but they said they would be watching, in secret, and would be gathering evidence to prove this mysterious person's guilt. I never did make out how they were going to expose him, but they said that wasn't really my concern. I could accept the offer as they posed it, or not at all, and just pay Rourke the twelve thousand."

Marcus massaged his brow wearily with one hand. "They set a trap for you, Rourke and the lot."

"Of course they did," David snapped. "I didn't realize that until later, though. At the time . . ." He made a helpless gesture. "At the time it seemed like an easy way out of a scrape."

Marcus felt a pinch of guilt. He had been responsible for that. All the times David had come to him for help, he had given it, but only with scoldings and lectures. It was only a matter of time before his brother agreed to something stupid to avoid him.

"For a fortnight it was easy," David continued. "No matter how much I lost, another bundle of notes would arrive with a new jacket or waistcoat. They never asked for an accounting. I had the worst run of luck, couldn't win a shilling. But then . . ." He hesitated. "Well, I had bills to pay, and the notes just arrived right on schedule. So I paid a few merchants with them. I told the fellows I'd gambled it away, of course. My luck improved, I won most of it back, and then I suppose I thought I'd pushed my luck far enough. I told them they ought to have enough proof by now, and I wanted out. They refused. That was when they hinted that I might have been doing something illegal. I'm no scholar, but I began to suspect what the notes where. It seemed a hopeless coil. I didn't know what to do."

His voice fell. "I knew it was foolhardy to carry on with Jocelyn, but my position was desperate. I almost didn't care if Barlow found out and killed me. I'm sorry I cut up at you for telling me to leave London. It really was the answer to my prayers, simply to disappear without notice, and if anyone questioned me, I could blame it on you."

"How convenient," Marcus murmured dryly.

"Well, yes." David raised his hands and let them drop, looking guilty for the first time. "As for the rest, well, if you'd known what Hannah was facing, you'd have understood. She was so kind to me, understanding and sympathetic but not condescending or coddling. I broke my leg and wrenched my shoulder in a carriage accident, and she nursed me back to health. And I wanted to help her—truly I did. You must believe me, Marcus. I did mean to marry her and reform my life to be a good husband, when I asked her."

For some reason this didn't sit very well with Marcus, even though David's motives had been far nobler than expected. He shifted in his seat and said nothing.

"But you know what I am. A husband and a father, all at once? I began to doubt. And then I began to panic. Percy brought your letter, and I realized I should have to give up all my mates to be the sort of husband Hannah deserved. She deserved someone better. Someone more like you."

Marcus only just kept his jaw from dropping.

"I didn't know how to get out of it, though, without publicly humiliating her. It was the night before the wedding; what was I to do?" David pushed one hand through his hair in frustration. "I know I owe you an apology for it, but I couldn't think of any other way."

"Do you know how she discovered what you'd done?" asked Marcus, recovering his self-possession. David shook his head with an apprehensive glance. "When I told her. And presented the marriage register I'd fetched from Middleborough. I have never seen anyone look so horrified."

David shifted his legs restlessly beneath the covers. "You could have gotten that register changed."

"And the notice in the *Times?* The letter to Rosalind?"

David flushed dark red. "I wanted to make certain you gave Hannah a handsome settlement. I never imagined you would . . ." His voice trailed off.

"I planned to. But, perhaps you might have guessed, Rosalind came to London to see for herself, and despite Hannah's protestations to the contrary, she believed the marriage was real. What was *I* to do then?"

David looked at him for a long moment. "Thank you," he said humbly at last. "It was a terrible trick to play."

Marcus raised a brow. "On Hannah, or on Rosalind and Celia?"

"All of them."

Marcus exhaled slowly and evenly. "Then perhaps I am not the only one who should hear the apology."

David nodded miserably. "I'll speak to them. I swear." His color had faded, and he looked tired again. Marcus had seen his brother in many states and situations, and yet never had David looked so defeated.

"How are you feeling?" Marcus asked, a little more kindly.

David lifted one shoulder, then winced. "No worse than I deserve. Rourke and his mates tracked me down the second I set foot in London again. I came here only because I knew they wouldn't dare follow."

Marcus got to his feet, and clapped his brother's shoulder. "Then get some rest. I assume the ladies will be by at some point, to check on your health." David nodded, eyes fixed on his hands. "We'll deal with Rourke and his lot later. No doubt between your reckless daring and my coldhearted calculation, we'll come up with something."

His brother looked up in shock. Marcus grinned a little. "It's a jest, David." And David was only just beginning to laugh as he left.

CHAPTER 19

If Hannah hadn't been starving, but too self-conscious to ring for Lily, she might have spent the entire day in bed. Every servant, she was sure, would know that she and Marcus had spent the night together. Hannah had almost gotten used to the servants, but felt awkward all over again now that her most personal relationship was gossip fodder.

But once Marcus had gone, the allure of staying in bed faded, and reality intruded again. What would she say to Rosalind and Celia? Would she ever be able to look Lily in the face again? And was she even prepared to be a duchess indefinitely? Part of what had gotten her through the last few weeks was the fact that she was just acting, and for only a short time. Could she possibly keep it up for months and even years?

Then she got out of bed, and caught sight of her dressing table. All the bottles of perfume and cosmetics still lay in a jumble on the floor, and the table itself stood at a crazy angle to the wall, the chair lying on its side a few feet away. Remembering what had happened to the table—and to her, on the table—made her blush, and smile, and feel rather recklessly ready to be Marcus's duchess for the rest of her life.

Bravado carried her through getting dressed and brushing out her hair, a task that again made her blood heat from the memories of how it had gotten into such a dreadful snarl. She was utterly smitten, and even laughed out loud at her own ridiculously happy reflection. Anyone who hadn't heard about it through the servants' quarters would most likely guess just from looking at her that she had spent the night making love.

The second she set foot in the breakfast room, she knew the news had gotten about. Both Rosalind and Celia were sitting quietly at the table, eating. Neither looked up at her entrance. Hannah grinned. She knew for a fact they would have been both still abed had they no idea, and wondered how long they'd been sitting here waiting for her. She went to fill her plate, her step lighter.

"Good morning."

"Good morning, Hannah." Rosalind looked up at once with a beaming smile. "How are you this morning? Did you sleep well?"

Hannah glanced at Celia, who was slicing her ham into minute pieces, listening so hard her ears were practically red. "Yes, thank you, very well." The footman pulled out a chair for her, and she took up her napkin.

"You may go," said Rosalind to the footman, a little too eagerly. Hannah took a bite of toast and tried to pretend she didn't know what was afoot. "Have you seen Marcus this morning?" continued Rosalind. "I had an important question to discuss with him, but he seems to have gone missing. I shall have to send for Telman to track him down."

Hannah swallowed her toast and took a sip of tea. For the first time she didn't feel like a guest at this table, like an imposter. "I believe he mentioned going to speak to David," she said.

Celia dropped her knife with a clank. Rosalind sucked in a noisy breath. Hannah poured a spoonful of sugar into her tea, then added another spoonful. Why not?

"Then you've seen him."

"Yes." She took another egg as well, and some bacon. For some reason she was starving hungry.

"And . . . and has he decided everything from last night?" Rosalind asked cautiously. Hannah could see she was almost holding her breath.

She chewed her bite of bacon. "I believe so."

"Well?" burst out Celia at last. "What have you decided? Are you staying? Did you speak to him?"

"Celia!" Rosalind glared at her daughter before turning to Hannah. "Did you speak to him? Are you staying?"

Hannah took another sip of tea, watching them over the rim of her cup. Rosalind was concealing her desire to know only slightly better than Celia was. And the sight of such hope, such delight, made Hannah's heart swell with happiness at the thought of being part of their family. "Yes," she said, setting down her cup. "I spoke to him." Among other things. "And I shall stay in London—"

At that, Celia shrieked and bounded out of her chair to throw her arms around Hannah. "Oh, that's wonderful! So very, very wonderful! Did you take my advice?" she demanded, pulling back to peer eagerly at Hannah's face. "Did you tell him?"

"Ah . . ." Her face warm, Hannah tried to remember just what she had said. Neither of them had mentioned love, exactly. "In a manner of speaking."

"Really? What man—?"

"Celia!" Rosalind exclaimed. "Your manners!"

Celia grinned widely, but didn't press it. "Well, I am very happy you're to stay, no matter what you told him! I knew he would never let you just walk away; Marcus is far too clever to do that. Even if he won't admit it out loud, he must know how he feels, and sooner or later he'll tell you—"

"Celia," cried Rosalind again. "That is quite enough."

Celia pursed her lips, not looking too regretful. "Yes, Mama."

"This is indeed wonderful, wonderful news. Oh, Hannah!" And now Rosalind couldn't contain herself any longer, and Hannah was hugged all over again.

"Oh dear." Rosalind released her and dabbed at her eyes. "What a wonderful relief! Why, when I think of how we fussed at you—but we shan't dwell on that," she finished hastily. "And now we simply must have a ball. In case any wretched lies spread about town regarding this. Poor David, to return home so ill! I vow, the boy was out of his mind in a delirium to say such things! From the moment I saw him I knew he was feverish, and didn't trust a word he said!"

"Mama, may I have a blue gown this time, instead of white?" Celia asked eagerly. Her mother smiled at her.

"Yes, my child, this time you may have whatever you like. Do ring for Mrs. Potts at once. We shall have the ball in a week's time—now Hannah, you mustn't worry a bit," she warned Hannah, who had opened her mouth. "It is absolutely vital to have as grand a ball as possible. Marcus will agree with me on this. And the sooner we have it, the sooner any . . . unpleasantness will fade away and be forgotten."

Hannah shook her head, grinning. "I wasn't about to protest. I wanted to thank you, Rosalind. For everything."

The older woman blinked several times, then threw her arms around Hannah again. "I shall have Madame

Lescaut here within an hour," she declared. "We shall order a gown worthy of any duchess's presentation ball!"

Thinking of all the magnificent gowns upstairs that she had yet to wear, Hannah mentally groaned. The last thing she felt like doing was ordering more clothing today. Today she was too happy, too light, to sit indoors and examine fabric swatches. She wanted to take Molly and go running and screaming in the park. She wanted to climb trees and wade in the lake and have an absolutely smashing good time, and then come home. Home, to Marcus. "I haven't yet told Molly," she said to Rosalind, easing free of her embrace.

"She'll be delighted," said Celia with a whoop. "As am I! Lord, Hannah, I just can't believe it! First it was such a surprise, when we first got David's letter, and then to find out he was—well—and then this morning!"

"But of course you must tell Molly," Rosalind cut in. "I shall start the preparations for the ball. You mustn't worry at all about it! Oh, my dear! I've longed to plan this ball for years!" And she threw her arms around Hannah one last time.

After breakfast Hannah skipped up the stairs and opened the nursery door, her heart light. At her entrance, Lily whirled around with a gasp. She lowered her eyes and stepped back, revealing Molly, dressed and ready to go out.

She beamed and waved. "Good morning, Mama! Lily is taking me to see the ducks this morning! Do you want to come with us, Mama?"

Hannah glanced at the maid in surprise; Lily had never taken Molly to the park before without being asked. Even with her face tucked down, Lily seemed to sense the question. "I thought it best, madam. I thought perhaps you wouldn't want to be disturbed for the rest of the day."

Oh. Right. The last time she had seen Lily had been

over Marcus's naked shoulder, right after he made love to her. Hannah tried not to smile at the memory. "Thank you, Lily, but I shall take Molly today. You are dismissed."

The maid didn't move as Molly jumped up and down and clapped her hands. "Dismissed, madam?"

"Yes, until dinner." Hannah caught up her daughter and swung her around, making Molly shriek. "Today shall be my Molly day: all day with Molly."

"And may we have a picnic?" Hannah nodded, and Molly shrieked with glee, flinging her arms around Hannah's neck, her sturdy little legs kicking.

"Oh, Mama, it will be so much fun! Shall we see the ducks? And watch the fancy carriages? And pet some dogs? And fly my kite?"

"Enough!" Hannah laughed. "We only have a few hours, Molly; we may have to save some fun for tomorrow. But I see you are already dressed to go, so shall we be on our way?"

Molly nodded, eyes glowing, and Hannah hugged her close. Turning toward the doorway, she paused. Lily still stood where she had been, head bowed and hands clenched. Hannah stepped closer and lowered her voice.

"Don't worry, Lily; all is well." On impulse, she added, "You may have the rest of the day free, to do as you like."

The maid raised her red-rimmed eyes. "Yes, madam," she whispered. "Thank you, madam."

Hannah smiled encouragingly at her, then hurried out the door to ward off the creeping discomfort. Heavens, it would take her a long time not to be self-conscious around Lily! But it wouldn't be fair to sack the girl for innocently walking into the room, so Hannah supposed she would just have to get over it.

"Molly," Hannah began, after they had eaten their

picnic, fed the crumbs to the ducks, and petted four passing dogs. "Would you like to stay here in London?"

"Oh, yes, Mama." Molly didn't look up from where she was tracking a trail of ants through the grass. "I like it here."

"Well, I believe we shall," Hannah said. "Indefinitely."

Molly looked up. "What's indebitately?"

Hannah smiled. "Indefinitely means forever."

"Hurray!" said Molly with a sunny smile. "And now that David is back, will he be my papa again?"

Hannah's mouth opened, then closed without a word. Why hadn't she expected that question? "No," she said carefully. "Not David. He was never going to be your new papa. But what do you think about his brother, the duke? Do you like him?"

"Oh, I like Extera," said Molly at once. "Will he let me dig in the garden, if we stay?"

Hannah cleared her throat. "Well, perhaps. We may ask him."

"All right." Molly had found a stick and started poking at the ants. "Look, Mama!" she squealed. "I can make them go around it!"

Hannah stared at her daughter, bemused. So much for the questions she'd feared. And the thought of Molly asking Marcus if she could dig in his garden was just too funny. She dutifully leaned over to see what Molly was inflicting on the hapless ants of Hyde Park.

The rest of the day sped by. Marcus returned home with a satisfied look in his eyes, and murmured to her that he had something to share with her over dinner— in their suite. Hannah blushed, agreed, and went to say good night early to Molly. Her daughter had been tired out by the day in the park, and could stand an early night. Humming under her breath, Hannah hurried up the stairs to the nursery.

The room was empty. All the toys were neatly put away, the table cleared of dinner. Hannah went across the room to the little bedroom where Molly slept. She had resisted moving Molly up here at first, but her little girl loved it, with the big sunny room filled with toys, her own little bed rather than the trundle under Hannah's bed at the vicarage, and of course a staircase of her very own, opening into the duchess's suite. Hannah made a mental note to make sure that door was closed, so she and Marcus would have a moment's warning in case Molly came down in the night.

She opened Molly's door. This room was also empty. Hannah frowned, looking around. Had Celia taken Molly out? Then she saw the paper on the pillow.

Her steps weighted with dread, Hannah crossed the room. There was something wrong about that scrap of paper, lying where her child should be. She lifted the paper as if it might bite her, and read. Her breath stopped in her throat at the words it held.

Blindly she groped her way to the door, unable to look away from those terrible words. Her heart had stopped beating and was now wedged in her throat—she couldn't breathe—she felt faint.

The door opened before her hand and Marcus stepped into the breach. "There you are," he said with a hint of smile that quickly disappeared. "What's the matter?"

Mute, Hannah held out her trembling hand. Shooting her a concerned look, he took the paper and read it.

"My baby," she choked out, before he seized her in his arms, holding her tightly against him. Hannah clutched at his arms as a sob of terror burst from her throat.

"Shh," Marcus said, pressing her face into his shoulder as he scanned the room over her head. The nursery was clean and tidy, with the last sunlight of the afternoon illuminating the shelves of books and dolls. Through the open doorway, he could see a little bed, neatly made. Nothing seemed out of place, and yet . . .

His eyes dropped to the coarse scrap of paper in his hand. *We have the brat,* said the fairly undistinguished handwriting. Why would someone take Molly?

Hannah shuddered in his arms again, and he forced the thought away. Why didn't matter—it was who, and how to get her back, that mattered. And he couldn't deal with that until he got Hannah settled.

Keeping her tight in his arm, he guided her down the stairs to her room. He rang for the housekeeper, instructing her to send for a doctor and to send a maid for tea. Hannah, blank-faced with shock, let him tuck her into a chair with a blanket around her legs. He knelt beside her, his stomach seized with fear at the horrible look in her eyes.

"Hannah," he said softly, taking her hand. "I promise I will find her, darling."

She looked at him with wide, tear-filled eyes, and Marcus felt his own throat tighten. He clasped her hand between his, and pressed his lips to her knuckles. "As God is my witness, you shall have her back soon," he vowed in a silent whisper.

At that moment, Rosalind rushed through the door. "What is wrong? Marcus, has something happened?"

He laid Hannah's hand back on her knee and got to his feet. "Yes. Stay with her, Rosalind." Ignoring his stepmother's startled exclamations, he went into his suite and closed the door. He took a deep breath and closed his eyes. Then he took out the note and read it again.

He summoned the butler, but Harper knew nothing. Marcus dispatched several servants to search the grounds, but he didn't expect them to find much. The ticking of the clock seemed loud and strident; he couldn't sit around and wait for the servants to search. The grounds of Exeter House were too expansive. He couldn't waste the time, and he had a good idea who was behind it anyway. Moments later, he stepped into his brother's room. David, cushioned on a heap of pillows, looked up from a book, eyebrows raised in question.

"Tell me where to find Rourke and his rabble," said Marcus.

Hannah was barely aware of Rosalind's presence. Her mind seemed to be stuck revolving around two words: Molly's missing, Molly's missing, Molly's missing . . .

Rosalind left after a while, saying something about a tisane. Hannah hardly noticed. Lily came in with a pot of tea, but Hannah ignored it. Tea wasn't going to help anything.

"Your Grace?" Hannah forced her eyes up at Lily's hesitant voice. Her maid was holding out Missy, Molly's battered doll.

Tears pooled in her eyes. She took the doll, smoothing the worn cotton dress she'd made for Missy out of scraps from the vicarage curtains. Molly would be terrified without Missy. The tears ran down her face. Who had stolen her baby? And why?

"Please, Your Grace, don't weep," pleaded Lily, on her knees at Hannah's feet. She clutched Hannah's arm. "She's fine, I'm sure of it. You mustn't make yourself ill." Clutching Missy to her breast, Hannah wept, barely listening.

But this was indulgent. For once in her life her father's words rang through her mind helpfully. Why cry about it, girl, she could almost hear him say; do something. Yes, Hannah thought hazily, she must do something. Molly needed her. She couldn't sit here and weep; she must try to find her daughter. But how? Her mind felt thick and muddled as she prodded it to work.

"Please, Your Grace," said Lily again, growing more distraught as she made no response. "Please! Listen to me. Your daughter is well. She is unharmed. I know it."

Something about that broke through Hannah's daze. "What? How do you know?"

"I know it, I do," declared the maid passionately. "You'll have her returned to you soon, I'm sure of it."

"How do you know?" repeated Hannah, less stunned and more confused. "Why would you say that, Lily?"

The girl opened her mouth, then hesitated. She took a closer look at Hannah's expression and gave a tiny shake of her head. "I—I am sure she will be found soon. You must believe that. . . ."

"Why, Lily?" She lurched to her feet, setting Lily off balance. The maid tumbled over backward, then scrambled awkwardly to her knees. "Why are you so sure?"

"I . . . I . . . Ooh!" Hannah grabbed hold of Lily's arm and gave her a terrific shake. "Please, madam!" cried the girl.

"Where is my daughter?" Hannah demanded with another shake. "What do you know, Lily? Why are you so sure she'll be returned soon and is unharmed? You were watching her, Lily. Where is my baby?"

Tears sprang up in Lily's eyes as Hannah's voice rose. She twisted under Hannah's hand, still gripping her shoulder. "I can't say, Your Grace! I can't tell you!"

Hannah seized the closest thing at hand on the dressing table, the engraved silver hairbrush, and raised it over Lily's head in threat. Only a very small part of her was really aware of what she was doing; the other part was ready to beat Lily until she got her daughter back. If Lily had been responsible—if she had put Molly in harm's way . . . "Where is she, Lily? Did you have anything to do with her going missing?"

Lily let out a terrified squeak. "No! I mean, I only kept her safe! I would never let anyone harm Miss Molly—"

"Where is my child?" shrieked Hannah. Lily also shrieked, and ducked a little.

"I'm sorry," she sobbed, cowering. "I'm sorry. She's not hurt, I promise!"

Hannah dragged her to her feet. "Take me to her, *now*." She kept the hairbrush in her hand. Clutching her apron to her face, Lily led the way, up the servants' stair into a part of the house Hannah had never seen. At the end of a long corridor, Lily opened the door of a small room. Several irons sat on the hearth, and a large sewing basket sat near a straight-backed chair next to a narrow window. As Hannah watched in amazement, the maid pressed hard against a carved rose on a wall panel, and lowered the panel to a horizontal position as it came out of the wall. There was a cavity behind it, dark but warm. Hannah could feel the warmth. She stepped closer and peered in.

"Molly?" she called. Silence. She turned a dangerous glare on Lily. The maid moistened her lips and leaned forward, into the space.

"Miss Molly!" she called softly. "The game is over. You've won."

There was a clunk, and a scramble, and then Molly's blond head popped out, her face wreathed in smiles. "I won, Mama!" she crowed.

Hannah dropped the hairbrush and reached for Molly, pulling her out of the wall and into her arms. "You did, darling, you won." Her arms shook as she held her daughter close. When her voice was steady enough to speak aloud, she smoothed back Molly's tangled curls and searched her face. Molly was already in her nightclothes; how long had she been here?

"How did you think to hide here? I never would have found you."

Molly beamed, not at all hurt or scared. Thank heavens for that. "Lily showed me the best hiding place, Mama. Even Celia doesn't know about this one! Only now it's no good, because you found me and now you'll know where to look when I hide."

"Oh, Molly." Words failed her again, and Hannah hugged her, too relieved to scold her. Lily, on the other hand . . .

Setting Molly down, but holding her hand tightly, Hannah turned to the maid, who now stood against the wall, her fists clenched in her apron. She looked terrified and belligerent and remorseful, all at once. "Come with us, Lily," she said as calmly as she could. Lily's chin dropped, but she nodded, and trailed quietly after them back to the family quarters.

At Celia's door, Hannah knocked, and a moment later Celia's face appeared. She had started getting ready for bed. "Yes?"

"Celia, may Molly sleep in your room tonight?"

Celia's eyes widened as Molly gave a little cry of joy. "Of course," she said, her eyes flickering past Hannah to Lily. "Come in, Molly." Molly bounded through the door, leaping into the middle of Celia's bed. Celia leaned forward. "Is something wrong, Hannah?"

Hannah gave her a tight smile. "I shall tell you in the morning. But if you would keep Molly with you, it would be a great help."

A moment of disappointment crossed Celia's face, but she masked it well. "Of course. You will tell me, won't you? Marcus always promises to tell me in the morning, and by then he's come up with a reason why he should not tell me after all."

On impulse Hannah gave her a quick hug. "I do promise. But keep Molly with you at all times. And ring for help if there is anything troubling or alarming, anything at all."

Celia nodded, solemn-faced. Hannah bid Molly good night, which her daughter returned with a cheery wave, and turned to Lily as Celia closed, and locked, her door.

"Now, you come with me."

"Where, madam?" Lily's voice quavered.

"To see the duke." Hannah ignored the girl's frightened gasp and marched off to the duke's study.

"Oh, madam, please," begged Lily as Hannah rapped on Marcus's door. "He'll send me to prison. I brought her back to you, I would never have let anyone hurt her. . . ."

"Lily, you hid my child from me and left a note saying she had been kidnapped." Hannah knocked again, "I don't trust myself to decide what to do with you."

Lily swallowed, her eyes huge.

"Is everything all right, Hannah?" At Rosalind's concerned voice behind her, Lily screamed and jumped as if she'd been shot. Hannah whirled around and grabbed the maid by the arm, to keep her from falling or running away. Rosalind's eyebrows shot up.

"Where is Marcus?" Hannah asked before Rosalind could say anything. "I must see him at once."

"I saw him at David's door not half an hour past. Why, Hannah, what is the matter? Are you feeling better?"

Hannah gave a distracted nod. Still holding Lily, she turned around and went toward David's room, Rosalind staring after them in amazement.

When she peered into the room, David was alone, dozing propped up by several pillows. Someone, probably Telman, had already shaved him and even trimmed his hair, which was still damp. Already he looked much better.

But Marcus was not there. Hannah started to step back out of the room, but David stirred, blinking awake. "What? Who's there?"

"I was looking for Marcus," she said quietly. "I'm sorry I disturbed you."

"Quite all right." He sighed, settling into the pillows again. "You just missed him. He was here not long ago." A frown flitted over his face, then he sat upright again. "I'm glad you've come, though. Hannah, what I did—"

"I'm sorry, David but I really must find Marcus at once." She wasn't in the mood to listen to his apology now.

"It was unpardonable—"

"Really, David—"

"I deserve to be shot—"

"Please, David," said Hannah desperately. "I must find Marcus—Lily's been working with the people who tried to kidnap Molly!"

His eyebrows shot up. "Molly? Kidnapped?"

Hannah nodded. "Yes, I found a note saying they'd taken her—didn't Marcus tell you? But then Lily let slip that she'd taken Molly, and only hidden her instead of handing her over to whomever wanted to snatch her. And I must find Marcus to tell him—" The hysteria she thought she'd tamped down bubbled up again, and she covered her mouth with one hand, feeling just as sick as she had the moment she'd comprehended the note's meaning. She needed Marcus, needed his advice and reassurance that things would be fine. Not being able to find him was shredding her nerves. What if the kidnappers came back, when Lily didn't deliver Molly to them? What if they were armed? What if—what if—

"Hannah." David had gotten out of bed and put on his dressing gown. "I didn't know. What happened?"

Hannah heaved a sigh. "Someone tried to kidnap Molly. But my maid, Lily, was working with them. She was supposed to take Molly to them, I think, but she didn't—but she must know something about the people who tried." She took another deep breath and tried to gather her scrambled thoughts. "Marcus will want to question her, don't you think? I'm so worried they may come back, or try again. But I don't know where he is."

David looked mildly dazed, but he nodded. "No doubt. Here, calm yourself." He pulled the bell. "But everyone is well, aren't they? You said Molly is safe?" Hannah nodded, closing her eyes in relief. There was a light tap at the door, and David ordered the servant to go fetch Marcus at once.

"Have you had some tea?" Hannah opened her eyes to see David looking a bit unsure of himself. She swiped at her eyes, and forced a laugh.

"No, thank you. I don't need tea. I just need—that is, I need to speak to Marcus. Your brother," she amended hastily, but not before a knowing look crossed David's face.

"Ah. I see." He cleared his throat. "So, shall I wish you—"

"No," she said firmly.

"Yes, of course." David looked away, although she saw his smirking grin, and then the servant reappeared, saying his grace had gone out. David glanced at Hannah. "Send Telman in," he directed the servant, who nodded and vanished. David shuffled his feet. "May I apologize now?"

Hannah glared at him. "No."

He closed his mouth with a mumbled, "Sorry."

"David!"

"Sorry, sorry," he said hastily. "I wasn't apologizing for that! Not at all, no, for the—the other thing!" He stopped, looking at her, and then they both choked back nervous laughter.

This was better. Hannah relaxed a little bit in her chair, her heart beginning to slow down. Surely if she could laugh with David, everything else would turn out right.

CHAPTER 20

Telman made his appearance in short order, but had nothing useful to tell them. "He has gone out, my lord," was his reply to David's question.

"Where?" David prodded.

"I cannot tell you, my lord. I do not know."

"What *do* you know?"

Telman stood a little straighter at the impatience in David's question. "Not much, my lord. But I do know he left the house attired in your clothing."

Hannah blinked. She turned to David. "Why would he do that?"

David was watching Telman with narrowed eyes. "Did he say anything at all?"

Telman swallowed. "I have always prided myself on my discretion, my lord, in serving His Grace, and I—"

"What is it, man?" barked David.

"He said nothing to me of where he meant to go or what he would do," finished Telman rapidly, glancing at Hannah, "but I believe he did say something, rather to himself, about your daughter, madam."

Hannah frowned in confusion and instinctive alarm. David swore, then threw off his dressing gown. "Bring a suit of my brother's clothing, *now*," he ordered Telman. The valet bolted for the door, letting it slam behind him. David peeled the sticking plaster from his forehead. "Can your maid cover this?" he asked Hannah, pointing at the cut.

"Yes." Still not understanding completely, Hannah ran into the hall where Lily still stood, her eyes scared and her apron rumpled. "Fetch the cosmetics at once," she ordered. The girl nodded and fled. Hannah ran back.

"What are you going to do, David?" she asked anxiously. "You know something, don't you?"

Looking grim, David nodded. "I told Marcus everything he would need to know to find the fellows who beat me. He must think they took Molly—God, Hannah, I'm so sorry—that's the only reason he would go off in my clothing." A bitter smile twisted his mouth. "What a turnabout, hmm? Marcus posing as me, instead of the other way 'round."

"But Molly is here," Hannah pointed out, confused and approaching hysteria again.

"Marcus doesn't know that." Telman flew back through the door, one of Marcus's finest coats and waistcoats draped over his arm, boots and trousers and shirt in his other hand. David stepped into the trousers, then yanked the nightshirt over his head without a trace of embarrassment and reached for the linen shirt.

Hannah pressed one hand to her mouth and closed her eyes. Marcus was running headlong after the men who had tried to kill David, dressed as David. To save her child. "What will they do to him?" she asked in a shaky voice.

David shrugged, pulling on the waistcoat as Telman tried to knot his cravat. "There's no saying. They weren't too pleased with me, but I can't imagine why they would have tried to steal Molly. You're not my wife after all, and . . ." Lily hurried in then, the cosmetics case in her hands. David pinned her with a cool look. "What do you know about this, girl?"

He sounded so much like Marcus, and had just the right expression on his face, that Lily let out a terrified squeak, stopping in her tracks. Even Hannah, who knew for certain it was David and not Marcus, looked at him in amazement.

"Nothing," Lily stammered. "I—I don't know anything! I was just supposed to b-bring the baby to them, but I couldn't. I didn't! I would never hurt her—"

"To whom were you supposed to bring the child?"

Lily wet her lips, looking to Hannah in mute appeal. "Mr. Reece, madam."

"What?" said Hannah, caught completely off guard. Lily flushed scarlet, the case shaking in her grip. Then David slammed his fist into the wall and muttered, "God damn it all!"

Hannah gave up trying to follow the tangled stories. "Hide the cut on his forehead," she commanded Lily. "I'm coming with you," she said to David as he sat on the bed to pull on the boots.

"The devil you are," he retorted.

"You'll be a better duke with a duchess," she called back as she ran from the room. "Do not leave without me!"

Hannah changed into one of her new dresses in record time. She pinned back the curls that had come loose, and put on her old half boots, in case she needed to run like a country girl instead of stroll like a duchess. Then she hurried back to David's room, where Lily was just finishing. The wound was well concealed, looking more like a shadow on David's forehead, an impression Telman reinforced by quickly combing David's hair a bit forward. It wasn't quite the way Marcus wore his hair, but it was close, and when David faced her, Hannah had to admit he looked very much like the duke of Exeter.

"You're not coming with me," he said.

"I most certainly am." She turned to Lily. "This way."

Lily turned white. "Oh, madam, please! Haven't I tried to help, as much as I can? Please forgive me, I beg you—"

Hannah pushed her into the dressing room that adjoined David's room. "I shall deal with you when I come back." She closed the door on her frightened maid, locked it, and handed the key to the thunderstruck Telman. "Do not let her out."

"No, madam," said the valet faintly. Hannah swept out the door, David in her wake.

They didn't speak again until they were in the carriage, rattling along toward whatever destination David had given the driver. Marcus, they learned, had hailed a cab.

"Are you sure?" Hannah asked at last.

David was staring out the window, his face stony. "Yes."

"But why?" she ventured a moment later. "I don't see what Mr. Reece trying to kidnap Molly has to do with the men who beat you."

David turned. "The men who beat me are counterfeiters," he said. "It's too long to relate now, but I didn't know what they were until I was too far involved to get out easily—as you saw. Bentley must be the one running things; I always suspected Rourke reported to someone else. Using me must have been a grand joke to Bentley. Christ!" He shoved one hand through his hair, uncovering the cut. Hannah leaned forward to brush his hair back into place, and he winced. "He's always been jealous of Marcus," David went on more calmly. "When we were younger, he'd make jokes about how close he was to being a duke, and yet was still just a penniless nobody. Marcus never liked him, and just ignored him, and I . . . well, I just thought he was jealous. But he's not penniless, or never seems to be—"

"Forged money," said Hannah, beginning to understand. "He's spending the counterfeit notes."

David shook his head. "*I* was spending the counterfeit notes, and passing them to other people through card games."

"But . . ." She shook her head, confused again. "What does that have to do with Molly? Why would they want to steal her?"

David sighed. "I don't know. It would make sense if they wanted to get at Marcus instead of at me."

"Does he?" asked Hannah in a shocked voice. "Could that be Bentley's goal all along, Marcus?" David frowned. "If he did," Hannah went on slowly, trying to fit the pieces together as she went, "it might make sense that he used you; if you were convicted of counterfeiting, you would be hanged—"

"Transported," David corrected. "Close enough."

"And then Marcus would have no heir," Hannah continued. "At least not one nearby . . . unless people thought he would have a son. . . ."

"Most likely Bentley planned to keep that from happening. Of course, Marcus showed no inclination to marry—"

"Lady Willoughby!" declared Hannah. "She used to be Marcus's mistress."

David stared. "How the bloody hell do you know that?"

"Rosalind told me. And Lady Willoughby was with Bentley Reece! I saw them one day!"

David blinked, then shook his head. "So what does Susannah have to do with it?"

"Well." Hannah pondered a moment. "She wanted to marry Marcus—Rosalind told me," she said as his eyes widened again. "Perhaps, when I . . . turned up, she was upset—"

"Viciously disappointed, more like," David muttered.

"And then she decided to help Bentley . . . ?" Hannah stopped, too confused. That didn't make sense. David frowned, then leaned forward.

"Bentley would have sought her out. He would have known how much she must have hated Marcus then—and she would have hated him, believe me. And at the same time, his plans must have been altered by Marcus's apparent marriage. For if Marcus fathered a child . . ." His voice trailed off as Hannah gaped.

"Do you suppose Lady Willoughby was working with Bentley all along, hoping to marry Marcus and never to bear him a child?"

David shook his head. "I can credit that she could contrive to marry him and enjoy being a duchess without wanting to become a mother; she's as vain as the very devil. But that would take too long for Bentley. Marcus could live to be ninety and thwart his plan. No, if Susannah were in league with Bentley, you can be sure she planned to be the widowed duchess of Exeter before too long."

Hannah digested that. "She could have killed him," she whispered. "And then Bentley . . ."

"Bentley would be the duke, and if she exercised enough pull over him, Susannah could make him marry her. Or she could just keep her title, and the generous settlement Bentley would be sure to give her."

"If that had ever come to pass," said Hannah in a voice low with fury, "I hope they both would have wondered every moment if the other might kill them, too."

David snorted. "No doubt. But we have to make

sure it doesn't come to pass." He took another look out the window.

"But Lily," Hannah went on. "What was Lily's role?"

David lifted one shoulder. "No idea."

"We saw her going into Marcus's study one night," she continued to think aloud. "But she didn't take anything, not that Marcus could see. And when I wanted to question her, he said no, he preferred to watch her and see what she did next."

"Steal Molly away, that's what she did," said David under his breath. Hannah put up one hand to quiet him.

"But she didn't. Money, then. Could he have paid her to be a spy in Marcus's household?"

"Of course he could have." David frowned. "He would have taken an awful risk, though. Marcus demands, and rewards, unwavering loyalty, and most of the staff have been with the family for years, if not generations. She could have told Marcus everything. Either Bentley did something to Lily that made her more likely to agree to his plan, or she already bore some grudge and he just stumbled across her. She had to have known what Marcus would do to her if she were discovered."

"Yes, I think she did," murmured Hannah, remembering Lily's expression when she had said they were going to the duke. "He'll send me to prison," the maid had said. Lily had known, so why did she do it?

"Well, she may have saved herself by not handing over Molly," said David, cutting into her thoughts. "And no doubt we'll never know the whole story unless Bentley tells us, although I would be delighted to choke it out of him personally. We're almost there."

Hannah started, and lifted the curtain to peer out. The fog was drifting in thicker now, and streetlamps were much scarcer in this part of town. "What will we do, David?"

"You," he said with a stern look, "will follow my lead. Marcus will have my head for bringing you into this, so don't make it worse for me by getting hurt. Remember, he is David. Call me Exeter, or nothing at all. You're supposed to be angry at him for being such an idiot"—David grimaced—"and endangering your daughter. Don't say too much, and don't look at Marcus any more than you have to. Your heart is in your eyes when you do that."

Hannah blushed. "All right. I'll do my best."

He threw her a glance over his shoulder, as he turned to the window again. "You'll do fine. Trust me."

She swallowed nervously. There was one last thing worrying her, something they couldn't do a thing about. "What will Marcus do? What if they discover he's not you, and you're not he?"

David grinned. "I can't answer for what Marcus will do, but if he's smart, he'll play a half-drunk, surly ne'er-do-well ready for his wealthy, powerful brother to step in and save his skin again." She shivered as the carriage slowed to a halt. David let the curtain fall and shrugged. "Only fair, don't you think, after all the times he's saved me? Are you ready?" Hannah nodded, and he pushed open the door.

Marcus had found David's assailants without much difficulty. Two hulking shadows descended on him almost the minute he set foot out of the hired hack. Pushed and jostled, protesting loudly the whole way, he allowed himself to be directed down a narrow, twisted lane past hulking warehouses to a falling-down building right on the water's edge. The docks groaned and creaked behind it, and the faint sound of the tide lapping at the pilings reached his ears. An old harbormaster's lodge, he guessed. No sooner had he stumbled through the door than two more thugs had leaped forward to shove him into a chair, then bind him to it. Water from the leaking roof dripped down the back of his neck, and the ropes bit into his wrists.

As he sat there, protesting for appearances' sake, a fifth man strolled in, a short, stout man with bushy blond hair, an enormous red nose, and a cruel, twisted mouth. Without a word he sat in the other chair. This must be Rourke. His accomplices flexed their arms threateningly.

"Why din't ye keep yer appointment?" one of them sneered.

Marcus let his head loll to one side and pasted a smirk on his face. "Why, I was taking advantage of my brother's hospitality. He's got the finest stock of whiskey. . . ."

One man cuffed him on the back of the head as the others snorted, laughing at him in contempt. "Well, now that y've had yer drink, ye'll be ready t' take yer medicine like a man, I 'ope."

Marcus heaved a sigh, as if the whole thing were painfully boring, even though his ears rang from the clout. "Yes. Right. But see, I know you really want money. It's rather unsporting of you to steal a child to get it, I must say, but now that it's done, shall we fix a price? My brother will pay, of course."

All of them suddenly went quiet. Rourke leaned forward in his chair. "The child?" he asked suspiciously.

Marcus nodded. "The old stick'll give good value. His wife's child, and all that."

Rourke glanced at his henchmen. They turned and left the room, although Marcus didn't doubt they were right outside the door. "He wants the child back, does 'e?" Rourke murmured. "What about you?"

Marcus pulled a face. "Give her back. She screams and cries; never quiet. Makes Marcus's life a living hell, so why he wants her back I don't know. Must be to keep her grace happy."

"No," said Rourke with a curl of his lip. "What would 'e pay to have *you* back?"

Marcus pretended to think. "Two shillings?"

Rourke's mouth curled further, into a menacing smile. "Nah. You're worth more'n that. You'd better 'ope, anyway." He stood suddenly. "All right. We'll send back the brat, in due time. It just remains to be seen what to do with you."

Marcus sighed again and shifted his legs. "You could cut them all out, you know. We could make a deal, just between the two of us." Rourke's soulless black eyes rested on him.

"Nah." The twisted grin flashed again. "Not just yet."

Marcus thought hard. He didn't dare mention Molly again, even though he was desperate to. Rourke didn't seem to be in any hurry to dispose of him, though, or to make any demands. In fact, he seemed to be . . . waiting. For what? Or whom?

He considered again David's words. A counterfeiting ring that worked through a tailor's shop, serving gentlemen. Forged notes passed to the upper class. A maid in his own household spying. What did it all mean? Why had they taken Molly?

He knew he must be the real focus of all this, somehow; as far as anyone knew, David had never even seen Molly. Celia or Rosalind would have been a more logical choice if these men wanted someone to hold over David's head. So he, Marcus, was the one they really wanted, but why? Rourke hadn't batted an eye at the mention of money. Something Lily had been looking for in his study? Perhaps he should have heeded Hannah's instinct to call the maid down and question her.

So they were waiting. He refused to think about Hannah, how she was or what she was feeling. Hopefully Rosalind had persuaded her to drink something so she could sleep. If all went well, Molly would be safely home by the time she woke. If all went really well, he would be home in time to wake her with the news.

One of the men outside opened the door after a while, poking his head in. He murmured something to Rourke, whose eyebrows went up, then he slowly nodded. The door closed for a second, then opened again. Marcus looked up and saw, with a jolt of astonishment, himself.

Marcus had been keenly aware, his whole life, of each and every difference between him and his brother. They had been hammered into him from an early age: he was the heir, David was the spare. He was the responsible one, David was the scoundrel. He must always look out for David, and David must always be in trouble. And yet, here he was, tied to a chair by some very shady characters, and there was David, looking as proper as could be, right down to the lady on his arm.

At the sight of Hannah, Marcus tensed. What the bloody hell was she doing here, he wondered furiously. He couldn't stop David from jumping headfirst into trouble, but he'd wring his brother's neck for bringing her here. He couldn't bear to think of anything happening to her, and for the first time Marcus felt a chill of fear. He didn't know what David was about, but if it went wrong, and Hannah got hurt . . .

He forced his eyes away from her, to David. His brother stood staring down at him with cool, expressionless eyes. He held himself stiffly erect, his arm barely crooked at Hannah's hand. He looked like . . .

It hit Marcus then. David was playing him, just as he was playing David. David had posed as him before, of course, but never for a selfless reason. Marcus didn't agree with Hannah being here, but he had no choice but to play along now. He slouched in the chair and huffed, "About bloody time," by way of greeting.

David's eyebrow arched, slowly. "Indeed," he said in a chilly voice. "Perhaps if you had seen fit to notify me of your intentions, it would not have taken so long to find you." He flicked a dismissive glance at the two men lurking in the doorway behind him. "Leave us."

Rourke climbed to his feet. "Not just yet, mates," he said. "What brings you here, Yer Grace?"

David's mouth lifted in a half smile. "We both know the answer to that."

"How could you?" said Hannah then in a deeply disappointed voice. Marcus avoided meeting her eyes. If he looked at her too long, he would surely give himself away.

"Didn't bring her just to scold me, did you? This really isn't a good time, old chap."

"For some reason, unknown to me, she cared enough to see that you were returned home in relatively good order." David let out his breath slowly, his chilly stare still fixed on Marcus, and Marcus glared back from under his eyebrows. David turned away and murmured something to Hannah, then faced Rourke.

"How much do you want?" David asked, his expression bored.

Rourke gave a short bark of laughter. "Not me, mate. I don't want nuffin." He glanced fleetingly at the door. "Not yet."

"Ah." That dry, humorless smile curled David's mouth again. "Shall we wait for Bentley, then?"

Rourke blinked. Marcus almost fell off his chair. Or would have, had he not been tied to it. Bentley? Of course—it made sense, he thought, thinking through things with growing fury and elation. So much sense, he should have figured it out himself. "Aye," growled Rourke. "We'll wait for 'im."

"Hmm." David stared down at Rourke with unreadable eyes. "Mustn't move without your master's permission, I see." The Irishman bristled. David folded his arms. "Let's speed things along, shall we? You've already given my brother a good thumping; that's about as much as he can take—"

"Oh, now really," whined Marcus, lapsing obediently back into silence as David cut him a cold glance.

"What more do you expect of him?" This time David flashed a smile at him, filled with contempt. It was a little shocking to Marcus, that this was how he appeared to his brother, but he pushed aside that thought and rolled his eyes exactly as he had seen David do many times before, after every little question and correction. "Bentley's gotten far more out of him than most of us have. You'd best wash your hands of him."

"Nay." Rourke showed his yellowing teeth. "Not on your life."

David's eyebrows climbed higher. "Indeed. You have something else planned for him? I assure you, he's not clever enough or reliable enough. Gambling is his main talent, and you've already exploited that."

"This is fine thanks I get," began Marcus indignantly. "After I came all the way out here, just to get the child back—"

"Don't you dare," Hannah interrupted him, her voice trembling. "If not for you, she would never have been in danger."

He ducked away from her gaze, not daring to let anything about her distract him. "Well, yes, sorry about that," he mumbled.

"Yes, you always are," said David dryly. "After the

fact." He turned to Hannah. "Do not trouble yourself, my dear. I shall deal with this." Now he looked to Rourke, pacing across the room, hands clasped behind his back. Marcus could just see a faint, condescending smile on his brother's face. "We both know you won't get anything from Bentley for the child," he said, so quietly Marcus had to strain to hear. "And as for my brother, I wouldn't give a farthing, but Her Grace wished to see him once more. Now that she's seen for herself what he's been up to, even she may not want him. My escort will come after me if either the duchess or I do not tell them otherwise. Shall we both profit, and send them out?"

Rourke was thinking about this, Marcus could tell. What was David planning? He obviously wanted Marcus to go free, but then what? Marcus knew, as David did not, that Timms and Stafford could be summoned with a dozen armed men ready to round up the counterfeiters. But it would take time to fetch them, and David would be alone. . . .

He flinched then as Hannah's hand brushed over his temple. He had been so deep in his thoughts, he hadn't noticed her approach. Now she was bending solicitously over him, her blue eyes unnervingly close to his, and his heart leaped in his chest, with a terrifying mixture of love and fear. "Don't worry," she breathed. Then, loudly and indignantly, "He's hurt!"

Rourke and David both turned to look at them. "How dare you," she went on, glaring at Rourke. "He's hurt, and I believe he has a fever coming on. Have you no decency, to leave him sitting here all wet? I must take him home at once. Your mother will be so concerned," she added to Marcus, who didn't have to pretend his astonishment. "She's been so worried about you, and now you return home only to go out seeking trouble! David, you really aren't competent to care for yourself."

She called him David. He was David. Marcus scowled. "I'm fine," he grumbled. "And I'm more than capable of handling things! Well, I might need a spot of money, of course, but nothing much—say, five thousand—" Rourke's eyes sparkled at the amount.

"Do you think me mad?" David gave a contemptuous snort. "Give you five thousand! It will never be enough. I might as well throw it on the fire."

Marcus glanced at Rourke. "Two thousand, then? For the child, I mean. You came all the way here, might as well make a bid."

"Not a farthing," said David swiftly. Marcus didn't know what he was up to, but he didn't have another bluff. He sagged in his seat, and tried to look sulky.

"Can't blame me, then. I tried to get her back. Not my fault he won't help."

Rourke was looking back and forth between them, calculation mixed with a bit of uncertainty. Marcus guessed he was wishing he'd had a chance to take the five thousand pounds, Bentley's orders or not.

"No, I am done giving you money," David said with a thin smile. "This time, I shall deal with your creditors directly." He glanced at Rourke. "How long must I wait in this hovel?"

The Irishman scowled. "I'd not be worrying about the accommodations, Yer Grace."

"No." David's tone was icy. He took out his watch and studied it. "You're running out of time."

For a moment the only sound was the *plip plip* of water dripping through the roof. Marcus could hardly breathe, racking his brain for something, anything to get them all free.

Rourke's gaze flickered away from David, back to Marcus. "All right," he growled. "Take him."

"That's more like it," David murmured, standing by and watching as one of the men sawed through the ropes around Marcus. Free at least, he lurched to his feet, taking care to stumble his first step. Hannah touched his arm.

"Are you well enough to walk?"

"Yes, yes," he blustered. His heart seemed to pound with the force of an army drum, marking off the seconds. Bentley could arrive at any moment, and Bentley would deduce what Rourke never would, that he and David had switched places. Their cousin knew them too well to be fooled for very long. And with Hannah right in the middle of things, Marcus knew they had to get out as soon as they could; if Bentley managed to get all three of them under his control, they were dead. "Let's go, then." He glanced at David as he jerked at his jacket, fussing unnecessarily with the cuffs. "Good show, Exeter."

David exhaled slowly through his nostrils. "See Her Grace safely home," he snapped. "After all I've gone through to spare your wretched neck, it is the least you can do."

"Er . . . Right, then." Marcus forced a bitter smile and made a show of offering Hannah his arm. No more maintaining appearances, it was time to beat a strategic retreat. The instant her fingers touched his sleeve, he scooped his hat off the floor and slapped it on his head before strolling toward the door. "Stand aside," he said to the man there, who curled his lip but did step aside. Sweeping the door open, Marcus managed to exchange one last fleeting glance with David. His brother stood tall and proud, unafraid to all appearances, except for his eyes.

I'll be back, he silently told his brother.

Hurry, said David's eyes. Marcus pulled the door closed, and hurried Hannah down the dock.

CHAPTER 21

Hannah somehow managed to walk back to the carriage in an almost normal manner, even though she was trembling horribly. She could hear and feel Marcus close beside her, his hand closed tightly over hers. She hadn't thought past anything but getting him safely out of that terrible shack, where he was tied to a chair, ruffled and scuffed—but now it was David in danger, and she didn't see how they could rescue him.

"What were you thinking?" she burst out the second they were alone in the carriage. "Marcus, you might have—"

He pulled her into his arms and kissed her soundly. When he lifted his head, she could only look at him through misty eyes. "I could never have survived it," she said brokenly. "If they had killed you."

His smile was tender. "I never intended to die, my dear."

"But why?" She clutched at his arms. "Why did you go?"

He put a finger on her lips. "To save Molly? I couldn't not go."

Tears spilled out of her eyes, and she gave a shaky

laugh. "Molly is safe at home. Lily hid her—Lily was working for Bentley Reece. But even if she had been missing . . ."

"Safe at home?" he echoed, startled. "Thank God; that will make things easier." He frowned slightly. Hannah gripped him harder.

"How could you do that, without telling me?"

His gaze focused on her once more. "I didn't want to worry you any more. I thought Molly had been kidnapped. There was no time to be lost."

"But . . . but . . ." Hannah covered her face with her hands, too distraught to make sense. "But why must *you* go?" He said nothing until she uncovered her eyes.

"I know," he began haltingly, not quite meeting her eyes, "I am not an easy man to love." He paused. "I am stiff and cold and proud, as people believe me to be."

"No!" she protested.

He glanced up at her. "To most I am. I always believed I was. A duke does not trifle with emotions." Another fleeting frown. "But you have shown me what it is to feel so strongly. . . . For you, I would do anything. To get Molly safely back to you, to keep her from harm, I would do anything. After what you have given me . . ."

"But I have nothing to give you," said Hannah tearfully.

His smile was crooked, almost hesitant. "Your heart?"

Her laugh caught in her throat, and came out half sob. "How could you not know you already have it?"

He hauled her across the seat into his arms, holding her tightly. "No one has ever given me her heart before," he whispered.

"No one!" She touched his face. "Any woman in London—"

He turned his head, pressing his lips to her palm. "That," he said with a wry, rueful look, "is not the same kind of love." He hesitated. "They wanted to be a duchess, not my wife."

"I told you there was a difference," she reminded him with a spark of humor. He looked back at her with an expression of such unguarded emotion, she almost burst into tears. Instead she kissed him again.

"What will we do about David?" she asked a moment later, feeling strangely calmer and clear-headed. Hannah lifted her head from his shoulder. "They already beat him. They tried to kill him—"

Marcus set her back on the opposite seat. "They threatened to kill him," he corrected. "There is a great difference. If they had wanted to kill him, why not do so when they had the chance? No, they didn't want him dead, not yet. They wanted something else from him, and I believe I don't presume too far to say it was money. Bentley's playing a deeper game, but Rourke and his lot want money, which they stood a much better chance of getting from a David very much alive."

"Oh, thank heavens," she sighed, closing her eyes in relief. "I was so afraid for him—"

"You were right," Marcus interrupted grimly. "It was a foolish idea. David should not have done it." He opened a door hidden in the carved mahogany paneling, and took out a pair of pistols. Hannah's eyes popped wide open in renewed alarm.

"But you said they would want him alive!"

"Yes, at first." He took out powder and began loading the pistols. "But the one they really want is the duke of Exeter." He sat forward, his dark eyes deadly serious. Hannah gripped her hands together, utterly terrified again. "Don't you see why they let us walk out so easily? They think they've got him, and had no need for a good-for-nothing wastrel and a woman. Once they realize we tricked them, David will be in grave danger."

"Perhaps they won't realize," Hannah began. Marcus shook his head.

"Bentley will. He knows us well enough to catch on eventually."

"Of course." She shuddered. "I should have never let him go!"

"Well." He gave a small shrug. "It can't be undone, so we must use everything it's gained us." He tucked the pistols into the pockets of his coat, then opened another panel and took out a wicked knife, which he slid into his boot. Then he swept back the curtain at the window and peered out. "This should be far enough." He turned back to her. "I need you to find a man named Timms. I'll give Harris the direction. Tell him—"

"Where are you going?" she cried.

"David," he said simply.

"You can't go back there alone!" she said, her face ashen. "Summon the Runners, or the watch at least! Let me come with you!"

"I can't help my brother if I must worry about you," he said, cutting short her protest. "Hannah, they want to kill him. If they discover he's David instead of the duke of Exeter . . ." She closed her mouth at his expression, desperate to protest but unable to do it. "I need you to go to Mr. Timms and tell him where Rourke and Bentley are. Tell him to bring as many men as he can summon in an instant, and bring them all back here. There is only so much I can do by myself."

Hannah nodded, her heart tight with fear. He gave her a smile meant to be encouraging, cupping her cheek in one hand. "I love you," he said, surprising her before he pressed a quick, hard kiss on her mouth.

"I love you, too," she said, but he was gone, slipping out of the carriage as it rolled along. She heard a rumble of voices outside for a moment, then the driver snapped the whip and the carriage sped up a little. Hannah scrambled to the window and tore open the curtain, but saw nothing in the dense fog. Marcus was gone.

That was good, she told herself nervously, refusing to let herself think about that last rushed exchange. If she couldn't see him, no one else could, either. How far had they come from the dock? She hadn't the faintest idea. She thought of the two pistols—two shots—and the knife. Against five armed men, who could hold David hostage.

She lunged onto the forward seat and hammered on the front of the carriage. "Hurry!" No response. "Faster!" she screamed, and this time the driver must have heard her, for the carriage lurched forward, clattering over the bumpy streets at a fearful pace. Hannah was thrown back into the rear seat, where she wrapped her arms around herself and tried not to shake.

When the carriage halted, she flung open the door and jumped down. Ignoring the driver's startled protest, she hiked up her skirts and ran up the steps, pounding on the door until a footman jerked it open.

"Where is Mr. Timms?" she demanded, barging past him.

"I say, madam," said the disconcerted servant. "He is not receiving visitors."

"He'll receive me." She gave him a push in the direction of the stairs. "Tell him the duchess of Exeter needs his assistance at once."

The title confused the footman; he paused, looking at her as if wondering whether she were actually a duchess, or a duchess's servant. "Go!" Hannah shrieked.

"May I help you?" inquired an icy voice. Hannah

whirled around to see the butler, looking as though he would like to throw her back out into the street.

"I must see Mr. Timms at once," she said over the murmurs of the footman. "It's a matter of life and death!"

The butler hesitated. "Your Grace?" he asked carefully.

"Yes!" She could scream from impatience, they were being so slow. "Will you fetch Mr. Timms, or must I run through the house and find him myself?"

The butler pursed his lips as though he would still like to throw her out, but he bowed very briefly. "I shall tell him, madam. Smith will see you into the drawing room to wait." He vanished, thankfully walking quickly. The footman, Smith, approached her again, a little more deferentially.

"This way, Your Grace," he said. Hannah glared at him.

"I shall wait here."

He blinked. "May I take your cloak?"

"No!"

The young man swallowed. If she hadn't been so afraid, Hannah would have apologized for being such a shrew; as it was, all she could think of was how long it was taking. Mr. Timms would still have to summon his men, then there was the journey back to the docks. She wrung her shaking hands, pacing the hall in a fever pitch of anxiety. What was Marcus doing now? Where was he? And David—was he still alive, still unhurt? It seemed a decade at least since Marcus had jumped out of the carriage and disappeared into the fog.

"Your Grace." She spun around to see a tall, barrel-chested man with a dinner napkin still tucked into his waistcoat striding toward her. His round, genial face was creased with wary concern. "My butler said you were here on an urgent matter."

"Yes. You must come at once—bring soldiers or the

watch—Marcus and David have found them—the men you are seeking," she said in a rush. "It is beyond urgent, it's life and death. They have them—David, I mean—and Marcus has gone to rescue him but there are at least five men, armed . . ."

"I see." Blessedly, Mr. Timms made enough sense of it to understand. He pulled off the napkin and thrust it into the footman's hands. "Where are they?" he demanded of Hannah.

"At the docks. Harris will know exactly where."

Timms wheeled around to his servant. "Ask Her Grace's coachman the direction," he snapped. "Find Stafford's man at Bow Street and bring a dozen men, more if you can get them, and meet us there at once. Run, man!" The footman nodded once before flinging open the door and taking off. Timms was already beckoning to the butler. "What happened?"

Hannah pressed a hand to her forehead, trying to force her thoughts into order. "David returned—he'd been beaten, and was ill. Then tonight my daughter went missing. But she wasn't, the maid who had pretended to kidnap her only hid her. Marcus thought she was gone, though, and went to ransom her back, and then David and I went to help him, only David merely traded places with Marcus. They've still got him and Marcus has gone back to help him. Please, Mr. Timms, we must *hurry!*"

Mr. Timms looked utterly flummoxed by this, but nodded as his butler rushed up with a polished wooden box, a coat, and a hat. "Right." He pulled on the coat, slapped the hat on his head, and took the box before waving her out the door ahead of him. Hannah clambered into the carriage as he had a quick word with Harris, then they were off, Timms slamming the door shut behind him.

He unlatched the wooden box, revealing two pistols.

He took one out and began loading it. "Now," he said, fixing a keen gaze on her, "tell me again everything that's happened, and what you know of his grace's investigations."

Hannah told him what she knew and what they suspected. The carriage careened along at an impressive rate, and more than once she had to pause in her story to grab on to the seat as they took corners practically on two wheels. By the end, Timms was frowning as he checked his loaded pistols.

"Bentley Reece, eh? I never should have suspected."

Hannah lifted one hand. "No one did. Rosalind told me he was a dandy, a charming and amusing flirt. Even Marcus dismissed him as a frippery."

Timms grunted. "The cleverest disguise: a useless man."

The carriage was slowing down. Before it even halted, Hannah had the door open and leaped down, looking around in confusion. This wasn't where she and Marcus had left David.

Timms jumped down beside her, shoving his pistols into the pockets of his greatcoat. "Now, Your Grace, I must ask you to wait in the carriage."

"No." She tugged up the hood of her cloak. "I shall be silent, I shall obey your orders, but I am not waiting in the carriage. This isn't the right place at all."

He heaved a sigh, but said nothing more of her waiting behind, possibly because at that moment a man slipped out of the shadows and murmured something to him. Timms nodded once, then took Hannah's arm.

"We'll walk the rest of the way," he said quietly. "With no idea of who might be there or how many men may be about, it's best to surprise them." Hannah nodded. Timms lifted one hand and gave a little wave. She became aware of more shadowy figures, gliding quietly through the fog. Keeping a firm grip on her arm, Timms began walking. Hannah obediently hustled along, her heart about to expire from pounding so hard. Let us be in time, she prayed as they hurried along.

Marcus made it back to the crumbling dock without trouble. The fog enabled him to slide right past the lone sentry at the end of the lane, even though he hated to leave the man behind him. He couldn't risk giving an alarm before he'd even seen if David were still alive. Moving slowly and deliberately, he crept past the warehouses to the house.

It was a rickety old structure, apparently on the verge of collapse. One man leaned against the doorway, and even through the fog Marcus could see the gleam of a pistol barrel. He watched for several minutes, until another man emerged from the shadows. The first stepped closer, and they talked for some time until Marcus became convinced they were the only two men outside.

He eased around a corner of the building. Light shone from cracks between the bricks, and through a grimy window he caught a glimpse of David.

Marcus pressed his eye to the glass. David was sitting in a chair opposite him, looking bored and haughty. Rourke was cleaning his fingernails with a wicked-looking little knife. A third man stood near the door, a pistol prominently displayed in his belt.

He left out a silent sigh of relief. Bentley hadn't arrived yet; their deception was still working. He took a closer look around him, trying to find a place to hide while still allowing him to see and hear. With any luck at all, Hannah and Timms would arrive with a brigade of Runners before long, and he wouldn't need to do anything but watch. Marcus wasn't so foolish as to want to take on four armed men himself.

Around the back, he found his place. The water came almost to the foundation here, and even lapped at some moss-covered stone steps sloping into the river. But at the top of the slippery steps was a door, a door that was warped enough to allow a good view of the room within. Placing his feet carefully, he was able to get right up against the door and monitor everything that happened.

For a long time there was nothing to see or hear. Periodically Rourke would mutter something to his man, who would peer out the window and shake his head. David usually greeted these exchanges with acerbic comments, once even pointedly checking his pocket watch. Outside, Marcus silently wished Rourke's greed would get the better of him; he'd appeared inclined to bargain earlier, but now he seemed content to wait.

Wedged into the doorframe, he had time to think. What was Bentley's plan? His cousin had wanted the duke; now he would think he had him. Bentley must know by now as well that Lily had failed to kidnap Molly, but perhaps that had only been a plot all along to lure him—or David—here. Bentley must want money, to pay Rourke if nothing else. Ransom? But surely Rourke would have simply demanded it when David and Hannah arrived, instead of letting his prisoner go. The question chased round and round in his mind, taunting him: what did Bentley want from him?

He was still considering possibilities when the faraway sound of a carriage approaching penetrated the fog. Marcus pricked up his ears expectantly, edging around the side of the house to see. Timms would know to approach quietly, though, so he waited, silent and hidden.

His fear was justified when the slim figure of his

cousin came striding down the path. Bentley said something to the men outside the door, then all three went inside. That made five inside with David, and a sixth down the lane. Marcus let out his breath in disappointment and slid back to his vantage point on the shoreside.

He could see Bentley across the room, in the doorway. David, his back to Marcus, still sat in the chair. His cousin wore a small, pleased smile, and said nothing for a long moment, as though savoring it.

"Fashionably late, as usual," said David coolly.

Bentley smiled, pulling off his gloves. "Perhaps I enjoy making you wait."

David let out a weary sigh. "Do let me know when we're to conduct business, won't you? I've been cooling my heels an age already."

The smile vanished from Bentley's face. "On your feet," he snapped. "Your manners, Exeter."

David tilted back his head, "How remiss of me," he said. But he got to his feet.

Slapping his gloves into his palm, Bentley smiled again, more forced this time. "I've looked forward to this conversation for a very long time."

"You might have called on me at any time, and in far more comfortable quarters," David shot back. Bentley's face darkened, but his smile didn't waver.

"Someday you shall call on *me* in more comfortable quarters," he said. "Or, perhaps not." Rourke let out a bark of a laugh, then tried to cover it with a cough. Bentley shot him a sharp frown, then smoothed his face again. "Imagine my surprise, dear cousin, to find you instead of your useless brother."

"Imagination," replied David, "was never your weakness."

A muscle twitched in Bentley's jaw. "No. You'll discover just how much imagination I possess very soon."

"At last," drawled David. "Something will occur *soon*."

Bentley's chest filled. He removed his hat and shoved it at one of the men, smoothing one hand over his golden hair. Deliberately, he shed his greatcoat and handed it over as well. He was making David wait, Marcus realized; just what David had intended. "Well, there's no real hurry," said Bentley, confirming his suspicions. "In fact, now that the moment is at hand, I cannot decide exactly what I shall do first."

"Get the money," rumbled Rourke.

"Silence," snapped Bentley, "or you'll not see a bloody farthing."

"Tsk, tsk," said David. "And you could have had so much more." Rourke cursed, but closed his mouth.

Visibly mastering himself again, Bentley turned back to David. "My first thought was just to kill you. I've thought of it for a long time."

"A similar thought had crossed my mind," interjected David.

"But I have reconsidered," said Bentley a little more loudly. "Perhaps I ought to bide my time, hold you for ransom first. I could put the Exeter fortune to good use immediately." He began pacing, hands clasped behind his back, an expression of vile satisfaction on his face. "How wrong that it should devolve onto just one person—"

"Who supports hundreds of others," David said.

"When I have lived with so little for so long. I am a Reece as well, am I not? We had the same grandfather, yet you have lived in splendor all your days, the chosen one, the anointed head of the family, while I scrape by on pennies."

"Rather more than pennies, I think," David said. "Pound notes as well, although not perhaps authentic ones." Bentley glared at him. David shifted his weight, and Marcus caught a glimpse of his brother's profile. "Enough gossiping," said David, sounding bored again. "What do you want?"

Bentley drew a deep breath. "What do I want? I want it all. And I shall have it, too." Rourke stirred, and Bentley slashed one hand at him. "And you yours, yes. But first," he said to David, a malicious, excited note in his voice, "to business."

David simply cocked his head. Marcus longed to slip around the front again, but didn't dare leave. Bentley began pacing again, toward Marcus and then away, tapping his finger on his lips. David turned as well, and Marcus saw the strain on his face. He hoped Bentley only took it for impatience.

"First," said Bentley thoughtfully as he paced, "the ransom. Some of my debts are . . . most pressing"— Rourke grinned—"and I require funds at once. Once that's paid, I'll set the rest of my plan in motion."

"My brother, no doubt, will suspect."

Bentley laughed. "Your brother will be in the dock for your murder," he returned. "An argument over money, perhaps. Yes, I see just how it went. The wastrel demands money, the duke refuses. The wastrel kills his brother in a fit of rage and takes the money anyway, though it is never found. Everyone knows gamblers can lose everything in a single night."

"The duchess might protest that story." Rourke grunted as though prodded.

"That's true, Mr. Reece. There was a woman here earlier."

Bentley swore, then calmed himself, beginning to pace again. "That's no concern. It's not a love match; she conspired with the wastrel, perhaps. London already believes she duped you into marriage."

"Framing a woman for murder," said David acidly. "How gallant of you, Bent."

From where he was, Marcus couldn't see Bentley's face. Instead he saw the sudden stiffening of his cousin's shoulders, the way he raised his head with a jerk. Marcus caught his breath. No, he prayed, please God, no . . . But he had never called his cousin Bent. Only David had ever teased him with that nickname.

Slowly Bentley turned. He looked David up and down, realization dawning in his face. "Lying, conniving bastard," he said incredulously.

David, either not grasping Bentley's meaning or trying to bluff, simply raised an eyebrow. Marcus tensed, straining his ears for any sounds of help approaching, and heard nothing.

"Kill him," snarled Bentley. Rourke blinked.

"What fer? He ain't signed—"

"He's not Exeter," Bentley ground out, his face taut with rage. "He's the damned younger brother! Didn't you recognize the man you beat to a bloody mess? It's Reece, you incompetent fool!"

Rourke lurched to his feet. "Why, ye blasted bugger—" He took a step toward David, looking for himself. David merely raised his chin, staring the man full in the face. Marcus felt a surge of helpless pride in his brother; he was playing his role to the end. "What was with the woman?" Rourke whined. "He'd a right proper-looking duchess with him!"

"Stupid!" hissed Bentley. "She tricked you, too. Kill him and be done with it! We'll have to do something else to get Exeter, now that you've let him escape; perhaps his brother's dead body will bring him."

Marcus hesitated one more second, listening in vain for the sound of a carriage or soldiers or anyone who could aid him. On the other side of the door, David stood proud and alone. Marcus took a tighter grip on his pistols, drew a deep breath, and shouldered open the rotting door.

* * *

After they had walked for what seemed like forever, Mr. Timms abruptly stopped, forcing Hannah to a halt as well. "What is it?" she whispered anxiously. She had begun to recognize their surroundings. They were very close, almost upon the lane, in fact.

He hesitated, looking over her head. Hannah turned to follow his gaze, and just caught sight of two shadows closing in on a man leaning against a nearby wall and swigging from a flask. They seemed to speak to him, then he lurched upright before apparently collapsing into the arms of one of Timms's men. She muffled a gasp behind her hand. "Is he dead?" she demanded of Timms in a whisper.

Just then the report of a pistol echoed through the night, muffled by fog. Everyone froze. Hannah's heart fell halfway to her feet, it seemed. Who had fired it, and at whom?

With renewed urgency, Timms waved the Runners onward. Hannah broke into a near run, trying to keep up with his pace. With a few whispered words, she directed Timms along the lane to the ramshackle building where she'd last seen David.

They stopped well back, in the shadow of one of the warehouses just as a second shot sounded. Hannah closed her eyes, biting down on her fist to keep from crying out. Timms told her, in no uncertain terms, to stay where she was and not to make a sound. She nodded, huddling into her cloak against the chill of the fog and her own fear. She longed to creep forward and peer in the window—she remembered one right beside the door—but didn't dare. She had given her word, and besides, the Runners were already flitting forward to look inside. After a moment one dashed back to them.

"Trouble, sir," he whispered. "We can't see much; it looks like there's been a struggle. There's a body on the floor."

"Dark-haired? Well-dressed?" asked Hannah anxiously in spite of herself. He shook his head.

"Can't tell, ma'am. The window's thick with dirt."

Timms let out a hiss of frustration. "We must know what's going on inside! I dare not burst in and put two noblemen at risk—it would be the end of my career!"

Hannah, about to tear into him for considering his career at a moment like this, stopped short. Her eyes climbed the crumbling stone chimney, all the way to the gently sloping roof. She remembered the plop, plop of water dripping through the rafters. She seized Timms's arm. "The roof," she whispered.

He looked. "What of it? None of my men can get up there," he said. "They'd fall through, even if they could."

"I can," said Hannah.

He looked at her in amazement. "You most certainly cannot."

"Yes, I can, and I will, unless you have a better idea." He hesitated. Hannah stripped off her cloak and shoved it at him. "There are holes in the roof. I'll be able to see in, or at least hear, and signal down to you. Have your men ready."

"See here," he said, but Hannah was off, running stealthily over to the chimney. One of the Runners caught up to her as she twisted up a handful of skirt. "Try to signal the first clear opportunity," he said to her quietly. "When no one is in immediate danger. But don't wait, if you suspect anyone's about to die."

"I won't," she promised him, setting her foot into a crack in the pocked stone.

He stepped back, drawing his pistol. "Be careful,

ma'am." Hannah nodded, wiped her hands on her skirt, and began to climb.

It went about as he'd expected. Marcus had aimed his first shot at Rourke, sending the Irishman to the floor with a thud. David, recovering from any surprise, took on the man nearest him. Marcus felled a gaping Bentley with a single blow, then fired his other pistol at the men by the door. But he and David were severely outnumbered, and Marcus soon found himself disarmed and gasping from the fists of Rourke's men.

"Get back there," grunted one of them, waving a pistol at him.

Marcus backed up, closer to his brother. David had gone a pasty shade of white. He was listing to one side, braced against the wall with one hand and clutching his side with the other. "All right, David?" he asked, keeping his eyes on the man with the gun.

"Simply splendid," gasped David. They must have hit him in his broken rib. Marcus stepped in front of him. His head throbbed and his left hand was numb, but he was still in better shape than David.

"Yes, isn't it splendid," spat Bentley, dabbing at his split lip as he climbed back to his feet. "The Reece brothers, united in death as never in life. What made you stupid enough to come after him?"

"He's my brother," said Marcus evenly.

"Not you," snarled his cousin. "Him." He jerked his head toward David. "I know you're the sort to martyr yourself for the family, but he doesn't serve any but himself." David glared at Bentley murderously, but said nothing.

"Perhaps you don't know us as well as you thought," Marcus taunted. Bentley had always been a braggart; perhaps he could be maneuvered into gloating some more, which would buy them time if nothing else. Where was Hannah, he wondered desperately. He'd sent her to Timms, certain Timms would be able to summon the Runners more easily than if Hannah just went to Bow Street. But if Timms weren't home . . .

Bentley scowled at them, then put out his hand. One of the thugs handed over his gun. "I know you both well enough to be standing here holding a pistol to your heads," he snapped.

"Damned . . . coward," wheezed David.

Bentley's eyes glittered with malice. "Damned fool," he replied softly. "Never willing to take the help that's offered." David growled. He was swaying slightly now, and Marcus tried not to think of the wounds that could be leeching his brother's life away. He needed a doctor at once, it was clear. Bentley seemed to know this as well. A cold smile crept over his face, as if he enjoyed seeing David suffer and Marcus agonize. "That was what made my plan work so well," he went on, addressing David. "I knew you hated his interference. I knew you would do anything to spare yourself crawling back to the almighty duke of Exeter for help. And look." He snorted contemptuously. "You've got both yourself and him killed with your stubbornness, to say nothing of your gullibility. If you were going to live, I'd warn you against propositions that sound too good to be true, but you're not, so I won't." He raised the gun. "I've waited a long time to be a duke."

"You'll wait a while longer," Marcus said tightly.

His cousin's smile widened. "No more than a few minutes," he said pleasantly. "I'll be merciful in that."

"Closer to seven months," Marcus shot back. Bentley's smile froze, then slipped. "The title will be held in suspense until my child is born, after all," Marcus supplied.

"Twins, with any luck," added David weakly. "They do seem to run in the family."

Bentley's narrow eyes flicked from David back to Marcus. "It's a lie," he said almost to himself. "She can't be increasing."

"Rosalind will see to it that the world knows," said Marcus. He was grasping at straws, but he had nothing left to grasp. "With us dead, she'll devote herself to the well-being of my wife and son."

"The woman should have had a dozen children," David mumbled. "A veritable force of nature, protecting her own." Marcus kept his eyes on Bentley. Whatever else Bentley might believe, he would know Rosalind would behave just as they said, and unlike Hannah, Rosalind was widely known in London, including by highly placed people in the government. Killing Marcus and David would by no means assure Bentley the title, for Rosalind, once Hannah had enlightened her about their cause of death, would stop at nothing to keep it from him.

"She's only a woman," Bentley said, more as though to reassure himself. "And she has her own daughter to care for."

"You thought you had nothing to fear from her, didn't you?" Marcus pressed on. "Because she has no son. But David and I have been her sons for over twenty years. And whom, pray, do you think her daughter will marry? By this time next year, an entirely different family will stand against you."

"It will be Avenall," said David, naming the Prime Minister's nephew. "He's asked after her every year since she was thirteen."

"Avenall?" Marcus exaggerated his interest. "Do you really think so? Ware asked me to send his regards the other night."

"Ware? Jack would be a capital choice."

"She won't marry either of them!" shrieked Bentley. His face was mottled red, and he looked half-mad.

"Silence, both of you! I must think for a moment!"
Marcus fell silent, conscious of David's raspy breathing behind him. He had shot his every arrow; the
notion of Celia marrying into a powerful family had
given Bentley pause, but Marcus didn't believe for a
moment that Bentley would allow him or David to
walk free, not even if they claimed Celia was be-
trothed to a royal prince. He felt hope slipping away.
Something must have delayed Hannah. She was too
late. He could only be glad he hadn't changed that
wedding register from the Middleborough church,
that she would be his legal widow—

Something hit the floor in the center of the room.
In the tense silence, it plinked loudly against the
floorboard. Marcus didn't dare take his eyes off
Bentley, even though he knew it would be hopeless
whenever Bentley decided to fire. Something else fell,
then rolled, followed by another plink. Bentley, his
face still screwed up in thought, frowned viciously.
"What the devil is that?" he cried, looking at the floor.
Then he stopped, his expression going slack. Warily,
Marcus dared a quick glance down.

It was a pearl. Three perfect lustrous pearls, lying
on the scarred wooden planks of the floor.

Astonishment and suspicion warred in Bentley's
face. "Don't move," he snapped, waving the pistol.
Marcus put up his hands in a defenseless gesture,
trying to hide any sign of his racing thoughts. She was
here. He distinctly remembered those pearls around
Hannah's neck, could feel them under his fingers as
he pulled her close for his kiss just before he leaped
from the carriage. But where was she? And why was
she throwing pearls?

Bentley inched forward, still frowning at the pearls
on the floor. He jerked the pistol threateningly at

Marcus again, then looked up, just in time to catch the falling brick right in the forehead.

Marcus was on him by the time his cousin hit the floor, unconscious. "Stay!" he shouted at Bentley's stunned accomplices, aiming his cousin's pistol at them. As if on cue, the door behind them burst open, and half a dozen armed Runners bounded in.

There was a great deal of shouting and a few punches, but as Bentley was senseless on the floor, Rourke's men lost their stomach for fight. It could only have been a matter of seconds before Timms appeared behind his men in the doorway, striding into the room and announcing in a booming voice his intention to have them all arrested. Marcus surrendered Bentley's pistol to one of the Runners and got to his feet.

"Exeter, by God!" Timms slapped his shoulder. "Damned fine work!"

Marcus waved it off. "My brother needs a doctor at once." He swung around in search of David. His brother was still leaning against the wall, holding his ribs. His eyes met Marcus's, tired and glazed with pain, but he gave a triumphant grin in spite of that.

"Of course. What about this fellow?" Timms asked the Runner now crouching over the prostrate Bentley. "Does he need the leech or the bone wagon?"

"The leech, sir." The man looked up. "The lady caught 'im just a glancin' blow. He's alive."

"Excellent," said Timms as Marcus seized him by the arms.

"Where is she? My wife?" Timms hesitated, then raised his eyes to the crumbling ceiling. Marcus followed suit instinctively, just as a tumult erupted outside the door. His heart leaping, Marcus shouldered Timms aside in time to see Hannah as she charged into the room, disheveled and dirty, her eyes wild with anxiety.

She froze for a second when she saw him, then flung herself at him with an inarticulate cry. Marcus met her halfway, catching her in his arms. The reality of how close he had come to never holding her again made his arms tremble, and he held her tighter.

"Oh, heavens, are you hurt?" She leaned back, running her hands down his face, over his shoulders, gripping his arms. "They said someone was shot— I didn't know—"

He cut her off with a kiss, long and hard and filled with relief that she was unhurt and that he was alive to know it. "I'm fine," he broke off the kiss to say. "But what on earth have you been up to?"

She smiled, a little self-consciously through her tears. "They needed to know what was going on inside, and I remembered the leaking roof. But none of the men could climb the chimney, and they might have been too heavy for the roof to bear in any event. So I did it."

"And dropped priceless pearls into a rat's hole," added Marcus with a grin. She laughed shakily.

"I didn't know what else to do—the necklace was the only thing I had to catch his attention and get him to move to where I could hit him—" He threw back his head and laughed, and Hannah clung to him, weak with relief. He was safe. She'd been sick with fear they'd been too late.

"I don't give a damn about the pearls," Marcus murmured against her hair. "I daresay it's the best use they've been put to in centuries."

Hannah started to smile, then caught sight of David over Marcus's shoulder. "David," she gasped.

Marcus whipped around at once. A Runner was crouching over David, who had slumped down the wall and was now sprawled on the floor. "Move," he ordered the man, stepping over to crouch beside his brother. "David," he said, touching his brother's shoulder. "Can you hear me?"

Hannah let out her breath as David nodded once, without opening his eyes. "Bloody rib," he muttered.

Marcus's face grew grim. "Let's go home," he said. He and the Runner each grasped one of David's arms, and helped him to his feet. Then Marcus wound David's arm around his neck, and David himself waved the Runner aside.

"Miserable place to receive guests anyway," he said, his words slurred. Hannah hurried over to David's other side, taking his arm across her shoulders. Moving slowly, they walked past Rourke's body, the bound and sullen thugs, and Bentley, who was just starting to come around as Timms emptied a bucket of river water on his head.

Marcus stopped outside, looking back at the little house. "How on earth did you do it?" he asked. She followed his gaze, to the rock chimney. Now that she looked at it again, it did seem rather unlikely that anyone could scale it.

"I don't really know," she said in surprise. It tilted alarmingly to one side, and all the missing rocks that had looked like toeholds and footholds before now looked like omens of impending collapse. "I had to, so I did."

"Dashed brave of you," said David feebly.

"Oh, no," she said at once. "Not compared to what you did."

"Hannah." Marcus stopped her. "It was heroic."

"It was not," she said again, blushing scarlet now. Climbing onto a roof and destroying a priceless necklace didn't seem half as brave as facing down five murderous cutthroats alone.

"Well, you're *my* bloody heroine," coughed David.

Over his head, Marcus gave Hannah a slow smile. "No," he said, "she's mine."

CHAPTER 22

They arrived back home to a tempest quite unlike anything Hannah had ever seen. Before the carriage had even reached the steps of Exeter House a dozen servants burst from the doors, followed by Rosalind, her face drawn and pale. Without a word she pushed past all the footman and threw herself at her two stepsons as they climbed from the carriage. Marcus embraced her for a moment before stepping away, leaving David to lean on their stepmother alone. David nodded a few times, in response to whatever she said to him, then released her and hobbled slowly into the house, assisted by a pair of servants.

"Hannah." Rosalind's face crumpled as she turned to Hannah. "Oh, goodness," she choked. "I didn't realize—I never imagined—not until Celia told me she had Molly, and Telman said there was a maid locked in a dressing room."

"Is everyone here well?" Hannah took the other woman's hands in hers. "Did anything happen while we were gone?"

Rosalind shook her head. "No. Everything here is fine. I told Harper to bar all the doors and windows until you returned, and had him search the house from top to bottom." She let out a weak laugh. "He's no doubt reached the wine cellar by now."

Hannah heaved a deep heartfelt sigh. That had been her last worry, that Bentley might have set some of his accomplices to causing trouble at the house. She and David had been in such a rush to leave, they'd told no one to be on guard.

"Shall we go in?" asked Marcus. "We'll explain everything, Rosalind." She nodded and they all went in, Marcus's hand reassuringly at Hannah's back. Inside, David had already gone up the stairs. Telman was sitting in the hall looking dazed and lost. At their approach, he leaped to his feet.

"Your Grace!" He bowed, his eyes darting anxiously from Marcus to Hannah and then back. "I did as you asked." He thrust a key at Hannah as if he couldn't wait to be rid of it. She took it, clasping his hand as she did so.

"Thank you, Telman. Your aid was invaluable. I shall be eternally grateful."

"Oh, madam. That is such a relief." He started to smile at her, then glanced at Marcus and all expression left his face.

"No need for that, Telman," said Marcus. "I imagine we're all rather dizzy with relief." He took the key from Hannah. "I shall not forget your service tonight." His valet blinked, then bowed, the beginnings of another smile on his face.

"Thank you, Your Grace," he murmured.

"You are dismissed," Marcus added. "I shan't need you tonight."

Telman bowed again, stepped backward, and hurried off past Harper, who had just come rushing into the hall, slightly disheveled. He came to a halt in front of them with a quick bow. "The house is secure, Your

Grace," he said breathlessly. "I have searched every room personally."

"Well done, Harper," said Marcus, a thread of amusement in his voice. The butler bowed his head. "Send someone for the surgeon to see to Lord David, and have tea sent to my study." Harper nodded and hurried away. Marcus turned to Rosalind. "Rosalind, will you assure Celia and Molly everyone is well?"

"Of course," Rosalind said, hesitating. "But . . ."

"Never fear, I shall tell you everything. But first there is a maid we must speak to." Marcus looked at the cluster of waiting servants, and one of them came forward. Marcus handed him the key. "Bring the maid who is locked in Lord David's dressing room to my study at once." The footman bowed and left. Hannah felt a wave of exhaustion crash over her; she closed her eyes, too tired to face Lily, too weak with relief to do much of anything. She just wanted to see Molly once more and fall into bed.

Marcus's hand came to rest at the back of her waist. "Can you bear up a little longer?" he murmured next to her ear. "I should like your assistance with Lily."

Hannah took a deep breath and nodded, opening her eyes to meet his. For a moment all she saw was Marcus, his dark eyes warm with affection, looking down at her. Then she recalled that they were standing in the middle of the hall surrounded by people, and tore her eyes away.

"Rosalind," she began. The other woman, who had been watching them avidly, jumped.

"Oh! I must see to Celia now," she exclaimed. "She'll be so worried. And now that I know everyone is safe and well . . ." She turned and all but ran up the stairs. Hannah blinked after her in surprise.

Marcus steered her toward his study with a low laugh. "Never mind her, darling," he said, as if he knew what she was thinking. "Come with me." Hannah let herself be guided. Inside the study, the heavy oak door closed behind them, he pulled her gently into his arms and just held her. Hannah went limp against him, unable to speak. He had almost died. To save her daughter he had put himself in great peril, and then to save his brother he had done it again. A man incapable of love, people had called him, but they were wrong; he had proved himself capable of the greatest possible love. And he loved *her.* Her throat felt tight.

"You saved me," he whispered. Hannah gave a sniffling laugh.

"Barely. Mr. Timms must think I'm quite a shrew, after the way I railed at him."

"Timms, of all people, will appreciate what you did. He's been trying to stop the counterfeiting ring for months." He smoothed the tangled hair back from her face. "Are you sure you're unhurt?"

She nodded, her heart turning over at the concern in his face. A tapping at the door interrupted before either could speak, but when she made to step away from him, Marcus didn't let her go. "Come," he called.

A servant brought in the tea tray. "You may go," Marcus said, and the footman bowed out again. "Sit down." Marcus finally released her. Hannah thankfully sank into a nearby chair. He crossed the room to the walnut cabinet and came back with a bottle of brandy. Pulling another chair close, he poured a cup of tea, then added some liquor. "Drink," he commanded, wrapping her hands around the teacup and waiting until she obeyed.

"Now." He sat forward, his eyes intent. "I intend to question Lily. She's more likely to tell us much more than Bentley ever will, and is therefore my main hope of answering my questions. I know you must have

some questions as well for her, but will you allow me
to proceed first?"

Hannah nodded, taking another sip of the brandy-
spiked tea. He was Lily's employer, after all, and had
the right to do with her as he saw fit.

"Even if you disagree with my methods?" he pressed.
Hannah opened her mouth to protest, rather indignantly, then remembered the Redleys, and closed it.
He grinned at her. "If you have anything to add, I shall
yield to you," he said. "Rest assured, I want to know
everything she has to tell us."

Hannah nodded again. After urging her to finish
the tea, Marcus went behind his desk, taking something out of the cabinet behind it. He flipped open a
file and sat down at the desk just as a knock sounded.

He looked up; his eyes met hers. Hannah put down
her empty cup and nodded once. Marcus smiled encouragingly, then called, "Come."

Lily edged into the room, as fearful as a woman
climbing the guillotine steps. Her eyes flicked from
Hannah to Marcus. "Your Grace." She curtseyed.

"Sit," he said, the imposing duke once more. Head
down, Lily scurried across the room and took the
chair he indicated. For a long moment Marcus just
studied her as he leaned back in his chair, his gaze
piercing. The silence stretched to an unnerving
length. Hannah barely kept herself from leaping up
and screeching at Lily, but she had promised him she
wouldn't. And to be honest, she didn't particularly
mind that he was scaring the girl.

"So," he said suddenly, making Lily jump. "I have a
spy in my household."

The maid cast a fleeting, agonized glance at Hannah, but said nothing.

"A spy who not only sneaks into my private office in
the dead of night to commit who knows what mis-

chief, but who kidnaps innocent children and conspires with murderers and thieves," he went on in the same deadly soft voice. "I doubt Bentley told you the penalty for murder, particularly that of a duke, is to be hanged. The rest would no doubt land you in prison for a great many years, assuming you would survive that long." He clasped his hands before him on the desk. "The only reason the Runners have not arrived yet is that I want answers. What made you betray me and my family?"

Lily looked frightened enough to faint. "Please, Your Grace," she whimpered. "I didn't steal the baby, I didn't, I kept her safe. . . ."

"Answer me!" he snapped. "Why did you betray me?"

The maid flinched, giving a small squeak of terror. "Mr. Reece, sir," she said, her voice trembling. "He—he told me—"

Marcus didn't say a word, but he leaned forward with a black look on his face. Lily went even paler, and started speaking much more quickly. "He told me th-that his f-father was really the firstborn, before your father, Your Grace, sir, and that there were documents here in your office that would prove he, I mean Mr. Reece, sir, had been cheated. He s-said he should be the duke, and that you and your father had hidden the evidence, and if I just helped him find it he would . . ." She swallowed hard. "He would take care of me," she finished. "Because he said he knew we shared the same f-father."

If Marcus were as surprised as Hannah was by this, he didn't show it. "Rubbish," he said disdainfully. "Think of a better story."

"Oh, no, it's true!" the girl exclaimed. "I mean, that's what he told me. And I said I couldn't do it at first, but then . . . he knew about my mother, and he said he was so sorry for the way his father treated her, that he knew I was his sister, and he wanted to do right by me." She flushed. "And I never knew my father. My mum told me he died when I was a baby, but she never talked about him. And now I got no one but myself, and . . . and . . ." She huddled on the chair, her voice small and unhappy. "I didn't know about no murder, and if there really was proof he should be the duke, it was rightfully his, weren't it? I never thought he meant to hurt anyone, just make things right. It was so easy, what he asked me to do, until he wanted the baby. That I couldn't do, no matter what." She swung around to Hannah. "I swear I wouldn't have let him hurt your little girl, madam," she pleaded.

Marcus made a quiet growl of disapproval. "What did he ask you to do?"

Lily wiped at her eyes with the back of her hand. "All I was to do was unlock the window there," she said, pointing to the French windows across from the desk. "That, and answer his questions every now and then. Mostly about you, madam," she added to Hannah. "He was terribly interested in you."

"What did he want to know?"

The maid thought for a second. "What Her Grace was like," she said. "What sort of woman was she, were the rumors of a love match true." She flushed pink again. "I said I thought not," she whispered. "Or else that there had been a quarrel, because of how I never saw—well—in your room, madam—"

"Yes, I understand," Hannah cut her off, trying not to turn pink herself. Lily had never seen Marcus in her room until that morning, when he'd been naked in her bed. No wonder Lily had dropped the breakfast tray. Hannah ignored the subtle flicker of amusement in Marcus's eyes when he glanced at her.

"And you told him about Molly," he said, switching his attention back to Lily.

The maid nodded miserably. "To my everlasting shame, madam. That's how he knew you loved your baby so much."

"Hmph." Marcus leaned back, not willing to let the girl off the hook yet. He believed her, though. It fit with everything he'd overheard between David and Bentley, and what he'd pieced together on his own. He'd forgotten his father and Bentley's father had also been twins; unlike Marcus and David, they'd been as different as the sun and moon. So Bentley thought—or had persuaded himself—that he was the rightful duke, and didn't care how he made it reality. He wondered if Bentley truly suspected there were documents suggesting it in the study, or if he'd just wanted a chance to dig through Marcus's affairs.

And playing on a young woman's desire to know her true father was something Bentley would do without qualm, manipulating her and using her for his own purposes. Marcus wasn't sure his cousin wouldn't have ended up trying to frame Lily for murder, if his plan had succeeded. A bastard daughter nursing a grudge against the family that kept her a lowly maid by murdering the head of that family? Yes, Bentley was capable of that, probably even handing her over to the authorities himself and claiming to have discovered her plot.

"He said his father was also your father," he repeated. "What proof did he offer?"

She blinked at him. "Why, he . . ." She faltered. "He admitted it. He said he'd found his father's journal, and read the whole story there, how his father had seduced my mother when she was a maid at Ainsley Park. He . . . he said he was appalled," she mumbled, looking disillusioned. "He told me he couldn't do anything to publicly name me his sister, but that he considered me such, and would provide for me as a brother should. And as a sister, I should help him."

"Did he show you the journal?"

"No, Your Grace," she whispered.

"Did he offer anything but his word?"

She shook her head. Marcus took a deep breath and let it out.

"My uncle has been dead for several years," he told her. "From what I remember of Bernard, he was not the sort to leave anything of the kind in a journal. Bernard was a dreamer, an artist who had no head for anything but painting and drawing. And if he had trifled with one of the maids at Ainsley Park, my father would have held him accountable for it." He paused. "I expect Bentley knew this."

Lily nodded. "Yes, Your Grace," she mumbled. "I was a bloody fool to listen."

He couldn't help a pinprick of sympathy. That was Hannah's fault, he thought to himself, although without malice. Before her, he'd not have spared a thought for Lily. "How old are you?" he asked in a clipped voice. Even though Bentley's story was highly unlikely, he probably couldn't prove it false, but he would try. If nothing else, it would drive home to Lily that she had betrayed her employer for a string of lies.

Lily swallowed. "Near three-and-twenty, Your Grace."

He thought back for a moment. "Twenty-two years ago my father married Rosalind. Bernard would have been at Exeter then. But the year before . . ." He shook his head, remembering. "No, he was not at Exeter. He was on the Continent for almost two years previous. I remember listening to his stories of Italy and Greece the following summer, during the wedding festivities."

Lily bowed her head, her clenched hands trembling in her lap. Hannah saw her blink several times before a single tear splashed onto her skirt. Almost unwillingly, she felt her anger ebbing. Lily had done something terribly wrong, but she had had a compelling reason. And in the end, not even wanting to discover her father had let her give Molly to Bentley.

She glanced at Marcus, and knew from his expression that he didn't care what had made Lily do it. He only cared that she had betrayed him, spied on him, and cooperated with the man who had wanted to kill him. He would probably send her to prison, Hannah realized, a girl not even twenty-three years old. It seemed terrible, and yet, Lily had no one to blame but herself.

But then Marcus met her eyes, and the grim look faded a little. "What will you do with her?" he asked evenly. Lily gave a muffled gasp. Hannah's lips parted in surprise.

"I?"

He inclined his head, his gaze never leaving hers. "You."

For a moment she didn't know what to do. How could she decide Lily's punishment, when she was sitting here feeling sorry for the girl? Didn't he want to send her to Newgate? It was perfectly within his right. . . . But then, he knew that. He was letting her decide because of Molly. Hannah got to her feet, thinking. "Do you remember what you offered me, when I first arrived?" A quick frown touched his brow, then vanished. He nodded. "May I have it now?"

He gave her a piercing look, but finally nodded again. Pulling out a small book, he wrote for a moment, then handed a paper to her. Hannah took it and turned to Lily.

The maid looked up at her fearfully. "It was a

wicked thing you did," Hannah began. "And not even Mr. Reece's story should have made you spy on His Grace and on me. You know you cannot remain in this house." Another tear slipped down Lily's cheek, but she said nothing. "But you didn't give my daughter to Mr. Reece, and for that I must forgive you the rest. You may go." She handed Lily the bank draft. "This is for you to make a fresh, honest, start somewhere else."

Lily took the paper as if afraid it might bite her. "You—you won't send me to prison?" she asked in a quavering voice.

"No. But you should know it was a close call. You would do best not to tempt fate again."

"No, madam." Lily fingered the draft gingerly, her eyes widening at the amount, then carefully tucked it into the pocket of her apron. She got to her feet. "Thank you, madam. Thank you, Your Grace. I shan't—"

"Go," said Marcus. Lily closed her mouth at once, bobbed a quick curtsey, and fled. Hannah watched her go, hoping she had done the right thing. Marcus would have been completely justified to send for the Runners and have Lily dragged away, and perhaps she had been too lenient. But after her pose as the duchess of Exeter, Hannah didn't feel she was in a position to cast stones at others for lying. If Lily hadn't cooperated with Bentley by spying on Marcus, Bentley wouldn't have asked her to help kidnap Molly; he would have sent someone else who wouldn't have hesitated a second. Hannah didn't have it in her to repay that by sending the maid to prison.

Impulsively, she turned to Marcus. "Thank you."

He raised one brow. "For what?"

She put her head to one side and smiled. "You know what."

Now his eyes glittered with mirth. "Ah, for last night. You are most welcome."

"Wretch!" she exclaimed, laughing. "I meant for not sending Lily to prison."

He got to his feet with a shrug. "Bentley fooled many more astute people. I myself never would have believed he'd have the intelligence to plan such a scheme, let alone execute it. Bentley's the one I want rotting in prison, not a girl who fell for a story she wanted to believe."

"I know. But thank you all the same."

He regarded her for a moment, one corner of his mouth tugging upward. "You've too kind a heart. Redley, David, Lily . . . everyone wins your forgiveness."

"Stop," she said, shaking her head.

"Even I." The laughter had faded from his tone, and when she looked up at him, his expression was serious once more. "I really was abominable to you at the beginning," he added softly. "I am sorry for it."

"I was not very kind to you, either," she said, suddenly remembering all the things she had said to him and the even worse things she had thought about him. She'd been angry, no question, but she'd lost her temper many times and said things she shouldn't have.

He waved it away. "I gave you no cause to be. And I was glad you weren't." She blinked in astonishment. "I would have seen it as proof you wanted to be the duchess in truth. After Susannah . . ." He cleared his throat and looked uncomfortable. "I was too accustomed to women who lied to get what they wanted. I would have believed any kindness on your part to be an act, a pretense meant to establish yourself so that I could never get rid of you."

She shook her head in bemusement. "I shall never understand London ladies."

"Nor I," he said fervently, adding under his breath, "thank God."

Before she could ask what that meant, there was a tap on the door and Rosalind peered in at them. "I've spoken to Celia; Molly is sound asleep. Is everything settled here?" she asked.

Marcus looked at Hannah, who smiled widely. It seemed everything was, finally, settled: David and Marcus had patched up some of their differences, Bentley and his accomplices were on their way to prison, and David would be cleared of any charges. Molly was safely tucked in Celia's bed, and no one was seriously wounded. Things had settled rather well indeed. "No," he said, to her surprise. "There is one vital question left."

"What is it?" asked Rosalind anxiously, as Hannah turned alarmed eyes on him. "Is David—?"

"No, it's naught to do with David." He cleared his throat, then shot Hannah an unreadable glance. "There's one more thing I must do, but it must be handled with some delicacy."

There was a moment of silence. Then Rosalind clapped her hands, a brilliant smile creeping over her face. "Oh, Marcus! Do you mean you haven't already? What are you waiting for?"

"For you to close the door behind you," he said.

His stepmother made one last chirp of glee, then closed the door softly. Mouth suddenly dry, Hannah hardly dared look at him.

He seemed just as nervous. He leaned over, bracing his hands on his desk, then straightened and put them in his pockets. Then he cleared his throat again and darted a quick glance at her.

"What I said in the carriage this evening," he began, "I should not have said."

Her heart dropped a foot. Good heavens. He'd said he loved her.

"It was not the right time or place," he went on, "to say such a thing. In a speeding carriage, sending you off to summon the Runners alone while I tried to keep David from an early death in my place. I should not have said . . ." He hesitated.

Hannah cleared her throat. "When did you plan to say it?" she asked softly, barely able to hear her own voice over the thudding of her heart.

He was fiddling with a paper. "Tonight. I planned to arrange a private dinner in my suite—knowing Rosalind would be ecstatic not to dine with us—and then . . ." He smiled slightly, unfolding a special license to marry. "I always was a great one for plans, and yet since you've arrived, not a one of them has gone off as I expected."

"Yes," she murmured. "I know just what you mean."

His smile grew rueful. "Do you? I wonder why."

She heaved a sigh. "Yes, I've learned so very much since I came to London."

He chuckled. "And I am hoping to teach you so much more."

Hannah grinned. "I shall do my best to learn." He surprised her then by grabbing her around the waist, swinging her up to sit on his desk.

"It may require many"—he cupped her face in his hands—"many, many lessons."

She met his eyes, now alight with that warmth she loved so well. "I hope so. In fact, I demand it."

All the teasing left his face, replaced by an expression of such longing and love, Hannah felt the backs of her eyelids prickle with tears. "I think . . ." he said haltingly. "I believe this is the right time to say it. I do love you, Hannah Jane Preston, more than I ever thought I could love a woman. I want you for my duchess, my wife in every way." He paused, searching her face. "If that is agreeable to you."

"Well, I don't know," she said slowly. "I haven't any wealth."

"Do you require any?" he exclaimed, looking severely nonplussed.

"Nor any consequence," she went on. "In fact, the only standing I may have in town is as a figure of fun, for my freckles and common, country ways."

"No one would dare—" he began swiftly, then stopped short, a knowing look creeping over his face.

"And if anyone were to find I climbed a chimney only to ruin some of the Exeter pearls, I fear not a lady in London would speak to me again." She peeked at Marcus, to see if he were following her. A faint smile tugged at his mouth, and that devilish light glowed in his eyes.

"Then we shan't have to waste our time attending their inconsequential little routs and balls. I've a fancy to stay home at nights more, anyway," he said.

"That is very fortunate, for I have no connections, either," she finished with a theatrical sigh. "None at all. Quite likely we'll never be invited anywhere again."

"Hmm." He rested his hands behind her hips, angling her back on the tabletop. "You shall be connected to me," he murmured. "Quite . . . intimately." Then he cocked his head, as if listening. "But you've not yet mentioned your one asset, poor though it may be."

Now it was her turn to blink at him in bemusement. Gently, Marcus took her hand in his and placed it on his chest, pressing it flat with his own hand until she could feel the steady thump of his heart.

For a moment they just stared at each other. Hannah felt herself falling all over again at the expression on his face. "Yes," she whispered. "All that would be most agreeable to me."

His grip on her hand tightened for a second. "Can you truly love an arrogant, heartless beast?"

She smiled back at him. "Can you truly love a plain, provincial girl?"

He pondered a moment. "Forever more, or here and now, on this desk?" Hannah's eyes popped open in surprise, and then Marcus shrugged, pressing her back, crawling on top of the desk above her. "Never mind, for the answer's the same." Hannah gave a little shriek, losing her balance and ending up sprawled across his desk. With a wicked gleam in his eyes, Marcus shoved his ledgers and papers to the floor. "I seem to have a problem with tables lately. Every time I see one, I think of making love to you on it."

Hannah thought of the dozens of tables in Exeter House. She slid her arms around his neck as he bent over her. "I may hold you to that."

He laughed, his breath warm against her lips. "Just so long as you hold me, darling."